Bluegate Fields

Anne Perry was born in London and lived in California and Northumberland before moving to Scotland, her present home. She worked in a variety of jobs before becoming a full-time writer. Her first book was published in 1978, and she enjoys a growing reputation for her novels of crime and detection set in Victorian London.

ANNE PERRY

BLUEGATE FIELDS

HarperCollins*Publishers*

HarperCollins*Publishers*
77–85 Fulham Palace Road,
Hammersmith, London W6 8JB

The HarperCollins website address is:
www.**fire**and**water**.com

This paperback edition 1995
7 9 8 6

First published in Great Britain by
Souvenir Press 1992

Copyright © Anne Perry 1984

The Author asserts the moral right to
be identified as the author of this work

ISBN 0 00 647905 7

Set in Baskerville

Printed and bound in Great Britain by
Omnia Books Limited, Glasgow

All rights reserved. No part of this publication may be
reproduced, stored in a retrieval system, or transmitted,
in any form or by any means, electronic, mechanical,
photocopying, recording or otherwise, without the prior
permission of the publishers.

This book is sold subject to the condition that it shall not,
by way of trade or otherwise, be lent, re-sold, hired out or
otherwise circulated without the publisher's prior consent
in any form of binding or cover other than that in which it
is published and without a similar condition including this
condition being imposed on the subsequent purchaser.

. . . dedicated to the members of the John Howard Society, who practice their founder's belief in the right to dignity of all people.

A. P.

BLUEGATE FIELDS

1

*I*nspector Pitt shivered a little and stared unhappily while Sergeant Froggatt lifted the manhole cover and exposed the opening beneath. Iron rungs led downward into a hollow chasm of stone that echoed the distant slither and drip of water. Did Pitt imagine the scutter of clawed feet?

A breath of damp air drifted up, and immediately he tasted the sourness below. He sensed the labyrinth of tunnels and steps, the myriad layers, and even more tunnels of slimy bricks that stretched out under the whole of London and carried away the waste and the unwanted, the lost.

"Down 'ere, sir," Froggatt said dolefully. "That's where they found 'im. Odd, I calls it—very odd."

"Very," Pitt agreed, pulling his scarf tighter around his neck. Though it was only early September, he felt cold. The streets of Bluegate Fields were dank and smelled of poverty and human filth. It had once been a prosperous area, with high, elegant houses, the homes of merchants. Now it was one of the most dangerous of all the portside slums in England, and Pitt was about to descend into its sewers to examine a corpse that had been washed up

1

against the great sluice gates that closed off the Thames' tides.

"Right!" Froggatt stood aside, determined not to go first into the gaping hole with its wet, dark caverns.

Pitt stepped resignedly backward over the edge, grasped hold of the rungs, and began his careful descent. As the gloom closed in on him, the coursing water below sounded louder. He could smell the stale, entombed old water. Froggatt was also climbing down, his feet a rung or two beyond Pitt's hands.

Standing on the wet stones at the bottom, Pitt hunched his coat higher onto his shoulders and turned to look for the sewer cleaner who had reported the discovery; he was there, part of the shadows—the same colors, the same damp, blurred lines. He was a little sharp-nosed man. His trousers, cobbled together from several other pairs, were held up by rope. He carried a long pole with a hook on the end, and around his waist was a large sacking bag. He was used to the darkness, the incessantly dripping walls, the smell, and the distant scurrying of rats. Perhaps he had already seen so many signs of the tragic, the primitive, and the obscene in human life that nothing shocked him anymore. There was nothing in his face now but a natural wariness of the police and a certain sense of his own importance because the sewers were his domain.

"You come for the body, then?" He craned upward to stare at Pitt's height. "Rum thing, that. Can't 'ave bin 'ere long, or the rats'd 'ave got it. Not bitten, it ain't. Now who'd want to do a thing like that, I ask yer?" Apparently, it was a rhetorical question, because he did not wait for an answer but turned and scurried along the great tunnel. He reminded Pitt of a busy little rodent, his feet clattering along the wet bricks. Froggatt followed behind them, his bowler hat jammed fiercely on his head, his galoshes squelching noisily.

Around the corner they came quite suddenly upon the great river sluice gates, shut against the rising tide.

"There!" the sewerman announced proprietarily, pointing to the white body that lay on its side as modestly as could be managed. It was completely naked on the dark stones at the side of the channel.

Pitt was startled. No one had told him the body was without the ordinary decency of clothes—or that it was so young. The skin was flawless, no more than a fine down on the cheeks. The stomach was lean, the shoulders slight. Pitt knelt down, momentarily forgetting the slimy bricks.

"Lantern, Froggatt," he demanded. "Bring it over here, man! Hold it still!" It was unfair to be angry with Froggatt, but death—especially useless, pathetic death—always affected him this way.

Pitt turned the body over gently. The boy could not have been more than fifteen or sixteen years old, his features still soft. His hair, though wet and streaked with filth, must have been fair and wavy, a little longer than most. By twenty he might have been handsome, when his face had had time to mature. Now he was pallid, a little swollen with water, and his pale eyes were open.

But the dirt was only superficial; underneath he was well-cared-for. There was none of the ingrained grayness of those who do not wash, whose clothes stay on from one month to another. He was slender, but it was only the lissomeness of youth, not the wasting of starvation.

Pitt reached for one of the hands and examined it. Its softness was not due only to the flaccidity of death. The skin had no calluses, no blisters, no lines of grime such as the skin of a cobbler, a ragpicker, or a crossing sweeper would have. His nails were clean and well clipped.

Surely he did not come from the seething, grinding poverty of Bluegate Fields? But why no clothes?

Pitt looked up at the sewer cleaner.

"Are the currents strong enough down here to rip off a man's clothes?" he asked. "If he were struggling—drowning?"

3

"Doubt it." The cleaner shook his head. "Mebbe in the winter—lot o' rains. But not now. Any'ow, not boots—never boots. 'E can't 'ave bin down 'ere long, or rats'd 'ave bin at 'im. Seen a sweeper's lad eaten to the bone, I 'ave, wot slipped and drowned a couple o' year ago."

"How long?"

He gave it some thought, allowing Pitt to savor the full delicacy of his expertise before he committed himself.

"Hours," he said at last. "Depends where 'e fell in. Not more than hours, though. Current won't take off boots. Boots stay on."

Pitt should have thought of that.

"Did you find any clothes?" he asked, although he was not sure he could expect an honest reply. Each sewerman had his own stretch of channel, jealously guarded. It was not so much a job as a franchise. The reward lay in the pickings garnered under the gratings: coins, sometimes a gold sovereign or two, the occasional piece of jewelry. Even clothes found a good market. There were women who spent sixteen or eighteen hours a day sitting in sweatshops unpicking and resewing old clothes.

Froggatt hopefully swung the lantern out over the water, but it revealed nothing but the dark, oily, unbroken surface. If the depths held anything, it was sunken out of sight.

"No," the sewerman answered indignantly. "I ain't found nuffink at all or I would 'ave said. An' I searches the place reg'lar."

"No boys working for you?" Pitt pressed.

"No, this is mine. Nobody else comes 'ere—and I ain't found nuffink."

Pitt stared at him, uncertain whether he dared believe him. Would the man's avarice outmatch his natural fear of the police if he withheld something? As well-cared-for a body as this might have been dressed in clothes that would fetch a fair price.

4

"I swear! God's oath!" the sewerman protested, self-righteousness mixed with the beginnings of fear.

"Take his name," Pitt ordered Froggatt tersely. "If we find you've lied, I'll charge you with theft and obstructing the police in the investigation of a death. Understand me?"

"Name?" Froggatt repeated with rising sharpness.

"Ebenezer Chubb."

"Is that with two 'b's?" Froggatt fished for his pencil and wrote carefully, balancing the lamp on the ledge.

"Yes, it is. But I swears—"

"All right." Pitt was satisfied. "Now you'd better help us get this poor creature up and outside to the mortuary wagon. I suppose he drowned—he certainly looks like it. I don't see any marks of anything else, not even a bruise. But we'd better be sure."

"Wonder who 'e was?" Froggatt said dispassionately. His beat was in Bluegate Fields, and he was used to death. Every week he came across children dead of starvation, piled in alleys or doorways. Or he found the old, dead of disease, the cold, or alcohol poisoning. "Suppose we'll never know now." He wrinkled his face. "But I'm damned if I can think 'ow 'e came to be down 'ere stark as a babe!" He gave the sewerman a sour look. "But I've got your name, my lad—and I'll know where to find you again—if as I should want to!"

When Pitt went home that evening to his warm house, with its neat window boxes and scrubbed step, he did not mention the matter. He had met his wife, Charlotte, when he had called at her parents' extremely comfortable, respectable home to investigate the Cater Street murders five years ago, in 1881. He fell in love with her then, never believing a lady of such a house would consider him as more than a painful adjunct to the tragedy, something to be borne with as much dignity as possible.

5

Incredibly, she had learned to love him as well. And although her parents hardly found the match fortunate, they could not refuse a marriage desired by a daughter so willful and disastrously outspoken as Charlotte. The alternative to marriage was to remain at home in genteel idleness with her mother or to engage in charitable works.

Since then, she had taken an interest in several of his cases—often to her own considerable peril. Even when she had been expecting Jemima, it had not deterred her from joining her sister Emily in meddling in the affair in Callander Square. Now their second child, Daniel, was only a few months old, and even with the full-time help of the maid, Gracie, she had plenty to occupy her. There was no purpose in distressing Charlotte with the story of the dead youth found in the sewers below Bluegate Fields.

When he came in, she was in the kitchen bending over the table with the flat iron in her hand. He thought again how handsome she was—the strength in her face, the high cheekbones, and the richness of her hair.

She smiled at him, and there was the comfort of friendship in her glance. He felt her warmth, as if in some secret way she knew not what he thought but what he felt inside, as if she would understand anything he said, whether his words were fluent or not, easy or awkward. It was a sense of coming home.

He forgot the boy and the sluice gates, the smell of the water. Instead, the quiet certainties washed over him, driving out the cold. He kissed Charlotte, then looked around at all the safe, familiar things: the scrubbed table, white with wear, the vase of late daisies, Jemima's playpen in the corner, the clean linen waiting to be mended, a small pile of colored bricks he had painted as a toy—Jemima's favorite.

Charlotte and he would eat and then sit by the old stove and talk of all kinds of things: memories of past pleasures or pains, new ideas struggling to find words, small incidents of the day.

But by noon the next day, the body under Bluegate Fields was forced back to his mind sharply and unpleasantly. He was sitting in his untidy office looking at the papers on his desk, trying to decipher his own notes, when a constable rapped on the door and, without waiting for an answer, came straight in.

"Police surgeon to see you, sir. Says it's important." Ignoring any acknowledgment, he opened the door wider and ushered in a neat, solid man with a fine gray beard and a marvelous head of curling gray hair.

"Cutler," he announced himself smartly. "You're Pitt? Been looking at your corpse from Bluegate Fields sewers. Miserable business."

Pitt put down his notes and stared at him.

"Indeed." He forced himself to be civil. "Extremely unfortunate. I suppose he drowned? I saw no marks of any kind of violence. Or did he die naturally?" He did not believe that. For one thing, where were the clothes? What was he doing down there at all? "I suppose you haven't any idea who he was? No one claimed him?"

Cutler pulled a face. "Hardly. We don't put them up for public exhibition."

"But he drowned?" Pitt insisted. "He wasn't strangled or poisoned or suffocated?"

"No, no." Cutler pulled himself out a chair and sat down as though preparing for a long stay. "He drowned."

"Thank you." Pitt meant it as a dismissal. Surely there was nothing more to be said. Perhaps they would find out who he was, perhaps not. It depended on whether his parents or guardians reported him missing and set up any inquiries before it was too late to identify the corpse. "Good of you to come so soon," he added as an afterthought.

7

Cutler did not move. "He didn't drown in the sewer, you know," he announced.

"What?" Pitt sat upright, a chill running through him.

"Didn't drown in the sewer," Cutler repeated. "Water in his lungs is as clean as my bath! In fact, it could have come out of my bath—even got a little soap in it!"

"What on earth do you mean?"

There was a wry, sad expression on Cutler's face.

"Just what I say, Inspector. The boy drowned in bathwater. How he got into the sewer, I haven't the faintest idea. Fortunately that's not my task to discover. But I should be very surprised indeed if he had ever been in Bluegate Fields in his life."

Pitt absorbed the information slowly. Bathwater! Not someone from the slums. He had half known that much from the clean, firm flesh of the body—it should not have been any surprise.

"Accident?" It was only a formal question. There had been no mark of violence, no bruises on the throat or on the shoulders or arms.

"I think not," Cutler answered gravely.

"Because of where he was found?" Pitt shook his head, dismissing the thought. "That doesn't prove murder, only the disposal of the body—which is an offense, of course, but not nearly as serious."

"Bruises." Cutler raised his eyebrows a little.

Pitt frowned. "I saw none."

"On the heels. Quite hard. If you came upon a man in his bath, it would be far easier to drown him by grasping hold of his heels and pulling them upward, thereby forcing his head under the water, than it would be to try forcing his shoulders down, leaving his arms free to struggle with you."

Pitt imagined it against his will. Cutler was right. It would be an easy, quick movement. A few moments' hold and it would all be over.

"You think he was murdered?" he said slowly.

"He was a strong youth, apparently in excellent health"—Cutler hesitated, and a shadow of distress flickered across his face—"but for one thing, which I shall come to. There were no marks of injury except for those on his heels, and he was certainly not concussed by any fall. Why should he drown?"

"You said except for one thing. What was it? Could he have fainted?"

"Not from this. He was in the very early stages of syphilis—just a few lesions."

Pitt stared at him. "Syphilis? But he was of good background, you said—and not more than fifteen or sixteen!" he protested.

"I know. And there's more than that."

"What more?"

Cutler's face looked suddenly old and sad. He rubbed his hand across his head as if it hurt. "He had been homosexually used," he answered quietly.

"Are you sure?" Still Pitt struggled, unreasonably. His sense knew better, but his emotions rebelled.

Irritation flashed in Cutler's eyes.

"Of course I'm sure. Do you think it's the sort of thing I'd say on speculation?"

"I'm sorry," Pitt said. It was stupid—the boy was dead now anyway. Perhaps that was why Pitt was so upset by Cutler's information. "How long?" he asked.

"Not long, about eight or ten hours when I saw him, as far as I can tell."

"Sometime the night before we found him," Pitt remarked. "I suppose that was obvious. I imagine you've no idea who he was?"

"Upper middle class," Cutler said, as if thinking aloud. "Probably privately educated—a little ink on one of his fingers. Well fed—shouldn't think he'd gone hungry a day in his life or done a day's hard work with his hands. The odd sports, probably cricket or something of that

9

kind. Last meal was expensive—pheasant and wine and a sherry trifle. No, very definitely not Bluegate Fields."

"Damnation," Pitt said under his breath. "Someone must miss him! We'll have to find out who he was before we can bury him. You'll have to do the best you can to make him fit to be seen." He had been through it all before: the white-faced, stomach-clenched parents coming, ravaged by hope and fear, to stare at the dead face; then the sweat before they found the courage to look, followed by the nausea, the relief, or the despair—the end of hope, or back again into unknowing, waiting for the next time.

"Thank you," he said formally to Cutler. "I'll tell you as soon as we know anything."

Cutler stood up and took his departure silently, also aware of everything that lay ahead.

It would take time, Pitt thought, and he must have help. If it was murder—and he could not ignore the probability—then he must treat it as such. He must go to Chief Superintendent Dudley Athelstan and ask for men to find this boy's identity while he was still recognizable.

"I suppose all this is necessary?" Athelstan leaned back in his padded chair and looked at Pitt with open skepticism. He did not like Pitt. The man had ideas above himself, just because his wife's sister had married some sort of title! He always had an air about him as if he had no respect for position. And this whole business of a corpse in the sewer was most unsavory—not the sort of thing Athelstan wished to know about. It was considerably beneath the dignity he had risen to—and far below what he still intended to achieve with time and judicious behavior.

"Yes, sir," Pitt said tartly. "We can't afford to ignore it. He may be the victim of kidnapping and almost certainly of murder. The police surgeon says he is of good family, probably educated, and his last meal was of pheasant and sherry trifle. Hardly a workingman's dinner!"

"All right!" Athelstan snapped. "Then you'd better take what men you need and find out who he is! And for heaven's sake try to be tactful! Don't offend anyone. Take Gillivray—at least he knows how to behave himself with quality people."

Quality people! Yes, Gillivray would be Athelstan's choice to be sure of soothing the outraged sensibilities of the "quality" obliged to face the distasteful necessity of receiving the police.

To begin, there was the perfectly ordinary task of checking with every police station in the city for reports of youths missing from home or educational establishments who fitted the description of the dead boy. It was both tedious and distressing. Time after time they found frightened people, heard stories of unresolved tragedy.

Harcourt Gillivray was not a companion Pitt would have chosen. He was young, with yellow hair and a smooth face that smiled easily—too easily. His clothes were smart; his jacket was buttoned high, the collar stiff—not comfortable and somewhat crooked, like Pitt's. And he seemed always able to keep his feet dry, while Pitt forever found himself with his boots in a puddle.

It was three days before they came to the gray stone Georgian home of Sir Anstey and Lady Waybourne. By now Gillivray had become used to Pitt's refusal to use the tradesman's entrance. It pleased his own sense of social standing, and he was quite ready to accept Pitt's reasoning that on such a delicate mission it would be tactless to allow the entire servants' hall to be aware of their purpose.

The butler suffered them to come in with a look of pained resignation. Better to have the police in the morning room where they could not be seen than on the front step for the entire street to know about.

"Sir Anstey will see you in half an hour, Mr.—er—Mr.

11

Pitt. If you care to wait here—" He turned and opened the door to leave.

"It is a matter of some urgency," Pitt said with an edge to his voice. He saw Gillivray wince. Butlers should be accorded the same dignity as the masters they represented, and most were acutely aware of it. "It is not something that can wait," Pitt continued. "The sooner and the more discreetly it can be dealt with, the less painful it will be."

The butler hesitated, weighing what Pitt had said. The word "discreetly" tipped the balance.

"Yes, sir. I shall inform Sir Anstey of your presence."

Even so, it was a full twenty minutes before Anstey Waybourne appeared, closing the door behind him. His eyebrows were raised inquiringly, showing faint distaste. He had pale skin and full, fair side-whiskers. As soon as Pitt saw him, he knew who the dead boy had been.

"Sir Anstey." Pitt's voice dropped; all his irritation at the man's patronage vanished. "I believe you reported your son Arthur as missing from home?"

Waybourne made a small deprecatory gesture.

"My wife, Mr.—er." He waved aside the necessity for recalling a name for a mere policeman. They were anonymous, like servants. "I'm sure there is no need for you to concern yourself. Arthur is sixteen. I have no doubt he is up to some prank. My wife is overprotective—women tend to be, you know. Part of their nature. Don't know how to let a boy grow up. Want to keep him a baby forever."

Pitt felt a stab of pity. Assurance was so fragile. He was about to shatter this man's security, the world in which he thought he was untouchable by the sordid realities Pitt represented.

"I'm sorry, sir," he said even more quietly. "But we have found a dead boy whom we believe may be your son." There was no point in spinning it out, trying to come to it slowly. It was no kinder, just longer.

"Dead? Whatever do you mean?" He was still trying to dismiss the idea, to repudiate it.

"Drowned, sir," Pitt repeated, aware of Gillivray's disapproval. Gillivray would like to skirt around it, to come at it obliquely, which seemed to Pitt like crushing someone slowly. "He is a fair-haired boy of about sixteen years, five-feet-nine-inches tall—of good family, to judge by his appearance. Unfortunately he has no identification on him, so we do not know who he is. It is necessary for someone to come and look at the body. If you prefer not to do it yourself—if it turns out not to be your son, we could accept the word of—"

"Don't be ridiculous!" Waybourne said. "I'm sure it is not Arthur. But I shall come and tell you so myself. One does not send a servant on such a task. Where is it?"

"In the morgue, sir. Bishop's Lane, in Bluegate Fields."

Waybourne's face dropped—it was inconceivable.

"Bluegate Fields!"

"Yes, sir. I'm afraid that is where he was found."

"Then it cannot possibly be my son."

"I hope not, sir. But whoever he is, he would appear to be a gentleman."

Waybourne's eyebrows rose.

"In Bluegate Fields?" he said sarcastically.

Pitt did not argue anymore. "Would you prefer to come in a hansom, sir, or in your own carriage?"

"In my own carriage, thank you. I do not care for public conveyances. I shall meet you there in thirty minutes."

Pitt and Gillivray excused themselves and found a hansom to take them to the morgue, since Waybourne was obviously not willing to have them accompany him.

The drive was not long. They were quickly out of the fashionable squares and into the narrow, grimy streets of the portside, enveloped by the smell of the river, the drift of fog in their throats. Bishop's Lane was anonymous; gray men came and went about their business.

The morgue was grim: less effort made to be clean

than in a hospital—less reason. There was no humanity here except one brown-faced little man with faintly Eastern eyes and curiously light hair. His manner was suitably subdued.

"Yes, sir," he said to Gillivray, who led the way in. "I know the body you mean. The gentleman to see it has not arrived yet."

There was nothing to do but wait for Waybourne. It turned out to be not thirty minutes but very nearly an hour. If Waybourne was aware of the time elapsed, he gave no sign. His face was still irritated, as though he had been called out on an unnecessary duty, required only because someone had made a foolish error.

"Well?" He came in briskly, ignoring the morgue attendant and Gillivray. He faced Pitt with raised eyebrows, hitching the shoulders of his coat into better position. The room was cold. "What is it you want me to see?"

Gillivray shifted his feet uncomfortably. He had not seen the corpse, nor did he know where it had been found. Oddly, he had not inquired. He regarded the whole task as something he was seconded to because of his superior manners, a task to be fulfilled and forgotten as soon as possible. He preferred the investigation of robbery, particularly robbery from the wealthy and the lesser aristocracy. The quiet, discreet association with such people when he was assisting was a rather pleasing way to advance his career.

Pitt knew what was to come—the inescapable pain, the struggle to explain away the horror, the denial right up to the last, inevitable moment.

"This way, sir. I warn you." He suddenly regarded Waybourne levelly, as an equal, perhaps even condescendingly; he knew death, he had felt the grief, the anger. But at least he could control his stomach through sheer habit. "I'm afraid it is not pleasant."

"Get on with it, man," Waybourne snapped. "I have not all day to spend on this. And I presume when I have

14

satisfied you it is not my son, then you will have other people to consult?"

Pitt led the way into the bare white room where the corpse was laid out on a table, and gently removed the covering sheet from the face. There was no point in showing the rest of the body with its great autopsy wounds.

He knew what was coming; the features were too alike: the fair wavy hair, the long soft nose, the full lips.

There was a faint sound from Waybourne. Every vestige of blood vanished from his face. He swayed a little, as though the room were afloat and had shifted under his feet.

Gillivray was too startled to react for an instant, but the morgue attendant had seen it more times than he could recall. It was the worst part of his job. He had a chair ready, and as Waybourne's knees buckled he eased him into it as if it were all one natural movement—not a collapse but a seating.

Pitt covered the face.

"I'm sorry, sir," he said quietly. "You identify this as the body of your son Arthur Waybourne?"

Waybourne tried to speak but at first his voice would not come. The attendant gave him a glass of water and he took a sip of it.

"Yes," he said at last. "Yes, that is my son Arthur." He grasped the glass and drank some more of it slowly. "Would you be so good as to tell me where he was discovered and how he died?"

"Of course. He was drowned."

"Drowned?" Obviously, Waybourne was startled. Perhaps he had never seen a drowned face before and did not recognize the puffy flesh, marble white.

"Yes. I'm sorry."

"Drowned? How? In the river?"

"No, sir, in a bath."

"You mean he—he fell? He hit his head or something?

15

What a ridiculous accident! That's the sort of thing that happens to old men!" Already the denial had begun, as if its ridiculousness could somehow make it untrue.

Pitt took a breath and let it out slowly. Evasion was not possible.

"No, sir. It seems he was murdered. His body was not found in a bath—not even in a house. I'm sorry—it was found in the sewers below Bluegate Fields, up against the sluice gates to the Thames. But for a particularly diligent sewer cleaner, we might not have found him at all."

"Oh, hardly!" Gillivray protested. "Of course he would have been found!" He wanted to contradict Pitt, prove him wrong in something, as if it could even now in some way disprove everything. "He could not have disappeared. That's nonsense. Even in the river—" He hesitated, then decided the subject was too unpleasant and abandoned it.

"Rats," Pitt said simply. "Twenty-four hours more in the sewer and he would not have been recognizable. A week, and there would have been nothing but bones. I'm sorry, Sir Anstey, but your son was murdered."

Waybourne bridled visably, his eyes glittering in the white face.

"That's preposterous!" His voice was high now, even shrill. "Who on earth would have any reason to murder my son? He was sixteen! Quite innocent of anything at all. We lead a perfectly proper and orderly life." He swallowed convulsively and regained a fraction of his control. "You have mixed too much among the criminal element and the lower classes, Inspector," he said. "There is no one whatsoever who would wish Arthur any harm. There was no reason."

Pitt felt his stomach tighten. This was going to be the most painful of all: the facts Waybourne would find intolerable, beyond acceptance.

"I'm sorry." He seemed to be beginning every sentence with an apology. "I'm sorry, sir, but your son was suffering from the early stages of veneral disease—and he had been homosexually used."

Waybourne stared at him, scarlet blood suffusing his skin.

"That's obscene!" he shouted, starting from the chair as if to stand up, but his legs buckled. "How dare you say such a thing! I'll have you dismissed! Who is your superior?"

"It's not my diagnosis, sir. It is what the police surgeon says."

"Then he is a mischievous incompetent! I'll see he never practices again! It's monstrous! Obviously, Arthur was kidnapped, poor boy, and murdered by his captors. If—" He swallowed. "If he was abused before he was killed, then you must charge his murderers with that also. And see to it that they are hanged! But as for the other"—he made a sharp slicing motion with his hand in the air—"that is—that is quite impossible. I demand that our own family physician examine the—the body and refute this slander!"

"By all means," Pitt agreed. "But he will find the same facts, and they are capable of only one diagnosis—the same as the police pathologist."

Waybourne gulped and caught his breath awkwardly. His voice, when it came, was tight, scraping.

"He will not! I am not without influence, Mr. Pitt. I shall see that this monstrous wrong is not done to my poor son or to the rest of his family. Good day to you." He stood a little unsteadily, then turned and walked out of the room, up the steps, and into the daylight.

Pitt ran his hand through his hair, leaving it on end.

"Poor man," he said softly, to himself rather than to Gillivray. "He's going to make it so much harder for himself."

"Are you sure it really is—?" Gillivray said anxiously.

"Don't be so stupid!" Pitt sank down with his head in his hands. "Of course I'm damned well sure!"

17

2

There was not time for the decencies of mourning to be observed. People's memories were short; details passed from mind. Pitt was obliged to return to the Waybourne family the next morning and begin the inquiries that could not wait upon grief or the recapturing of composure.

The house was silent. All the blinds were partway down, and there was black crepe on the front door. Straw was spread on the road outside to reduce the sound of carriage wheels passing. Gillivray had come in the soberest of garb, and stayed, grim-faced, two steps behind Pitt. He reminded Pitt irritatingly of an undertaker's assistant, full of professional sorrow.

The butler opened the door and ushered them in immediately, not allowing them time to stand on the doorstep. The hall was somber in the half-light of the drawn blinds. In the morning room, the gas lamps were lit and a small fire burned in the grate. On the low, round table in the center of the room were white flowers in a formal arrangement: chrysanthemums and thick, soft-fleshed lilies. It all smelled faintly of wax polish and old sweet flowers, just a little stale.

Anstey Waybourne came in almost immediately. He

looked pale and tired, his face set. He had already prepared what he intended to say and did not bother with courtesies.

"Good morning," he began stiffly. Then, without waiting for a response, he continued: "I assume you have certain questions it is necessary for you to ask. I shall do my best, of course, to give you the small amount of information I possess. I have given the matter some considerable thought, naturally." He clasped his hands together and looked at the lilies on the table. "I have come to the conclusion that my son was quite certainly attacked by strangers, perhaps purely from the base motives of robbery. Or I admit it is marginally possible that abduction was intended, although we have received no indication that it was so—no demand for any kind of ransom." He glanced at Pitt, and then away again. "Of course it may be that there was not time—some preposterous accident occurred, and Arthur died. Obviously, they then panicked." He took a deep breath. "And the results we are all painfully aware of."

Pitt opened his mouth, but Waybourne waved his hand to silence him.

"No, please! Allow me to continue. There is very little we can tell you, but no doubt you wish to know about my son's last day alive, although I cannot see of what use it will be to you.

"Breakfast was perfectly as normal. We were all present. Arthur spent the morning, as is customary, with his younger brother Godfrey, studying under the tutelage of Mr. Jerome, whom I employ for that purpose. Luncheon was quite unremarkable. Arthur was his usual self. Neither his manner nor his conversation was in any way out of the ordinary, and he made no mention of any persons unknown to us, or any plans for unusual activity." Waybourne did not move in all the time he spoke, but stood in exactly the same spot on the rich Aubusson carpet.

"In the afternoon, Godfrey resumed his studies with

19

Mr. Jerome. Arthur read for an hour or two—his classics, I believe—a little Latin. Then he went out with the son of a family friend, a boy of excellent background and well known to us. I have spoken to him myself, and he is also unaware of anything unusual in Arthur's behavior. They parted at approximately five in the afternoon, as near as Titus can remember, but Arthur did not say where he was going, except that it was to dine with a friend." Waybourne looked up at last and met Pitt's eyes. "I'm afraid that is all we can tell you."

Pitt realized that there was already a wall raised against investigation. Anstey Waybourne had decided what had occurred: a chance attack that might have happened to anyone, a tragic but insoluble mystery. To pursue a resolution would not bring back the dead, and would only cause additional and unnecessary distress to those already bereaved.

Pitt could sympathize with him. He had lost a son, and in extraordinarily painful circumstances. But murder could not be concealed, for all its anguish.

"Yes, sir," he said quietly. "I would like to see the tutor, Mr. Jerome, if I may, and your son Godfrey."

Waybourne's eyebrows rose. "Indeed? You may see Jerome, of course, if you wish. Although I cannot see what purpose it will serve. I have told you all that he knows. But I'm afraid it is quite out of the question that you should speak with Godfrey. He has already lost his brother. I will not have him subjected to questioning— especially as it is completely unnecessary."

It was not the time to argue. At the moment, they were all just names to Pitt, people without faces or characters, without connections except the obvious ones of blood; all the emotions involved were not yet even guessed.

"I would still like to speak to Mr. Jerome," Pitt repeated. "He may recall something that would be of use. We must explore every possibility."

"I cannot see the purpose of it." Waybourne's nose

flared a little, perhaps with irritation, perhaps from the deadening smell of the lilies. "If Arthur was set upon by thieves, Jerome is hardly likely to know anything that might help."

"Probably not, sir." Pitt hesitated, then said what he had to. "But there is always the possibility that his death had something to do with his—medical condition." What an obscene euphemism. Yet he found himself using it, painfully aware of Waybourne, the shock saturating the house, generations of rigid self-discipline, imprisoned feelings.

Waybourne's face froze. "That has not been established, sir! My own family physician will no doubt find your police surgeon is utterly mistaken. I daresay he has to do with a quite different class of person, and has found what he is accustomed to. I am sure that when he is aware of who Arthur was, he will revise his conclusions."

Pitt avoided the argument. It was not yet necessary; perhaps it never would be if the "family physician" had both skill and courage. It would be better for him to tell Waybourne the truth, to explain that it could be kept private to some degree but could not be denied.

He changed the subject. "What was the name of this young friend—Titus, sir?"

Waybourne let out his breath slowly, as if a pain had eased.

"Titus Swynford," he replied. "His father, Mortimer Swynford, is one of our oldest acquaintances. Excellent family. But I have already ascertained everything that Titus knows. He cannot add to it."

"All the same, sir, we'll speak to him," Pitt insisted.

"I shall ask his father if he will give you permission," Waybourne said coldly, "although I cannot see that it will serve any purpose, either. Titus neither saw nor heard anything of relevance. Arthur did not tell him where he intended to go, nor with whom. But even if he had, he was obviously set upon by ruffians in the street, so the information would be of little use."

"Oh, it might help, sir." Pitt told a half lie. "It might tell us in what area he was, and different hooligans frequent different streets. We might even find a witness, if we know where to look."

Indecision contorted Waybourne's face. He wanted the whole matter buried as quickly and decently as possible, hidden with good heavy earth and flowers. There would be proper memories draped with black crepe, a coffin with brass handles, a discreet and sorrowful eulogy. Everyone would return home with hushed voices to observe an accepted time of mourning. Then would follow the slow return to life.

But Waybourne could not afford the inexplicable behavior of not appearing to help the police search for his son's murderer. He struggled mentally and failed to find words to frame what he felt so that it sounded honorable, something he could accept himself as doing.

Pitt understood. He could almost have found the words for him, because he had seen it before; there was nothing unusual or hard to understand in wanting to bury pain, to keep the extremity of death and the shame of disease private matters.

"I suppose you had better speak to Jerome," Waybourne said at last. It was a compromise. "I'll ask Mr. Swynford if he will permit you to see Titus." He reached for the bell and pulled it. The butler appeared as if he had been at the door.

"Yes, sir?" he inquired.

"Send Mr. Jerome to me." Waybourne did not look at him.

Nothing was said in the morning room until there was a knock on the door. At Waybourne's word, the door opened and a dark man in his early forties walked in and closed it behind him. He had good features, if his nose was a little pinched. His mouth was full-lipped, but

pursed with a certain carefulness. It was not a spon-
taneous face, not a face that laughed, except after consideration, when it believed laughter advisable—the thing to
do.

Pitt looked at him only from habit; he did not expect
the tutor to be important. Maybe, Pitt reflected, if he had
worked teaching the sons of a man like Anstey Waybourne, imparting his knowledge yet knowing they were
growing up only to inherit possessions without labor and
to govern easily, by right of birth, he would be like
Jerome. If Pitt had spent his life as always more than a
servant but less than his own man, dependent on boys of
thirteen and sixteen, perhaps his face would be just as
careful, just as pinched.

"Come in, Jerome," Waybourne said absently. "These
men are from the police. Er—Pitt—Inspector Pitt, and
Mr.—er—Gilbert. They wish to ask you a few questions
about Arthur. Pointless, as far as I can see, but you had
better oblige them."

"Yes, sir." Jerome stood still, not quite to attention. He
looked at Pitt with the slight condescension of one who
knows that at last he addresses someone beyond argument his social inferior.

"I have already told Sir Anstey all I know," Jerome said
with a slight lift of his eyebrows. "Naturally, if there were
anything, I should have said so."

"Of course," Pitt agreed. "But it is possible you may
know something without being aware of its relevance. I
wonder, sir," he looked at Waybourne, "if you would be
good enough to ask Mr. Swynford for his permission to
speak with his son?"

Waybourne hesitated, torn between the desire to stay
and make sure nothing was said that was distasteful or
careless, and the foolishness of allowing his anxiety to be
observed. He gave Jerome a cold, warning look, then
went to the door.

When it was closed behind him, Pitt turned to the tutor. There was really very little to ask him, but now that he was here, it was better to go through the formalities.

"Mr. Jerome," he began gravely. "Sir Anstey has already said that you observed nothing unusual about Mr. Arthur's behavior on the day he died."

"That is correct," Jerome said with overt patience. "Although there could hardly be expected to have been, unless one believes in clairvoyance"—he smiled faintly, as though at a lesser breed from whom foolishness was to be expected—"which I do not. The poor boy cannot have known what was to happen to him."

Pitt felt an instinctive dislike for the man. It was unreasonable, but he imagined Jerome and he would have no belief or emotion in common, not even their perceptions of the same event.

"But he might have known with whom he intended to have dinner?" Pitt pointed out. "I presume it would be someone he was already acquainted with. We should be able to discover who it was."

Jerome's eyes were dark, a little rounder than average.

"I fail to see how that will help," he answered. "He cannot have reached the appointment. If he did, then the person would no doubt have come forward and expressed his condolences at least. But what purpose would it serve?"

"We would learn where he was," Pitt pointed out. "It would narrow the area. Witnesses might be found."

Jerome did not see any hope in that.

"Possibly. I suppose you know your business. But I'm afraid I have no idea with whom he intended to spend the evening. I presume, in view of the fact that the person has not come forward, that it was not a prearranged appointment, but something on the spur of the moment. And boys of that age do not confide their social engagements to their tutors, Inspector." There was a faint touch of irony in his voice—something less than self-pity, but more sour than humor.

"Perhaps you could give me a list of his friends that you are aware of?" Pitt suggested. "We can eliminate them quite easily. I would rather not press Sir Anstey at the moment."

"Of course." Jerome turned to the small leather-topped writing table by the wall and pulled out a drawer. He took paper and began to make notes, but his face expressed his disbelief. He thought Pitt was doing something quite useless because he could think of nothing else, a man clutching at straws to appear efficient. He had written half a dozen lines when Waybourne came back. He glanced at Pitt, then immediately at Jerome.

"What is that?" he demanded, hand outstretched toward the paper.

Jerome's face stiffened. "Names of various friends of Mr. Arthur's, sir, with whom he might have intended to dine. The inspector wishes it."

Waybourne sniffed. "Indeed?" He looked icily at Pitt. "I trust you will endeavor to be discreet, Inspector. I should not care for my friends to be embarrassed. Do I make myself clear?"

Pitt had to force himself to remember the circumstances in order to curb his rising temper.

But Gillivray stepped in before he could answer.

"Of course, Sir Anstey," he said smoothly. "We are aware of the delicacy of the matter. All we shall ask is whether the gentlemen in question was expecting Mr. Arthur for dinner, or for any other engagement that evening. I'm sure they will understand it is important that we make every effort to discover where this appalling event took place. Most probably it was just as you say, a chance attack that might have happened to any well-dressed young gentleman who appeared to have valuables on him. But we must do what little we can to ascertain that this was so."

Waybourne's face softened with something like appreciation.

"Thank you. I cannot think it will make the slightest difference, but of course you are right. You will not discover who did this—this thing. However, I quite see that you are obliged to try." He turned to the tutor. "Thank you, Jerome. That will be all."

Jerome excused himself and left, closing the door behind him.

Waybourne looked from Gillivray back to Pitt, his expression changing. He could not understand the essence of Gillivray's social delicacy, or of Pitt's brief, sharp compassion that leaped the gulf of every other difference between them; to him, the men represented the distinction between discretion and vulgarity.

"I believe that is all I can do to be of assistance to you, Inspector," he said coldly. "I have spoken to Mr. Mortimer Swynford, and if you still feel it necessary, you may speak to Titus." He ran his hand through his thick, fair hair in a tired gesture.

"When will it be possible to speak to Lady Waybourne, sir?" Pitt asked.

"It will not be possible. There is nothing she can tell you that would be of any use. Naturally, I have asked her, and she did not know where Arthur planned to spend his evening. I do not intend to subject her to the ordeal of being questioned by the police." His face closed, hard and final, the skin tight.

Pitt drew a deep breath and sighed. He felt Gillivray stiffen beside him and could almost taste his embarrassment, his revulsion for what Pitt was going to say. He half expected to be touched, to feel a hand on his arm to restrain him.

"I'm sorry, Sir Anstey, but there is also the matter of your son's illness and his relationships," he said quietly. "We cannot ignore the possibility that they were connected to his death. And the relationship is in itself a crime—"

"I am aware of that, sir!" Waybourne looked at Pitt as if

26

he himself had participated in the act merely by mentioning it. "Lady Waybourne will not speak with you. She is a woman of decency. She would not even know what you were talking about. Women of gentle birth have never heard of such—obscenities."

Pitt knew that, but pity overruled his resentment.

"Of course not. I was intending only to ask her about your son's friends, those who knew him well."

"I have already told you everything you can possibly find of use, Inspector Pitt," Waybourne said. "I have no intention whatsoever of prosecuting whoever"—he swallowed—"whoever abused my son. It's over. Arthur is dead. No raking over of personal"—he took a deep breath and steadied himself, his hand gripping the carved back of one of the chairs—"depravities of—of some unknown man is going to help. Let the dead at least lie in peace, man. And let those of us who have to go on living mourn our son in decency. Now please pursue your business elsewhere. Good day to you." He turned his back and stood, his body stiff and square-shouldered, facing the fire and the picture over the mantelshelf.

There was nothing for Pitt or Gillivray to do but leave. They accepted their hats from the footman in the hall and went out the front door into the sharp September wind and the bustle of the street.

Gillivray held up the list of friends written by Jerome. "Do you really want this, sir?" he said doubtfully. "We can hardly go around asking these people much more than if they saw the boy that evening. If they knew of anything"—his face wrinkled slightly in distaste, reflecting just such an expression as Waybourne himself might have assumed—"indecent, they are not going to admit it. We can hardly press them. And, quite honestly, Sir Anstey is right—he was attacked by footpads or hooligans. Extremely unpleasant, especially when it happens to a good family. But the best thing we can do is let it lie for a while, then discreetly write it off as insoluble."

Pitt turned on him, his anger at last safe to unloose.

"Unpleasant?" he shouted furiously. "Did you say 'unpleasant,' Mr. Gillivray? The boy was abused, diseased, and then murdered! What does it have to be before you consider it downright vile? I should be interested to know!"

"That's uncalled for, Mr. Pitt," Gillivray said stiffly, repugnance in his face rather than offense. "Discussing tragedy only makes it worse for people, harder for them to bear, and it is not part of our duty to add to their distress—which, God knows, must be bad enough!"

"Our duty, Mr. Gillivray, is to find out who murdered that boy and then put his naked body down a manhole into the sewers to be eaten by the rats and left as anonymous, untraceable bones. Unfortunately for them, it was washed up to the sluice gates and a sharp-eyed sewerman, on the lookout for a bargain, found him too soon."

Gillivray looked shaken, the pink color gone from his skin.

"Well—I—I hardly think it is necessary to put it quite like that."

"How would you put it?" Pitt demanded, swinging around to face him. "A little gentlemanly fun, an unfortunate accident? Least said the better?" They crossed the road and a passing hansom flung mud at them.

"No, of course not!" Gillivray's color flooded back. "It is an unspeakable tragedy, and a crime of the worst kind. But I honestly do not believe there is the slightest chance whatever that we shall discover who is responsible, and therefore it is better we should spare the feelings of the family as much as we can. That is all I meant! As Sir Anstey said, he is not going to prosecute whoever—well—that's a different matter. And one that we have no call in!" He bent and brushed the mud off his trousers irritably.

Pitt ignored him.

*   *   *

By the end of the day, they had separately called on the few names on Jerome's list. None had admitted expecting or seeing Arthur Waybourne that evening, or having had any idea as to his plans. On returning to the police station a little after five o'clock, Pitt found a message awaiting him that Athelstan wished to see him.

"Yes, sir?" he inquired, closing the heavy, polished door behind him. Athelstan was sitting behind his desk, with a fine leather set of inkwells, powder, knife, and seals beside his right hand.

"This Waybourne business." Athelstan looked up. A shadow of annoyance crossed his face. "Well, sit down, man! Don't stand there flapping about like a scarecrow." He surveyed Pitt with distaste. "Can't you do something about that coat? I suppose you can't afford a tailor, but for heaven's sake get your wife to press it. You are married, aren't you?"

He knew perfectly well that Pitt was married. Indeed, he was aware that Pitt's wife was of rather better family that Athelstan himself, but it was something he chose to forget whenever possible.

"Yes, sir," Pitt said patiently. Not even the Prince of Wales's tailor could have made Pitt look tidy. There was a natural awkwardness about him. He moved without the languor of a gentleman; he was far too enthusiastic.

"Well, sit down!" Athelstan snapped. He disliked having to look up, especially at someone who was taller than he was, even when standing. "Have you discovered anything?"

Pitt sat obediently, crossing his legs.

"No, sir, not yet."

Athelstan eyed him with disfavor.

"Never imagined you would. Mostly unsavory affair, but a sign of the times. City's coming to a sad state when gentlemen's sons can't take a walk in the evening without being set upon by thugs."

29

"Not thugs, sir," Pitt said precisely. "Thugs strangle from behind, with scarves. This boy was—"

"Don't be a fool!" Athelstan said furiously. "I am not talking of the religious nature of the assailants! I am talking of the moral decline of the city and the fact that we have been unable to do anything about it. I feel badly. It is the job of the police to protect people like the Waybournes—and everyone else, of course." He slapped his hand on the burgundy leather surface of his desk. "But if we cannot discover even the area in which the crime was committed, I don't see what we can do, except save the family a great deal of public notice which can only make their bereavement the harder to bear."

Pitt knew immediately that Gillivray had already reported to Athelstan. He felt his body tighten with anger, the muscles cord across his back.

"Syphilis may be contracted in one night, sir," he said distinctly, sounding each word with the diction he had learned with the son of the estate on which he had grown up. "But the symptoms do not appear instantly, like a bruise. Arthur Waybourne was used by someone long before he was killed."

The skin on Athelstan's face was beaded with sweat; his mustache hid his lip, but his brow gleamed wet in the gaslight. He did not look at Pitt. There were several moments of silence while he struggled with himself.

"Indeed," he said at last. "There is much that is ugly, very ugly. But what gentlemen, and the sons of gentlemen, do in their bedrooms is fortunately beyond the scope of the police—unless, of course, they request our intervention. Sir Anstey has not. I deplore it as much as you do." His eyes flickered up and met Pitt's with a flash of genuine communication, then slid away again. "It is abominable, repugnant to every decent human being."

He picked up the paper knife and fiddled with it, watching the light on the blade. "But it is only his death we are concerned with, and that would seem to be insolu-

30

ble. Still, I appreciate that we must appear to try. Quite obviously the boy did not come to be where he was by accident." He clenched his hand until his knuckles showed white through the red skin. He looked up sharply. "But for God's sake, Pitt—use a little discretion! You've moved in society before with investigations. You ought to know how to behave! Be sensitive to their grief, and their horrible shock in learning the other—facts. I don't know why you felt it necessary to tell them! Couldn't it have been decently buried with the boy?" He shook his head. "No—I suppose not. Had to tell the father, poor man. He has a right to know—might have wanted to prosecute someone. Might have known something already—or guessed. You won't find anything now, you know. Could have been washed to Bluegate Fields from anywhere this side of the city. Still—we have to make it seem as if we've done all we can, if only for the mother's sake. Wretched business—most unpleasant crime I've ever had to deal with.

"All right, you'd better get on with it! Do what you can." He waved his hand to indicate that Pitt could leave. "Let me know in a day or two. Good night."

Pitt stood up. There was nothing else to say, no argument that was worth making.

"Good night, sir." He went out of the polished office and closed the door behind him.

When Pitt arrived home, he was tired and cold. Indecision was no more than a shadow at the back of his mind, disturbing his certainty, spoiling the solidity of his will. It was his job to resolve mysteries, to find offenders and hand them over to the law for trial. But he had seen the damage that the resolution of all secrets could bring; every person should have the right to a certain degree of privacy, a chance to forget or to overcome. Crime must be paid for, but not all sins or mistakes need be made public and explained for everyone to examine and re-

31

member. And sometimes victims were punished doubly, once by the offense itself, and then a second and more enduring time when others heard of it, pored over it, and imagined every intimate detail.

Could that be so with Arthur Waybourne? Was there any point now in exposing his weakness or his tragedy?

And if answers were dangerous, half answers were worse. The other half was built by the imagination; even the innocent were involved and could never disprove what was not real to begin with. Surely that was a greater wrong than the original crime, because it was not committed in the heat of emotion or by instinct, but deliberately, and without fear of danger to oneself. There was almost an element of voyeurism, a self-righteousness in it that sickened him.

Were Gillivray and Athelstan right? Was there no chance of finding the person who had murdered Arthur? If it had nothing to do with his private weaknesses, his sins, or sickness, then the investigation would only publicize the pain of a lot of men and women who were probably no more to blame than most people, for one omission or another.

At first he said nothing about it to Charlotte. In fact, he said very little at all, eating his meal in near silence in the parlor, which was soft in the evening gaslight. He was unaware of his withdrawal until Charlotte put it into words.

"What is the decision?" she asked, as she laid down her knife and fork and folded her napkin.

He looked up, surprised.

"Decision? About what?"

Her mouth tightened in a tiny smile. "Whatever it is that has been tormenting you all evening. I've watched it wavering back and forth across your face ever since you came in."

He relaxed with a little sigh.

"I'm sorry. Yes, I suppose I have been. But it's an unpleasant case. I'd rather not discuss it with you."

She stood, picked up the plates, and stacked them on the sideboard. Gracie worked all day, but she was permitted to leave the dinner dishes until the following morning.

Pitt went to sit by the fire. He eased into the fat, padded chair with relief.

"Don't be ridiculous," she said briskly, coming to sit opposite him. "I've already been involved with all sorts of murders. My stomach is as strong as yours."

He did not bother to argue. She had never even imagined most of the things he had seen in the rookery slums: filth and misery beyond the imagination of any sane person.

"Well?" she came back and sat down, looking at him expectantly.

He hesitated. He wanted her opinion, but he could not tell her the dilemma without the details. If the disease or the homosexuality was omitted, there would be no problem. Eventually he gave in to his need and told her.

"Oh," she said when he finished. She sat without saying anything more for so long that he was afraid he had distressed her too deeply, perhaps confused or disgusted her.

He leaned forward and took her hand.

"Charlotte?"

She looked up. There was pain in her eyes, but it was the pain of pity, not confusion or withdrawal. He felt an overwhelming surge of relief, a desire to hold on to her, feel her in his arms. He wanted even just to touch her hair, to pull out its neat coils and thread his fingers through its softness. But it seemed inappropriate; she was thinking of a dead boy, hardly more than a child, and of the tragic compulsions that had driven someone to use him, and then destroy him.

"Charlotte?" he said again.

Her face was screwed up with doubt as she met his eyes.

"Why should ruffians put him down into the sewers?" she said slowly. "In a place like Bluegate Fields, what would it matter if he were found? Don't you find bodies there anyway? I mean—wouldn't ruffians have hit him over the head, or stabbed him? Kidnappers might drown him! But there's no point in kidnapping someone if you don't know who he is—because whom do you ask for a ransom?"

He stared at her. He knew what her answer was going to be long before she framed it in words herself.

"It had to be someone who knew him, Thomas. For it to have been strangers doesn't make any sense! They'd have robbed him and left him there in the street, or in an alley. Maybe—" She frowned; she did not believe it herself. "Maybe it has nothing to do with whoever used him—but don't you think it has? People don't just suddenly stop having 'relationships.'" She used a delicate word, but they both knew what she meant. "Not where there isn't love. Whoever it is, he'll find someone else now this boy is dead—won't he?"

He sat back wearily. He had been deceiving himself because it would be easier, would avoid the unpleasantness and the pain.

"I expect so," he admitted. "Yes, I suppose he will. I can't take the chance. You're right," he sighed. "Damn."

Charlotte could not put the boy's death out of her mind. She did not speak of it again that evening to Pitt; he was already full of the knowledge of it and wanted to bar it from his thoughts, to have some hours to restore his emotions and revitalize.

But through the night she woke often. As she lay staring at the ceiling, Pitt silent beside her in the sleep of exhaustion, her mind compelled her to think over and over what sort of tragedy had finally ended in this dreadful manner.

Of course she did not know the Waybournes—they were hardly within her social circle—but her sister Emily might. Emily had married into the aristocracy and moved in high society now.

Then she remembered that Emily was away in the country, in Leicestershire, visiting a cousin of George's. They were to go hunting, or something of the sort. She could picture Emily in immaculate riding habit as she sat perched on her sidesaddle, heart in her throat, wondering whether she could take the fences without falling off and making a fool of herself, yet determined not to admit defeat. There would be an enormous hunt breakfast: two hundred people or more, the master in glorious pink, hounds milling around the horses' feet, chatter, shouts to order, the smell of frost—not, of course, that Charlotte had ever been to a hunt! But she had heard from those who had.

And neither could she turn to Great-Aunt Vespasia—she had gone to Paris for the month. She would have been ideal; she had known absolutely everyone that mattered over the last fifty years.

But then, according to Pitt, Waybourne was only a baronet, a very minor title—it could even have been bought in trade. Her own father was a banker and man of affairs; her mother might know Lady Waybourne. It was at least worth trying. If she could meet the Waybournes socially, when they were not guarding themselves against the vulgarity and intrusion of the police, she might learn something that would be of use to Pitt.

Naturally, they would be in mourning now, but there were always sisters or cousins, or even close friends—people who would, as a matter of course, know of relationships that would never be discussed with persons of the lower orders, such as professional investigators.

Accordingly, without mentioning it to Pitt, she took an omnibus just before lunch the following day and called on her mother at her home in Rutland Place.

"Charlotte, my dear!" Her mother was delighted to see her; it seemed she had completely forgiven her for that miserable affair over the Frenchman. There was nothing but warmth in Caroline's face now. "Do stay for luncheon—Grandmama will be down in half an hour, and we shall have lunch. I am expecting Dominic any moment." She hesitated, searching Charlotte's eyes for any shadow of the old enchantment when she had been so in love with the husband of her eldest sister, Sarah, when Sarah was still alive. But she found nothing; indeed, Charlotte's feelings for Dominic had long since faded into simple affection.

The anxiety disappeared. "It will be an excellent party. How are you, my dear? How are Jemima and Daniel?"

For some time they discussed family affairs. Charlotte could hardly launch instantly into inquiries her mother would be bound to disapprove of. She had always found Charlotte's meddling in Pitt's affairs both alarming and in the poorest possible taste.

There was a thump on the door. The maid opened it, and Grandmama swept in, wearing dourest black, her hair screwed up in a style that had been fashionable thirty years before, when society, in her opinion, had reached its zenith—it had been on the decline ever since. Her face was sharp with irritaiton. She eyed Charlotte up and down silently, then whacked the chair nearest to her with her stick to make sure it was precisely where she supposed, and sat down in it heavily.

"Didn't know you were coming, child!" she observed. "Have you no manners to inform people? Don't suppose you have a calling card either, eh? When I was young, a lady did not drop in to a person's house without due notice, as if she were a piece of unsolicited postage! No one has any manners these days. And I take it you will be getting one of these contraptions with strings and bells, and the good Lord knows what else? Telephones! Talking to people on electric wires, indeed!" She sniffed loudly, "Since dear Prince Albert died, all moral sensibility has declined. It is the Prince of Wales' fault—the scandals one hears are enough to make one faint! What about Mrs. Langtry? No better than she should be, I'll be bound!" She squinted at Charlotte, her eyes bright and angry.

Charlotte ignored the matter of the Prince of Wales and returned to the question of the telephone.

"No, Grandmama, they are very expensive—and, for me, quite unnecessary."

"Quite unnecessary for anyone!" Grandmama snorted. "Lot of nonsense! What's wrong with a perfectly good letter?" She swiveled a little to glare at Charlotte face to face. "Though you always wrote a shocking hand! Emily was the only one of you who could handle a pen like a lady. Don't know what you were thinking of, Caroline! I brought up my daughter to know all the arts a lady should, the proper things—embroidery, painting, singing and playing the pianoforte pleasingly—the sort of occupations proper for a lady. None of this meddling in other people's affairs, politics and such. Never heard such nonsense! That's men's business, and not good for the health or the welfare of women. I've told you that before, Caroline."

Grandmama was Charlotte's father's mother, and never tired of telling her daughter-in-law things should be done to conform with standards as they used to be in her own youth, when things were conducted properly.

Mercifully they were saved any further pursuance of the subject by Dominic's arrival. He was as elegant as always but now the grace of his movement, the way his dark hair grew to his quick smile stirred no pain in Charlotte at all. She felt only the pleasure of seeing a friend.

He greeted them all charmingly, even Grandmama, and as always she dissembled in front of him. She examined him for something to criticize and failed to find anything. She was not sure whether she was pleased or disappointed. It was not desirable that young men, however attractive, should be too satisfied with themselves. It did them no good at all. She looked at him again, more carefully.

"Is your barber indisposed?" she said at last.

Dominic's black eyebrows rose a little.

"You consider my hair ill-cut, Grandmama?" He still gave her the courtesy title, even though his membership of the family was far more distant since Sarah's death and his move from the house in Cater Street to his own lodgings.

"I had not realized it had been cut at all!" she replied, screwing up her face. "At least not recently! Have you considered joining the army?"

"No, never," he said, affecting surprise. "Are their barbers good?"

She snorted with infinite contempt and turned to Caroline.

"I'm ready for luncheon. How long am I obliged to wait? Are we expecting yet another guest I have not been told of?"

Caroline opened her mouth to argue, then resigned herself to the futility of it.

"Immediately, Mother-in-law," she said, standing up and reaching for the bell. "I will have it served now."

Charlotte did not find an opportunity to raise the name of the Waybournes until after soup had been served and eaten, the plates removed, and the fish set on the table.

"Waybourne?" Grandmama balanced an enormous portion on her fork, her eyes like black prunes. "Waybourne?" The fish overbalanced and fell on her plate into a pile of sauce. She scooped it up again and put it into her mouth, her cheeks bulging.

"I don't think so." Caroline shook her head. "Who was Lady Waybourne before she was married, do you know?"

Charlotte had to admit that she had no idea.

Grandmama swallowed with a gulp and coughed violently.

"That's the trouble with the world these days!" she snapped when she had caught her breath. "Nobody knows who anyone is any more! Society has gone to the dogs!" She took another huge mouthful of fish and glared at each of them in turn.

"Why do you ask?" Caroline inquired innocently. "Are you considering whether to pursue an acquaintance?"

Dominic appeared lost in his own thoughts.

"Are they people you have met?" Caroline continued.

Grandmama swallowed. "Hardly!" she said with considerable acid. "If they are people we might be acquainted with, then they would not move in Charlotte's circle. I told her that when she insisted on running off and marrying that extraordinary creature from the Bow Street runners, or whatever they call them these days! I don't know what you were thinking of, Caroline, to allow such a thing! If one of my daughters had even entertained such an idea, I'd have locked her in her bedroom until she came out of it!" She spoke as if it were some kind of fit.

Dominic covered his face with his napkin to hide his smile, but it still showed in his eyes as he looked up quickly at Charlotte.

"A lot of things were done in your day that are impractical now," Caroline said crossly. "Times change, Mama-in-law."

Grandmama banged her fork on her empty plate and her eyebrows rose almost to her hair.

"The bedroom door still has a lock on it, has it not?" she demanded.

"Vanderley," Dominic said suddenly.

Grandmama swung around to face him. "What did you say?"

"Vanderley," he repeated. "Benita Waybourne was Vanderley before she married. I remember because I know Esmond Vanderley."

Charlotte instantly forgot about Grandmama and her insults, and looked at him with excitement.

"Do you? Could you possibly find a way to introduce me—discreetly, of course? Please?"

He looked a bit startled. "If you wish—but whatever for? I don't think you would like him. He is fashionable, and quite amusing—but I think you would find him very light."

"All young men are light-minded these days!" Grandmama said morosely. "No one knows their duty anymore."

Charlotte ignored her. She had already thought of her excuse. It was a complete lie, but desperate situations occasionally call for a little invention.

"It is for a friend," she said, looking at no one in particular. "A certain young person I know—a romantic affair. I would rather not divulge the details. They are"—she hesitated delicately—"most personal."

"Indeed!" Grandmama scowled. "I hope it is nothing sordid."

"Not in the least." Charlotte jerked her head up and faced her, finding suddenly that it gave her great pleasure to lie to the old lady. "She is of good family but slight resources, and she wishes to better herself. I'm sure you would sympathize with that, Grandmama."

Grandmama gave her a suspicious look, but did not argue. Instead she glanced across at Caroline.

"We are all finished! Why don't you ring the bell and have them dish the next course? I presume we are to have a next course? I don't want to sit here all afternoon! We may have callers. Do you wish them to find us still at luncheon?"

Resignedly, Caroline reached out and rang the bell.

When it was time to leave, Charlotte bade her mother and grandmother goodbye. Dominic escorted her out and offered to take her home in a hansom. He knew her circumstances: that otherwise she would have to walk to an omnibus. She gratefully accepted, both for the comfort and because she wished to pursue the matter of a meeting with Esmond Vanderley, who must be, if Dominic was correct, the dead boy's uncle.

Inside the hansom, he looked at her skeptically.

"It's unlike you to interfere in other people's romances, Charlotte. Who is she, that her 'betterment' has engaged your assistance?"

She debated rapidly whether it would be advisable to continue the lie or to tell him the truth. On the whole, the truth was better—at least it was more consistent.

"It isn't a romance at all," she confessed. "It is a crime."

"Charlotte!"

"A very serious one!" she said hastily. "And if I learn something of the circumstances, I may prevent its happening again. Truly, Dominic, it is something Thomas would never learn in the way we could!"

He looked at her sideways. "We?" he said cautiously.

"We who are placed so as to be socially acquainted with the family!" she explained with a fairly successful attempt at innocence.

"Well, I can't just take you round to Vanderley's rooms and present you," he protested reasonably.

"No, of course not." She smiled. "But I'm sure you could find an occasion, if you tried."

He looked dubious.

"I am still your sister-in-law," she pressed. "It would all be quite proper."

"Does Thomas know about this?"

"Not yet." She evaded the truth with uncharacteristic skill. "I could hardly tell him before I knew that you were

41

able to help." She did not mention that she had no intention of telling him afterward either.

Her ability to deceive was entirely new, and he was not used to it. He took her remarks at face value.

"Then I suppose it is all right. I'll arrange it as soon as I can without being crass."

She reached out her hand and clasped his impulsively, giving him a radiant smile that unnerved him a little.

"Thank you, Dominic. That really is most generous of you! I'm sure if you knew how important it is, you would be happy to help!"

"Humph." He was unprepared to commit himself any further; perhaps he was not entirely wise to trust Charlotte when she was embarked upon an attempt at detection.

When he returned to the Waybournes' home three days later, Pitt had made an effort to find witnesses—anyone who had heard of an attack, a kidnapping, any event in Bluegate Fields that might have relevance to Arthur Waybourne's death. But none of his usual sources of information offered him anything.

He was inclined to believe there was nothing to know. The crime was a domestic one, and not of the streets.

He and Gillivray were received, to their surprise, in the withdrawing room. Not only Anstey Waybourne was present, but two other men. One was lean, in his early forties, with fair, heavily waving hair and regular features. His clothes were excellently cut, but it was the elegance with which he held himself that gave the clothes distinction. The other man was a few years older, thicker of body, but still imposing. His rich side-whiskers were touched with gray, his nose fleshy and strong.

Waybourne was somewhat at a loss to know how to introduce them. One did not treat policemen as social entities, but he obviously needed to inform Pitt who the others were, though apparently they were expecting Pitt.

He resolved the problem by nodding toward the older man with a brief indicative gesture.

"Good afternoon, Inspector. Mr. Swynford has been good enough to give his permission, if you still find it necessary, for you to speak to his son." His arm moved slightly to include the younger man. "My brother-in-law Mr. Esmond Vanderley—to comfort my wife, at this extremely difficult time." Perhaps it was intended as an introduction; more likely it was a warning of the family solidarity that was massing against any unwarranted intrusion, any excess of duty that verged on mere curiosity.

"Good afternoon," Pitt replied, then introduced Gillivray.

Waybourne was a little surprised; it was not the reply he had foreseen, but he accepted it.

"Have you discovered anything further about my son's death?" he inquired. Then, as Pitt glanced at the others, he smiled very bleakly. "You may say whatever you have to tell me in front of these gentlemen. What is it?"

"I'm sorry, sir, but we have found no information at all—"

"I hardly expected you would," Waybourne interrupted him. "But I appreciate it was your duty to try. I'm obliged to you for informing me so promptly."

It was a dismissal, but Pitt could not leave it so easily, so comfortably.

"I'm afraid we do not believe strangers would have tried to hide your son as they did," he went on. "There was no purpose. It would have been simpler to let him lie where he was attacked. It would have aroused less remark, which could only be to their advantage. And street robbers do not drown people—they use a knife or a club."

Waybourne's face darkened. "What are you trying to say, Inspector? It was you who told me my son was drowned. Do you now dispute that?"

"No, sir, I dispute that it was a casual attack."

"I don't know what you mean! If it was premeditated, then obviously someone intended to kidnap him for ransom, but there was some sort of an accident—"

"Possibly." Pitt did not think there had ever been ransom planned. And although he had mentally rehearsed how he would tell Waybourne it was a deliberate murder—neither an accident nor anything as relatively clean as a kidnapping for money—now, faced with Vanderley and Swynford as well as Waybourne, all three watching, listening, the tidy phrases escaped him. "But if it was so designed," he continued, "then we should be able to find out quite a lot if we investigate. They will almost certainly have cultivated his acquaintance, or that of someone close to him."

"Your imagination is running away with you, Inspector!" Waybourne said icily. "We do not take up acquaintances as casually as you appear to imagine." He glanced at Gillivray, as if he hoped he might have a better understanding of a social circle of finer distinctions, where people did not make such chance friendships. One required to know who people were—indeed, who their parents were.

"Oh." Vanderley's expression changed slightly. "Arthur might have. The young can be very tolerant, you know. Met some odd people myself, from time to time." He smiled a little sourly. "Even the best families can have their problems. Could even have been a prank that went wrong."

"A prank?" Waybourne's entire body stiffened with outrage. "My son molested in his—his innocence, robbed of—" A muscle jumped in his cheek; he could not bring himself to use the words.

Vanderley flushed. "I was suggesting the intention, Anstey, not the result. I take it from your remark that you believe the two are connected?"

Now it was Waybourne's turn to color with awkwardness, even anger with himself.

"No—I—"

For the first time, Swynford spoke; his voice was rich, full of confidence. He was used to being listened to without the need to seek attention.

"I'm afraid, Anstey, it does look inevitably as if someone of poor Arthur's acquaintance was perverted in the most appalling fashion. Don't blame yourself—no man of decency would conceive of such an abominable thing. It doesn't enter the mind. But now it has to be faced. As the police say, there doesn't appear to be any other rational explanation."

"What do you suggest I do?" Waybourne demanded sarcastically. "Allow the police to question my friends, to see if any of them seduced and murdered my son?"

"I hardly think you will find him among your friends, Anstey." Swynford was patient. He was dealing with a man in the extremities of grief. Outbursts that at another time would be frowned upon were now quite naturally excused. "I would begin by looking a little more closely at some of your employees."

Waybourne's face fell. "Are you suggesting Arthur was—was consorting with the butler or the footman?"

Vanderley looked up. "I remember I used to be great friends with one of the grooms when I was Arthur's age. He could do anything with a horse, rode like a centaur. Lord, how I wanted to do that myself! I was a damned sight more impressed by his talents than any of the dry political skills my father practiced." He made a face. "One is, at sixteen."

A flicker of light shone in Waybourne's eyes. He looked up at Pitt.

"Never thought of that. I suppose you'd better consider the groom, although I've no idea whether he rides. He's a competent driver, but I never knew Arthur had any interest. . . ."

Swynford leaned on the back of one of the chairs.

"And of course there's always the tutor—whatever his

name is. A good tutor can become a great influence on a boy."

Waybourne frowned. "Jerome? He had excellent references. Not a particularly likable man, but extremely competent. Fine academic record. Keeps good discipline in the schoolroom. Has a wife. Good woman—spotless reputation. I do take certain care, Mortimer!" The criticism was implicit.

"Of course you do. We all do!" Swynford said reasonably, even placatingly. "But then a vice of that sort would hardly be known! And the fact that the wretched man has a wife is no proof of anything. Poor woman!"

"Good God!"

Pitt remembered the tutor's tight, intelligent face reflecting a painful knowledge of his position, of what it would always be, and why. There was nothing wrong with his talent or his diligence; it was just his birth that was wrong. Now, perhaps, the slow growth of sourness had warped his character as well, probably permanently after all these years.

It was time to interrupt. But before Pitt spoke, Gillivray cut in.

"We'll do that, sir. I think there's every chance we shall discover something. You may well have found the answer already."

Waybourne let out his breath slowly. The muscle in his face calmed.

"Yes. Yes, I suppose you'd better. Most unpleasant, but if it cannot be avoided . . ."

"We'll be discreet, sir," Gillivray promised.

Pitt felt irritation wash over him. "We'll investigate everything," he said a little sharply. "Until we have either discovered the truth or exhausted every possibility."

Waybourne looked at him with disapproval, his eyes sharp under the sweeping, fair lashes.

"Indeed! Then you may return tomorrow and begin with the groom and Mr. Jerome. Now I think I have said everything that I have to say to you. I will instruct the appropriate servants for your convenience tomorrow. Good day to you."

"Good day, gentlemen." Pitt accepted dismissal this time. He had much to consider before he spoke to the groom, Jerome, or anyone else. There was already an ugliness in it beyond the tragedy of death itself. Tentacles of the compulsions that had led to the death were beginning to surface, assaulting his senses.

3

The Waybourne family doctor had asked to see the body and make an examination; he came away silent, shaking his head, his face drawn. Pitt did not know what he said to Waybourne, but there was never any further suggestion of incompetence by the police surgeon, and no other explanation for the symptoms was put forward. In fact, they were not mentioned.

Pitt and Gillivray returned at ten o'clock in the morning; they interviewed the grooms and the footmen, which proved fruitless. Arthur's tastes had been more sophisticated than anything the stables or the mews had to offer. He had liked to be well driven, and admired a handsome rig, but he had never shown the least desire to take the reins himself. Even good bloodstock moved him to no more than a passing appreciation, like good boots or a well-tailored coat.

"This is all a waste of time," Gillivray said, poking his hands in his pockets and stepping up into the areaway. "He probably fell into bad company with some older boy—a single experience—and then he reverted to quite natural relationships. After all, he was sixteen! I daresay he contracted the disease from a street woman or some other miserable initiation. Perhaps someone gave him a little too much to drink—you know how these things can end up. I don't suppose he had the least idea, poor little devil. And we certainly won't do any good pursuing it." He raised his eyebrows and gave Pitt a warning glance. "None of those men," he said, jerking his head back toward the stables, "would dare touch the son of the house! And I don't imagine they'd want to. They'd stick to their own class—more fun and less dangerous. We could probably find out about that from the maids, if it matters. A groom would have to be insane to risk his livelihood. He'd probably never get another place with a decent family anywhere in the country if he was caught! No man in his right mind is going to risk that for a bit of foolery."

Pitt had no argument; he had already thought the same things himself. Added to which, by all accounts so far, neither Arthur nor his brother had been in the habit of visiting the stables. Carriages were brought to the front door and there was no occasion for them to go to the mews except from personal interest. And that, apparently, had not existed.

"No," Pitt agreed tersely, cleaning his feet against the iron boot-scraper at the back door. "Now we'd better try the rest of the staff to see what they can tell us."

"Oh, come on!" Gillivray protested. "Boys like that don't spend their spare time—or their affection—in the servants' hall!"

"Clean your boots," Pitt ordered. "Anyway, it was you who wanted to check on the grooms," he added spitefully. "Just ask them. The butler or the valet may know where the boys went visiting, other houses they stayed at. Families go away for weekends or longer, you know. Strange things happen at country houses on occasion."

Gillivray scraped his boots obediently, taking off some straw and, to his surprise, manure. He wrinkled his nose.

"Spent many weekends in the country, have you, Inspector?" he asked, permitting a faint touch of sarcasm into his voice.

"More than I can count," Pitt replied with a very small smile. "I grew up on a country estate. The gentlemen's gentlemen could tell a few tales, if they were plied with a little of the butler's best port."

Gillivray was caught between distaste and curiosity. It was a world he had never entered, but had watched avidly from the first time he glimpsed its color and ease, and the grace with which it hid its frailties.

"I hardly think the butler will give me the keys to his cellar for that purpose," he said with a touch of envy. It smarted that Pitt, of all people, should have seen inside such a society, even if only from the vantage of an outdoor servant's son. The mere knowledge was something Gillivray did not have.

"We won't do any good raking it all over," Gillivray repeated.

Pitt did not bother to argue anymore. Gillivray was obliged to obey. And, to be honest, Pitt did not believe there was any purpose in it either, except to satisfy Waybourne—and perhaps Athelstan.

"I'll see the tutor." He opened the back door and went into the scullery. The kitchenmaid, a girl of about fourteen, dressed in gray stuff and a calico apron, was scrubbing pots. She looked up, her hands dripping soap, her face full of curiosity.

"You get on with your work, Rosie," the cook ordered, scowling at the intruders. "And what'll you be wanting now?" she demanded of Pitt. "I've no time to be getting you anything to eat, or cups of tea either! I've never seen the like of it. Police indeed! I've luncheon to get for the family, and dinner to think of, I'll have you know. And Rosie's much too busy to be bothering with the likes of you!"

Pitt looked at the table and at a glance he could see the ingredients for pigeon pie, five types of vegetables, some

50

sort of whitefish, a fruit pudding, trifle, sherbet, and a bowl full of eggs that could have been for anything—perhaps a cake or a soufflé.

The downstairs maid was polishing glasses. The light caught on the cut designs, sending prisms of color into the mirror behind her.

"Thank you," Pitt said dryly. "Mr. Gillivray will talk to the butler, and I am going through to speak to Mr. Jerome."

The cook snorted, dusting flour from her hands.

"Well, you'll not do it in my kitchen," she snapped. "You'd best go and see Mr. Welsh in his pantry, if you must. Where you see Mr. Jerome is nothing to do with me." She bent to her pastry again, sleeves rolled up, hands strong and thick, powerful enough to wring a turkey's neck.

Pitt walked past her, along the passage and through the baize door into the hallway. The footman showed him to the morning room, and five minutes later, Jerome came in.

"Good morning, Inspector," he said with a faintly supercilious half smile. "I really cannot add anything to what I have already told you. But if you insist, I am prepared to repeat it."

Pitt could not feel any liking for the man, in spite of an empathy for his situation; but it was an intellectual understanding, an ability to imagine how Jerome felt—the scraping of the emotions with every small reminder of dependence, of inferiority. Facing him in the flesh—seeing his bright, guarded eyes, the pursed mouth, the precise collar and tie, hearing the edge to his voice—Pitt still disliked him.

"Thank you," he said, forcing himself to be patient. He wanted to let Jerome know that they were both there under compulsion: Pitt of duty, Jerome because Waybourne required it. But that would have been to give way to himself, and would defeat his objective. He sat down to indicate that he intended to take some time.

Jerome sat also, arranging his coat and trousers with care. Opposite Pitt, who spread out like dumped laundry, Jerome was meticulous. He raised his eyebrows expectantly.

"How long have you taught Arthur and Godfrey Waybourne?" Pitt began.

"Three years and ten months," Jerome replied.

"Then Arthur would have been twelve and Godfrey nine?" Pitt calculated.

"Bravo." Jerome's voice went down at the end in weary sarcasm.

Pitt restrained his inclination to retaliate.

"Then you must know both boys well. You have observed them through most important years, the change from child to youth," he said instead.

"Naturally."

There was still no interest in Jerome's face, no anticipation of what was to come. Had Waybourne told him anything of the details of Arthur's death or merely of the death itself? Pitt watched him more closely, waiting for surprise in the round eyes, disgust—or any kind of fear.

"You are aware of their friends, even if you do not know them personally?" he continued.

"To a limited extent." This time Jerome was more guarded, not willing to commit himself where he could not foresee.

There was no delicate way of approaching the subject. If Jerome had observed any strange personal habits in either of his charges, he could hardly afford to admit it now. And a wise tutor who wished to retain his position made it his business not to see the less attractive attributes of his employers or their friends. Pitt understood before he asked. Anything must be framed in such a way that Jerome could pretend only now to understand the meaning of what he had seen.

To be direct seemed the only avenue. He tried to make himself sound frank, to hide his instinctive dislike.

"Did Sir Anstey tell you the cause of Arthur's death?" he asked, leaning forward in an unconscious attempt to do physically what he could not do emotionally.

Jerome sat back at the same moment, viewing Pitt with a frown.

"I believe he was attacked in the street," he replied. "I haven't heard more than that." His nostrils flared delicately. "Are the details important, Inspector?"

"Yes, Mr. Jerome, they are very important indeed. Arthur Waybourne was drowned." He watched closely: Was the incredulity feigned, a little too much?

"Drowned?" Jerome regarded him as if he had made an attempt at humor that was repellent. Then comprehension flashed across his face. "You mean in the river?"

"No, Mr. Jerome, in a bath."

Jerome spread out his manicured hands. His eyes were bleak.

"If this sort of idiocy is part of your method of interrogation, Inspector, I find it unnecessary and most unpleasant."

Pitt could not disbelieve him. Such a dry, sour man could not be so consummate an actor, or he would have shown humor, learned charm to make his own path easier.

"No," Pitt answered him. "I mean it quite literally. Arthur Waybourne was drowned in bathwater, and his naked body put down a manhole into the sewers."

Jerome stared at him. "In God's name! What's happening? Why—I mean—who? How could—for heaven's sake, man, it's preposterous!"

"Yes, Mr. Jerome—and very ugly," Pitt said quietly. "And there is worse than that. He was homosexually used sometime before he was killed."

Jerome's face was absolutely still, as if he either did not understand or could not believe it as any kind of reality.

Pitt waited. Was the silence caution, a consideration what to say? Or was it genuine shock, the emotion any decent man would feel? He watched every flicker—and still he had no idea.

"Sir Anstey did not tell me that," Jerome said at last. "It is perfectly dreadful. I suppose there is no question?"

"No." Pitt allowed himself the shadow of a smile. "Do you think Sir Anstey would concede it if there were?"

Jerome took his point, but the irony passed him by.

"No—no, of course not. Poor man. As if death were not enough." He looked up quickly, hostile again. "I trust you are going to treat the matter with discretion?"

"As far as possible," Pitt said. "I would prefer to get all the answers I can from within the household."

"If you are suggesting that I have any idea who might have had such a relationship with Arthur, you are quite mistaken." Jerome bristled with offense. "If I had had even the least suspicion of such a thing, I should have done something about it!"

"Would you?" Pitt said quickly. "Upon suspicion—and without proof? What would you have done, Mr. Jerome?"

Jerome saw the trap instantly. A flicker of self-mockery moved in his face, and then vanished.

"You are quite right, Mr. Pitt. I should have done nothing. However, disappointing as it is, I had no suspicion at all. Whatever occurred, it was quite beyond my knowledge. I can tell you all the boys of similiar age that Arthur spent time with. Although I don't envy you trying to discover which of them it was—if indeed it was any of his friends and not just some acquaintance. Personally, I think you are probably mistaken in supposing it to have any connection with his death. Why should anyone indulging in such a—a relationship commit murder? If you are suggesting some sort of an affair, with passion and jealousy or anything of the sort, I would remind you that Arthur Waybourne was barely sixteen."

This was something that had troubled Pitt. Why should

anyone have killed Arthur? Had Arthur threatened to disclose the relationship? Was he an unwilling partner, and the strain had become too great? That seemed the more likely answer. If it was someone who knew him, robbery would be pointless. Anything he would carry would be far too trivial for a boy of that social circle to covet so violently—a few coins, probably not even a watch or a ring.

And would another youth, even in panic, have the physical strength to murder, or afterward have the coolheadedness to dispose of the body so skillfully? And it was skillful: for all but mischance, it would never have been identified. An older man was a far more probable suspect: a man with more weight, more inured to his appetite, and better able to deal with the results of satisfying it—perhaps a man who had even foreseen this very danger arising one day.

Would such a man be fool enough, fragile enough, to become infatuated with a youth of sixteen? It was possible. Or perhaps it was a man who had only just discovered his own weakness, maybe through constant companionship, a proximity forced upon him by circumstances? He might still have the cunning to hide the body in the labyrinth of the sewers, trusting that by the time it was found it would be past connecting with the disappearance of Arthur Waybourne.

He looked up at Jerome. That careful face might hide anything. He was trained by a lifetime of masking his feelings so that they never offended, and his opinions so that they never clashed with those of his social superiors—even when he was perhaps better informed, or just quicker-witted. Was it possible?

Jerome was waiting, overtly patient. He had scant respect for Pitt, and he was enjoying the luxury of affording to show it.

"I think you would be better advised to leave the matter alone." Jerome sat back and crossed his legs, folding his hands fingertip to fingertip. "It was probably a single instance of excess, certainly repellent." His face was marked momentarily by a shadow of disgust; could the man really be an actor of such subtlety, such polish? "But not to be repeated," he went on. "If you persist in trying to discover who it was, apart from the fact that you will almost certainly fail, you will bring a great deal of distress, not least to yourself."

It was a fair warning, and Pitt was already aware of how the whole social caste would close its ranks against such an inquiry. To defend themselves they would defend each other—at any expense. After all, one moment of youthful vice was not worth exposing the follies or pains of a dozen families. Memories in society were long. Any youth marred by the stain might never marry within his own class, even if nothing was ever proved.

And perhaps Arthur had not been so very innocent. After all, he had contracted syphilis. Maybe his education had included women of the streets, an initiation into the other side of appetite.

"I know that," Pitt said quietly. "But I cannot overlook murder!"

"Then you would do better to concentrate on that and leave the other to be forgotten," Jerome expounded as if it were advice Pitt had sought from him.

Pitt felt his skin tighten in anger. He changed the subject, returning to facts: Arthur's daily routine, his habits, his friends, his studies, his likes and dislikes—every clue to character he could think of. But he found himself weighing the answers as much for what they said of Jerome as of Arthur.

It was over two hours later when he stood facing Waybourne in his library.

"You were an uncommonly long time with Jerome," Waybourne said critically. "I cannot imagine what he can have had to say to you of such value."

56

"He spent a great deal of time with your son. He must have known him well," Pitt began.

Waybourne's face was red. "What did he tell you?" He swallowed. "What did he say?"

"He had no knowledge of any impropriety," Pitt answered him, then wondered why he had given in so easily. It was a momentary thing—a flash of sensitivity, more instinct than thought; he had no warmth for the man.

Waybourne's face relaxed. Then incredulity flashed across his eyes, and something else.

"Good God! You don't really suspect him of—of—"

"Is there any reason why I should?"

Waybourne half rose from his chair.

"Of course not! Do you think if I—" He sank down again and covered his face with his hands. "I suppose I could have made a most ghastly mistake." He sat without moving for several seconds, then suddenly looked up at Pitt. "I had no idea! He had the most excellent references, you know?"

"And he may be worthy of them," Pitt said a little sharply. "Do you know something to his discredit you have not told me?"

Waybourne remained perfectly still for so long that Pitt was about to prompt him, when at last he replied.

"I don't know anything—at least not on the surface of my mind. Such an idea never occurred to me—why should it? What decent man entertains suspicions like that? But knowing what I do now"—he took a deep breath and let it out in a sigh—"I may remember things and understand them differently. You must allow me a little time. All this has been a very profound shock." There was finality in his voice. Pitt was dismissed; it was only a matter of whether he was delicate enough not to require that it be put into words.

There was nothing left to insist on. There was justice in

Waybourne's request for time to consider, to weigh memories in the light of understanding. Shock drove out clarity of thought, blurred the edges, distorted recall. He was not unusual; he needed time, and sleep, before he committed himself.

"Thank you," Pitt answered formally. "If you should think of anything relevant, I'm sure you will let us know. Good day, sir."

Waybourne, lost in his dark reflections, did not bother to reply, but continued to frown, staring at a spot on the carpet by Pitt's feet.

Pitt went home at the end of the day with a feeling not of satisfaction but of conclusion. The end was in sight; there would be no surprises, nothing more to discover but the pain-ridden details to dovetail into one another and complete the pattern. Jerome, a sad, unsatisfied man, cramped into a livelihood that stifled his talents and curbed his pride, had fallen in love with a boy who promised to be all the things Jerome himself might have been. Then, when all that envy and hunger had spilled over into physical passion, what? Perhaps a sudden revulsion, a fear—and Arthur had turned on him, threatening exposure? Searing shame for Jerome, all his private weakness torn apart, laughed at. And then dismissal without hope of ever finding another position—ruin. And doubtless the loss of the wife, who was—what? What was she to him?

Or had Arthur been more sophisticated than that? Was he capable of blackmail, even if it consisted of only the gentle, permanent pressure of his knowledge and its power? The slow smiles, the little cuts of the tongue.

From what Pitt had learned of Arthur Waybourne, he was neither so ingenious nor so enamored of integrity that the thought could not have occurred to him. He seemed to have been a youth determined to wade into adulthood with all its excitements as soon as chance al-

58

lowed. Perhaps that was not uncommon. For most adolescents, childhood hung on like old clothes, when new and glamorous ones, more flattering ones, were waiting.

Charlotte met him as soon as he walked in the door.

"I heard from Emily today, and you'll never believe—" She saw his face. "Oh. What is it?"

He smiled in spite of himself. "Do I look so grim?"

"Don't evade me, Thomas!" she said sharply. "Yes, you do. And what has happened? Is it something to do with that boy who was drowned? It is, isn't it?"

He took off his coat and Charlotte put it on the peg for him. She remained in the middle of the hallway, determined on an explanation.

"It appears as if it was the tutor," he replied. "It's all very sad and grubby. Somehow I can't be outraged with any pleasure anymore when it stops being anonymous and I can attach a face to it and a life before it. I wish I could find it incomprehensible—it would be so much damnably easier!"

She knew he was referring to the emotions, not the crime. He had no need to explain. She turned in silence, just offering him her hand, and led the way into the warm kitchen—its blacked stove open, with live embers behind the bars, its wooden table scrubbed white, gleaming pans, blue-ringed china set out on the dresser, ironing waiting over the rails to be taken upstairs. Somehow it seemed to him to be the heart of the house, the living core that only slept but was never empty—unlike the parlor or bedrooms when there was no one in them. It was more than just the fire; it was something to do with the smell of the room, the love and the work, the echo of voices that laughed and talked there.

Had Jerome ever had a kitchen like this that was his own to sit in for as long as he wanted, where he could put things into perspective?

He eased comfortably into one of the wooden chairs, and Charlotte put the kettle on the hob.

"The tutor," she repeated. "That was quick." She got down two cups and the china teapot with the flowers on it. "And convenient."

He was stung. Did she imagine he was trimming the case to suit his comfort or his career?

"I said it appears as if it was," he retorted sharply. "It's far from proven! But you said yourself that it was unlikely to have been a stranger. Who would be more likely than a lonely, inhibited man, forced by circumstances to be always more than a servant and less than an equal, neither in one world nor the other? He saw the boy every day, worked with him. He was constantly and subtly patronized, one minute encouraged for his knowledge, his skills, and the next rebuffed because of his social status, set aside as soon as school was out."

"You make that sound awful." She poured milk from the cooler at the back door into a jug and set it on the table. "Sarah and Emily and I had a governess, and she wasn't treated like that at all. I think she was perfectly happy."

"Would you have changed places with her?" he asked.

She thought for only a moment; then her face shadowed very slightly.

"No. But then a governess is never married. A tutor can be married because he doesn't have to look after his own children. Didn't you say this tutor was married?"

"Yes, but he has no children."

"Then why do you think he's lonely or dissatisfied? Maybe he likes teaching. Lots of people do. It's better than being a clerk or a shopboy."

He thought. Why had he supposed Jerome was lonely or dissatisfied? It was an impression, no more—and yet it was deep. He had felt a resentment around him, a hunger to have more, to *be* more.

"I don't know," he answered. "Something about the man; but it's no more than informed suspicion so far."

60

She took the kettle off the hob and made the tea, sending steam up in a sweet-smelling cloud.

"You know, most crimes are not very myserious," he went on, still a little defensively. "The most obvious person is usually the one responsible."

"I know." She did not look at him. "I know that, Thomas."

Two days later, any doubts he had were dismissed when a constable met him with the message that Sir Anstey Waybourne's footman had called, and Pitt was required at the house because a most serious turn of events had taken place; new and extremely disturbing evidence was to hand.

Pitt had no choice but to go immediately. It was raining, and he buttoned up his coat, tied his scarf tighter, and pushed his hat down on his head. It took only moments to find a hansom and clatter over the wet stones to the Waybourne house.

A serene-faced parlormaid let him in. Whatever had happened, it seemed she was unaware of it. She showed him straight into the library, where Waybourne was standing in front of the fire, clasping and unclasping his hands. His head jerked up and he faced Pitt even before the maid had closed the door.

"Good!" he said quickly. "Now perhaps we can get this whole dreadful business over with and bury the tragedy where it belongs. My God, it's appalling!"

The door closed with a faint snap and they were alone. The maid's footsteps clicked away on the parquet floor outside.

"What is the new evidence, sir?" Pitt asked guardedly. He was still sensitive to Charlotte's implication of convenience, and it would have to be more than suspicion or malice before he regarded it with any credence.

Waybourne did not sit down or offer Pitt a seat.

"I have learned something most shocking, quite—" His face creased with distress, and again Pitt was suddenly caught by a sense of pity that surprised and disconcerted him. "Quite dreadful!" Waybourne finished. He stared at the Turkish carpet, a rich red and blue. Pitt had once recovered one like it in a robbery case, and so knew its worth.

"Yes, sir," he said quietly. "Perhaps you would tell me what it is?"

Waybourne found the words difficult; he searched for them awkwardly.

"My younger son, Godfrey, has come to me with a most distressing confession." He clenched his knuckles. "I cannot blame the boy for not having told me before. He was . . . confused. He is only thirteen. Quite naturally, he did not understand the meaning, the implication." Finally he looked up, though only for a moment. He seemed to desire Pitt's understanding, or at least his comprehension.

Pitt nodded but said nothing. He wanted to hear whatever it was in Waybourne's own words, without prompting.

Waybourne went on slowly. "Godfrey has told me that Jerome has, on more than one occasion, been overly familiar with him." He swallowed. "That he has abused the boy's trust, quite natural trust, and—and fondled him in an unnatural fashion." He shut his eyes and his face twisted with emotion. "God! It's revolting! That man—" He breathed in and out, his chest heaving. "I'm sorry. I find this—extremely distasteful. Of course Godfrey did not understand the nature behind these acts at the time. He was disturbed by them, but it was only when I questioned him that he realized he must tell me. I did not let him know what had happened to his brother, only that he should not be afraid to tell me the truth, that I should not be angry with him. He has committed no sin whatsoever—poor child!"

Pitt waited, but apparently Waybourne had said all he

wished to. He looked up at Pitt, his eyes challenging, waiting for his response.

"May I speak to him?" Pitt said at last.

Waybourne's face darkened. "Is that absolutely necessary? Surely now that you know what Jerome's nature is, you will be able to find all the other information you need without questioning the boy. It is all most unpleasant, and the less said about it to him, the sooner he may forget it and begin to recover from the tragedy of his brother's death."

"I'm sorry, sir, but a man's life may depend on it." There was no such easy escape for either of them. "I must see Godfrey myself. I shall be as gentle as I can with him, but I cannot accept a secondhand account—even from you."

Waybourne glared at the floor, weighing in his mind one danger against another; Godfrey's ordeal against the possibility of the case dragging on, further police investigations. Then he jerked his head up to face Pitt, trying to judge if he could prevail on him by force of character if necessary. He knew it must fail.

"Very well," he said at last, his anger rasping through his voice. He reached for the bell and pulled it hard. "But I shall not permit you to harass the boy!"

Pitt did not bother to answer. Words were of no comfort now; Waybourne would not be able to believe him. They waited in silence until the footman came. Waybourne told him to fetch Master Godfrey. Some moments later, the door opened and a slender, fair-haired boy stood in the entrance. He was not unlike his brother, but his features were finer; when the softness of childhood was gone, Pitt judged they would be stronger. The bones in the nose were different. He would like to have seen Lady Waybourne, just from curiosity, to complete the family, but he had been told she was still indisposed.

"Close the door, Godfrey," Waybourne ordered. "This is Inspector Pitt, from the police. I'm afraid he insists that you repeat to him what you have told me about Mr. Jerome."

The boy obeyed, but his eyes were on Pitt, wary. He walked in and stood in front of his father. Waybourne put his hand on the boy's arm.

"Tell Mr. Pitt what you told me yesterday evening, Godfrey, about Mr. Jerome touching you. There is no need to be afraid. You have done nothing wrong or shameful."

"Yes, sir," Godfrey replied. But he hesitated and seemed unsure how to begin. He appeared to think of several words and discard them all.

"Did Mr. Jerome embarrass you?" Pitt felt a rush of sympathy for the boy. He was being asked to recount to a stranger an experience that was profoundly personal, confusing, and probably repellent. It should have been allowed to remain a secret within his family, a secret to be told or not as he chose, perhaps a little at a time, at whatever moments it came easily. Pitt hated having to extract it this way.

The boy's face showed surprise; his blue eyes widened into a frank stare.

"Embarrass?" he repeated, considering the word. "No, sir."

Apparently, Pitt had chosen the wrong word, although it seemed a particularly appropriate one to him.

"He did something that caused you to feel uncomfortable because it was overfamiliar, unusual?" he said, trying again.

The boy's shoulders lifted and tightened a little.

"Yes," he said very quietly, and for a second his eyes went up to his father's face, but for so short a time that there was no communication between them.

"It's important." Pitt decided to treat him as an adult. Perhaps candor would be less distressing than an attempt to skirt around the issue, which would make it seem that there was shame or crime attached to it, leaving the boy to seek his own words for something he did not understand.

"I know," Godfrey replied soberly. "Papa said so."

"What happened?"

"When Mr. Jerome touched me?"

"Yes."

"He just put his arm around me. I slipped and fell, and he helped me up."

Pitt curbed his impatience. For all his confusion perhaps a natural denial, a retreat, the boy must be embarrassed.

"But it was unusual this time?" he encouraged.

"I didn't understand." Godfrey's face puckered. "I didn't know there was anything wrong—till Papa explained."

"Of course," Pitt agreed, watching Waybourne's hand clench on his son's shoulder. "How was it different from other times?"

"You must tell him," Waybourne said with an effort. "Tell him that Mr. Jerome put his hand on a most private part of your body." His face colored with his own discomfort.

Pitt waited.

"He touched me," Godfrey said reluctantly. "Sort of felt around."

"I see. Did that only happen once?"

"No—not really. I—honestly, sir—I don't understand—"

"That's enough!" Waybourne said harshly. "He's told you—Jerome interfered with him, more than once. I cannot permit you to pursue it any further. You have what you need. Now do your job. For heaven's sake, arrest the man and get him out of my house!"

"Of course, sir, you must dismiss him from your employ, if you think fit," Pitt answered with unhappiness growing inside him. A feeling of certainty was drawing close in a sad, imprisoning circle. "But I have not yet enough evidence to charge him with murder."

Waybourne's face convulsed, the muscles of his body knotting. Godfrey winced under his hand.

"Good God, man! What more do you want? An eyewitness?"

Pitt tried to keep calm. Why should this man understand police necessities? One son had been murdered, the other distressed by perverted attentions, and the offender was still under his roof. Why should he be reasonable? His emotions were raw. His whole family had been violated in one way after another, robbed and betrayed.

"I'm sorry, sir." He was apologizing for the whole crime: for its nature, its obscenity, for his own intrusion into it, for the grief still to come. "I'll be as quick and as discreet as I can. Thank you, Godfrey. Good day, Sir Anstey." He turned and went out of the library into the hall where the parlormaid was waiting, still serene and unknowing, with Pitt's hat in her hand.

Pitt was dissatisfied without reason. There was not yet enough known for grounds to arrest Jerome, but there was too much to justify keeping it from Athelstan any longer. Jerome had said he spent the evening at a musical recital, and had had no idea where Arthur Waybourne had been or intended to be. Perhaps if it was carefully checked, Jerome's time could be accounted for. It was possible an acquaintance had seen him, and if he had returned home with someone—perhaps his wife—it would be impossible to prove beyond a very reasonable doubt that he had then gone out to some unknown place and murdered Arthur Waybourne.

That was a weakness in the case. They had no idea whatsoever where the murder had taken place. There was without question much to do before they had grounds for arrest.

He quickened his step. He could face Athelstan with a report; there was progress, but they were a long way from certainty.

*   *   *

Athelstan was smoking an excellent cigar, and his room was pungent with the smell of it. The furniture gleamed a little in the gaslight, and the brass doorknob was bright, without a fingermark.

"Sit down," Athelstan invited comfortably. "Glad we're getting this thing tidied up. Very nasty, very painful. Well, what did Sir Anstey have to tell you? Deciding factor, he said. What was it, man?"

Pitt was surprised. He had not known that Athelstan was even aware of the call from Waybourne.

"No," he said quickly. "Not that. Indicative, certainly, but not enough for an arrest."

"Well, what was it?" Athelstan said impatiently, leaning forward over the desk. "Don't just sit there, Pitt!"

Pitt found himself inexplicably reluctant to tell him, to repeat the sad, frail story. It was nothing, and everything—indefinite and at the same time undeniable.

Athelstan's fingers drummed with irritation on the burgundy leather surface.

"The younger brother, Godfrey," Pitt replied wearily. "He says that the tutor Jerome was overfamiliar with him, that he touched him in a homosexual manner." He took a breath and let it out slowly. "More than once. Of course he did not mention it at the time because—"

"Of course, of course." Athelstan dismissed it with a wave of his thick hand. "Probably didn't realize at the time what it meant—only makes sense in the light of his brother's death. Dreadful—poor boy. Take a while to get over it. Well!" He spread his hand flat on the desk, as if closing something, the other hand still held the cigar. "At least we'll be able to tidy it all up now. Go and arrest the fellow. Wretched!" His face curled in distaste and he let out his breath in a little snort through his nose.

"We haven't enough for an arrest," Pitt argued. "He may be able to account for his time the whole night."

"Nonsense," Athelstan said briskly. "Says he was out at

a musical event of some sort. Went alone, saw no one, and came back alone after his wife had gone to bed. And he didn't wake her. No account at all! Could have been anywhere."

Pitt stiffened.

"How do you know?" He had not known that much himself, and he had told Athelstan nothing at all.

A slow smile touched the corners of Athelstan's mouth.

"Gillivray," he answered. "Good man, that. He'll go a long way. Has a good manner about him. He makes the whole investigation as civilized as possible and gets on with what really matters—gets to the core of a case."

"Gillivray," Pitt repeated with a tightening at the back of his neck. "You mean Gillivray checked up on where Jerome said he was that night?"

"Didn't tell you?" Athelstan said casually. "Should have done. Bit keen—can't blame him. Felt for the father—very nasty case this." He frowned to show his own sympathy. "Still, glad it's over now. You can go and make the arrest. Take Gillivray with you. He deserves to be in at the kill!"

Pitt felt hopelessness and anger boil up inside him. Jerome was probably guilty, but this was not sufficient. There were still too many other possibilities unexplored.

"We haven't got a good enough case," he said sharply. "We don't know where the crime took place! There's no circumstantial evidence, nothing to put Jerome anywhere but where he says he was. Where did this relationship take place—in Jerome's house? Where was his wife? And why, of all things, should Arthur Waybourne be taking a bath in Jerome's house?"

"For heaven's sake, Pitt!" Athelstan interrupted angrily, clenching his hand on the cigar till it bent. "These are details! They can be found out. Perhaps he hired a room somewhere—"

"With a bath in it?" Pitt said with scorn. "Not many

bawdy houses or cheap rooms have a private bath where you can comfortably murder someone!"

"Then it won't be hard to find, will it?" Athelstan snapped. "It's your job to unearth these things. But first you'll arrest Jerome and put him where he can't escape and do any more harm! Or next thing we know he'll be on the Channel steamer and we'll never see him again! Now do your duty, man. Or must I send Gillivray to do it for you?"

There was no point in arguing. Either Pitt did it or someone else would. And, in spite of the case being far from proved, there was justice in what Athelstan said. Other answers were possible, even though Pitt knew in his mind they were unlikely. Jerome had every likely trait; his life and his circumstances were susceptible to the emptiness, the warping. It needed only the physical hunger—and no one could explain whence that might grow or whom it might tempt.

And if Jerome had been driven to murder once, he could, as he felt the police coming closer to him, easily be forced to panic, to run or, far worse, to kill again.

Pitt stood up. He had nothing to fight Athelstan with, but then, perhaps there was nothing to fight him about either.

"Yes, sir," he acceded quietly. "I'll take Gillivray and go tomorrow morning, as soon as it won't cause a stir." He looked at Athelstan wryly, but Athelstan saw no humor in Pitt's statement.

"Good," he said, sitting back with satisfaction. "Good man. Be discreet—family's been through a bad time, very bad. Get it over with now. Warn the man on the beat to keep an eye tonight, but I don't suppose he'll run. Not close enough yet."

"Yes, sir," Pitt said, going to the door. "Yes, sir."

4

Pitt set out the following morning with Gillivray, bright and spring-stepped beside him. He hated Gillivray for his demeanor. An arrest for so intimately personal a crime was only the middle of a tragedy, the time when it became public and the wounds were stripped of their privacy. He wanted to say something to lacerate Gillivray's comfortable, clean-faced satisfaction, something to make him feel the real, twisting pain in his own belly.

But no words came to mind that were broad enough to encompass the reality, so he strode on in silence, faster and faster with his long, gangling legs, leaving Gillivray to trot inelegantly to keep up. It was a small satisfaction.

The footman let them in with an air of surprise. He had the look of a well-bred person who observes someone else commit a gross breach of taste, but whose own code obliges him to pretend not to have noticed.

"Yes, sir?" he inquired without permitting them inside.

Pitt had already decided he ought to inform Waybourne before actually making the arrest; it would be easier as well as courteous, a gesture that might well repay itself later—they were far from the end. There was high suspicion, justification that necessitated arrest. There was only one reasonable solution, but there were hours of investigation before they could expect proof. There were many things still to be learned, such as where the crime had taken place, and why precisely now? What had precipitated the explosion into violence?

"It is necessary that we speak to Sir Anstey," Pitt replied, meeting the footman's eyes.

"Indeed, sir?" The man was flat-faced, as expressionless as a china owl. "If you care to come in, I shall inform Sir Anstey of your request. He is at breakfast at the moment, but perhaps he will see you when he is finished." He stepped back and permitted them to pass, closing the door behind him with smooth, silent weight. The house still smelled of mourning, as though there were lilies somewhere just out of sight, and baked meats left over. There was a dimness from half-drawn blinds. Pitt was reminded of the pain of death again, that Waybourne had lost a son, a boy scarcely out of childhood.

"Will you please tell Sir Anstey that we are ready to make an arrest," he said. "This morning. And we would prefer to acquaint him fully with the situation beforehand," he added less coldly. "But we cannot afford to wait."

The footman was startled out of his calm at last. Pitt was irritably pleased to see his jaw sag.

"An arrest, sir? In the matter of Mr. Arthur's death, sir?"

"Yes. Will you please tell Sir Anstey?"

"Yes, sir. Of course." He left them to make their own way into the morning room, went smartly toward the dining room doors, and knocked and went in.

Waybourne appeared almost immediately, crumbs in the folds of his waistcoat, a napkin in his hand. He discarded it and the footman picked it up discreetly.

Pitt opened the morning room door and held it as Waybourne walked in. When they were all inside, Gillivray closed the door and Waybourne began urgently.

"You're going to arrest Jerome? Good. Wretched busi-

ness, but the sooner it's over the better. I'll send for him."
He reached out and yanked at the bellpull. "I don't suppose you need me here. Rather not be. Painful. I'm sure you understand. Obliged you let me know first, of course. You will take him out through the back, won't you? I mean he'll be somewhat—well, er—don't want to make a scene. Quite—" His face colored and there was a blurring of distress over his features, as if at last his imagination had pierced the misery of the crime and felt a brush of its invading coldness. "Quite unnecessary," he finished lamely.

Pitt could think of nothing appropriate to say—in fact nothing that was even decent, when he thought about it.

"Thank you," Waybourne fumbled on. "You've been most—considerate, all things—well—taken into account, the—"

Pitt interrupted before he thought. He could not stand the comfortable ignorance.

"It's not over yet, sir. There will be much more evidence to collect, and then of course the trial."

Waybourne turned his back, perhaps in some attempt at momentary privacy.

"Of course." He invested his reply with certainty, as if he had been aware of it all along. "Of course. But at least the man will be out of my house. It is the beginning of the end." There was insistence in his voice, and Pitt did not argue. Perhaps it would be simple. Maybe now that they knew so much of the truth, the rest would follow easily, in a flood, not an extraction forced piece by piece. Jerome might even confess. It was possible the burden had grown so heavy he would be relieved, once there was no hope of escape anymore, just to be able to share it, to abandon the secrecy and its consuming loneliness. For many, that burden was the worst pain of all.

"Yes, sir," Pitt said. "We'll take him away this morning."

"Good—good."

There was a knock on the door, and on Waybourne's

command Jerome came in. Gillivray automatically moved closer to the door, in case he should try to get out again.

"Good morning." Jerome's eyebrows rose in surprise. If it was feigned, it was superbly well done. There was no uncertainty in him, no movement of eye or muscle, no twitch, not even a paleness to the skin.

It was Waybourne's face that glistened with sweat. He looked at one of the dozen photographs on the wall as he spoke.

"The police wish to see you, Jerome," he said stiffly. He then turned and left, Gillivray opening the door and closing it behind him.

"Yes?" Jerome inquired coolly. "I cannot imagine what you want now. I have nothing to add."

Pitt did not know whether to sit or remain standing. It seemed vaguely irreverent to tragedy itself to be comfortable at such a moment.

"I'm sorry, sir," he said quietly. "But we have more evidence now, and I have no choice but to make an arrest." Why did he still refuse to commit himself? He was keeping the man hanging like a fish safe on the hook, not yet feeling the tear in the mouth, not aware of the line and its long, relentless pull.

"Indeed?" Jerome was uninterested. "Congratulations. Is that what you wish me to say?"

Pitt felt as though his skin were scraped every time he met the man, and yet he was still reluctant to arrest him. Perhaps it was the very absence of guilt in him, of any sense of fear or even anticipation.

"No, Mr. Jerome," he replied. He must make the decision. "It is you I have the warrant for." He took a breath and removed the piece of paper from his pocket. "Maurice Jerome, I arrest you for the assault and murder of Arthur William Waybourne on or about the night of September 11, 1886, and I warn you that anything you say will be recorded and may be given in evidence at your trial."

Jerome did not seem to understand; his face was perfectly blank. Gillivray, watching, stood stiffly by the door, his fist loosely knotted as if ready for sudden violence.

Pitt wondered for a ridiculous moment if he should repeat it. He then realized that of course it was not the words themselves that were unclear; it was simply that they had not had time to deliver their meaning. The impact was too immense, too totally inconceivable to be grasped in an instant.

"W—What?" Jerome stammered at last, still too staggered to be aware of real fear. "What did you say?"

"I am arresting you for the murder of Arthur Waybourne," Pitt repeated.

"That's ridiculous!" Jerome was angry, contemptuous of Pitt's stupidity. "You can't possibly believe I killed him! Why on earth should I? It makes no sense." Suddenly, his face was sour. "I imagined you to have more integrity, Inspector. I see I was mistaken. You are not stupid—at least not as stupid as this. Therefore, I must assume you to be a man of convenience, an opportunist—or simply a coward!"

Pitt was stung by Jerome's accusations. They were unfair. He was arresting Jerome because there was too much evidence to leave him free. It was a necessary decision; it had nothing to do with self-interest. It would have been irresponsible to allow him to remain free.

"Godfrey Waybourne has said that you have interfered with him on several occasions, in a homosexual manner," he said stiffly. "That is a charge we cannot ignore, or set aside."

Jerome's face was white, slack, as the horror dawned on him and he accepted its reality.

"That's preposterous! It's—it's—" His hands moved up as if to cover his face, then fell away again weakly. "Oh, my God!" He looked around, and Gillivray stepped in front of the door.

Pitt felt the twinge of unease again; could not so superb

an actor, so subtle and complete, have smoothed his way through life with a performance of charm? He could have won himself so much more than he now possessed; his influence could have been immense if he had wooed with friendship or a little humor, instead of the wall of pomposity he had consistently shown Pitt.

"I'm sorry, Mr. Jerome, but we must take you with us now," Pitt said helplessly. "It would be far better for everyone if you would come without resistance. You'll only make it worse for yourself if you don't."

Jerome's eyebrows rose in amazement and anger.

"Are you threatening me with violence?"

"No, of course not!" Pitt said furiously. It was a ridiculous suggestion, and totally unjust. "I was thinking of your own embarrassment. Do you want to be hauled out struggling and yelling for the scullery maid and the boot-boy to gawp at?"

Jerome's face flamed but he found no words to answer. He was in a nightmare that moved too rapidly for him; he was left floundering, still trying to argue the original charge.

Pitt took a step closer.

"I didn't touch him!" Jerome protested. "I never touched either of them! It's a base slander! Let me speak to him—I'll soon sort it out."

"That's not possible," Pitt said firmly.

"But I—" Then he froze, his head jerking up sharply. "I'll see you are reprimanded for this, Inspector. You can have no possible grounds for this charge, and if I were a man of private means, you would not dare do this to me! You are a coward—as I said! A coward of the most contemptible sort!"

Was there truth in that? Was the feeling Pitt had mistaken for compassion for Waybourne and his family really only relief at finding an easy answer?

Walking side by side, they took Jerome along the hallway, through the green baize door, the passage, and the kitchen, then up the areaway steps and into the waiting cab. If it was noticed that the police had come in by the front and left by the back, it might just have been attributed to the fact that they had asked first for Sir Anstey himself. And one had more control over the way by which people exited than entered. The cook nodded in approval. It was past time persons like the police were taught their place. And she had never cared for that tutor with his airs and criticisms, acting as if he was a gentleman just because he could read Latin—as if that was any use to a person!

They rode in silence to the police station, where the arrest was formally entered and Jerome was taken to the cells.

"Your clothes and toiletries will be sent for," Pitt said quietly.

"How very civilized—you make it sound almost reasonable!" Jerome snapped. "Where am I supposed to have committed this murder? In whose bath, pray, did I drown the wretched boy? Hardly his own—even you could not imagine that! I do not care to ask you why. Your mind will have conjured up enough obscene alternatives to make me sick. But I should like to know where? I should like to know that!"

"So should we, Mr. Jerome," Pitt replied. "The reasons are obvious, as you say. If you would care to talk about it, it might help."

"I should not!"

"Some people do—"

"Some people are no doubt guilty! I find the whole subject disgusting. You will very soon find out your mistake, and then I shall expect reparation. I am not responsible for Arthur Waybourne's death, or anything else that happened to him. I suggest you look among his own class for that sort of perversion! Or do I expect too much courage of you?"

"I have looked!" Pitt bit back at last, stung beyond con-

76

trol. "And all I have found so far is an allegation from Godfrey Waybourne that you interfered with him! It would seem you have the weakness which would provide the motive, and the opportunity. The means was simply water—anyone has that."

There was fear in Jerome's eyes this time—quick, before reason overrode it, but real enough. The taste of it was unique, unmistakable.

"Nonsense! I was at a musical recital."

"But no one saw you there."

"I go to musical recitals to listen to the music, Inspector, not to make idiotic conversation with people I barely know, and interrupt their pleasure by requiring them to mouth equal inanities back to me!" Jerome surveyed Pitt with contempt as one who listened to nothing better than public-house songs.

"Are there no intervals in your recitals?" Pitt asked with exactly the same chill. He had to look a little downward at Jerome from his superior height. "That's uncommon, surely?"

"Are you fond of classical music, Inspector?" Jerome's voice was sharp with sarcastic disbelief. Perhaps it was a form of self-defense. He was attacking Pitt, his intelligence, his competence, his judgment. It was not hard to understand; part of Pitt, detached, could even sympathize. A greater part of him was stung raw by the patronage.

"I am fond of the pianoforte when it is well played," he replied with open-eyed candor. "And I like a violin, on occasions."

For an instant there was communication between them, a little surprise; then Jerome turned away.

"So you spoke to no one?" Pitt returned to the pursuit, the ugliness of the present.

"No one," Jerome answered.

"Not even to comment on the performance?" He could believe it. Who would, after listening to beautiful music, want to turn to a man like Jerome? He would sour the magic, the pleasure. His was a mind without softness or laughter, without the patina of romance. Why did he like music at all? Was it purely a pleasure of the senses, the sound and the symmetry answered in the brain?

Pitt went out, and the cell door clanged behind him; the bolt shot home and the jailer pulled out the key.

A constable was dispatched to collect Jerome's necessary belongings. Gillivray and Pitt spent the rest of the day seeking additional evidence.

"I've already spoken to Mrs. Jerome," Gillivray said with a cheerfulness Pitt could have kicked him for. "She doesn't know what time he came in. She had a headache and doesn't like classical music very much, especially chamber music, which apparently was what this was. There was a program published beforehand, and Jerome had one. She decided to stay at home. She fell asleep and didn't waken until morning."

"So Mr. Athelstan told me," Pitt said acidly. "Perhaps next time you have such a piece of information you will do me the courtesy of sharing it with me as well?" Immediately he regretted allowing his anger to become so obvious. He should not have let Gillivray see it. He could at least have kept himself that dignity.

Gillivray smiled, and his apology was no more than the minimum of good manners.

They spent six hours and achieved nothing, neither proof nor disproof.

Pitt went home late, tired and cold. It was beginning to rain and scurries of wind sent an old newspaper rattling along the gutter. It was a day he was glad to leave behind, to close out with the door, leaving the space of the evening to talk of something else. He hoped Charlotte would not even mention the case.

He stepped into the hall, took his coat off, and hung it up, then noticed the parlor door open and the lamps lit. Surely Emily was not here at this time in the evening? He did not want to have to be polite, still less to satisfy Emily's inveterate curiosity. He was tempted to keep on walking to the kitchen. He hesitated for a moment, wondering if he could get away with it, when Charlotte pulled the door wide open and it was too late.

"Oh, Thomas, you're home," she said unnecessarily, perhaps for the benefit of Emily, or whoever it was. "You have a visitor."

He was startled. "I have?"

"Yes." She stepped back a little. "Mrs. Jerome."

The cold spread right through him. The familiarity of his home was invaded by futile and predictable tragedy. It was too late to avoid it. The sooner he faced her, explained the evidence as decently as he could to a woman, and made her understand he could do nothing, then the sooner he could forget it and sink into his own evening, into the safe, permanent things that mattered to him: Charlotte, the details of her day, the children.

He stepped into the room.

She was small, slender, and dressed in plain browns. Her fair hair was soft about her face and her eyes were wide, making her skin look even paler, almost translucent, as though he could see the blood beneath. She had obviously been weeping.

This was one of the worst parts of crime: the victims for whom the horror was only beginning. For Eugenie Jerome, there would be the journey back to her parents' house to live—if she was fortunate. If not, she would have to take whatever job she could find, as a seamstress, a worker in a sweatshop, a ragpicker; she might even end up at the workhouse or, out of desperation, in the streets. But all of that she would not yet even have imagined. She was probably still grappling with the guilt itself, still hanging on to the belief that things were the same, that it was all a mistake—a reversible mistake.

"Mr. Pitt?" She stepped forward, her voice shaky. He was the police—for her, the ultimate power.

He wished there was something he could say that would ease the truth. All he wanted was to get rid of her and forget the case—at least until he was forced to go back to it tomorrow.

"Mrs. Jerome." He began with the only thing he could think of: "We had to arrest him, but he is perfectly well and not hurt in any way. You will be permitted to visit him—if you wish."

"He didn't kill that boy." The tears shone in her eyes and she blinked without moving her gaze from his. "I know—I know he is not always very easy"—she took a deep breath, steeling herself for the betrayal— "not very easy to like, but he is not an evil man. He would never abuse a trust. He has far too much pride for that!"

Pitt could believe it. The man he thought he had seen beneath that mannered exterior would take a perverse satisfaction in his moral superiority in honoring the trust of those he despised, those who, for entirely different reasons, despised him equally—if they gave him any thought at all.

"Mrs. Jerome—" How could he explain the extraordinary passions that can suddenly arise and swamp all reason, all the carefully made plans for behavior? How could he explain the feelings that could drive an otherwise sane man to compulsive, wide-eyed self-destruction? She would be confused, and unbearably hurt. Surely the woman had more than enough to bear already? "Mrs. Jerome," he tried again, "a charge has been made against your husband. We must hold him under arrest until it has been investigated. Sometimes people do things in the heat of the moment that are quite outside their usual character."

She moved closer to him and he caught a waft of lavender, faint and a little sweet. She had an old-fashioned brooch in the lace at her neck. She was very young, very gentle. God damn Jerome for his cold-blooded, bitter loneliness, for his perversion, for ever having married this woman in the first place, only to tear her life apart!

"Mrs. Jerome—"

"Mr. Pitt, my husband is not an impulsive man. I have been married to him for eleven years and I have never known him to act without giving the matter consideration, weighing whether it would be fortunate or unfortunate."

That also Pitt found only too easy to accept. Jerome was not a man to laugh aloud, dance on the pavement, or sing a snatch of song. His was a careful face; the only spontaneity in it was of the mind. He possessed a sour appreciation for humor, but never impulse. He did not even speak without judging first what effect it would have, how it would profit or harm him. What extraordinary passions must this boy have tapped to break the dam of years in a torrent that ended in murder?

If Jerome *were* guilty . . .

How could so careful, so self-preserving a man have risked a clumsy fondling of young Godfrey for the few instants of slight gratification it might have afforded him? Was it a façade beginning to crack—a first breach of the wall that was soon going to explode in passion and murder?

He looked at Mrs. Jerome. She was close to Charlotte's age, and yet she looked so much younger, so much more vulnerable, with her slender body and delicate face. She needed someone to protect her.

"Have you parents near to you?" he asked suddenly. "Someone with whom you can stay?"

"Oh, no!" Her face puckered with consternation and she screwed up her handkerchief, absently letting her reticule slide down her skirt to the floor. Charlotte bent and picked it up for her. "Thank you, Mrs. Pitt, you are so kind." She took it back and clutched it. "No, Mr. Pitt, I couldn't possibly do that. My place is at home, where I

81

can be of as much support to Maurice as I am able. People must see that I do not for a single moment believe this dreadful thing that has been said about him. It is completely untrue, and I only beg that for justice's sake you will do everything you can to prove it so. You *will*, won't you?"

"I—"

"Please, Mr. Pitt? You will not allow the truth to be buried in such a web of lies that poor Maurice is—" Her eyes filled with tears and she turned away with a sob to rest in Charlotte's arms. She wept like a child, lost in her own desperation, unconscious of anyone else's thoughts or judgments.

Charlotte slowly patted her, her eyes meeting Pitt's helplessly. He could not read what she thought. There was anger, but was it at him, at circumstances, at Mrs. Jerome for intruding and disturbing them with her distress, or at their inability to do anything for her?

"I'll do my best, Mrs. Jerome," he said. "I can only find out the truth—I can't alter it." How abrasively cruel that sounded, and how sanctimonious!

"Oh, thank you," she said between sobs and gasps for breath. "I was sure you would—but I am so grateful." She clung to Charlotte's hands like a child. "So very grateful."

The more Pitt thought about it, the less did he find it within what he had observed of Jerome's character that he should be so impulsive and so inept as to pursue Godfrey while simultaneously conducting an affair with his elder brother. If the man was so driven by his appetite that he had lost all ordinary sense, surely others would have noticed it—many others?

He spent a miserable evening, refusing to talk about it with Charlotte. The next day, he sent Gillivray on what he sincerely believed would be a fool's errand, searching for a room rented by Jerome or Arthur Waybourne. In the meantime, he took himself back to the Waybournes' house to interview Godfrey again.

He was received with extreme disfavor.

"We have already been through this exceedingly painful matter in every detail!" Waybourne said sharply. "I refuse to discuss it any further! Hasn't there been enough—enough obscenity?"

"It would be an obscenity, Sir Anstey, if a man were hanged for a crime we believe he committed but are too afraid of our own distaste to make sure!" Pitt replied very quietly. "It's a crime of irresponsibility I am not prepared to commit. Are you?"

"You are damned impertinent, sir!" Waybourne snapped. "It is not my duty to see that justice is done. That is what people like you are paid for! You attend to your job, and remember who you are in my house."

"Yes, sir," Pitt said stiffly. "Now may I see Master Godfrey, please?"

Waybourne hesitated, his eyes hot, pink-rimmed, looking Pitt up and down. For several moments both men were silent.

"If you must," he said at last. "But I shall remain here, I warn you."

"I must," Pitt insisted.

They stood in mutual discomfort, avoiding each other's eyes, while Godfrey was sent for. Pitt was aware that his anger was born of confusion within himself, of a growing fear that he would never prove Jerome's guilt and thereby wipe away the memory of Eugenie's face, a face that reflected her conviction of the world as she knew it, and of the man whose life she shared in that world.

Waybourne's hostility was even easier to read. His family had already been mutilated—he was now defending it against any unnecessary turning of the knife in the wounds. Had it been his family, Pitt would have done the same.

Godfrey came in. Then, when he saw Pitt, his face colored and his body suddenly became awkward.

Pitt felt a stab of guilt.

"Yes, sir?" Godfrey stood with his back to his father, close, as if he were a wall, something against which he could retreat.

Pitt ignored the fact that he had not been invited, and sat down in the leather-covered armchair. His position made him look up slightly at the boy, instead of obliging Godfrey to crane up at him.

"Godfrey, we don't know Mr. Jerome very well," he began, in what he hoped was a conversational tone. "It is important that we learn everything we can. He was your tutor for nearly four years. You must know him well."

"Yes, sir—but I never knew he was doing anything wrong." The boy's clear eyes were defiant. His narrow shoulders were high and Pitt could imagine the muscles hunched underneath the flannel of his jacket.

"Of course not," Waybourne said quickly, putting his hand on the boy's arm. "No one imagines you knew about it, boy."

Pitt restrained himself. He must learn, fact by fact, small impressions that built a believable picture of a man who had lost years of cold control in a sudden insane hunger—insane because it defied reality, because it could never have achieved anything but the most transient, ephemeral of pleasures while destroying everything else he valued.

Slowly, Pitt asked questions about their studies, about Jerome's manner, the subjects he taught well and those that appeared to bore him. He questioned whether the tutor's discipline was good, his temper, his enthusiasms. Waybourne grew more and more impatient, almost contemptuous of Pitt, as if he were being foolish, evading the real issue in a plethora of trivialities. But Godfrey became more confident in his answers.

A picture emerged so close to the man Pitt had imagined that it gave him no comfort at all. There was nothing new to grasp, no new perspective to try on all the fragments he already possessed. Jerome was a good teacher, a disciplinarian with little humor. And what humor he had was far too dry, too measured through years of self-control, to be understandable to a thirteen-year-old born and bred in privilege. Ambition that to Jerome was unachievable was to Godfrey an expected part of the adult life he was being groomed for. He was unaware of any injustice in the relationship with his tutor. They belonged to different levels of society, and would always do so. That Jerome might resent him had never occurred to the boy. Jerome was a schoolmaster; that was not the same thing as possessing the qualities of leadership, the courage of decision, the innate knowledge and acceptance of duty—or the burden, the loneliness of responsibility.

The irony was that perhaps Jerome's very bitterness was partly born of a whisper at the back of his brain that reminded him of the gulf between them—not only because of birth but because he was too small of vision—too self-obsessed, too aware of his own position—to command. A gentleman is a gentleman because he lives unself-consciously. He is too secure to take offense, too certain of his finances to account for shillings.

All this went through Pitt's mind as he watched the boy's solemn, rather smug face. He was at ease now—Pitt was ineffectual, not to be feared after all. It was time to come to the point.

"Did Mr. Jerome show any consistent favoritism toward your brother?" he asked quite lightly.

"No, sir," Godfrey answered. Then confusion spread on his face as he realized what had half dawned on him through the haze of grief—hints of something that was unknown but abominably shameful, that the imagination hardly dared conjure up, and yet could not help but try. "Well, sir, not that I realized at the time. He was pretty—

sort of—well, he spent a lot of time with Titus Swynford, too, when he took lessons with us. He did quite often, you know. His own tutor wasn't any good at Latin and Mr. Jerome was very good indeed. And he knew Greek, too. And Mr. Hollins—that's Titus' tutor—was always getting colds in the head. We called him 'Sniffles.'" He gave a juicy, realistic imitation.

Waybourne's face twitched with disapproval of mentioning to a person of Pitt's social inferiority such details of frivolous and rather childish malice.

"And was he also overfamiliar with Titus?" Pitt inquired, ignoring Waybourne.

Godfrey's face tightened. "Yes, sir. Titus told me that he was."

"Oh? When did he tell you?"

Godfrey stared back at him without blinking.

"Yesterday evening, sir. I told him that Mr. Jerome had been arrested by the police because he had done something terrible to Arthur. I told him what I told you, about what Mr. Jerome did to me. And Titus said he'd done it to him, too."

Pitt felt no surprise, only a gray sense of inevitability. Jerome's weakness had shown itself after all. It had not been the secret thing, erupting without warning, that had struck Pitt as so unlikely. Perhaps surrender to it had been sudden, but once he had recognized it and allowed the hunger to release itself in action, then it had been uncontrollable. It could only have been a matter of time until some adult had seen it and understood it for what it was.

What a tragic mischance that the violence—the murder—had arisen so quickly. If even one of those boys had spoken to a parent, the greater tragedy could have been avoided—for Arthur, for Jerome himself, for Eugenie.

"Thank you." Pitt sighed and looked up at Waybourne. "I would appreciate it, sir, if you would give me Mr.

Swynford's address so that I can call on him and verify this with Titus himself. You will understand that secondhand testimony, no matter from whom, is not sufficient."

Waybourne took a breath as if to argue, then accepted the futility of it.

"If you insist," he said grudgingly.

Titus Swynford was a cheerful boy, a little older than Godfrey. He was broader, with a freckled, less handsome face, but he possessed a natural ease that Pitt found attractive. Pitt was not permitted to see his young sister Fanny. And since he could put forward no argument to justify insisting, he saw only the boy, in the presence of his father.

Mortimer Swynford was calm. Had Pitt been less aware of society's rules, he might have imagined his courtesy to be friendliness.

"Of course," he consented, in his rich voice. His manicured hands rested on the back of the tapestried antimacassar. His clothes were immaculate. His tailor had cut his jacket so skillfully it all but disguised the thickening of his body, the considerable swell of his stomach under his waistcoat, the heaviness of his thighs. It was a vanity that Pitt could sympathize with, even admire. He had no such physical defects to mask, but he would dearly like to have possessed even a fraction of the polish, the ease of manner with which Swynford stood waiting, watching him.

"I'm sure you won't press the matter any further than is absolutely necessary," he went on. "But you must have enough to stand up in court—we all understand that. Titus—" He gestured toward his son with an embracing sweep. "Titus, answer Inspector Pitt's questions quite frankly. Don't hide anything. It is not a time for false modesty or any misplaced sense of loyalty. Nobody cares for a telltale, but there are times when a man is witness to a crime that cannot be permitted to continue, or to go unpunished. Then it is his duty to speak the truth, without fear or favor! Is that not so, Mr. Pitt?"

"Quite so," Pitt agreed with less enthusiasm than he should have felt. The sentiment was perfect. Was it only Swynford's aplomb, his supreme mastery of the situation, that made the words sound unnatural? He did not look like a man who either feared or favored anyone. Indeed, his money and his heritage had placed him in a situation where, with a little judgment, he could avoid the need for pleasing others. As long as he obeyed the usual social rules of his class, he could remain exceedingly comfortable.

Titus was waiting.

"You were occasionally tutored by Mr. Jerome?" Pitt rushed in, aware of the silence.

"Yes, sir," Titus agreed. "Both Fanny and I were. Fanny's rather clever at Latin, although I can't see what good it will do her."

"And what will you do with it?" Pitt inquired.

Titus's face split with a broad grin.

"I say, you're rather odd, aren't you? Nothing at all, of course! But we aren't allowed to admit that. It's supposed to be fearfully good discipline—at least that's what Mr. Jerome said. I think that's the only reason he put up with Fanny, because she was better at it than any of the rest of us. It would make you sick, wouldn't it? I mean, girls being better at class, especially a thing like Latin? Mr. Jerome says that Latin is fearfully logical, and girls aren't supposed to have any logic."

"Quite sick," Pitt agreed, keeping a sober face with difficulty. "I gather Mr. Jerome was not very keen on teaching Fanny?"

"Not terribly. He preferred us boys." His eyes darkened suddenly, and his skin flushed red under his freckles. "That's what you're here about, isn't it? What happened to Arthur, and the fact that Mr. Jerome kept touching us?"

There was no point in denying it; apparently, Swynford had already been very frank.

"Yes. Did Mr. Jerome touch you?"

Titus pulled a face to express a succession of feelings.

"Yes." He shrugged. "But I never thought about it till Godfrey explained to me what it meant. If I'd known, sir, that it was going to end up with poor Arthur dead, I'd have said something sooner." His face shadowed; his gray-green eyes were hot with guilt.

Pitt felt a surge of sympathy. Titus was quite intelligent enough to know that his silence could have cost a life.

"Of course." Pitt put out his hand without thinking and clasped the boy's arm. "Naturally you would—but there was no way you could know. Nobody wishes to think so ill of someone, unless there is no possible doubt. You cannot go around accusing somebody on a suspicion. Had you been wrong, you could have done Mr. Jerome a fatal injustice."

"As it is, it's Arthur who's dead." Titus was not so easily comforted. "If I'd said something, I might have saved him."

Pitt felt compelled to be bolder and risk a deeper wound. "Did you know it was wrong?" he asked. He let go the boy's arm and sat back again.

"No, sir!" Titus colored, the blood rushing up again under his skin. "To be honest, sir, I still don't really know exactly. I don't know whether I wish to know—it sounds rather dirty."

"It is." Pitt was soiled himself, by all his knowledge, in the face of this child who would probably never know a fraction of the weakness and misery Pitt had been forced to see. "It is," he repeated. "I'd leave it well alone."

"Yes, sir. But do you—do you think I could have saved Arthur if I'd known?"

Pitt hesitated. Titus did not deserve a lie.

"Perhaps—but quite possibly not. Maybe no one would

have believed you anyway. Don't forget, Arthur could have spoken himself—if he'd wished to!"

Titus's face showed incomprehension.

"Why didn't he, sir? Didn't he understand? But that doesn't make any sense!"

"No—it doesn't, does it?" Pitt agreed. "I'd like to know the answer to that myself."

"No doubt frightened." Swynford spoke for the first time since Pitt had begun questioning Titus. "Poor boy probably felt guilty—too ashamed to tell his father. I daresay that wretched man threatened him. He would, don't you think, Inspector? Just thank God it's all over now. He can do no more harm."

It was far from the truth, but this time Pitt did not argue. He could only guess what the trial would bring. There was no need to distress them now, no need to tell them the sad and ugly things that would be exposed. Titus, at least, need never know.

"Thank you." Pitt stood up, and his coat fell in creases where he had been sitting on it. "Thank you, Titus. Thank you, Mr. Swynford. I don't think we shall have to trouble you again until the trial."

Swynford took a deep breath, but he knew better than to waste energy arguing now. He inclined his head in acknowledgment and pulled the bell for the footman to show Pitt out.

The door opened and a girl of about fourteen ran in, saw Pitt, and stopped with an instant of embarrassment. She then immediately composed herself, stood quite upright, and looked at him with level gray eyes—a little coolly, as if it were he who had committed the social gaffe, and not she.

"I beg your pardon, Papa," she said, with a little hitch of her shoulders under her lace-edged pinafore. "I didn't know you had a visitor." She had sized up Pitt already and knew he was not "company." Her father's social equals did not wear mufflers; they wore silk scarves, and they left them with whoever opened the door, along with their hats and sticks.

"Hello, Fanny," Swynford replied with a slight smile. "Have you come down to inspect the policeman?"

"Certainly not!" She lifted her chin and returned her gaze to Pitt, regarding him from head to toe. "I came to say that Uncle Esmond is here, and he promised me that when I am old enough to 'come out' he will give me a necklace with pearls in it for my seventeenth birthday, so I may wear it when I am presented at court. Do you suppose it will be to the Queen herself, or only the Princess of Wales? Do you imagine the Queen will still be alive then? She's fearfully old already, you know!"

"I have no idea," Swynford answered with raised eyebrows, meeting Pitt's glance with amusement. "Perhaps you could begin with the Princess of Wales, and progress from there—if the Queen survives long enough for you, that is?"

"You're laughing at me!" she said with a note of warning. "Uncle Esmond dined with the Prince of Wales last week—he just said so!"

"Then I've no doubt it's true."

"Of course it's true!" Esmond Vanderley appeared in the doorway behind Fanny. "I would never dare lie to anyone as perceptive or as unversed in the social arts as Fanny. My dear child." He put his arm on Fanny's shoulder. "You really must learn to be less direct, or you will be a social disaster. *Never* let people know that you know they have lied! That is a cardinal rule. Well-bred people never lie—they occasionally misremember, and only the ill-mannered are gross enough to remark it. Isn't that so, Mortimer?"

"My dear fellow, you are the expert in society—how could I dispute what you say? If you wish to succeed, Fanny, listen to your mother's cousin Esmond." His words were perhaps a little tart, but, looking at his face, Pitt could see only goodwill. He also noted the rela-

91

tionship with a lift of interest: so Swynford, Vanderley, and the Waybournes were cousins.

Vanderley looked over the girl's head at Pitt.

"Inspector," he said with a return to seriousness. "Still chasing up that wretched business about young Arthur?"

"Yes, sir, I'm afraid there is a lot more we need to know yet."

"Oh?" Vanderley's face showed slight surprise. "For example?"

Swynford made a slight movement with his arm. "You may leave us now, thank you, Titus, Fanny! If your Latin requires improvement, then you had best be about studying it."

"Yes, sir." Titus excused himself to Vanderley, then a little self-consciously to Pitt, aware it was a socially unmapped area. Did he behave as if Pitt were a tradesman, and take his departure as a gentleman would? He decided on the latter, and collecting his sister's hand, much to her annoyance because her curiosity was overwhelming, he escorted her out.

When the door was closed, Vanderley repeated his question.

"Well, we have no idea where the crime took place," Pitt began, hoping that with their knowledge of the family they might have some idea. A new thought occurred to him. "Did the Waybournes ever possess any other property that might have been used? A country house? Or did Sir Anstey and Lady Waybourne ever travel and leave the boys behind with Jerome?"

Vanderley considered for a moment, his face solemn, brows drawn down.

"I seem to remember them all going to the country in the spring. . . . They do have a place, of course. And Anstey and Benita came back to town for a while and left the boys up there. Jerome must have been there—he does go with them, naturally. Can't ignore the boys' education. Poor Arthur was quite bright, you know. Even considered

92

going up to Oxford. Can't think what for—no need to work. Rather enjoyed the classics. Think he was meaning to read Greek as well. Jerome was a good scholar, you know. Damn shame the fellow was a homosexual—damn shame." He said it with a sigh, and his eyes looked into some distance Pitt could see. His face was sad, but without anger or the harsh contempt Pitt would have expected.

"Worse than that." Swynford shook his head, his wide mouth somewhat curled, as if the sourness of it were in the room with them. "More than a damn shame. Anstey said he was riddled with disease. Gave it to Arthur—poor beggar!"

"Disease?" Vanderley's face paled a little. "Oh, God! That's awful. I suppose you are sure?"

"Syphilis," Swynford clarified.

Vanderley stepped backward and sat down in one of the big chairs, putting the heels of his hands over his eyes as if to hide both his distress and the vision that leaped to his mind.

"How bloody wretched! What—what a ghastly mess." He sat silent for a few more moments, then jerked up and stared at Pitt, his eyes as gray as Fanny's. "What are you doing about it?" He hesitated, fished frantically for words. "God in heaven, man—if all this is true, it could have gone anywhere—to anyone!"

"We are trying to find out everything about the man that we can," Pitt answered, knowing it was not enough, not nearly enough. "We know he was overfamiliar with other children, other boys, but we can't find out yet where he conducted the intimacies of this relationship with Arthur—or where Arthur was killed."

"What the hell does that matter?" Vanderley exploded. He shot to his feet, his clean, chisel-boned face flushed, his muscles tight. "You know he did it, don't you? For pity's sake, man, if he was that far demented in his obsession he could have hired rooms anywhere! You can't be naïve enough not to know that—in your business!"

"I do know it, sir." Pitt tried to keep his own voice from rising, from betraying his revulsion or his growing sense of helplessness. "But I'd still feel we had a better case if we could find it—and someone who has seen Jerome there—perhaps the landlord, someone who took money—anything more definite. You see, so far all we can prove is that Jerome interfered with Godfrey Waybourne and with Titus."

"What do you want?" Swynford demanded. "He's hardly likely to have seduced the boy with witnesses! He's perverted, criminal, and spreading that filthy disease God knows where! But he's not foolish—he's never lost sight of the smaller sanities, like tidying up after himself!"

Vanderley ran his fingers through his hair. Suddenly he was calm again, in control.

"No—he's right, Mortimer. He needs to know more than that. There are tens of thousands of rooms around London. He'll never find it, unless he's lucky. But there may be something he can find, somebody—somebody who knew Jerome. I don't suppose poor Arthur was the only one." He looked down and his face was heavy, his voice suddenly even quieter. "I mean—the man was in bondage to a weakness."

"Yes, of course," Swynford said. "But that's the police's job, thank God; not ours. We don't need to concern ourselves with whatever else he needs—or why." He turned to Pitt. "You've talked to my son—I would have thought that was enough, but if it isn't, then you must pursue whatever else you want—in the streets, or wherever. I don't know what else you think there is."

"There must be something more." Pitt felt confused, almost foolish. He knew so much—and so little: explanations that fitted—a growing desperation he could understand, a loneliness, a sense of having been cheated. Would it be enough to hang a man, to hang Maurice

Jerome for the murder of Arthur Waybourne? "Yes, sir," he said aloud. "Yes—we'll go and look, everywhere we can."

"Good." Swynford nodded. "Good. Well, get on with it! Good day, Inspector."

"Good day, sir." Pitt walked to the door and opened it silently. He went out into the hall to collect his hat and coat from the footman.

Charlotte had sent an urgent letter to Dominic to ask him to hasten his efforts for a meeting with Esmond Vanderley. She had little idea what she expected to learn, but it was more important than ever that she try.

Today, at last, she had received a reply that there was an afternoon party of sorts to which, if she wished, Dominic would escort her, although he doubted she would find any enjoyment in it whatsoever; and did she possess anything she cared to wear for the occasion, because it was fashionable and a little risqué? He would call by in his carriage at four o'clock, in case she chose to go.

Her mind whirled. Of course she chose to go! But what gown had she that would not disgrace him? Fashionable and risqué! Emily was still out of town, and so could not be borrowed from, even had there been time. She raced upstairs and pulled open her wardrobe to see what it presented. At first it was hopeless. Her own clothes were all, at best, last year's styles, or the year before. At worst, they were plain sensible—and one could hardly say less for a gown that that! Whoever wished to seem sensible, of all things?

There was the lavender of Great-Aunt Vespasia's that she had been given for a funeral. With black shawl and hat it had been half mourning, and suitable. She pulled it out and looked at it. It was definitely magnificent and very formal—a duchess' gown, and an elderly duchess at that! But if she were to cut off the high neck and make it daringly low, take out the sleeves below the shoulder drape, it would look far more modern—in fact a little avante-garde!

Brilliant! Emily would be proud of her! She seized the nail scissors from the dresser and began before she could reconsider. If she were to stop and think what she was doing, she would lose her nerve.

It was completed in time. She coiled her hair high (if only Gracie were a lady's maid!), bit her lips and pinched her cheeks to give herself a little more color, and splashed on some lavender water. When Dominic arrived, she sailed out, head high, teeth clenched, looking neither to right nor left, and certainly not at Dominic to see what he thought of her.

In the carriage, he opened his mouth to comment, then smiled faintly, a little confused, and closed it again.

Charlotte prayed that she was not making a complete fool of herself.

The party was like nothing she had ever attended before. It was not in one room but in a series of rooms, all lavishly decorated in styles she considered a trifle obtrusive, with vague suggestions of the last courts of France in one and of the sultans of the Turkish Empire in another; a third seemed Oriental, with red lacquer and silk-embroidered screens. It was rather overwhelming and a little vuglar; she began to have serious misgivings about the wisdom of having come.

But if she had been concerned about her dress, that at least was needless; some of the fashions were so outrageous that she felt quite mildly dressed by comparison. Indeed, her gown was low over the bosom and a little brief around the shoulders, but it did not look in any danger of sliding off altogether and producing a catastrophe. And, glancing around, that was more than she could say for some! Grandmama would have had apoplexy if she could have seen these ladies' attire! As Charlotte stood watching them, keeping one hand on Dominic's arm lest he leave her alone, their behavior was so brazen it would not have passed in the circles she was accustomed to before her marriage.

But Emily had always said high society made its own rules.

"Do you want to leave?" Dominic whispered hopefully.

"Certainly not!" she replied without giving herself time to consider, in case she accepted. "I wish to meet Esmond Vanderley."

"Why?"

"I told you—there has been a crime."

"I know that!" he said sharply. "And they have arrested the tutor. What on earth do you hope to achieve by talking to Vanderley?"

It was a very reasonable question and he did have a certain right to ask.

"Thomas is not really satisfied that he is guilty," she whispered back. "There is a great deal we do not know."

"Then why did he arrest him?"

"He was commanded to!"

"Charlotte—"

At this point, deciding that valor was the better part of discretion, she let go of his arm and swept forward to join in the party.

She discovered immediately that the conversation was glittering and wildly brittle, full of bons mots and bright laughter, glances with intimate meaning. At another time, she might have felt excluded, but today she was here just to observe. The few people who spoke to her she answered without effort to be entertaining, half her mind absorbed with watching everyone else.

The women were all expensively dressed, and seemed full of self-assurance. They moved easily from group to group, and flirted with a skill that Charlotte both envied and deplored. She could no more have achieved it than grown wings to fly. Even the plainest ones seemed peculiarly gifted in this particular skill, exhibiting wit and a certain panache.

The men were every bit as fashionable: coats exquisitely cut, cravats gorgeous, hair exaggeratedly long and with waves many a woman would have been proud of. For once, Dominic seemed unremarkable. His chiseled features were discreet, his clothes sober by comparison—and she discovered she greatly preferred them.

One lean young man with beautiful hands and a passionately sensitive face stood alone at a table, his dark gray eyes on the pianist gently rippling a Chopin nocturne on the grand piano. She wondered for a moment if he felt as misplaced here as she did. There was an unhappiness in his face, a sense of underlying grief that he sought to distract, and failed. Could he be Esmond Vanderley?

She turned to find Dominic. "Who is he?" she whispered.

"Lord Frederick Turner," he replied, his face shadowing with an an emotion she did not understand. It was a mixture of dislike and something else, indefinable. "I don't see Vanderley, yet." He took her firmly by the elbow and pushed her forward. "Let us go through the next room. He may be there." Short of pulling herself free by force, she had no choice but to move as he directed.

A few people drifted up and spoke with Dominic, and he introduced Charlotte as his sister-in-law Miss Ellison. The conversation was trivial and bright; she gave it little of her attention. A striking woman with very black hair addressed them and skillfully led Dominic off, grasping his arm in an easy, intimate gesture, and Charlotte found herself suddenly alone.

A violinist was playing something that seemed to have neither beginning nor end. Within moments, she was approached by a Byronically handsome man with bold eyes, full of candid humor.

"The music is inexpressibly tedious, is it not?" he remarked conversationally. "I cannot imagine why they bother!"

"Perhaps to give those who desire it some easy subject with which to open a conversation?" she suggested coolly. She had not been introduced, and he was taking something of a liberty.

It seemed to amuse him, and he regarded her quite openly, looking at her shoulders and throat with admiration. She was furious to realize from the heat she felt in her skin that she was blushing. It was the very last thing she wished!

"You have not been here before," he observed.

"You must come very regularly to know that." She allowed considerable acid into her tone. "I am surprised, if you find it so uninteresting."

"Only the music." He shook his head a little. "And I am an optimist. I come in permanent hope of some delightful adventure. Who could have foretold that I should meet you here?"

"You have not met me!" She tried to freeze him with an icy glance, but he was impervious; in fact, it appeared to entertain him the more. "You have scraped an acquaintance, which I do not intend to continue!" she added.

He laughed aloud, a pleasant sound of true enjoyment. "You know, my dear, you are quite individual! I believe I shall have a delicious evening with you, and you will find I am neither ungenerous nor overly demanding."

Suddenly it all became abominably clear to her—this was a place of assignation! Many of these women were courtesans, and this appalling man had taken her for one of them! Her face flamed with confusion for her own obtuseness, and rage with herself because at least half of her was flattered! It was mortifying!

"I do not care in the slightest what you are!" she said with a choking breath. She added, quite unfairly, "And I shall have most unpleasant words with my brother-in-law for bringing me to this place. His sense of humor is in the poorest possible taste!" With a flounce of her skirts, she swept away from him, leaving him surprised but delighted, with an excellent story to recount to his friends.

"Serves you right," Dominic said with some satisfaction when she found him. He half turned and moved his hand toward a man of casually elegant appearance, dressed in the height of fashion but managing to make it all seem uncontrived. His bones were good, his wavy, fair hair not especially long. "May I present Mr. Esmond Vanderley, my sister-in-law Miss Ellison!"

Charlotte was ill-prepared for it; her wits were still scattered from the last encounter.

"How do you do, Mr. Vanderley," she said with far less composure than she had intended. "Dominic has spoken of you. I am delighted to make your acquaintance."

"He was less kind to me," Vanderley answered with an easy smile. "He has kept you a total secret, which I consider perhaps wise, but most selfish of him."

Now that she was faced with him, how on earth could she bring up the subject of Arthur Waybourne or anything to do with Jerome? The whole idea of meeting Vanderley in this place had been ridiculous. Emily would have managed it with far more aplomb—how thoughtless of her to be absent just when she was needed! She should have been here in London to hunt murderers, not galloping about in the Leicestershire mud after some wretched fox!

She lowered her eyes for a moment, then raised them with a frank smile, a little shy. "Perhaps he thought with your recent bereavement you would find being bothered with new acquaintances tiresome. We have had such an experience in our own family, and know that it can take one in most unexpected ways."

She hoped the smile, the sense of sympathy, extended to her eyes, and that he understood it as such. Dear heaven! She could not bear to be misunderstood again! She plunged on, "One moment one wishes only to be left alone; the next, one desires more than anything else to be among as many people as possible, none of whom have the faintest idea of your affairs." She was proud of that— it was an embroidery of the truth worthy of Emily at her best.

Vanderley looked startled.

"Good gracious! How perceptive of you, Miss Ellison. I had no idea you were even aware of it. Dominic apparently was not. Did you read it in the newspapers?"

"Oh, no!" she lied instantly. She had not yet forgotten that ladies of good society would not do such a thing. Reading the newspaper overheated the blood; it was considered bad for the health to excite the mind too much, not to mention bad for the morals. The pages of social events might be read, perhaps, but certainly not murders! A far better answer occurred to her. "I have a friend who also has had dealings with Mr. Jerome."

"Oh, God, yes!" he said wearily. "Poor devil!"

Charlotte was confused. Could he possibly mean Jerome? Surely whatever sympathy he felt could only be for Arthur Waybourne.

"Tragic," she agreed, lowering her voice suitably. "And so very young. The destruction of innocence is always terrible." It sounded sententious, but she was concerned with drawing him out and perhaps learning something, not with creating a good impression upon him herself.

His wide mouth twisted very slightly.

"Would you consider me very discourteous to disagree with you, Miss Ellison? I find total innocence the most unutterable bore, and it is inevitably lost at one point or another, unless one abdicates from life altogether and withdraws to a convent. I daresay even there the same eternal jealousies and malice still intrude. The thing to desire is that innocence should be replaced with humor and a little style. Fortunately, Arthur possessed both of those." He raised his eyebrows slightly. "Jerome, on the other hand, has neither. And of course Arthur was charming, whereas Jerome is a complete ass, poor sod. He has neither lightness of touch nor even the most basic sense of social survival."

Dominic glared at him, but obviously could find no satisfactory words to answer such frankness.

"Oh." Vanderley smiled at Charlotte with candid charm. "I beg your pardon. My language is inexcusable. I have only just learned that the wretched man also forced his attentions upon my younger nephew and a cousin's boy. Arthur was dreadful enough, but that he should have involved himself with Godfrey and Titus I still find staggering. Put my appalling manners down to shock, if you will be so generous?"

"Of course," she said quickly, not out of courtesy but because she truly meant it. "He must be a totally depraved man, and to discover that he has been teaching one's family for years is enough to horrify anybody out of all thought of polite conversation. It was clumsy of me to have mentioned it at all." She hoped he would not take her at her word and let the subject fall. Was she being too discreet? "Let us hope that the whole matter will be proved beyond question, and the man hanged," she added, watching his face closely.

The long eyelids lowered in a movement that seemed to reflect pain and a need for privacy. Perhaps she should not have spoken of hanging. It was the last thing she wished herself—for Jerome, or anyone else.

"What I mean," she hastened on, "is that the trial should be brief, and there be no question left in anyone's conscience that he is guilty!"

Vanderley regarded her with a flash of honesty that was oddly out of place in this room of games and masquerades. His eyes were very clear.

"A clean kill, Miss Ellison? Yes, I hope so, too. Far better to bury all the squalid little details. Who needs to strip naked the pain? We use the excuse of the love for truth to inquire into a labyrinth of things that are none of our affair. Arthur is dead anyway. Let the wretched tutor be convicted without all his lesser sins paraded for a prurient public to feed its self-righteousness on."

She felt suddenly guilty, a raging hypocrite. She was trying to do precisely what he condemned and by silence she was agreeing with: the turning over of every private weakness in an endless search for truth. Did she really believe Jerome was innocent, or was she merely being inquisitive, like the rest?

She shut her eyes for a moment. That was immaterial! Thomas did not believe it—at least he had desperate doubts. Prurient or not, Jerome deserved an honest hearing!

"If he is guilty?" she said quietly.

"You think he is not?" Vanderley was looking at her narrowly now, unhappiness in his eyes. Perhaps he feared another sordid and drawn-out ordeal for his family.

She had trapped herself; the moment of candor was over.

"Oh—I have no idea!" She opened her eyes wide. "I hope the police do not often make mistakes."

Dominic had had enough.

"I should think it very unlikely," he said with some asperity. "Either way, it is a most unpleasant subject, Charlotte. I am sure you will be pleased to hear that Alicia Fitzroy-Hammond married that extraordinary American—what was his name? Virgil Smith! And she is to have a child. She has retired somewhat from public functions already. You do remember them, don't you?"

Charlotte was delighted. Alicia had had such a miserable time when her first husband died, just before the murders in Resurrection Row.

"Oh, I'm so glad!" she said sincerely. "Do you think she would recall me if I wrote to her?"

Dominic made a face. "I cannot conceive of her forgetting!" he said dryly. "The circumstances were hardly commonplace! One is not littered with corpses every week!"

A woman in hot pink buttonholed Vanderley and led him away. He glanced over his shoulder at them once, reluctantly, but his habitual good manners overcame his desire to avoid the new involvement, and he went gracefully.

"I hope you are satisfied now?" Dominic said waspishly. "Because if you are not, you are going to leave here unhappy. I refuse to stay any longer!"

She thought of arguing, as a matter of principle. But in truth, she was just as pleased to retreat as he was.

"Yes, thank you, Dominic," she said demurely. "You have been very patient."

He gave her a suspicious look, but decided not to question what seemed to be a compliment, and to accept his good fortune. They walked out into the autumn evening, each with a considerable sense of relief, for their separate reasons, and took the carriage home again. Charlotte had a profound desire to change out of this extraordinary gown before any necessity arose to explain it to Pitt—a feat that would be virtually impossible!

And Dominic had little wish for such a confrontation either, much as his regard had developed for Pitt—or perhaps because of it. He was beginning to grow suspicious that Pitt had not countenanced a meeting with Vanderley at all!

5

Several days passed in fruitless search for any further evidence. Landladies and landlords were questioned, but there were too many to make anything but a cursory attempt, in the hope that for a little reward someone would come forward. Three did. The first was a brothel-keeper from Whitechapel, rubbing his hands, eyes gleaming in anticipation of a little future leniency from the police in recompense for his assistance. Gillivray's delight was short-lived when the man proved unable to describe either Jerome or Arthur Waybourne with any accuracy. Pitt had never expected that he would, and was therefore left with a sense of superiority to soothe his irritation.

The second was a nervous little woman who let rooms in Seven Dials. Very respectable, she insisted—only let to gentlemen of the best moral character! She feared her good nature and innocence of the viler aspects of human nature had suffered her to be deceived in a most tragic manner. She moved her muff from one hand to the other, and beseeched Pitt to be assured of her total ignorance of the true purpose for which her house had been used; and was it not simply quite dreadful what the world was coming to these days?

Pitt agreed with her that it was, but probably no worse

than always. She roundly disagreed with him on that—it had never been like that in her mother's day, or that good woman, may her soul rest in peace, would have warned her not to let rooms to strangers.

However, she not only identified Jerome from a photograph shown her, but also three other people who were photographed for the purpose of just such identity quests—all of them policemen. By the time she got to the picture of Arthur—obtained from Waybourne—she was so confused she was quite sure the whole of London was seething with all manner of sin, and would be consumed like Sodom and Gomorrah before Christmas.

"Why do people do it?" Gillivray demanded furiously. "It's a waste of police time—don't they realize that? It ought to be punished!"

"Don't be ridiculous." Pitt lost his patience. "She's lonely and frightened—"

"Then she shouldn't let rooms to people she doesn't know!" Gillivray retorted waspishly.

"It's probably her only living." Pitt was getting genuinely angry now. It would do Gillivray good to walk the beat for a while, somewhere like Bluegate Fields, Seven Dials, or the Devil's Acre. Let him see the beggars piled in the doorways and smell the bodies and the stale streets. Let him taste the dirt in the air, the grime from chimneys, the perpetual damp. Let him hear the rats squealing as they nosed in the refuse, and see the flat eyes of children who knew they would live and die there, probably die before they were as old as Gillivray was now.

A woman who owned a little property had safety, a roof over her head, and, if she let out rooms, food and clothing as well. By Seven Dials standards, she was rich.

"Then she ought to be used to it," Gillivray replied, oblivious of Pitt's thoughts.

"I daresay she is." Pitt dug himself deeper into his feelings, glad to have the excuse to let go of the bridle he kept on them most of the time. "That hardly stops it

106

hurting! She's probably used to being hungry, and used to being cold, and used to being scared half the time she's conscious at all. And probably she deceives herself as to what her rooms are used for and dreams that she's better than she is: wiser, kinder, prettier, and more important—like the rest of humanity! Maybe all she wanted was for us to lend her a little fame for a day or two, give her something to talk about over the teacups—or the gin—so she convinced herself Jerome rented one of her rooms. What do you suggest we do—prosecute her because she was mistaken?" He let all his dislike for Gillivray and his comfortable assumptions thicken his voice with scorn. "Apart from anything else, that would hardly be conducive to having other people come forward to help us—now, would it?"

Gillivray looked at him, his face full of hurt.

"I think you are being quite unreasonable, sir," he said stiffly. "I can see that for myself. It does not alter the fact that she wasted our time!"

And so did the third claimant, who came to the police station saying he had let rooms to Jerome. He was a rotund personage with rippling jowls and thick white hair. He kept a public house in the Mile End Road, and said that a gentleman answering the murderer's description to a tee had rented rooms from him on numerous occasions, rooms immediately above his saloon bar. He had seemed perfectly respectable at the time, soberly dressed and well spoken, and had been visited while there by a young gentleman of good breeding.

But he also failed to identify Jerome among a group of photographs presented to him, and when he was questioned closely by Pitt, his answers became vaguer and vaguer, until finally he retreated altogether and said he thought after all that he had been mistaken. When he considered the matter more carefully, Pitt helped to bring back to mind that the gentleman in question had had a North Country accent, had been a little on the portly side, and was definitely bald over the major portion of his head.

"Damn!" Gillivray swore as soon as he was out of the room. "Now he really *was* wasting time! Just after a little cheap notoriety for his wretched house! What sort of people want to go drinking in a place where a murder's been committed anyway?"

"Most sorts," Pitt said with disgust. "If he spreads it around, he'll probably double his custom."

"Then we ought to prosecute him!"

"What for? The worst we could do is give him a fright—and waste a great deal more time, not only ours but the court's as well. He'd get off—and become a folk hero! He'd be carried down the Mile End Road shoulder high, and his pub would be crammed to the doors! He'd be able to sell tickets!"

Gillivray slammed his notebook down on the table, speechless because he did not wish to be vulgar and use the only words that sprang to his mind.

Pitt smiled to himself, and allowed Gillivray to see it.

The investigation continued. It was now October and the streets were hard and bright, full of the edge of autumn. Cold winds penetrated coats, and the first frost made the pavements slippery under one's boots. They had traced Jerome's career back through his previous employers, all of whom had found him of excellent scholastic ability. If admitting to no great personal liking for him, all felt definite satisfaction with his work. None of them had had the least notion that his personal life was anything but of the most regular—even, one might almost say, prim. Certainly he appeared to be a man of little imagination and no humor at all, except of the most perverse, which they failed to understand. As they had said: not likable, but of the utmost propriety—to the point of being a prig—and socially an unutterable bore.

On October 5, Gillivray came into Pitt's office without

knocking, his cheeks flushed either with success or by the sharpening wind outside.

"Well?" Pitt asked irritably. Gillivray might have ambition, and might consider himself a cut above the average policeman, as indeed he was, but that did not give him the right to walk in without the courtesy of asking.

"I've found it!" Gillivray said triumphantly, his face glowing, eyes alight. "I've got it at last!"

Pitt felt his pulse quicken in spite of himself. It was not entirely pleasure, which was unexplainable. What else should he feel?

"The rooms?" he asked calmly, then swallowed hard. "You've found the rooms where Arthur Waybourne was drowned? Are you sure this time? Could you prove it in a court?"

"No, no!" Gillivray waved his arms expansively. "Not the rooms. Far better than that, I've found a prostitute who swears to a relationship with Jerome! I've got times, places, dates, everything—and perfect identification!"

Pitt let out his breath with disgust. This was useless—and a sordid contradiction he did not want to know. He saw Eugenie Jerome's face in his mind, and wished Gillivray had not been so zealous, so self-righteously successful. Damn Maurice Jerome! And damn Gillivray. And Eugenie, for being so innocent!

"Brilliant," he said sarcastically. "And totally pointless. We are trying to prove that Jerome assaulted young boys, not that he bought the services of street women!"

"But you don't understand!" Gillivray leaned forward over the desk, his face, shining with victory, only a foot from Pitt's. "The prostitute is a young boy! His name is Albie Frobisher, and he's seventeen—just a year older than Arthur Waybourne. He swears he's known Jerome for four years, and been used by him all that time! That's all we need! He even says Arthur Waybourne took his place—Jerome admitted as much. That's why Jerome was never suspected before—he never bothered anyone else! He paid for his relationship—until he became infatuated with Arthur. Then, when he seduced Arthur, he stopped seeing Albie Frobisher—no need! It explains everything, don't you see? It all fits into place!"

"What about Godfrey—and Titus Swynford?" Why was Pitt arguing? As Gillivray said, it all fell into place; it even answered the question of why Jerome had never been suspected before, why he had been able to control himself so completely that his appearance was perfect—until Godfrey. "Well?" he repeated. "What about Godfrey?"

"I don't know!" Gillivray was confused for a moment. Then comprehension flashed into his eyes, and Pitt knew exactly what he was thinking. He believed Pitt was envious because it was Gillivray who had found the essential link, and not Pitt himself. "Perhaps once he'd seduced someone he resented paying for it?" he suggested. "Or maybe Albie's prices had gone up. Maybe he was short of money? Or, most likely, he'd developed a taste for a higher class of youth—a touch of quality. Perhaps he preferred seducing virgins to the rather shop-soiled skills of a prostitute?"

Pitt looked at Gillivray's smooth, clean face and hated it. What he said might well be true, but his satisfaction in it, the ease with which the words came out between his perfect teeth, was disgusting. He was talking of obscenity, of intimate human degradation, with no more pain or difficulty than if they had been items on a bill of fare. Shall we have the beef or the duck tonight? Or the pie?

"You seem to have thought of every aspect of it," he said with a curl of his lip, at once bracketing Gillivray with Jerome in intent—in nature of thought, if not in act. "I should have dwelt on its possibilities longer, then maybe I would have thought of these things for myself."

Gillivray's face flamed as sharp red as the blood rose, but he could think of no reply that did not involve language that would only confirm Pitt's charge.

"Well, I suppose you have an address for this prostitute?" Pitt went on. "Have you told Mr. Athelstan yet?"

Gillivray's face lightened instantly, satisfaction returning like a tide.

"Yes, sir, it was unavoidable. I met him as I was coming in, and he asked me what progress we had made." He allowed himself to smile. "He was delighted."

Pitt could imagine it without even looking at the pleasure in Gillivray's eyes. He made an immense effort to hide own feelings.

"Yes," he said. "He would be. Where is this Albie Frobisher?"

Gillivray handed him a slip of paper and he took it and read it. It was a rooming house of known reputation—in Bluegate Fields. How appropriate, how very suitable.

The following day, late in the afternoon, Pitt finally found Albie Frobisher at home and alone. It was a seedy house up an alley off one of the wider streets, its brick front grimy, its wood door and window frames peeling and spongy with rot from the wet river air.

Inside there was a hempen mat for a distance of about three yards, to absorb the mud from boots, and then a well-worn carpet of brilliant red, giving the hallway a sudden warmth, an illusion of having entered a cleaner, richer world, an illusion of promises behind the closed doors, or up the dim stairs to the gaslit higher floors.

Pitt walked up quickly. In spite of all the times he had been inside brothels, bawdy houses, gin mills, and workhouses, it made him unusually uncomfortable to be visiting a house of male prostitution, especially one that employed children. It was the most degrading of all human abuses, and that anyone, even another customer, should imagine for an instant that he had come for that purpose made his face flush hot and his mind revolt.

He took the last stairs two at a time and knocked sharply on the door of room 14. He was already shifting his weight and turning his shoulder toward the door in preparation to force it if it was not opened. The thought of standing here on the landing begging for admittance sent the sweat trickling down his chest.

But it was unnecessary. The door opened a crack almost immediately, and a light, soft voice spoke.

"Who is it?"

"Pitt, from the police. You spoke to Sergeant Gillivray yesterday."

The door swung wide without hesitation and Pitt stepped inside. Instinctively he looked around, first of all to make sure they were alone. He did not expect violence from a protector, or the procurer himself, but it was always possible.

The room was ornate, with fringed covers and cushions in crimson and purple, and gas lamps with faceted pendants of glass. The bed was enormous, and there was a bronze male nude on the marble-topped side table. The plush curtains were closed, and the air smelled stale and sweet, as though perfume had been used to mask the smells of bodies and human exertion.

The feeling of nausea Pitt experienced lasted only for an instant; then it was overtaken by a suffocating pity.

Albie Frobisher himself was smaller than Arthur Waybourne had been—perhaps as tall, although it was hard to tell, since Pitt had never seen Arthur alive—but far lighter. Albie's bones were as fragile as a girl's, his skin white, face beardless. He had probably grown up on such scraps of food as he could beg or steal, until he had been old enough to be sold or to find his way into the care of a procurer. By then chronic malnutrition had doubtless already taken its toll. He would always be undersized. He might become soft in old age—although the chances of his living to reach it were negligible—but he would never be rounded, plump. And he was probably worth far more in his profession if he kept this frail, almost childlike look. There was an illusion of virginity about him—physically, at least—but his face, when Pitt regarded it more carefully, was as weary and as bleached of innocence as the face of any woman who had plied her trade in the streets for a lifetime. The world held no surprises for Albie, and no hope except of survival.

"Sit down," Pitt said, closing the door behind him. He balanced himself unhappily on the red plush seat as if he were the host, yet it was Albie who made him nervous.

Albie obeyed without moving his eyes from Pitt's face.

"What do you want?" he asked. His voice was curiously pleasing, softer, better educated than his surroundings suggested. Probably he had clients from a better class of person and had picked up their tricks of speech. It was an unpleasant thought, but it made sense. Men of Bluegate Fields had no money for this kind of indulgence. Had Jerome unintentionally schooled this child as well? If not Jerome, then others like him: men whose tastes could only be satisfied in the privacy of rooms like this, with people for whom they had no other feelings, shared no other side of their lives.

"What do you want?" Albie repeated, his old woman's eyes tired in his beardless face. With a shiver of revulsion, Pitt realized what he was thinking. He straightened up in the chair and sat back as if he were at ease, although he felt furiously uncomfortable. He knew his face was hot, but perhaps the lights were too dim for Albie to see it.

"To ask you about one of your customers," he answered. "You told Sergeant Gillivray yesterday. I want you to repeat it to me today. A man's life might depend on it—we have to be sure."

Albie's face stiffened but there was too little color in the skin to see, in this yellow gaslight, if he paled even more.

"What about him?"

"You know the man I mean?"

"Yes. Jerome, the tutor."

"That's right. Describe him for me." He would have to allow some leniency. Customers to places like these often did not wish to be seen closely. They preferred the lights dim, and came in heavily muffled even in summer. It would be cool enough down in these dank, riverside streets any night. It would not be remarked. "Well?"

"Fairly tall." Albie did not seem hesitant or confused. "On the lean side, dark hair that was always short and neat, mustache. Sort of pinched face, sharp nose, pursed-up mouth as if he smelled something bad, brown eyes. I can't describe his body because he always liked the lights off before that part, but he felt strong, and sort of bony—"

Pitt's stomach lurched, his imagination was too vivid. This boy had been thirteen when it started!

"Thank you," he stopped Albie. It was Jerome, exactly; he could not have phrased it better himself. He took half a dozen photographs out of his pocket, including one of Jerome, and passed them over one by one. "Any one of these?"

Albie looked at them each until he came to the right one. He hesitated only for a moment.

"That one," he said with certainty. "That's him. I've never seen any of the others."

Pitt took it back. It was a picture taken in the police cells, stiff and unwilling, but it was a clear likeness.

"Thank you. Did he ever bring anyone else with him when he came?"

"No." Albie smiled very slightly, a wan ghost of expression full of self-knowledge. "People don't, when they come to places like this. With women they might—I don't know many women. But they come here alone, especially the gentry, and they're mostly the ones who can afford it. Others with that sort of taste exercise it with whoever they can find with the same inclination. Usually the higher they are, the quieter they come, the lower their hats and the tighter their collars to their chins. There's more than one wears false whiskers till he gets inside, and always wants the lamps so low he's fallen over the fur-

114

niture before now." His face was cold with scorn. In his opinion, a man should at least have the courage of his sins. "The more I accommodate them, the worse they hate me for it," he went on harshly, suddenly finding anger because he was despised and knew it, for all their begging and added money. Sometimes, when he had had a good week and he did not need the funds, he turned someone away for the sheer luxury of humiliating him, of stripping naked his need and exposing it. Next time, and perhaps even for a month or two, the man remembered to say please and thank you, and did not drop the guineas quite so offhandedly on the table.

It was not necessary to put his thoughts into words for Pitt. Similar ideas had been running through Pitt's imagination: the two bodies locked together in passionate intimacy, the physical need of the man and Albie's need to survive—each despising the other, and in their hearts hating! Albie, because he was used like a public convenience in which you relieve yourself and then leave for the next man; the other, whatever dim figure it was, because Albie had seen his dependence—his naked soul— and he could not forgive that. Each was master and slave, and each knew it.

Pitt felt a sudden pity and anger—pity for the men, because they were imprisoned in themselves, but anger for Albie, because he had been made into what he was not by nature but by man, and for money. He had been taken as child and set into this mold. He would almost certainly die in it, probably within a few years.

Why couldn't Jerome have stayed with Albie, or someone like him? What was it Jerome felt for Arthur Waybourne that Albie had not been able to satisfy? He would probably never know.

"Is that all?" Albie asked patiently. His mind was already somewhere else.

"Yes, thank you." Pitt stood up. "Don't go away, or we'll

be obliged to look for you and keep you safe in jail so we have you for the trial."

Albie looked uncomfortable. "I gave Sergeant Gillivray a statement. He wrote it all down."

"I know. But we'll need you all the same. Don't make things harder for yourself—just be here."

Albie sighed. "All right. Where have I got to go, anyway? I have clients here. I couldn't afford to start all over again somewhere else."

"Yes," Pitt said. "If I thought you would go, I'd arrest you now." He walked to the door and opened it.

"You don't want to do that." Albie smiled with wan humor. "I've too many other clients who wouldn't like it if I was arrested. Who knows what I might say—if I was questioned too hard? You're not free either, Mr. Pitt. All sorts of people need me—people far more important than you are."

Pitt did not grudge him his brief moment of power.

"I know," he said quietly. "But I wouldn't remind them of it, Albie—not if you want to stay safe." He went out and closed the door, leaving Albie sitting on the bed, his arms wrapped around his body as he stared at the prisms on the gaslight.

When Pitt got back to his office, Cutler, the police surgeon, was waiting for him, his face wrinkled in puzzlement. Taking his hat off and flinging it at the stand, Pitt closed the office door. The hat missed and fell on the floor. He pulled his muffler undone and threw it as well. It hung over the antler like a dead snake.

"What is it?" he asked, undoing his coat.

"This man of yours," Cutler replied, scratching his cheek. "Jerome, the one who is supposed to have killed your body from the Bluegate Fields sewer—"

"What about him?"

"He infected the boy with syphilis?"

"Yes—why?"

"He didn't, you know! He doesn't have it. Clean as a whistle. Given him every test I know of—twice. Difficult disease, I know. Goes dormant—can stay like that for years. But whoever gave it to that boy was infectious within the last few months—even weeks—and this man is as clean as I am! I'd swear to that in court—and I'll have to. Defense will ask me—and if they don't, I'll damn well tell them!"

Pitt sat down and shook off his coat, leaving it sprawled over the back of his chair.

"No possibility of a mistake?"

"I told you—I did it twice, and had my assistant check me. The man has not got syphilis or any other venereal disease. Done all the tests on him there are."

Pitt looked at him. He had a strong face but it was not overbearing. There were lines of humor around the mouth and eyes. Pitt found himself wishing he had time to know him better.

"Have you told Athelstan?"

"No." This time there was a smile. "I will if you like. I thought you might prefer to do that yourself."

Pitt stood up and reached out his hand for the written report. His coat slid to the floor in a heap but he did not notice it.

"Yes," he said, without knowing why. "Yes, I would. Thank you." He went to the door, and the doctor left to go back to his work.

Upstairs in his polished and gleaming room, Athelstan was leaning back in his chair contemplating the ceiling when he gave Pitt permission to come in.

"Well?" he said with satisfaction. "Good job young Gillivray did turning up the prostitute, eh? Watch him—he'll go a long way. Wouldn't be surprised if I have to promote him in a year or two. Treading on your tail, Pitt!"

"Possibly," Pitt said without pleasure. "The police surgeon has just given me his report on Jerome."

"Police surgeon?" Athelstan frowned. "What for? Fellow's not ill, is he?"

"No, sir, he's in excellent health—not a blemish, apart from a little dyspepsia." Pitt felt satisfaction welling up inside him. He looked straight at Athelstan, meeting his eyes. "Perfect health," he repeated.

"God dammit, man!" Athelstan sat upright sharply. "Who cares if he has indigestion or not! The man perverted, contaminated, and then murdered a decent boy, a good boy! I don't give a fig if he's doubled up in agony!"

"No, sir, he's in excellent health," Pitt repeated. "The doctor gave him every test he knows of, and then did it again to make sure."

"Pitt, you're wasting my time! As long as he's kept alive and fit for trial, and then hanging, his health is of no interest to me whatsoever. Get on with your job!"

Pitt leaned forward a little, keeping the smile from his face with an effort.

"Sir," he said carefully. "He doesn't have syphilis—not a trace!"

Athelstan stared at him; it was a second or two before the meaning of the statement dawned on him.

"Not got syphilis?" he repeated, blinking.

"That's right. He's clean as a whistle. Hasn't got it now—never has had."

"What are you talking about? He must have it! He gave it to Arthur Waybourne!"

"No, sir, he can't have. He doesn't have it," Pitt repeated.

"That's absurd!" Athelstan exclaimed. "If he didn't give it to Arthur Waybourne, then who did?"

"I don't know, sir. That's a very interesting question."

Athelstan swore viciously, then colored with anger because Pitt had seen him lose control of himself and sink to obscenity.

"Well, get out and do something!" he shouted. "Don't leave everything to young Gillivray! Find out who did give it to that wretched boy! Someone did—find him! Don't stand there like a fool!"

Pitt smiled sourly, his pleasure sharply diluted with the knowledge of what lay ahead.

"Yes, sir. I'll do what I can."

"Good! Get on with it then! And close the door behind you—it's damn cold out there in the passage!"

The end of the day brought the worst experience of all. He arrived home late, to find Eugenie Jerome waiting in the parlor again. She was sitting on the edge of the sofa with Charlotte, who was pale-faced and, for once, obviously uncertain what to do or say. She stood up the moment she heard Pitt at the door, and rushed to greet him—or perhaps to warn him.

As Pitt entered the room, Eugenie stood up, her body tense, her face composed with an effort that was painful.

"Oh, Mr. Pitt, it is so kind of you to see me!"

He had no choice; he would like to have avoided her. That knowledge made him feel guilty. He could see nothing in his mind's eye but Albie Frobisher—what a ridiculous name that was for a prostitute!—sitting in the gaslight in his disgusting room. He felt obscurely guilty for that, too, although it was nothing to do with him. Perhaps the guilt was because he knew about it, and had done nothing to fight it, to wipe it out forever.

"Good evening, Mrs. Jerome," he said gently. "What can I do for you?"

Her eyes filled with tears, and she had to struggle for several seconds to master herself before she could speak distinctly.

"Mr. Pitt, there is no way that I can prove that my husban was at home with me all the night that poor child was killed, because I was asleep and I cannot truly say I know where he was—except that I have never known Maurice to lie about anything, and I believe him." She pulled a little face as she recognized her own naïveté. "Not that I suppose people would expect me to say anything else—"

"That's not so, Mrs. Jerome," Charlotte interrupted. "If you believed he was guilty, you might feel betrayed and wish to see him punished. Many women would!"

Eugenie turned around, her face aghast.

"What a dreadful thought! Oh, how terrible! I do not for even an instant believe it to be true. Certainly Maurice is not an easy man, and there are those who dislike him, I know. He holds very definite opinions, and they are not shared by everyone. But he is not evil. He has no—no appetites of the vile nature they are accusing him of. Of that I am perfectly sure. It is just not the sort of person he is."

Pitt hid his feelings. She was remarkably innocent for a woman married eleven years. Did she really imagine that Jerome would have permitted her to learn of it if he had?

And yet it surprised him also. Jerome seemed too—too ambitious, too rational to fill the picture that was emerging of him as an emotional, sensual man. Which proved what? Only that people were far more complex, more surprising than it was so easy to suppose.

There was no point in hurting her the more by arguing. If it was better for her to go on believing in his innocence, cherishing the good in what she had had, then why insist on trying to shatter it?

"I can only uncover evidence, Mrs. Jerome," he said weakly. "It is not in my power to interpret it, or to hide it again."

"But there must be evidence to prove him innocent!" she protested. "I know he is! Somewhere there must be a way to show that! After all, someone did kill that boy, didn't they?"

"Oh, yes, he was murdered."

"Then find who really did it! Please, Mr. Pitt! If not for the sake of my husband, then for the sake of your own conscience—for justice. I know it was not Maurice, so it must be somebody else." She stopped for a moment, and a more forceful argument came to her mind. "After all if he is left to go free, he may abuse some other child in the same manner, may he not?"

"Yes, I suppose so. But what can I look for, Mrs. Jerome? What other evidence do you think there could be?"

"I don't know. But you are far cleverer at that sort of thing. It is your job. Mrs. Pitt has told me about some of the marvelous cases you have solved in the past, when it seemed quite hopeless. I'm sure if anyone in London can find the truth, it is you."

It was monstrous, but there was nothing he could say. After she had gone, he turned on Charlotte furiously.

"What in God's name have you been telling her?" he demanded, his voice rising to a shout. "I can't do anything about it! The man's guilty! You have no right to encourage her to believe—it's grossly irresponsible—and cruel. Do you know who I saw today?" He had not planned to tell her anything about it. Now he was smarting raw, and he did not want to be alone in his pain. He lashed out with all the clarity of new memory. "I saw a prostitute, a boy who was probably sold into homosexual brothels when he was thirteen years old. He sat there on a bed in a room that looked like a cheap copy of a West End whorehouse—all red plush and gilt-backed chairs, and gas lamps dim in the middle of the day. He was seventeen, but his eyes looked as old as Sodom. He'll probably be dead before he's thirty."

Charlotte stood silent for so long that Pitt began to regret having said what he had. It was unfair; she could not have known what had happened. She was sorry for Eugenie Jerome, and he could hardly blame her for that. So was he—painfully so.

"I'm sorry. I shouldn't have told you that."

"Why?" she demanded, moving suddenly. "Isn't it true?" Her eyes were wide and angry, her face white.

"Yes, of course it's true, but I shouldn't have told you."
Now her anger, fierce and scalding, was directed at him.

"Why not? Do you think I need to be protected, politely deceived like some child? You used not to treat me so condescendingly! I remember when I lived in Cater Street, you forced me to learn something of the rookeries, whether I would or not—"

"That was different! That was starvation. It was poverty you knew nothing of. This is perversion."

"And I ought to know about people starving to death in the alleys, but not about children being bought to be used by the perverted and the sick? Is that what you're saying?"

"Charlotte—you can't do anything about it."

"I can try!"

"You can't possibly make any difference!" He was exasperated. The day had been long and wretched, and he was in no mood for high-flown moral rhetoric. There were thousands of children involved, maybe tens of thousands; there was nothing any one person could do. She was indulging in a flight of imagination to salve conscience, and nothing more. "You've simply no idea of the enormity of it." He waved his hands.

"Don't you dare talk down at me like that!" She caught up the cushion from the sofa and flung it at him as hard as she could. It missed, flew past him, and knocked a vase of flowers from the sideboard onto the floor, spilling water on the carpet but fortunately not breaking the vase.

"Damnation!" she said loudly. "You clumsy creature! You could have at least have caught it! Now look what you've done! I'll have to clean all that up!"

It was grossly unjust of her, but it was not worth arguing about.

She picked up her skirts and swept out to the kitchen, then returned with the dustpan and brush, a cloth, and a jug of fresh water. She silently tidied up, refilled the vase with water from the jug, set the flowers back in, and replaced them on the sideboard.

"Thomas!"

"Yes?" He was deliberately cool, but ready to accept an apology with dignity, even magnanimity.

"I think you may be wrong. That man may not be guilty."

He was stunned. "You what?"

"I think he might not be guilty of killing Arthur Waybourne," she repeated. "Oh, I know Eugenie looks as if she couldn't count up to ten without some man helping her, and she goes dewy-eyed at the sound of a masculine voice, but she puts it all on—it's an act. She's as sharp underneath as I am. She knows he's humorless and full of resentment, and that hardly anybody likes him. I'm not even sure if she likes him very much herself. But she does know him! He has no passion, he's as cold as a cod, and he didn't particularly like Arthur Waybourne. But he knew that working in the Waybourne house was a good position. Actually, the one he preferred was Godfrey. He said Arthur was a nasty boy, sly and conceited."

"How do you know that?" he asked. His curiosity was roused, even though he thought she was being unfair to Eugenie. Funny how even the nicest women, the most levelheaded, could give way to feminine spite.

"Because Eugenie said so, of course!" she said impatiently. "And she might be able to play you like a three-penny violin, but she doesn't pull the wool over my eyes for a moment—she has too much wit to try! And don't look at me like that!" She glared at him. "Just because I don't melt into tears in front of you and tell you you're the only man in London who is clever enough to solve a case! That doesn't mean I don't care. I care very much indeed. And I think it's all frighteningly convenient for everyone else that it's Jerome. So much tidier—don't you think? Now you can leave all the important people alone to get on with their lives without having to answer a lot of very personal and embarrassing questions, or have the police in their houses for the neighbors to gawp at and speculate about."

"Charlotte!" Indignation welled up inside him. She was being wildly unfair. Jerome was guilty; everything pointed to it, and nothing whatsoever pointed to anyone else. She was sorry for Eugenie and she was upset over the boy prostitute; she was letting her emotions run all over the place. It was his fault; he should not have told her about Albie. It was stupid and self-indulgent of him. Worse than that, he had known it was stupid all the time, even as he heard his own voice saying the words.

Charlotte stood still, waiting, staring at him.

He took a deep breath. "Charlotte, you do not know all the evidence. If you did, then you would know that there is enough to convict Maurice Jerome, and there is none at all—do you hear me?—none at all to indicate anyone else knew anything, or had any guilt or complicity in any part of it. I cannot help Mrs. Jerome. I cannot alter or hide the facts. I cannot suppress witnesses. I cannot and *will* not try to get them to alter their evidence. That is the end of the matter! I do not wish to discuss the subject any further. Where is my dinner, please? I am tired and cold, and I have had a long and extremely unpleasant day. I wish to be served my dinner, and to eat it in peace!"

Unblinking, she stared at him while she absorbed what he had said. He stared straight back at her. She took a deep breath and let it out.

"Yes, Thomas," she answered. "It is in the kitchen." She switched her skirts sharply and turned and led the way out and down the hallway.

He followed with a very slight smile that he did not intend her to see. A little of Eugenie Jerome would not hurt her at all!

Just short of a week later, Gillivray came up with his second stroke of brilliance. Admittedly—and he was

124

obliged to concede it—he made the discovery following an idea Pitt had given him and insisted he pursue. All the same, he contrived to tell Athelstan before he reported to Pitt himself. This was achieved by the simple stratagem of delaying his return to the police station with the news until he knew Pitt would be out on another errand.

Pitt came back, wet to the knees from the rain, and with water dripping off the edge of his hat and soaking his collar and scarf. He took off his hat and scarf with numb fingers and flung them in a heap over the hatstand.

"Well?" he demanded as Gillivray stood up from the chair opposite. "What have you got?" He knew from Gillivray's smug face that he had something, and he was too tired to spin it out.

"The source of the disease," Gillivray replied. He disliked using the name of it and avoided it whenever he could; the word seemed to embarrass him.

"Syphilis?" Pitt asked deliberately.

Gillivray's nose wrinkled in distaste, and he colored faintly up his well-shaven cheeks.

"Yes. It's a prostitute—a woman called Abigail Winters."

"Not such an innocent after all, our young Arthur," Pitt observed with a satisfaction he would not have cared to explain. "And what makes you think she is the source?"

"I showed her a picture of Arthur—the photograph we obtained from his father. She recognized it, and confessed she knew him."

"Did she indeed? And why do you say 'confessed'? Did she seduce him, deceive him in some way?"

"No, sir." Gillivray flushed with annoyance. "She's a whore. She couldn't ever find herself in his society."

"So he took himself to hers?"

"No! Jerome took him. I proved that!"

"Jerome took him?" Pitt was startled. "Whatever for?

Surely the last thing he would want would be for Arthur to develop a taste for women? That doesn't make any sense!"

"Well, whether it makes sense or not—he did!" Gillivray snapped back with satisfaction. "Seems he was a voyeur as well. He liked to sit there and watch. You know, I wish I could hang that man myself! I don't usually go to watch a hanging, but this is one I won't miss!"

There was nothing for Pitt to say. Of course he would have to check the statement, see the woman himself; but there was too much now to argue against. It was surely proved beyond any but the most illusory and unrealistic of doubts.

He reached out and took the name and address from Gillivray's hand. It was the last piece necessary before trial.

"If it amuses you," he said harshly. "Can't say I ever enjoyed seeing a man hanged, myself. Any man. But you do whatever gives you pleasure!"

6

The trial of Maurice Jerome began on the second Monday in November. Charlotte had never before been in a courtroom. Her interest in Pitt's cases had been intense in the past; indeed, on several occasions she had actively and often dangerously engaged herself in discovering the criminal. But it had always come to an end for her with the arrest; once there was no mystery left, she had considered the matter finished. To know the outcome had been sufficient—she did not wish to see it.

This time, however, she felt a strong need to attend as a gesture of support to Eugenie in what was surely one of the worst ordeals a woman could face—whatever the verdict. Even now, she was not sure what she expected the verdict to be. Usually she had entire confidence in Pitt, but in this case she had sensed an unhappiness in him that was deeper than his usual distress for the tragedy of crime. There was a sense of dissatisfaction, an air of something unfinished—answers he needed to have, and did not.

And yet if it was not Jerome, then who? There was no one else even implicated. All the evidence pointed to Jerome; why should everyone lie? It made no sense, but still the doubts were there.

She had, in her mind, formed something of a picture

of Jerome, a little blurred, a little fuzzy in the details. She had to remind herself it was built on what Eugenie had told her, and Eugenie was prejudiced, to say the least. And, of course, on what Pitt had said; perhaps that was prejudiced too? Pitt had been touched by Eugenie as soon as he had seen her. She was so vulnerable; his pity was reflected in his face, his desire to protect her from the truths he knew. Charlotte had watched it in him, and felt angry with Eugenie for being so childlike, so innocent, and so very, very feminine.

But that was not important now. What was Maurice Jerome like? She had gathered that he was a man of little emotion. He displayed neither superficial emotions nor the emotions that smolder beneath an ordinary face, surfacing only in privacy in moments of unbearable passion. Jerome was cold; his appetites were less sensual than intellectual. He possessed a desire for knowledge and the status and power it afforded, for the social distinctions of manner, speech, and dress. He felt proud of his diligence and of possessing skills that others did not. He was proud, too, in an obscure way, of the satisfying totality of such branches of mental discipline as Latin grammar and mathematics.

Was that all merely a superb mask for ungovernable physical hungers beneath? Or was he precisely what he seemed: a chilly, rather incomplete man, too innately self-absorbed for passion of any sort?

Whatever the truth, Eugenie could only suffer from it. The least Charlotte could do was to be there, so that the crowd of inquisitive, accusing faces would contain at least one that was neither, that was a friend whose glance she could meet and know she was not alone.

Charlotte had put out a clean shirt for Pitt, and a fresh cravat, and she sponged and pressed his best coat. She did not tell him that she intended to go as well. She kissed him goodbye at quarter past eight, straightening his collar one last time. Then, as soon as the door closed, she whirled around and ran back to the kitchen to instruct Gracie in meticulous detail on the duties of caring for the house and the children for every day that the trial should last. Gracie assured Charlotte that she would perform every task to the letter, and be equal to any occasion that could arise.

Charlotte accepted this and thanked her gravely, then went to her room, changed into the only black dress she possessed, and put on a very beautiful, extravagant black hat that was a cast-off from Emily. Emily had worn it at some duchess's funeral, and then, on hearing of the woman's excessive parsimony, had taken such a dislike to her that she got rid of the hat immediately and bought another, even more expensive and stylish.

This one had a broad, rakish brim, plenty of veiling, and quite marvelous feathers. It was wildly flattering, accenting the bones of Charlotte's face and her wide gray eyes, and was as glamorous as only a touch of mystery could be.

She did not know if one was supposed to wear black to a trial. Decent society did not attend trials! But after all it was for murder, and that necessarily had to do with death. Anyway, there was no one she could ask, at this late date. They'd probably say she should not attend at all, and make it difficult fo her by pointing out to Pitt all the excellent reasons why she should not. Or they'd say that only women of scandalous character, like the old women who knitted at the foot of the guillotine in the French Revolution, attended such things.

It was cold, and she was glad she had saved enough from the housekeeping money to pay for fare in a hansom cab both ways, every day of the week, should it be necessary.

She was very early; hardly anyone else was there—only court officials dressed in black, looking a little dusty like summer crows, and two women with brooms and dusters. It was bleaker than she had imagined. Her footsteps echoed on the wide floors as she followed directions to the appropriate room and took her seat on the bare wooden rows.

She stared around, trying to people the room in her mind. The rails around the witness box and the dock were dark now, worn by the hands of generations of prisoners, of men and women who had come here to give evidence, nervous, trying to hide private and ugly truths, telling tales about others, evading with lies and half lies. Every human sin and intimacy had been exposed here; lives had been shattered, deaths pronounced. But no one had ever done the simple things here—eaten or slept, or laughed with a friend. She saw only the anonymous look of a public place.

Already there were others coming in, with bright, sneering faces. Hearing snatches of conversation, she instantly hated them. They had come to leer, to pry, to indulge their imaginations with what they could not possibly know. They would come to their own verdicts, regardless of the evidence. She wanted Eugenie to know there was at least one person who would keep pure friendship, whatever was said.

And that was odd, because her feelings for Eugenie were still very confused. Charlotte was irritated by her saccharine feminity; not only did it scrape Charlotte raw, but it was a perpetuation of all that was most infuriating in men's assumptions about women. She had been aware of such attitudes ever since the time her father had taken a newspaper from her, and told her it was unsuitable for a lady to be interested in such things, and insisted she return to her painting and embroidery. The condescension of men to female frailty and general silliness made her temper boil. And Eugenie pandered to it by pretending to be exactly what they expected. Perhaps she had learned to act that way as a form of self-protection, as a way of getting what she wanted? That was a partial excuse, but it was still the coward's way out.

And the worst thing about it all was that it worked—it worked even with Pitt! He melted like a complete fool! She had watched it happen in her own parlor! Eugenie, in her own simpering, self-deprecating, flattering way, was socially quite as clever as Emily! If she had started from as good a family and had been as pretty as Emily, perhaps she too might have married a title.

What about Pitt? The thought sent a chill throughout her body. Would Pitt have preferred someone a little softer, a little subtler at playing games; someone who would remain at least partly a mystery to him, demanding nothing of his emotions but patience? Would he have been happier with someone who left him at heart utterly alone, who never really hurt him because she was never close enough, who never questioned his values or destroyed his self-esteem by being right when he was wrong and letting him know it?

Surely to suspect Pitt of wanting such a woman was the most supreme insult of all. It assumed he was an emotional child, unable to stand the truth. But we are all children at times, and we all need dreams—even foolish ones.

Perhaps she would be wiser if she bit her tongue a little more often, let truth—or her understanding of the truth—wait its time. There was kindness to consider—as well as devotion to honesty.

The court was now full. In fact, when she turned around there were people being refused entrance. Curious faces crowded at the doorways, hoping for a glimpse of the prisoner, the man who had murdered an aristocrat's son and stuffed his naked body down a manhole to the sewers!

The proceedings began. The clerk, somber in old black, wearing a gold pince-nez on a ribbon around his neck, called for attention in the matter of the Crown versus Maurice Jerome. The judge, his face like a ripe plum beneath his heavy, horsehair wig, puffed out his cheeks and sighed. He looked as if he had dined too well the evening before. Charlotte could imagine him in a velvet jacket, with crumbs on his waistcoat, wiping away the last remnants of the Stilton and upending the port wine. The fire would be climbing the chimney and the butler standing by to light his cigar.

Before the end of the week, he would probably put on the black three-cornered cap and sentence Maurice Jerome to be hanged by the neck until he was dead.

She shivered and turned to look for the first time at the man standing in the dock. She was startled—unpleasantly so. She realized what a precise mental picture she had built of him, not so much of his features, but of the sense of him, the feeling she would have on seeing his face.

And the picture vanished. He was larger than her pity had allowed; his eyes were cleverer. If there was fear in him, it was masked by his contempt for everyone around him. There were ways in which he was superior—he could speak Latin and considerable Greek; he had read about the arts and the cultures of ancient peoples, and this rabble below him had not. They were here to indulge a vuglar curiosity; he was here by force, and he would endure it because he had no choice. But he would not descend to be part of the emotional tide. He despised the vulgarity, and in his slightly flared nostrils, his pursed mouth that destroyed any lines of softness or sensitivity, in the slight movement of his shoulders that prevented him from touching the constables at either side, he silently made it understood.

Charlotte had begun with sympathy for him, thinking she could understand, at least in part, how he could have come to such a depth of passion and despair—if he was guilty. And surely he was deserving of every compassion and effort at justice if he was innocent?

And yet looking at him, real and alive, only yards away, she could not like him. The warmth faded and she was left with discomfort. She must begin all over again with her feelings, build them for an entirely different person from the one her mind had created.

The trial had begun. The sewer cleaner was the first witness. He was small, narrow as a boy, and he blinked, unaccustomed to the light. The counsel for the prosecution was a Mr. Bartholomew Land. He dealt with the man quickly and straightforwardly, drawing from him the very simple story of his work and his discovery of the corpse, the body surprisingly unmarked by injury or attacks by rats—and the fact that, remarkably, it had kept none of its clothes, not even boots. Of course he had called the police immediately, and certainly not, me lud, he had removed nothing whatsoever—he was not a thief! The suggestion was an insult.

Counsel for the defense, Mr. Cameron Giles, found nothing to contest, and the witness was duly excused.

The next witness was Pitt. Charlotte bent a little to hide her face as he passed within a yard of her. She was amused and felt a small quake of uncertainty when, even at a time like this, he glanced for a moment at her hat. It was beautiful! Though of course he did not know it was she who was wearing it! Did he often notice other women with that quick flash of appreciation? She drove the idea from her mind. Eugenie had worn a hat.

Pitt took the witness stand and swore to his name and occupation. Though she had pressed his jacket before he left the house, it sat slightly lopsided already, his cravat was crooked, and, as usual, he had run his fingers through his hair, leaving it on end. It was a waste of time even trying! Heaven only knew what he had in his pockets to make them hang like that! Stones, by the look of it!

"You examined the body?" Land asked.

"Yes, sir."

"And there was no identification on it whatsoever? How did you then learn who he was?"

Pitt outlined the process, the elimination of one possibility after another. He made it sound very routine, a matter of common sense anyone might have followed.

"Indeed." Land nodded. "And in due course Sir Anstey Waybourne identified his son?"

"Yes, sir."

"What did you do then, Mr. Pitt?"

Pitt's face was blank. Only Charlotte knew that it was misery that took away his normal expression, the consuming interest that was usually there. To anyone else he might simply have appeared cold.

"Because of information given me by the police surgeon"—he was far too used to giving evidence to repeat hearsay—"I began to make investigations into Arthur Waybourne's personal relationships."

"And what did you learn?"

Everything was being dragged out of him; he volunteered nothing.

"I learned of no close relationships outside his own household that fitted the description we were looking for." What a careful answer, all in words that gave nothing away. He had not even implied there was any sort of sexuality involved. He could have been talking of finance, or even some trade or other.

Land's eyebrows shot up and his voice showed surprise. "No relationships, Mr. Pitt! Are you sure?"

Pitt's mouth curled down. "I think you will have to ask Sergeant Gillivray for the information you are fishing for," he said with thinly concealed acidity.

Charlotte closed her eyes for a moment, even behind her veiling. So he was going to make Gillivray tell all about Albie Frobisher and the woman prostitute with the disease. Gillivray would love that. He would be a celebrity.

Why? Gillivray would make it all so much more florid, so full of detail and certainty. Or was it that Pitt simply did not want to be part of it and this was his way of escaping—at least from saying the words himself, as if that made some difference? Left to Gillivray, they would be the more damning.

She looked up. He was terribly alone there in that wood-railed box; there was nothing she could do to help.

He did not even know she was here, understanding his fear because some part of him was still not entirely satisfied of Jerome's guilt.

What had Arthur Waybourne really been like? He was young, well-born, and a victim of murder. No one would dare to speak ill of him now, to dig up the mean or grubby truths. Maurice Jerome, with his cynical face, probably knew that, too.

She looked across at Pitt.

He was going on with his evidence, Land drawing it out of him a piece at a time.

Giles had nothing to ask. He was too skilled to try to shake him, and would not give him the opportunity to reinforce what he had already said.

Then it was the police surgeon's turn. He was calm, quite certain of his facts and impervious to the power or solemnity of the court. Neither the judge's flowing size and rippling wig nor Land's thundering voice made any impression on him. Under the pomposity of the court were only human bodies. And he had seen bodies naked, had taken them apart when they were dead. He was only too aware of their frailty, their common indignities and needs.

Charlotte tried to imagine members of the court in white dust sheets, without the centuries of dignity their robes lent them, and suddenly it all seemed faintly ridiculous. She wondered if the judge was hot under that great wig; did it itch?

Perhaps the white dust sheets would be just as delusionary as the gowns and robes?

The surgeon was talking. He had a good face, strong without arrogance. He told the truth, sparing nothing. But he stated it as fact, without emotion or judgment. Arthur Waybourne had been homosexually used. A ripple of disgust spread through the room. Everyone doubtless already knew, but it was a pleasure, a kind of catharsis to be able to express the feeling and wallow in it. After all, that was what they had come for!

Arthur Waybourne had recently contracted syphilis. Another wave of revulsion—this time also a shudder of surprise and fear. This was disease; it was contagious. There were things about it one knew, and decent people stood in no peril. But there was always mystery with disease, and they were close enough to it for a thrill of apprehension, the cold brush of real danger. It was a disease for which there was no cure.

Then came the surprise. Giles stood up.

"You say, Dr. Cutler, that Arthur Waybourne had recently contracted syphilis?"

"Yes, that is so."

"Unquestionably?"

"Unquestionably."

"You could not have made a mistake? It could not be some other disease with similar symptoms?"

"No, it could not."

"From whom did he contract this disease?"

"I have no way of knowing, sir. Except, of course, that it must have been someone who suffered from the disease."

"Precisely. That would not tell you who it was—but it would tell you undoubtedly who it was not!"

"Of course."

There was a shifting in the seats. The judge leaned forward.

"So much would appear to be obvious, Mr. Giles, even to the veriest imbecile. If you have a point, please come to it, sir!"

"Yes, my lord. Dr. Cutler, have you examined the prisoner with the purpose of determining whether he has or has ever had syphilis?"

"Yes, sir."

"And has he that disease?"

"No, sir, he has not. Nor has he any other communicable disease. He is in good health, as good as a man may be under such stress."

There was silence. The judge screwed up his face and stared at the doctor with dislike.

"Do I understand you to say, sir, that the prisoner did not pass on this disease to the victim, Arthur Waybourne?" he asked icily.

"That is correct, my lord. It would have been impossible."

"Then who did? How did he get it? Did he inherit it?"

"No, my lord, it was in the early stages, such as is found when it has been sexually transmitted. Congenital syphilis would betray entirely different symptoms."

The judge sighed heavily and leaned back, a look of long-suffering on his face.

"I see. And of course you cannot say from whom he did contract it!" He blew his nose. "Very well, Mr. Giles, you appear to have made your point. Pray continue."

"That is all, my lord. Thank you, Dr. Cutler."

Before he could go, however, Land shot to his feet.

"Just a moment, Doctor! Did the police subsequently ask you to verify a diagnosis of another person, who did have syphilis?"

Cutler smiled dryly. "Several."

"One with particular reference to this case?" Land said sharply.

"They did not tell me—it would be hearsay." The doctor seemed to find some pleasure in being obstructively literal.

"Abigail Winters?" Land's temper was rising. His case was flawless and he knew it, but he was being made to look inefficient in front of the court, and he resented it.

"Yes, I did examine Abigail Winters, and she does have syphilis," Cutler conceded.

"Communicable?"

"Certainly."

"And what is Abigail Winters's profession—or trade, if you prefer?"

"I have no idea."

"Don't be naïve, Dr. Cutler! You know as well as I do what her trade is!"

Cutler's wide mouth showed only the slightest of smiles.

"I'm afraid you have the advantage of me, sir."

There was a twitter around the court and Land's face flushed dull red. Even from behind him, Charlotte could see the color stain his neck. She was glad her veil hid her own expression. This was neither the place nor the time to be amused.

Land opened his mouth and closed it again.

"You are excused!" he said furiously. "I call Sergeant Harcourt Gillivray."

Gillivray took the stand and swore to his name and office. He looked freshly scrubbed and neat without losing the air of having attained the effect without labor. He could have passed for a gentleman, except for a slight unease in his hands and just a small, betraying air of self-importance. A true gentleman would not have worried about how others saw him; he would have known there was no need—and he would not have cared anyway.

Gillivray confirmed Pitt's evidence. Land then went on to question him about discovering Albie Frobisher, stopping short, of course, of Albie's evidence, which would have been hearsay from Gillivray. And Albie would be called in due course to give it himself—far more tellingly.

Charlotte sat cold; it was all so logical, it fitted so well. Thank heaven at least Eugenie was outside. As a witness, she was not permitted in until after she had testified.

Gillivray told how he had then pursued his investigations. He did mention Pitt's hand in them, or that he had been following Pitt's orders, Pitt's intuition of where he should look. He stood very straight. He told them how he

138

had found Abigail Winters and learned that she had a disease that on examination proved to be syphilis.

He left the stand pink-cheeked with pride, two hundred pairs of eyes watching his straight back and elegant shoulders as he returned to his seat.

Charlotte loathed him, because he was satisfied; to him this was an achievement, not a tragedy. He should have hurt! He should have felt pain and bewilderment welling up inside him.

The judge adjourned them for luncheon, and Charlotte huddled out with the crowd, hoping that Pitt would not see her. She wondered now if perhaps the vanity that had led her to wear the black hat was going to be her undoing.

Actually, it did not happen until she was returning—a little early, to be sure of claiming her seat again.

She saw Pitt as soon as she entered the hallway, and stopped. Then, realizing that stopping would only attract further attention, she tilted her chin higher and sailed down toward the courtroom door.

It was inevitable that Pitt should see her. She was dressed entirely in black, and the hat was quite marvelous. He would have looked had they been anywhere.

She considered inclining her head away and decided against it. It would be unnatural and arouse his suspicion.

Even so, it was a moment before he recognized her.

She felt his hand hard on her arm and was obliged to stop. She froze, then she turned to stare at him.

"Charlotte!" He was astonished, his face almost comical. "Charlotte? What on earth are you doing here? You can't help!"

"I wish to be here," she said reasonably, keeping her voice low. "Don't make a scene, or everyone will look at us."

"I don't give a damn if everyone looks at us! Go home. This is no place for you!"

"Eugenie's here—I think there is very good cause for me to remain. She may need a deal of comfort before this is through."

He hesitated. She took his hand off her arm gently.

"Wouldn't you want me to help her if I could?"

He could think of no answer and she knew it. She gave him a dazzling smile and swept into the courtroom.

The first witness in the afternoon was Anstey Waybourne. Suddenly, the room became aware of tragedy. There was no sound from the body of the court except a low mutter of sympathy. People nodded sagely, joining in a sort of mass awareness of death.

He had little of worth to add, just the identification of his son's body, an account of the boy's brief life and its day-to-day details, his studies with Jerome. He was asked by Giles how he had come to employ Jerome, about the excellence of his references and the fact that no previous employer had had any complaint about him. Jerome's academic qualifications were unquestionable; his discipline was exacting but without brutality. Neither Arthur nor Godfrey had especially liked him, but neither, Waybourne had to admit, had they expressed any but the natural resentment of young people for one in constant authority over them.

Questioned about his own opinion of Jerome, he had little to contribute. The whole matter had shocked him deeply. He had had no conception of what was happening to his sons. He could be of no assistance. The judge, in subdued voice, permitted him to be excused.

Godfrey Waybourne was called. There was an instant hum of anger against Jerome; he was to blame for such a child being required to suffer this ordeal.

Jerome sat motionless, staring straight ahead as if Godfrey had been a stranger and of no interest. Neither did he look at Land when he spoke.

The evidence was brief. Godfrey repeated what he had

140

told Pitt, all in genteel words—almost ambiguous, except to those who already knew what he was talking about.

Even Giles was gentle with him, not requiring him to repeat the painful details.

They finished for the day surprisingly early. Charlotte had had no idea courts closed at what for Pitt was barely more than halfway through the afternoon. She found herself a hansom and rode home. She had been there over two hours and had changed into a more modest dress when Pitt finally came in. She was at the stove with dinner simmering. She waited for the blast, but it did not come.

"Where did you get the hat?" he asked, sitting down in the kitchen chair.

She smiled with relief. She had not been aware of it, but her whole body had been tense, waiting for his anger. It would have hurt her more than she could easily accommodate. She poked the stew and took a little broth in her spoon, blowing on it to taste. She usually failed to put in sufficient salt. She wanted this to be especially good.

"Emily," she replied. "Why?"

"It looks expensive."

"Is that all?" She turned around to look at him, smiling at last.

He met her eyes without a flicker, reading her perfectly.

"And beautiful," he added, then said beaming, "Quite beautiful! But it would have suited Emily, too. Why did she give it to you?"

"She saw one she liked better," she said truthfully. "Although of course she said it was because she bought it for a funeral and then heard something unpleasant about the deceased."

"So she gave you the hat?"

"You know Emily." She sipped the broth and added

enough salt to suit Pitt's sharper tongue. "When does Eugenie give evidence?"

"When the defense starts. That may not be tomorrow—more probably the next day. You don't need to go."

"No, I suppose not. But I want to. I don't want just half an opinion."

"My dear, when did you ever have less than a total opinion? Whatever the issue!"

"Then if I'm going to have an opinion," she retorted instantly, "better it be an informed one!"

He had neither energy nor will to argue. If she wanted to go, it was her own decision. In a way there was comfort in sharing the burden of knowing; his aloneness melted away. He could not change anything, but at least he could touch her, and without words, explanations, she would understand exactly what he felt.

The following day, the first witness was Mortimer Swynford. His only purpose was to lay the ground for Titus, by testifying that he had employed Jerome to tutor both his son and his daughter. He had done so very soon after Jerome was engaged by Anstey Waybourne, to whom Swynford was related by marriage; it was Waybourne in fact, who had recommended Jerome to him. No, he had had no idea that Jerome was anything but of the most impeccable moral character. His intellectual record was excellent.

They kept Titus only a matter of minutes. Grave, but more curious than frightened, he stood straight in the stand. Charlotte immediately liked the boy because he gave her the feeling he was saddened by the whole thing, speaking only reluctantly of something he still found distressing and hard to believe.

After the luncheon adjournment, the atmosphere changed entirely. The sympathy, the sober silence, vanished and was replaced with a buzz of whisper, the rustling of clothes in seats as the spectators settled to enjoy a salacious superiority, a little voyeurism without the indignity of crouching at windows or peeping through holes.

Albert Frobisher was called to the stand. He looked small, a strange mixture of the weariness of great age and the vulnerability of a child. He did not surprise Charlotte; her imagination had already built a picture of him that was not far from the truth. Yet the reality did somehow shock her. There was something so much sharper about the voice, not just the mind. She sensed a being whose feelings she could not reach, who said things she had not thought of first.

He swore to his name and address.

"What is your occupation, Mr. Frobisher?" Land asked coolly. He needed Albie—indeed Albie was vital to the case—but Land could not keep the contempt out of his voice, the reminder to everyone that there was an unbridgeable gulf between them. He did not wish anyone, even in a moment's absence of mind, to imagine that they had any connection but this necessary one of duty.

Charlotte could understand. She would not have wished to be bracketed with him. Yet she was angry; perhaps it was unfair.

"I am a prostitute," Albie said with cold derision. He understood the niceties, too, and despised them. But at least he would not hide in a hypocrisy of ignorance.

"A prostitute?" Land's voice rose in pretended disbelief. "But you are a man?"

"I'm seventeen," Albie replied. "I began with my first customer when I was thirteen."

"I did not ask your age!" Land was annoyed. He was not interested in child prostitution—that was an entirely different matter, and one he was not concerned with. "Do you sell your services to some kind of depraved women whose appetites are so gross they cannot be satisfied within a normal relationship?"

Albie was tired of this playacting. His whole trade was

143

one long charade, a procession of people who pretended to be respectable.

"No, I don't," he said flatly. "I've never touched a woman. I sell myself to men, mostly rich men, toffs, who prefer boys to women and can't get them without paying, so they come to people like me. I thought you knew that—or why did you call me here? What use would I be to you if I didn't, eh?"

Land was furious. He turned to the judge.

"My lord! Will you order the witness to answer the questions and refrain from making impertinent observations that may well slander decent and honorable men, and can only distress the court! There are ladies present!"

Charlotte thought that was ridiculous, and would dearly like to have said so. Anyone attending this court—except witnesses, who were outside anyway—had come here precisely because they wanted to hear something shocking! Why else attend a murder trial where you know in advance the victim was abused and contaminated by a venereal disease? The hypocrisy was revolting; her whole body was rigid with anger.

The judge's face was even purpler than it had been.

"You will answer only the questions you are asked!" he said sharply to Albie. "I understand the police have laid no charges against you. Conduct yourself here in a manner to insure that that remains so! Do you understand me? This is not an opportunity for you to advertise your vile trade, or to slander your betters!"

Charlotte thought bitterly that the men who used him, far from being his betters, were considerably inferior. They did not go to Albie out of ignorance or the need to survive. Albie was not innocent, but he could plead some mitigation. They had none but the compulsion of their appetites.

"I shall mention no one who is better than I am, my lord," Albie said with a curl of his lip. "I swear."

The judge gave him a look of sour suspicion, but he had obtained the promise he had asked for. No complaint he could justify came to his mind.

Charlotte found herself smiling with sharp satisfaction. She would like to have been able to say exactly that.

"So your customers are men?" Land continued. "Just answer yes or no!"

"Yes." Albie omitted the 'sir.'

"Do you see anyone in this courtroom who has been a customer of yours at any time."

Albie's soft mouth widened into a smile and he began to look slowly, almost lingeringly around the room. His eyes stopped on one smart-suited gentleman after another.

Land saw the danger and his body stiffened in alarm.

"Has the prisoner ever been a customer of yours?" he said loudly. "Look at the prisoner!"

Albie affected surprise and removed his glance from the gallery to the dock.

"Yes."

"Maurice Jerome bought your services as a male prostitute?" Land said triumphantly.

"Yes."

"On one occasion or several?"

"Yes."

"Don't be obtuse!" Land allowed his temper to show at last. "You can be charged with contempt of court, and find yourself in jail if you are obstructive, I promise you!"

"Several." Albie was unruffled. He had a certain power and he meant to taste the full pleasure of it. It would almost certainly not arise again. Life would not be long, and he knew it. Few people's were, in Bluegate Fields, still fewer in his occupation. Today was for the savoring. Land was the one with status and possessions to lose; Albie had nothing anyway—he could afford to live dangerously. He faced Land without a quiver.

"Maurice Jerome came to your rooms on several occasions?" Land waited to make sure the jury had taken the point.

"Yes," Albie repeated.

"And did he have a physical relationship with you, and pay you for it?"

"Yes." His mouth curled in contempt and his eyes flickered over the gallery. "Good God, I don't do it free! You don't imagine I *like* it, do you?"

"I have no idea as to your tastes, Mr. Frobisher," Land said icily. There was a very small smile on his face. "They are quite beyond my imagination!"

Albie's face was white in the gaslight. He leaned forward a little over the railing.

"They're very simple. I expect they're much the same as yours. I like to eat at least once every day. I like to have clothes that keep me warm, and don't stink. I like to have a dry roof over my head and not have to share it with ten or twenty other people! Those are my tastes—sir!"

"Silence!" The judge banged his gavel. "You are being impertinent. We are not concerned with your life story or your desires. Mr. Land, if you cannot control your witness, you had better dismiss him. Surely you have elicited the information you require? Mr. Giles, have you anything to ask?"

"No, my lord. Thank you." He had already tried to shake Albie's identification and failed. There was no purpose in showing his failure to the jury.

Dismissed from the stand, Albie walked back along the aisle, passing within a few feet of Charlotte. His moment of protest was over, and he looked small and thin again.

The last witness for the prosecution was Abigail Winters. She was an ordinary-looking girl, a little plump but with fine, clear skin that many a lady would have envied. Her hair was frizzy and her teeth too large, and a little discolored, but she was handsome enough. Charlotte had seen daughters of countesses who had been less favored by nature.

146

The evidence was short and to the point. She had neither Albie's bitterness not his vicarious education. She was not ashamed of what she did. She knew gentlemen and judges, even bishops, had patronized her and girls like her, and a barrister without his gown and wig looks much the same as a clerk without his suit. If Abigail had few illusions about people, she had none at all about the rules of society. Those who wished to survive kept the rules.

She answered the questions soberly and directly, adding nothing. Yes, she knew the prisoner in the dock. Yes, he had patronized her establishment—not that he wished her services for himself, but for a young gentleman of about sixteen or seventeen years old that he had brought with him. Yes, he had asked her to initiate the young gentleman into the arts of such a relationship while he, the prisoner, sat in the room and watched.

There was a murmur of disgust around the court, a long letting out of breath in self-righteous horror. Then there was total silence, in case the audience should inadvertently miss the next revelation. Charlotte felt sick—for all of them. This should never have happened, and they should not be here willingly listening to it. How on earth was Eugenie going to bear it when she knew—some busybody would be bound to tell her!

Land inquired whether Abigail could describe the young gentleman concerned.

Yes, she could. He was slender, fair-haired, with light blue eyes. He was very good-looking, and spoke with a fine accent. He was definitely a person of good breeding and money. His clothes were excellent.

He showed her a picture of Arthur Waybourne. Was this he?

Yes, it was he, without doubt.

Had she known his name?

Only his Christian name, which was Arthur. The prisoner had addressed him by it on several occasions.

There was nothing Giles could do. Abigail was unshakable, and after a brief attempt he accepted the futility of it and gave up.

That evening, by strict consent, neither Charlotte nor Pitt referred to Jerome or anything to do with the trial. They ate silently, absorbed in thought. Occasionaly they smiled knowingly across the table.

After dinner they spoke quite casually of other things: a letter Charlotte had received from Emily, who had returned from Leicestershire, detailing social gossip, someone's outrageous flirtation, a disastrous party, a rival's most unflattering dress—all the pleasant trivia of daily life. She had been to a concert: there was an entertaining new novel—very risqué—and Grandmama's health had not improved. But then it never had done so since Charlotte could recall. Grandmama enjoyed poor health, and was determined to enjoy it to the last!

On the third day, the defense began its case. There was little enough to say. Jerome could not prove his innocence, or there would have been no prosecution. All he could do was deny, and hope to bring forward enough witnesses to his previously impeccable character that there would be reasonable doubt.

Sitting in her accustomed seat near the aisle, Charlotte felt a wave of pity and hopelessness that was almost physical as Eugenie Jerome walked past her to climb into the witness stand. Just once she lifted her chin and smiled across at her husband. Then quickly, before she had time to see if he smiled back or not, she averted her eyes to take the Bible in her hand for the oath.

Charlotte lifted her veil so Eugenie could see her face and know there was one friend there in that anonymous, inquisitive crowd.

The court heard her in absolute silence. They wavered between contempt for her as an accomplice, the wife of such a monster, and compassion for her as the most innocent and ill-used of his victims. Perhaps it was her narrow shoulders, her plain dress, her white face, her soft voice, the way she kept her eyes a little downcast, then slowly gathered courage and faced her questioner. It could have been any of these things—or none, simply a whimsy of the crowd. But suddenly, like the moment when the tide slackens and turns, Charlotte could feel their mood change and they were with her. They were burning with pity, with hunger to see her avenged. She, too, was a victim.

But there was nothing Eugenie could do. She had been in bed that night and did not know when her husband had come home. Yes, she had planned to go to the concert with him, but that afternoon had developed a severe headache and gone to her room instead. Yes, the tickets had been purchased beforehand and she had fully intended to go. She had to admit, though, she was not fond of classical music; she preferred ballads, something with melody and words.

Had her husband told her what was played that evening? Certainly he had, and that it was excellently performed. Could she recall what it was? She could and did. But was it not true that the program had been published, and anyone might know simply by reading one, without having attended the performance?

She had no idea; she did not read such things.

Land assured her that it was so.

She had married Maurice Jerome eleven years ago and he had been a good husband to her, had provided well. He was sober, industrious, and had never given her cause to complain in any way. He had certainly never mistreated her either verbally or physically; he had not forbidden her any friendships or the occasional outing. He had never embarrassed her by flirting with other women, or any manner of unseemly behavior; nor had he been coarse or overdemanding in private. And he had cer-

149

tainly never required of her any conjugal duties that were offensive or other than would be expected of any wife.

But then, as Land pointed out with something close to embarrassment, there was a great deal she did not know. And, being a lady of decent upbringing and gentle disposition, it would never have occurred to her to be jealous of a schoolboy! In face, she probably had not even known of the existence of such depraved practices.

No, she admitted, white to the lips, she had not. And she did not believe it now. It may be true of some, if Mr. Land said so; but it was not true of her husband. He was a decent man—indeed, highly moral. Even uncouth language offended him, and he never took alcohol. She had never known him to exhibit the least vulgarity.

They permitted her to go, and Charlotte wished she would leave the court. It was hopeless—nothing could save Jerome. It was pathetic, even vaguely revolting, to hope.

Nevertheless it ground on.

Another, less biased witness—a previous employer— was called regarding Jerome's character. He was embarrassed to be there and it was obviously very much against his wish. While he did not want to say anything that might ally him with Jerome in the public mind, he could hardly admit to having been aware of any long-standing flaw in Jerome's character. He had recommended him without reservation; he was now obliged to stand by that recommendation or appear a fool. And since he was an investment banker, that he could not possibly afford to do.

He duly swore that while living in his house and tutoring his sons, Jerome had appeared to be of exemplary character, and certainly he had never behaved improperly toward either of his sons.

And would the witness know if he had, Land inquired courteously.

There was a long hesitation while he weighed the consequences of either answer.

"Yes," he said firmly at last. "Certainly I would. I am naturally concerned with the welfare of my family."

Land did not pursue it. He nodded and sat down, knowing a fruitless course when he saw it.

The only other witness of character was Esmond Vanderley. It was he who had recommended Jerome to Waybourne. Like the previous witness, Vanderley was caught between two poles: appearing to support Jerome and—far worse than merely being a poor judge of character—having been the single individual who had more than any other precipitated the tragedy they were discussing. After all, it was he who had brought Maurice Jerome into the house and thus into Arthur Waybourne's life—and death.

He swore to his name and his relationship with the Waybourne household.

"Lady Waybourne is your sister, Mr. Vanderley?" Giles repeated.

"Yes."

"And Arthur Waybourne was your nephew?"

"Naturally."

"So you would not lightly or casually recommend a tutor for him, knowing the effect it would have on his personal and academic life?" Giles pressed.

There was only one answer that allowed self-respect.

"Of course," Vanderley said with a slight smile. He leaned elegantly over the rail. "I would make myself unpopular rather quickly if I were to recommend regardless. They come home to roost, you know!"

"Home to roost?" Giles was momentarily confused.

"Recommendations, Mr. Giles. People seldom remember the good advice you give them—they always take the credit themselves. But let them take your bad advice and they will instantly recall that it was not their own idea but yours that was to blame. Not only that, but they will make sure everyone else is made aware of it, too."

"May we take it, then, that you did not recommend Maurice Jerome without some considerable inquiry into his qualifications—and his character?"

"You may. His qualifications were excellent. His character was not especially pleasing, but then I was not intending to make a social acquaintance of him. His morality was impeccable, so far as it was discussed at all. One doesn't mention such things, you know, when talking of tutors. Underhousemaids one has to inquire into—or, rather, one has the housekeeper do it. But a tutor one expects to be satisfactory unless stated otherwise. In which case, of course, one doesn't employ him in the first place. Jerome was a little stuffy, if anything—rather a prig. Oh—and a teetotaler. He's the sort that would be."

Vanderly smiled a little tightly.

"Married to a pleasant woman," he went on. "Inquired into her reputation. Spotless."

"No children?" Now Land took over, attempting to shake him. He pressed the point, as if it had some meaning.

"Don't think so. Why?" Vanderly's eyebrows went up innocently.

"Possibly indicative." Land was not prepared to commit himself to something that might mar his case by being considered prejudicial. And of course he might also offend many others, dangerous others. "We are dealing with a man of most peculiar tastes!"

"Nothing peculiar about Mrs. Jerome," Vanderley answered, his eyes still wide. "At least not that I could see. Looked like an average sort of woman to me—quiet, sober, well mannered, pretty enough."

"But no children!"

"For heaven's sake, man, I only met her twice!" Vanderley sounded surprised and a little irritated. "I'm not her doctor! Thousands of people don't have children. Do you expect me to be able to account for the domestic lives of everyone else's servants? All I did was inquire as to the man's scholastic abilities and his suitable character. Both appeared to be excellent. What more do you want me to say?"

"Nothing, Mr. Vanderley. You may go." Land sat down, recognizing defeat.

Giles had nothing to put in re-examination, and Vanderley, with a faint sigh, found himself a seat in the body of the court.

Maurice Jerome was the last witness to be called in his own defense. As he walked from the dock to the stand, Charlotte realized with surprise that she had not yet heard him speak. Everything had been said about him; it was all other people's opinions, other people's words, their recollections of events. For the first time, Jerome would be real—a moving, feeling creature, not a two-dimensional picture of a man.

Like all the others, he began with the oath and identification. Giles worked hard to present him in a sympathetic light. It was all he had: the chance somehow to create the feeling in the jury that this man in reality was a far different person from the one the prosecution had drawn; he was ordinary, decent, everyday—like one of themselves—and could not have been guilty of such obscene offenses.

Jerome stared back at him with a cold, pursed face.

Yes, he answered, he had been employed for approximately four years as tutor to Arthur and Godfrey Waybourne. Yes, he taught them in all academic subjects, and on occasion a little sports as well. No, he did not favor one boy above the other; his tone expressed disdain for such unprofessional conduct.

Already Charlotte found him hard to like. She felt, without real reason, that he would have disliked her. She would not have met his standards of how a lady should conduct herself. For a start, she had opinions, and Jerome did not look like a man who found opinions acceptable when they were not his own.

Perhaps that was unfair. She was leaping to conclusions with just the sort of prejudice she condemned in others. The poor man was accused of a crime not only violent but disgusting, and if he was found guilty he would lose his life. He was entitled to less than the best behavior. Indeed, there must be some courage about him, for he was not screaming out or in hysteria. Maybe this icy calm was his way of controlling the inner terror. And who could claim to do it better, with more dignity?

There was no point in skirting the subject.

"Did you ever, at any time, have an indecent physical relationship with any of your pupils?"

Jerome's nostrils flared very slightly—the thought was distasteful.

"No, sir, I did not."

"Can you imagine why Godfrey Waybourne should lie about such a thing?"

"No, I cannot. His imagination is warped—how or why I do not know."

The additional comment did not further his cause. Any man asked such a question would deny it, yet the curling lip, the suggestion that somehow someone else was to blame engendered less sympathy than simple confusion would have done.

Giles tried again. "And Titus Swynford? Could he have misunderstood some gesture, or some remark?"

"Possibly—although what gesture or remark, I cannot think. I teach academic subjects, things of culture and of the brain. I am not accountable for the moral atmosphere in the house. What they may have learned in other areas was not my responsibility. Gentlemen of a certain class, at that age, have money and opportunity to discover the ways of the world for themselves. I should think a rather fevered adolescent imagination, coupled with a little look-

154

ing through keyholes, has conjured such stories. And people occasionally indulge in lewd conversation without realizing how much youths hear—and understand. I can offer no better explanation. It is otherwise to me both incomprehensible and disgusting!"

Land took a deep breath. "So both boys are either lying or mistaken?"

"Since it is not the truth, that is the obvious conclusion," Jerome replied.

Charlotte felt sympathy with him at last. He was being treated as if he were stupid, and although it was far from in his interest, it was understandable that he should want to retaliate. She would have stung under that patronage. But if only he would ease the sour look a little, or behave as if he sought mercy.

"Have you ever met a prostitute named Albie Frobisher?"

Jerome's chin came up.

"I have never to my knowledge, met a prostitute by any name at all."

"Have you ever been to Bluegate Fields?"

"No, there is nothing in that area that I should wish to see, and fortunately I have no business that requires me to go there, and most certainly no pleasure!"

"Albert Frobisher swears that you were a customer of his. Can you think of any reason why he should do so, if it is not true?"

"My education has been classical, sir—I have no knowledge whatever as to the mind or motives of prostitutes, male or female."

There was a titter of unsympathetic laughter around the court, but it died almost instantly.

"And Abigail Winters?" Giles still struggled. "She says that you took Arthur Waybourne to her establishment."

"Possibly someone did," Jerome agreed, a trace of venom showing through his voice, although he did not seek Waybourne's face among the crowd. "But it was not I."

"Why should anyone do that?"

Jerome's eyebrows shot up.

"Are you asking me, sir? One might equally ask why I should have taken him myself. Whatever purpose you imagine was good enough for me, surely that would serve for someone else as easily? In fact, there are more—perhaps purely for his education? A young gentleman"—he gave the word a curious accent— "must learn his pleasures somewhere, and it is most assuredly not among his own class! And on a tutor's salary, with a wife to keep, even if my taste or my ethics permitted my patronizing such a place, my purse would not!"

It was a telling point, and to her surprise Charlotte found herself glowing warm with satisfaction. Let them answer that! Where would Jerome have found the money?

But when it was Land's turn he was quick.

"Did Arthur Waybourne have an allowance, Mr. Jerome?" he inquired smoothly.

Jerome's face showed only the barest movement, but the point was not lost on him.

"Yes, sir, he said so."

"Have you cause to doubt it?"

"No—he appeared to have money to spend."

"Then he could have paid for his own prostitute, could he not?"

Jerome's full mouth curled down fractionally with sour humor.

"I don't know, sir, you will have to ask Sir Anstey what the allowance amounted to, and then discover—if you do not already know—what is the rate of a prostitute."

The back of Land's neck, where Charlotte could see it above his collar, flushed a dull red.

But it was suicidal. The court may not have had any love for Land, but Jerome had alienated himself entirely.

He continued to be a prig, and at the same time he did not clear himself of the most obscene charge of a crime against one who may have been overprivileged and unlikable, but was still—in memory, at least—a child. To the black-coated jury, Arthur Waybourne had been young and desperately vulnerable.

The summing-up for the prosecution reminded them of all this. Arthur was painted as fair, unblemished until Jerome contaminated him, poised on the verge of a long and profitable life. He had been perverted, betrayed, and finally murdered. Society owed it to his memory, to destroy from their midst the bestiality that had perpetrated these appalling acts. It was almost an act of self-cleansing!

There was only one verdict possible. After all, if Maurice Jerome had not killed him, who had? Well may they ask! And the answer was evident—no one! Not even Jerome himself had been able to suggest another answer.

It all fitted. There were no outstanding pieces, nothing that teased the mind or was left unexplained.

Did they ask themselves why Jerome had seduced the boy, used him, and then murdered him? Why not simply carry on with his base practice?

There were several possible answers.

Perhaps Jerome had grown tired of him, just as he had of Albie Frobisher. His appetite demanded constantly new material. Arthur was not easily discarded now that he was so debauched. He had not been bought, like Albie; he could not simply be dropped.

Could that be why Jerome had taken him to Abigail Winters? To try to stimulate in him more normal hungers?

But his own work had been too well done; the boy was debased forever—he wanted nothing from women.

He had become a nuisance. His love now bored Jerome; he was weary of it. He hungered for younger, more innocent flesh—like Godfrey or like Titus Swynford. They had heard the evidence of that for themselves. And Arthur was growing importunate, his persistence an embarrassment. Perhaps in his distress, in his desperate realization of his own perversion—yes his damnation!—that was not too strong a word—he had even become a threat!

And so he had to be killed! And his naked body disposed of in a place where, but for a monumental stroke of ill-fortune and some excellent police work, it would never have been identified.

Gentlemen, have you ever faced a clearer case—or a more tragic and despicable one? There can be but one verdict—guilty! And there can be but one sentence!

The jury were out for less than half an hour. They filed back stone-faced. Jerome stood, white and stiff.

The judge asked the foreman of the jury and the answer was what had long since been decided by the silent voice of the courtroom.

"Guilty, my lord."

The judge reached for the black cap and placed it on his head. In his thick, ripe voice he pronounced sentence.

"Maurice Jerome, a jury of your peers has found you guilty of the murder of Arthur William Waybourne. The sentence of this court is that you be returned to the place from whence you came, and in not less than three weeks from now you shall be taken to the place of execution, and there you shall be hanged by the neck until you are dead. May the Lord have mercy upon your soul."

Charlotte walked out into icy November winds that cut through her as if they had been knives. But her flesh was numb, already too preoccupied with shock and suffering to be aware of further pain.

7

*T*he trial should have been the end of the case for Pitt. He had found all the evidence he could, and had sworn to its truth in court without fear or favor. The jury had found Maurice Jerome guilty.

He had never expected to feel satisfaction. It was the tragedy of an unhappy man with a gift beyond his opportunity to use. The flaws in Jerome's character had robbed him of the chance to climb in academic fields where others of less offensive nature might have succeeded. He would never have been an equal—that was denied from birth. He had ability, not genius. With a smile, a little flattery now and then, he might have gained a very enviable place. If he could have taught his pupils to like him, to trust him, he might have influenced great houses.

But his pride denied him of it; his resentment of privilege burned through his every action. He seemed never to appreciate what he had, concentrating instead on what he had not. That surely was the true tragedy—because it was unnecessary.

And the sexual flaw? Was it of the body or the mind? Had nature denied him the usual satisfaction of a man, or was it fear in him that drove him from women? No, surely Eugenie would have known—poor creature. In eleven years, how could she not? Surely no woman could be so desperately ignorant of nature and its demands?

Was it something much uglier than that, a need to subjugate in the most intimate and physical manner the boys he taught, the youths who held the privileges he could not?

Pitt sat in the parlor and stared into the flames. For some reason, Charlotte had lit the fire in here tonight, instead of preparing dinner to be eaten in the kitchen, as they often did. He was glad of it. Perhaps she also felt like spending an evening by the warm open hearth, sitting in the best chairs, and all the lamps lit and sparkling, revealing the gleam and nap of the velvet curtains. They were an extravagance, but she had wanted them so much it had been worth the cheap mutton stews and the herrings they had eaten for nearly two months!

He smiled, remembering, then looked across at her. She was watching him, her eyes, steady on his face, almost black in the shadows from the lamp behind her.

"I saw Eugenie after the trial," she said almost casually. "I took her home and stayed with her for nearly two hours."

He was surprised, then realized he should not have been. That was what she had gone to the trial for—to offer Eugenie some fragment of comfort or at least companionship.

"How is she?" he asked.

"Shocked," she said slowly. "As if she could not understand how it had happened, how anyone could believe it of him."

He sighed, it was natural. Who ever does believe such a thing of a husband or a wife?

"Did he do it?" she asked solemnly.

It was the question he had been avoiding ever since he walked out of the courtroom. He did not want to talk about it now, but he knew she would insist until he gave her an answer.

"I imagine so," he said wearily. "But I am not part of the jury, so what I think doesn't matter. I gave them all the evidence I had."

She was not so easily put off. He noticed the sewing was idle in her lap. She had the thimble on her finger and had threaded the needle, but she had not put it through the cloth.

"That's not an answer," she said, frowning at him. "Do you believe he did it?"

He took a deep breath and let it out silently.

"I can't think of anyone else."

She was onto it immediately. "That means you don't believe it!"

"It doesn't!" She was being unfair, illogical. "It means just what I said, Charlotte. I cannot think of any other explanation, therefore I have to accept that it was Jerome. It makes excellent sense, and there is nothing whatsoever against it—no awkward facts that have to be faced, nothing unexplained, nothing to indicate anyone else. It's a pity about Eugenie, and I understand the way she feels. I'm as sorry as you are! Criminals sometimes have nice families—innocent and likable, and they suffer like hell! But that doesn't stop Jerome from being guilty. You can't fight it and you won't help by trying. You certainly can't help Eugenie Jerome by encouraging her to believe there is some hope. There isn't! Now accept it, and leave it alone!"

"I've been thinking," she replied, exactly as if he had not spoken.

"Charlotte!"

She took no notice of him.

"I've been thinking," she repeated. "If Jerome is innocent, then someone else must be guilty."

"Obviously," he said crossly. He did not want to think about it anymore. It was not a good case, and he wanted to forget it. It was finished. "And there isn't anyone else implicated at all," he added in exasperation. "No one else had any reason."

"They might have!"

"Charlotte—"

"They might have!" she insisted. "Let's imagine Jerome is innocent and that he is telling the truth! What do we know for a fact?"

He smiled sourly at the "we." But there was no purpose in trying any longer to evade talking about it. He could see she was going to follow it to the bitter end.

"That Arthur Waybourne was homosexually used," he answered. "That he had syphilis, and that he was drowned in bathwater, almost certainly by having his heels jerked up so his head went under the water and he couldn't get up again. And his body was put down a manhole into the sewers. It is almost impossible that he drowned by accident, and completely impossible that he put his own body into the sewer." He had answered her question and it told them nothing new. He looked at her, waiting for acceptance in her face.

It was not there. She was thinking.

"Then Arthur had a relationship with someone, or with several people," she said slowly.

"Charlotte! You're making the boy seem like—like a—" He struggled for a word that would not be too coarse or too extreme.

"Why not?" She raised her eyebrows and stared at him. "Why should we assume that Arthur was nice? Lots of people who get murdered have brought it upon themselves, one way or another. Why not Arthur Waybourne? We've been supposing he was an innocent victim. Well, perhaps he wasn't."

"He was sixteen!" His voice rose in protest.

"So?" She opened her eyes wide. "There's no reason why he couldn't have been spiteful or greedy, or thoroughly cunning, just because he's young. You don't know children very well, do you? Children can be horrible."

Pitt thought of all the child thieves he knew who were everything she had just said. And he could so easily understand why and how they were. But Arthur Waybourne? Surely he had only to ask for what he wanted and it was given him? There was no need—no cause.

She smiled at him with an oblique, unhappy satisfaction.

"You made me look at the poor, and it was good for me." She still held the needle poised. "Perhaps I ought to show you a little of another world—the inside of it—for your education!" she said quietly. "Society children can be unhappy too, and unpleasant. It's relative. It's only a matter of wanting something you can't have, or seeing someone else with something and thinking you should have it. The feeling is much the same, whether it's for a piece of bread or a diamond brooch—or someone to love. All sorts of people cheat and steal, or even kill, if they care enough. In fact"—she took a deep breath—"in fact, maybe people who are used to getting their own way are quicker to defy the law than those who often have to go without."

"All right," he conceded a little reluctantly. "Suppose Arthur Waybourne was thoroughly selfish and unpleasant—what then? Surely he wasn't so unpleasant that someone killed him for it? That might get rid of half the aristocracy!"

"There's no need to be sarcastic!" she said, her eyes glinting. She poked the needle into the cloth, but did not pull it through. "He may well have been just that! Suppose—" She scowled, concentrating on the idea, tightening it into words. "Suppose Jerome was telling the truth? He never went to Ablie Frobisher's, and he was never overfamiliar with any of the boys—not Arthur, not Godfrey, and not Titus."

"All right, we have only Godfrey and Titus's word for it," he argued. "But there was no doubt about Arthur. The police surgeon was positive about it. It couldn't be a mistake. And why should the other boys lie? It doesn't make sense! Charlotte, however much you don't like it, you are standing reason on its head to get away from Jerome! Everything points to him."

"You are interrupting." She put the sewing things on the table beside her and pushed them away. "Of course Arthur had a relationship—probably with Albie Frobisher—why not? Maybe that's where he got his disease. Did anyone test Albie?"

She knew instantly that she had struck home; it was in her face, a mixture of triumph and pity. Pitt felt a cold tide rush up inside him. No one had thought to test Albie. And since Arthur Waybourne was dead, murdered, Albie would naturally be loath to admit having known him! He would be the first suspect; if Albie could have been guilty, it would have suited everyone. None of them had even thought to test him for veneral disease. How stupid! How incredibly, incompetently stupid!

But what about Albie's identification of Jerome? He had picked out the likeness immediately.

But then what had Gillivray said when he first found Albie? Had he shown him pictures then, perhaps led him into identifying Jerome? It could so easily be done: just a little judicious suggestion, a slight turn of the phrase. "It was this man, wasn't it?" In his eagerness, Gillivray might not even have been aware of it himself.

Charlotte's face was puckered, a flush that could have been embarrassment on her cheeks.

"You didn't, did you." It was barely a question, more an acknowledgment of the truth. There was no blame in her voice, but that did nothing to assuage the void of guilt inside him.

"No."

"Or the other boys—Godfrey and Titus?"

The thought was appalling. He could imagine Waybourne's face if he asked for that—or Swynford's. He sat upright.

"Oh, God, no! You don't think Arthur took them—?" He could envision Athelstan's reaction to such an unspeakable suggestion.

She went on implacably. "Maybe it wasn't Jerome who molested the other boys—maybe it was Arthur. If he had a taste for it, perhaps he used them."

It was not impossible, not at all. In fact, it was not even very improbable, given the original premise that Arthur was as much sinning as sinned against.

"And who killed him?" he asked. "Would Albie care about one customer more or less? He must have had hundreds of people come and go in his four years in business."

"The two boys," she answered straightaway. "Just because Arthur had a liking for it doesn't mean they did. Perhaps he could dominate them one at a time, but when they each learned that the other was being similarly used, maybe they got together and got rid of him."

"Where? In a brothel somewhere? Isn't that a little sophisticated for—"

"At home!" she said quickly. "Why not? Why go anywhere else?"

"Then how did they get rid of the body without family or servants seeing? How did they get it to a manhole connected with the Bluegate sewers? They live miles from Bluegate Fields."

But she was not confused. "I daresay one of their fathers did that for them—or perhaps even both, although I doubt it. Probably the father in whose house it happened. Personally, I rather favor Sir Anstey Waybourne."

"Hide his own son's murder?"

"Once Arthur was dead, there was nothing he could do to bring him back," she said reasonably. "If he didn't hide it, he would lose his second son as well, and be left with no one! Not to mention a scandal so unspeakable the family wouldn't live it down in a hundred years!" She leaned forward. "Thomas, you don't seem to realize that

165

in spite of not being able to do up their own boot buttons or boil an egg, the higher levels of society are devastatingly practical when it comes to matters of survival in the world they understand! They have servants to do the normal things, so they don't bother to do them themselves. But when it comes to social cunning, they are equal to the Borgias any day!"

"I think you've got a lurid imagination," he answered very soberly. "I think I should take a closer look at what you are reading lately."

"I'm not a pantry maid!" she said with considerable acidity, the temper rising in her face. "I shall read what I please! And it doesn't take a lot of imagination to see three young boys playing around at a rather dangerous game of discovering appetites, and being drawn into perversion by an older boy they trust—and then finding it degrading and disgusting, but being too frightened to deny him. Then joining forces together, and one day, perhaps meaning to give him a good fright, they end up going too far and killing him instead."

Her voice gathered conviction as she pictured it. "Then of course they are terrified by what has happened, and appeal to the father of one of them, and he sees that the boy is dead and that it is murder. Perhaps it could have been hushed up, explained as an accident, but perhaps not. Under pressure, the ugly truth would come out that Arthur was perverted and diseased. Since nothing could be done now to help him, better to look to the living and dispose of the body where it will never be found."

She took a deep breath and continued. "Then, of course, when it was found, and all the ugliness comes out, someone has to be blamed. The father knows Arthur was perverted, but maybe he does not know who first introduced him to such practices, and does not wish to believe it was simply his own nature. If the other two boys—frightened of the truth, of saying that Arthur took them to prostitutes—say that it was Jerome, whom they do not like, it is easy enough to believe them, in which case then Jerome is morally to blame for Arthur's death—let him take the literal blame as well. He deserves to be hanged—so let him be! And by now the two boys can hardly go back on what they have said! How could they dare? The police and the courts have all been lied to, and believed it. Nothing to do but let it go on."

He sat and thought about it and the minutes ticked by. There was no sound but the clock and the faint hiss of the fire. It was possible—quite possible—and extremely ugly. And there was nothing of any substance to disprove any of it. Why had it not occurred to him before—to any of them? Was it just that it was more comfortable to blame Jerome? They would risk no disturbing reactions by charging him, no threat to any of their careers, even if by mischance they had not, at the last, been able to prove it.

Surely they were better men than that? And they were too honest, were they not, simply to have settled on Jerome because he was pompous and irritating?

He tried to recall every meeting he had had with Waybourne. How had the man seemed? Was there anything in him at all, any shadow of deceit, of extra grief or unexplained fear?

He could remember nothing. The man was confused, shocked because he had lost a son in appalling circumstances: He was afraid of scandal that would further injure his family. Wouldn't any man be? Surely it was only natural, only decent.

And young Godfrey? He had seemed open, as far as his shock and fear would allow him to be. Or was his singular guilelessness only the mask of childhood, the clear skin and wide eyes of a practiced liar who felt no shame, and therefore no guilt?

Titus Swynford? He had liked Titus, and unless he was very much mistaken, the boy was grieved by the whole course of events—a natural grief, an innocent grief. Was

Pitt losing his judgment, falling into the trap of the obvious and the convenient?

It was a distressing thought. But was it true?

He found it hard to accept that Titus and Godfrey were so devious—or, frankly, that they were clever enough to have deceived him so thoroughly. He was used to sifting lies from truth; it was his job, his profession, and he was good at it. Of course he made mistakes—but seldom was he so totally blinded as not even to suspect!

Charlotte was looking at him. "You don't think that's the answer, do you?" she said.

"I don't know," he admitted. "No—it doesn't feel right."

"And do you feel right about Jerome?"

He looked at her. He had forgotten lately how much her face pleased him, the line of her cheek, the slight upward wing of her brow.

"No," he said simply. "No, I don't think so."

She picked up the sewing again. The thread slipped out of the needle and she put the end in her mouth to moisten it, then carefully rethreaded it.

"Then I suppose you'll have to go back and start again," she said, looking at the needle. "There's still three weeks' time left."

The following morning, Pitt found a pile of new cases on his desk. Most of them were comparatively minor: thefts, embezzlement, and a possible arson. He detailed them to various other officers, one of the privileges of his rank that he made the most of; then he sent for Gillivray.

Gillivray came in cheerfully, his face glowing, shoulders square. He closed the door behind him and sat down before being asked, which annoyed Pitt quite out of proportion.

"Something interesting?" Gillivray inquired eagerly. "Another murder?"

"No." Pitt was sour. He had disliked the whole case,

and he disliked even more having to open it up again, but it was the only way to get rid of the crowding uncertainties in his mind, the vague possibilities that intruded every time his concentration lapsed. "The same one," he said.

Gillivray was perplexed. "The same one? Arthur Waybourne? You mean someone else was involved? Can we do that? The jury found its verdict. That closes the case, doesn't it?"

"It may be closed," Pitt said, keeping his temper with difficulty. He realized Gillivray annoyed him so much because he seemed invulnerable to the things that hurt Pitt. He was smiling and clean, and he walked through other people's tragedies and emotional dirt without being scathed by them at all.

"It may be closed for the court," Pitt said, starting, "but I think there are still things we ought to know, for justice's sake."

Gillivray looked dubious. The courts were sufficient for him. His job was to detect crime and to enforce the law, not to sit in judgment. Each arm of the machinery had its proper function: the police to detect and apprehend; the barristers to prosecute or to defend; the judge to preside and see that the procedures of the law were followed; the jury to decide truth and fact. And in due course, if necessary, the warders to guard, and the executioner to end life rapidly and efficiently. For any one arm to usurp the function of another was to put the whole principle in jeopardy. This was what a civilized society was about, each person knowning his function and place. A good man fulfilled his obligation to the limit of his ability and, with good fortune, rose to a better place.

"Justice is not our business," Gillivray said at last. "We've done our job and the courts have done theirs. We shouldn't interfere. That would be the same as saying that we don't believe in them."

Pitt looked at him. He was earnest, very composed.

There was a good deal of truth in what he said, but it altered nothing. They had been clumsy, and it was going to be painful to try to rectify it. But that did not alter the necessity.

"The courts judge according to what they know," he answered. "There are things they should have known, that they did not because we neglected to find them out."

Gillivray was indignant. He was being implicated in dereliction of duty, and not only him, but the entire police force above him, even the lawyers for the defense, who ought to have noticed any omission of worth.

"We didn't explore the possibility that Jerome was telling the truth," Pitt began, before Gillivray interrupted him.

"Telling the *truth*?" Gillivray exploded, his eyes bright and furious. "With respect, Mr. Pitt—that's ridiculous! We caught him in lie after lie! Godfrey Waybourne said he interfered with him, Titus Swynford said the same. Abigail Winters identified him! Albie Frobisher identified him! And Albie alone has to be damning. Only a perverted man goes to a male prostitute. That's a crime in itself! What else could you want, short of an eyewitness? It isn't even as if there was another suspect!"

Pitt sat back in his chair, and let himself slide down till he was resting on the base of his spine. He put his hands into his pockets and touched a ball of string he carried, a lump of sealing wax, a pocketknife, two marbles he had picked up in the street, and a shilling.

"What if the boys were lying?" he suggested. "And the relationship was among themselves, the three of them, and had nothing to do with Jerome?"

"Three of them?" Gillivray was startled. "All—" He did not like to use the word, and would have preferred some genteelism that avoided the literal. "All perverted?"

"Why not? Perhaps Arthur was the only one whose nature it was, and he forced the others to go along."

"Then where did Arthur get the disease?" Gillivray hit

170

on the weak point with satisfaction. "Not from two innocent young boys he drove into such a relationship by force! They certainly didn't have it!"

"Don't they?" Pitt raised his eyebrows. "How do you know?"

Gillivray opened his mouth; then realization flooded his face, and he closed it again.

"We don't—do we!" Pitt challenged. "Don't you think we should find out? He may have passed it on to them, however innocent they are."

"But where did he get it?" Gillivray still held to his objection. "The relationship can't have involved only the three of them. There must have been someone else!"

"Quite," Pitt conceded. "But if Arthur was perverted, perhaps he went to Albie Frobisher and contracted it there. We didn't test Albie either, did we?"

Gillivray was flushed. There was no need of admission; he saw the neglect immediately. He despised Albie. He should have been aware of the possibility and put it to the proof without being told. It would have been easy enough. And certainly Albie would have been in no position to protest.

"But Albie identified Jerome," he said, going back to more positive ground. "So Jerome must have been there. And he didn't recognize the picture of Arthur. I showed him one, naturally."

"Does he have to be telling the truth?" Pitt inquired with an affectation of innocence. "Would you take his word in anything else?"

Gillivray shook his head as if brushing away flies—something irritating but of no consequence. "Why should he lie?"

"People seldom want to admit to an acquaintance with a murder victim. I don't think that needs any explanation."

"But what about Jerome?" Gillivray's face was earnest. "He identified Jerome!"

"How did he recognize him? How do you know?"

"Because I showed him photographs, of course!"

"And can you be sure, absolutely sure, that you didn't say or do anything at all, even by an expression on your face—a lift in your voice, maybe—to indicate which picture you wanted him to choose?"

"Of course I'm sure!" Gillivray said instantly. Then he hesitated; he did not knowingly lie to himself, still less to others. "I don't think so."

"But you believed it was Jerome?"

"Yes, of course I did."

"Are you sure you didn't somehow betray that—in tone or look? Albie's very quick—he'd have seen it. He's used to picking up the nuance, the unspoken word. He earns his living by pleasing people."

Gillivray was offended by the comparison, but he saw the purpose of it.

"I don't know," he admitted. "I don't think so."

"But you could have?" Pitt pressed.

"I don't think so."

"But we didn't test Albie for disease!"

"No!" Gillivray flicked his hand to dispel the irritant again. "Why should we have? Arthur had the disease, and Arthur never had any relationship with Albie! It was Jerome who had the relationship with Albie, and Jerome was clean! If Albie had it, then presumably Jerome would have it too!" That was an excellent piece of reasoning, and Gillivray was pleased with it. He sat back in the chair again, his body relaxing.

"That is presuming that everyone is telling the truth except Jerome," Pitt pointed out. "But if Jerome is telling the truth, and someone else is lying, then it would be quite different. And, by the same line of logic you just put forward, since Arthur had it, then Jerome should have it also—shouldn't he? And we didn't think of that either, did we?"

Gillivray stared. "He didn't have it!"

172

"Precisely! Why not?"

"I don't know! Perhaps it just doesn't show yet!" He shook his head. "Perhaps he hasn't molested Arthur since he got it from the woman. How do I know. But if Jerome is telling the truth, then that means everyone else is lying, and that's preposterous. Why should they? And anyway, even if the relationship included Albie and all three boys, that still doesn't answer who killed Arthur, or why. And that's all that matters to us. We are back to Jerome just the same. You've told me yourself not to torture the facts to fit them into an unlikely theory—just take them as they are and see what they say." He looked satisfied, as if he had scored some minor victory.

"Quite," Pitt agreed. "But *all* the facts. That's the point—all of them, not just most of them. And in this case we haven't taken the trouble to discover all the facts. We should have tested Albie and the other boys as well."

"You can't!" Gillivray was incredulous. "You can't possibly mean to go to the Waybournes now and ask to test their younger son for syphilis? They'd throw you out— and probably protest to the Commissioner as well, if not all the way to Parliament!"

"Maybe. But that doesn't alter the fact that we should."

Gillivray snorted and stood up. "Well, I think you're wasting your time—sir. Jerome is guilty and will be hanged. You know, with respect, sir—sometimes I think you allow your concern for justice, and what you imagine to be equality, to override common sense. People are not all equal. They never have been, and they never will be— morally, socially, physically, or—"

"I know that!" Pitt interrupted. "I have no delusions about equality, brought about by man or nature. But I don't believe in privilege before the law—that's quite a different thing. Jerome doesn't deserve to be hanged for something he didn't do, whatever we think of him personally. And if you prefer to look at it from the other side, we don't deserve to hang him if he's innocent, and

173

let the guilty man go free. At least I don't! If you're the kind of man who can walk away from that, then you should be in another job, not the police."

"Mr. Pitt, that is quite uncalled for! You are being unjust. I didn't say anything like that. I think it's blinding your judgment—that's what I said, and that's what I mean! I think you lean over so far to be fair that you are in grave danger of falling over backwards." He squared his shoulders. "That's what you're doing this time. Well, if you want to go to Mr. Athelstan and ask for a warrant to test Godfrey Waybourne for venereal disease—go ahead. But I'm not coming with you. I don't believe in it, and I shall say so if Mr. Athelstan asks me! The case is closed." And he stood up and walked to the door, turning when he reached it. "Is that all you wanted me for?"

"Yes." Pitt stayed in his seat, sliding even farther down till his knees bent and touched the bottom of the desk drawer. "I suppose you'd better go and look at that arson—see if it really is. More probably some fool with a leaking lamp."

"Yes, sir." Gillivray opened the door and went out, closing it after him with a snap. Pitt sat for quarter of an hour arguing himself out of it and back in again before he finally accepted the inevitable and went up the stairs to Athelstan's office. He knocked and waited.

"Come!" Athelstan said cheerfully.

Pitt opened it and went in. Athelstan's face fell as soon as he saw him.

"Pitt? What is it now? Can't you handle it yourself, man? I'm extremely busy. Got to see a member of Parliament in an hour, most important matter."

"No, sir, I can't. I shall need some sort of authority."

"For what? If you want to search something, go ahead and search it! You ought to know how to go about your business by now! Heaven knows you've been at it long enough."

"No, I don't want to search anything—not a house,"

Pitt replied. He was cold inside. He knew Athelstan would be furious, caught in a trap of necessity, and he would blame Pitt for it. And that would be fair. Pitt was the one who should have thought of it at the right time. Not, of course, that it would have been allowed then either.

"Well, what do you want?" Athelstan said irritably, his face creased into a frown. "For heaven's sake, explain yourself! Don't just stand there like a fool, moving from one foot to the other!"

Pitt could feel his skin flush hot, and it seemed suddenly as if the room were getting smaller and if he moved at all he would knock against something with his elbows or his feet.

"We should have tested Albert Frobisher to see if he had syphilis," he began.

Athelstan's head jerked up, his face dark with suspicion.

"Why? Who cares if he has? Perverted men who patronize that sort of place deserve all they get! We're not the keepers of the public morals, Pitt—or of public health. None of our business. Homosexuality is a crime, and so it should be, but we haven't the men to prosecute it. Need to catch them at it if we're going to take it to court." He snorted with distaste. "If you haven't got enough to do, I'll find you something more. London's teeming with crime. Go out any door and follow your nose, you'll find thieves and blackguards all over the place." He bent down again over the letters in front of him, dismissing Pitt by implication.

Pitt stood motionless on the bright carpet.

"And Godfrey Waybourne and Titus Swynford also, sir."

For a second there was silence; then Athelstan raised his eyes very slowly. His face was purple; veins appeared that Pitt had never noticed before, plum-colored, on his nose.

"What did you say?" he demanded, sounding every word distinctly, as though he were talking to someone slow-witted.

Pitt took a deep breath. "I want to make sure that no other people have been infected by the disease," he said rephrasing it more tactfully. "Not only Frobisher, but the other two boys."

"Don't be ridiculous!" Athelstan's voice rose, a note of hysteria creeping into it. "Where on earth would boys like that contract such a disease? We're talking about decent families, Pitt—not something out of your bloody rookeries. Absolutely not! The very idea is an insult!"

"Arthur Waybourne had it," Pitt pointed out quietly.

"Of course he did!" Athelstan's face was suffusing with blood. "That perverted animal Jerome took him to a damned prostitute! We've proved that! The whole damnable affair is closed! Now get on with your job—get out and leave me to do some work myself!"

"Sir," Pitt persisted. "If Arthur had it—and he did—how do we know he didn't give it to his brother, or his friend? Boys of that age are full of curiosity."

Athelstan stared at him. "Possibly," he said coldly. "But no doubt their fathers are better acquainted with their aberrations than we are, and it is most certainly their business! There is no conceivable way, Pitt, in which it is yours!"

"It would put rather a different light on Arthur Waybourne, sir!"

"I have no desire to put any light on him whatever!" Athelstan snapped. "The case is closed!"

"But if Arthur had relationships with the other two boys, it would open up all kinds of possibilities!" Pitt pressed, taking a step forward to lean over the desk.

Athelstan sat as far away as he could, resting against the back of his chair.

"The private—habits—of the gentry are no business of ours, Pitt. You will leave them alone!" He spat out the

176

words. "Do you understand me? I don't care if every one of them got into bed with every other one—it doesn't alter the fact that Maurice Jerome murdered Arthur Waybourne. That is all that matters to us. We have done our duty and what happens now is their own concern—not yours and not mine!"

"But what if Arthur had relationships with the other boys?" Pitt clenched his fist on the desk, feeling the nails dig into his flesh. "Maybe it had nothing to do with Jerome."

"Rubbish! Absolute nonsense! Of course it was Jerome—there's evidence! And don't tell me we haven't proved where he did it. He could have hired a room anywhere. We'll never find it and no one expects us to. He is homosexual! He had every reason to kill the boy. If it came out, the best he could hope would be to be thrown onto the street without a job or a good reputation. He'd be ruined."

"But who says he is homosexual?" Pitt demanded, his voice rising as loudly as Athelstan's.

Athelstan's eyes were wide. There was a bead of sweat on his lip—and another.

"Both boys," he said with a catch in his voice. He cleared his throat. "Both boys," he repeated, "and Albert Frobisher. That's three witnesses. Good God, man, how many do you want? Do you imagine the creature went about exhibiting his perversion?"

"Both boys?" Pitt said again. "And what if they were involved themselves, wouldn't that be just the lie they would tell? And Albie Frobisher—would you take the word of a seventeen-year-old male prostitute against that of a respectable scholastic tutor at any other time? Would you?"

"No!" Athelstan was on his feet now, his face only a handspan from Pitt's, his knuckles white, arms shaking. "Yes!" he contradicted himself. "Yes—if it fits with all the other evidence. And it does! He identified him from photographs—that proves Jerome was there."

"Can we be sure?" Pitt urged. "Can we be sure we didn't put the idea into his mind, prompt him? Did we suggest the answer we wanted by the way we asked the questions?"

"No, of course we didn't!" Athelstan's voice dropped a little. He was regaining control of himself. "Gillivray is a professional." He took a deep breath. "Really, Pitt, you are allowing your resentment to warp you. I said Gillivray was treading on your heels, and now you're trying to discredit him. It's not worthy of you." He sat down again, straightening his jacket and stretching his neck to ease his collar.

"Jerome is guilty," Athelstan said. "He has been found guilty by the courts, and he will be hanged." He cleared his throat again. "Don't stand over me like that, Pitt—it's insolent! And the health of Godfrey Waybourne is his father's affair—similarly Titus Swynford. As far as the prostitute is concerned, he's lucky we didn't prosecute him for his filthy trade. He'll probably die of some disease or other in the end anyway. If he hasn't got it now, he soon will have! Now I warn you, Pitt, this matter is closed. If you insist on pursuing it any further, you will be jeopardizing your own career. Do you understand me? These people have suffered enough tragedy in their lives. You will now pursue the job you are paid for—and leave them alone. Have I made myself clear?"

"But, sir—"

"I forbid it! You do not have permission to harass the Waybournes any further, Pitt! The case is closed—finished! Jerome is guilty and that is the end of it. I don't want you to mention it again—to me or to anyone else. Gillivray is an excellent officer and his conduct is not open to question. I am perfectly satisfied he did everything necessary to determine the truth, and that he did determine it! I don't know how to make it any plainer to

you. Now get on with your job—if you want to keep it."
He stared at Pitt in challenge.

Suddenly it had become a test between them whose will
would prevail, and Athelstan could not afford to let it be
Pitt's. Pitt was dangerous because he was unpredictable;
he did not give respect where he ought to, and when his
sympathies were engaged, his good sense, even his self-
preservation, went out the window. He was a most uncomfortable person to have about; at the first available
opportunity, Athelstan decided, he would promote him
to someone else's area. Unless, of course, Pitt were to
press on in this wretched business of the Waybourne case,
in which event he could be reduced to walking the beat
again and Athelstan would be as easily rid of him.

Pitt stood still as the seconds ticked by. The room was
so silent he imagined he could hear the workings of the
gold watch hanging from Athelstan's waistcoat on the
thick, gold link chain.

To Athelstan, Pitt was a disturbing person because he
did not understand him. Pitt had married above himself,
and that was offensive as well as incomprehensible. What
did a wellborn woman like Charlotte want with an untidy,
erratic, and imaginative paradox like Pitt? A woman with
any dignity would have stuck to her own class!

Gillivray, on the other hand, was quite different; he
was easy to understand. He was an only son with three
sisters. He was ambitious, but he accepted that one must
climb the ladder rung by rung, everything in order, each
advance earned. There was comfort, even beauty, in observing order. There was safety in it for everyone, and
that was what the law was for—preserving the safety of
society. Yes, Gillivray was an eminently sane young man,
and very pleasing to have around. He would go far. In
fact, Athelstan had once even remarked that he would
not mind if one of his own daughters were to marry a
young man of such a type. He had already proved he
knew how to conduct himself with both diligence and dis-

cretion. He did not go out of the way to antagonize people, or allow his own feelings to show, as Pitt so often did. And he was extremely personable, dressed like a gentleman, neat and without ostentation—not a veritable scarecrow like Pitt!

All this passed through Athelstan's mind as he stared at Pitt, and most of it was plain in his eyes. Pitt knew him well. He ran the department satisfactorily. He seldom wasted time pursuing pointless cases; he sent his men into the witness box well prepared—it was a rare day they were made to look foolish. And no charge of corruption had been leveled against any man in his division for over a decade.

Pitt sighed and stood back at last. Athelstan was probably right. Jerome was almost certainly guilty. Charlotte was bending the facts to suppose otherwise. While it was conceivable that it could have been the two boys, it was not remotely likely; and quite honestly, he did not believe they had been lying to him. There was an innate sense of truth about them, and he could feel it, just as he could usually tell a liar. Charlotte was letting her emotions rule her head. That was unusual for her, but it was a feminine characteristic, and she was a woman! Pity was no bad thing, but it should not be allowed to distort the truth till it became disproportionate.

He resented Athelstan's use of force to prevent him from going back to Waybourne, but he was probably right in principle. Nothing would be served by it but to prolong the pain. Eugenie Jerome was going to suffer; it was time he accepted it and stopped trying to evade it, like some child that expects a happy ending to every story. False hope was cruel. He would have to have a long talk with Charlotte, make her see the harm she was doing by rigging up a preposterous theory like this. Jerome was a tragic man, tragic and dangerous. Pity him, by all means, but do not try to make other people pay even more dearly than they already have for his sickness.

180

"Yes, sir," he said aloud. "No doubt Sir Anstey will have his own physician make such checks as are advisable, without our saying anything."

Athelstan blinked. It was not the answer he had expected.

"No doubt," he agreed awkwardly. "Although I hardly think—well—that—be that as it may, it's none of our affair. Family problem—man has a right to his privacy— part of being a gentleman, the respecting of other men's privacy. Glad you understand that!" His eyes still held the last trace of uncertainty. It was a question.

"Yes, sir," Pitt repeated. "And, as you say, there's not much point in checking someone like Albie Frobisher—if he hasn't got it today, he could have by tomorrow."

Athelstan's face wrinkled in distaste.

"Quite. Now I'm sure you have something else to get on with? You'd better be about it, and leave me to deal with my appointment. I have a great many things to do. Lord Ernest Beaufort has been robbed. His town house. Bad thing to happen. I'd like to get it solved as soon as possible. Promised him I'd see to it myself. Can you spare me Gillivray? He's just the type to handle this."

"Yes, sir. Certainly I can," Pitt said with satisfaction sharply colored with spite. In the unlikely event they would ever find the thieves, the goods would be long gone by then, dispersed into a warren of silversmiths, pawnshops, and scrap dealers. Gillivray was too young to know them, too conspicuously clean to pass unremarked in the rookeries—as Pitt could, if he chose. The word would spread before Gillivray, with his pink face and white collar, as loudly as if he carried a bell around his neck. Pitt was ashamed of his satisfaction, but it did not stop the feeling or its warmth.

He walked out of Athelstan's office and back to his own. Passing Gillivray in the hallway, he sent him, face glowing in anticipation, up to Athelstan.

He went into his own office and sat down, staring at the

statements and reports. Then, half an hour later, he threw all of them into a wire basket marked "in," snatched his coat from the stand, jammed his hat on his head, and strode out the door.

He caught the first hansom that passed, and clambered in shouting at the driver, "Newgate!"

"Newgate, sir?" the cabbie said with a slight lift of surprise.

"Yes! Get on with it. Newgate Prison," Pitt said. "Hurry!"

"Ain't no 'urry there," the cabbie said dryly. "They ain't goin' nowhere. Less o' course they goin' ter be 'ung! And nobody due to be 'ung yet—not for near on three weeks. Always knows when there's an 'angin'. Guess there'll be farsands out fer vis 'un. I've seen 'em an 'undred farsand thick in years past, I 'ave."

"Get on with it!" Pitt snapped. The thought of a hundred thousand people milling around, pressing close to see a man hanged, was revolting. He knew it was true; it was even regarded as something of a sport by a certain set. Someone owning a room with a view over the front of Newgate could rent it out for twenty-five guineas for a good hanging. People would picnic with champagne and delicacies.

What is there in death, he wondered, that is so fascinating—in someone else's agony that is acceptable as public entertainment? Some sort of catharsis of all one's own fears—a kind of propitiation to fate against the violence that hangs over even the safest lives? But the idea of taking pleasure in it made him sick.

It was raining gently when the cabbie dropped him outside the great rusticated front of Newgate Prison.

He identified himself to the turnkey at the gate, and was let in.

"Who did you say?"

"Maurice Jerome," Pitt repeated.

"Goin' to be 'anged," the turnkey said unnecessarily.

"Yes." Pitt followed him into the gray bowels of the place; their feet echoed hollowly on the stone. "I know."

"Knows something, does 'e?" the turnkey went on, leading the way to the offices where they would have to obtain permission. Jerome was a man under sentence of death; he could not be visited at will.

"Maybe." Pitt did not want to lie.

"Mostly when you got 'em this far, I likes to see you rozzers leave them poor sods alone," the turnkey remarked, and spat. "But I can't stand a man wot kills children. Uncalled for, that is. Man's one thing—and there's a lot of women as can ask for it. But children's different—unnatural, that is."

"Arthur Waybourne was sixteen," Pitt found himself arguing. "That's not exactly a child. They've hanged people less than sixteen."

"Oh, yeah!" the turnkey said. "When they'd earned it, like. And we've 'ad 'em in the 'ouses o' correction for a spell, for being a public nuisance. And more than one in for spinnin' 'is top in the marketplace. Set a lot o' people a mess o' trouble. 'Ad 'em in the 'Steel'—down Coldbath Fields."

He was referring to one of the worst jails in London, the Bastille, where men's health and spirits could be broken in a matter of months on the treadmill or the crank, or the shot drill, passing iron cannonballs endlessly from one to the other along a line till their arms were exhausted, backs strained, muscles cracking. Picking oakum until the fingers bled was easy by comparison. Pitt made no reply to the turnkey—there were no words that would suffice. The Bastille had been like that for years, and it was better than it had been in the past; at least the stocks and the pillories were gone, for any difference that made.

He explained to the chief warder that he wanted to see Jerome on police business, because there were still a few questions that should be asked for the sake of the health of innocent parties.

183

The warder was sufficiently aware of the case not to need more detailed explanation. He was familiar with disease, and there was no perversion known to man or beast he had encountered.

"As you wish," he agreed. "Although you'll be lucky if you get anything out of him. He's going to be hanged in three weeks, whatever happens to the rest of us, so he's got nothing to gain or lose either way."

"He has a wife," Pitt replied, although he had no idea if it made any difference to Jerome. Anyway, he was answering the warder out of the necessity for appearance. He had come to see Jerome from a compulsion within himself, a need to try one more time to satisfy his own mind that Jerome was guilty.

Outside the office, another turnkey led him along the gray vaulted corridors toward the death cells. The smell of the place closed over him, creeping into his head and throat. He was assaulted by staleness, a dirt that carbolic never washed away; by a sense that everyone was always tired, and yet could not rest. Did men with the knowledge of certain death—at a given hour, a given minute—lie awake terrified lest sleep rob them of a single instant of the life left? Did they relive the past—all the good things? Or repent, full of guilt, beg forgiveness of a suddenly remembered God? Or weep—or revile?

The turnkey stopped. "'Ere we are," he said with a little snort. "Give me a shout when you've finished."

"Thank you." Pitt heard his voice answer as if it were someone else's. Almost automatically, his feet took him through the open door and into the dark cell. The door shut behind him with a sound of iron on iron.

Jerome was sitting on a straw mattress in the corner. He did not immediately look around. The key turned, leaving Pitt locked inside. At last Jerome appeared to register that it was not an ordinary check. He raised his head and saw Pitt; his eyes showed surprise, but nothing strong enough to be called emotion. He was oddly the same—

the stiffness, the sense of aloofness as if the past few weeks were something he had merely read about.

Pitt, dreading a change for the worse in him, had been prepared for all kinds of embarrassment. And now that it was not there, he was even more disconcerted. Jerome was impossible to like, but Pitt was forced into a certain admiration for his total self-control.

How very odd that such a man, seemingly untouched by such appalling circumstances, by physical deprivation, public shame, and the certain knowledge of one of the worst of human deaths only weeks away—how extraordinary that such a man should have been carried away by appetite and panic to his own destruction. So extraordinary that Pitt found himself opening his mouth to apologize for the squalid cell, the humiliation, as if he were responsible, and not Jerome himself.

It was ridiculous! It was the evidence. If Jerome felt nothing, or showed nothing, then it was because he was perverted, deranged in mind and body. One should not expect him to behave like a normal man—he was not normal. Remember Arthur Waybourne in the Bluegate sewers, remember that young, abused body, and get on with what you came for!

"Jerome," he began, taking a step forward. What was he going to ask now that he was here? It was his only chance; he must find out everything he wanted to know, everything that Charlotte had so unpleasantly conjured up. He could not ask Waybourne or the two boys; it must all come from this solitary interview, here in the gray light that filtered through the grating across the high window.

"Yes?" Jerome inquired coldly. "What more can you possibly want of me, Mr. Pitt? If it is ease of conscience, I cannot give it to you. I did not kill Arthur Waybourne, nor did I ever touch him in the obscene manner you have charged me with. Whether you sleep at night or lie awake

185

is your own problem. I can do nothing to help you, and I would not if I could!"

Pitt responded without thought. "You blame me for your situation?"

Jerome's nostrils flared; it was an expression at once of resignation and great distaste.

"I suppose you are doing your job within your limitations. You are so used to dealing with filth that you see it everywhere. Perhaps that is the fault of society at large. We must have police."

"I discovered Arthur Waybourne's body," Pitt answered, curiously unangered by the charge. He could understand it. Jerome would want to hurt someone, and there was no one else. "That's all I testified to. I questioned the Waybourne family, and I checked the two prostitutes. But I didn't find them, and I certainly didn't put words in their mouths."

Jerome looked at him carefully, his brown eyes covering Pitt's features as if the secret lay within them.

"You didn't discover the truth," he said at last. "Maybe that was asking too much. Maybe you're a victim as much as I am. Only, you are free to walk away and repeat your mistakes. I'm the one who will pay."

"You didn't kill Arthur?" Pitt put it forward as a proposition.

"I did not."

"Then who did? And why?"

Jerome stared at his feet. Pitt moved to sit on the straw beside him.

"He was an unpleasant boy," Jerome said after a few moments. "I've been wondering who did kill him. I've no idea. If I had, I would have offered it to you to investigate!"

"My wife has a theory." Pitt began.

"Indeed." Jerome's voice was flat, contemptuous.

"Don't be so bloody patronizing!" Pitt snapped. Suddenly his anger at the whole affair, the system, the monumental and stupid tragedy exploded in offense for the slight to Charlotte. His voice was loud and harsh. "It's more than you have—damn you!"

Jerome turned to look at him, his eyebrows high.

"You mean she doesn't think I did it?" He was still disbelieving, his face cold, eyes showing no emotion except surprise.

"She thinks that perhaps Arthur was the perverted one," Pitt said more coolly. "And that he drew the younger boys into his practices. They complied to begin with, and then when each learned the other was also involved, they banded together and killed him."

"A pleasant thought," Jerome said sourly. "But I can hardly see Godfrey and Titus having the presence of mind to carry the body to a manhole and dispose of it so effectively. If it had not been for an overdiligent sewerman, and indolent rats, Arthur would never have been identified, you know."

"Yes, I do know," Pitt said. "But one of their fathers might have helped."

For an instant Jerome's eyes widened; something flashed across them that could have been hope. Then his face darkened again.

"Arthur was drowned. Why not just say it was an accident? Easier, infinitely more respectable. It doesn't make any sense to put him down a sewer. Your wife is very imaginative, Mr. Pitt, but not very realistic. She has a lurid picture of the Anstey Waybournes of the world. If she had met a few, she would realize they do not panic and act in such an hysterical fashion."

Pitt was stung. Charlotte's breeding had never been more utterly irrelevant, and yet he found himself replying with all the resentment of the ambitious middle classes and the values he despised.

"She is perfectly well acquainted with them." His voice was acid. "Her family is of considerable means. Her sister is the Lady Ashworth. She is perhaps better aware than either you or I of the sort of thing that panics the socially élite—like discovering that your son is a carrier of venereal disease and is homosexual. Perhaps you do not know last year's amendment to the law? Homosexuality is a criminal offense now, and punishable by imprisonment."

Jerome turned sideways, his face against the light so Pitt could not read his expression.

"In fact," Pitt went on a little recklessly, "perhaps Waybourne discovered Arthur's practices and killed him himself. One's eldest son and heir, a syphilitic pervert! Better dead—far better dead. Don't tell me you don't know the upper classes well enough to believe that, Mr. Jerome?"

"Oh I believe it." Jerome let out his breath very slowly. "I believe it, Mr. Pitt. But not you, or your wife, or an angel of God will prove it! And the law won't try! I'm a far better suspect. Nobody'll miss me, nobody'll mind. This answer suits everyone who matters. You've less chance of changing their minds than you have of becoming Prime Minister." His mouth suddenly twisted with harsh mockery. "Not, of course, that I seriously imagined you meant to try! I can't think why you came. You'll only have more nightmares now—and for longer!"

Pitt stood up. "Possibly," he said. "But for your sake, not mine. I didn't try you, and I didn't twist or hide any of the evidence. If"—he hesitated, then repeated the word—"if there is a miscarriage of justice, it is in spite of me, not because of me. And I don't give a damn whether you believe that or not." He banged his clenched fist on the door. "Jailer! Let me out!"

The door opened and he walked into the dank, gray passage without looking back. He was angry, confused, and, as far as he could imagine, completely helpless.

8

Charlotte, too, was unable to dismiss the matter from her mind. She could not have given anyone reason for believing that Jerome was innocent; in fact, she was not sure that she believed it herself. But the law did not require you to prove yourself innocent; it was sufficient that there should be some reasonable doubt.

And she was sorry for Eugenie, even though a large part of her still could not really like the woman. Her presence was an irritant; she epitomized everything that Charlotte was not. But she could be quite wrong about her; maybe Eugenie was sincere. Perhaps she really was a gentle and patient woman who wished to obey, a woman to whom loyalty was the highest virtue. Perhaps she genuinely cared for her husband.

And if it was true that her husband was innocent, it must follow that the person who had killed Arthur Waybourne would remain free after having committed, in Charlotte's estimation, an even graver crime—because it was slower and there had been time to understand and to change—that of allowing Jerome to be convicted and hanged in his place! That was as close to unpardonable as any sanely committed human act could be. The thought

189

of it made her so angry she found herself clenching her teeth till they hurt.

And hanging was so final. What if Jerome was innocent and they found out too late?

Whatever Pitt was going to do, whatever he *could* do—and it might not be much—she must at least try herself. And now that Emily was back, and Great-Aunt Vespasia, they would help, too.

Gracie would have to look after Jemima and Daniel again. Only three weeks: no time for letters, calling cards, and social niceties. She would put on a morning dress and take an onmibus, and then a hansom cab to Paragon Walk and visit Emily. Ideas whirled around in her head: possibilities, unanswered questions, things the police could not do and probably would not even think of.

She shouted for Gracie, startling the girl to running, her feet clattering along the corridor. She flew into the parlor and arrived breathless to find Charlotte standing in the middle of the floor, perfectly composed.

"Oh! Ma'am!" Gracie's face fell in confusion. "I thought as you was hurt terrible, or something. Whatever's 'appened?"

"Injustice!" Charlotte said, with a sweep of her arm. Melodrama would be far more effective than reasonable explanations. "We must do something before it is too late." She included Gracie in the "we" to make her an instant party to it, and to secure her wholehearted cooperation. A great deal of it would be necessary in the next three weeks.

Gracie shivered with excitement and let out her breath in a little squeak. "Oh, ma'am!"

"Yes," Charlotte said firmly. She must move to the details while enthusiasm was hot. "You remember Mrs. Jerome who came here? Yes, of course you do! Good. Well, her husband has been sent to prison for something I don't think he did"—she didn't want to cloud the issue

190

with questions of reasonable doubt—"and he will be hanged if we do not discover the truth!"

"Ooh, ma'am!" Gracie was appalled. Mrs. Jerome was a real person, and just like a heroine should be: sweet and pretty, and obviously terribly in need of rescuing. "Ooh, ma'am. Are we going to help her then?"

"Yes, we are. The master will be doing what he can, of course—but that may not be enough. People keep secrets very close, and a man's life may depend on this—in fact, several people's lives. We shall need a lot of others to help, too. I am going to see Lady Ashworth, and while I am away I want you to look after Daniel and Miss Jemima." She fixed Gracie with a gaze that almost hypnotized her, so intense was Gracie's concentration. "Gracie, I do not want you to tell anyone else where I am, or why I have gone there. I am merely out visiting, do you understand? If the master should ask you, I have gone calling upon my family. That is the truth and you have no need to fear saying it."

"Oh, no, ma'am!" Gracie breathed out. "You're just gone calling! I won't say a word! It's secret with me. But do be careful, ma'am! Them murderers and the like can be terrible dangerous! What on earth should we all do if anything 'appened to you!"

Charlotte kept a perfectly sober face.

"I shall be very careful, Gracie, I promise you," she answered. "And I shall take care not to be alone with anyone in the least questionable. I am only going to inquire a little, see if I can learn rather more about a few people."

"Ooh—I shan't say a thing, ma'am. I'll look after everything 'ere, I swear. Don't you worry one bit."

"Thank you, Gracie." Charlotte smiled as charmingly as she could, then swept out and left Gracie, mouth agape from fearful thoughts, standing in the middle of the parlor.

Emily's maid received her with surprise well concealed

by years of training. There was nothing more than a slight lift of her eyebrows beneath the starched cap. The black dress and lace-trimmed apron were immaculate. Charlotte wished for a fleeting moment she could afford to dress Gracie that way, but it would be terribly impractical. Gracie had more to do than answer the door, even if anyone called. She had to scrub floors, sweep and beat carpets, clean out the grates and black them, wash dishes.

Parlormaids were part of another life, one Charlotte only regretted in silly, light-headed moments when she first walked into houses like this, before she remembered all the things about that life that were boring, the suffocating rituals she had not been able to keep with any skill when she herself was part of it.

"Good morning, Mrs. Pitt," the maid said smoothly. "Her Ladyship is not receiving yet. If you will sit in the morning room, the fire is lit, and I will ask if you may join Her Ladyship for breakfast, if you care to?"

"Thank you." Charlotte tilted her chin a little to show she was perfectly at ease, whatever the hour or its inconvenience. She had not broken convention; she was superior to it, and therefore not bound by such restrictions. The maid must understand that. "Will you please tell Her Ladyship it is a matter of the utmost urgency—a scandalous matter in which I need her assistance to prevent a great injustice from being enacted." That should bring Emily even if she was in bed!

The maid's eyes opened wide and bright. That gem of information would certainly find its way back to the servants' hall; and everyone who had the courage to listen at keyholes would most certainly do so, and relay with relish everything gleaned. Perhaps she had overdone it? They might be plagued with unnecessary messages all morning, and superfluous offers of tea.

"Yes, ma'am," the maid said a little breathlessly. "I shall inform Her Ladyship immediately!" She left, closing the door behind her very quietly. Then her heels clicked at so fast a pace along the passage she must have sent her skirts flying.

She reappeared in about four minutes.

"If you would care to join Her Ladyship in the breakfast room, ma'am?" She left no allowance for refusal, even if one had been contemplated.

"Thank you," Charlotte accepted and walked past her; it was nice to have doors held for one. She knew where the breakfast room was, and did not need to be shown.

Emily was sitting at the table, her fair hair already exquisitely dressed for the day; she wore a morning gown of water-green taffeta that made her look delicate and expensive. Charlotte was instantly conscious of her own drabness; she felt like a damp winter leaf next to a flower in bloom. The excitement drained out of her and she sat down heavily in the chair opposite Emily. Visions of a hot, perfumed bath floated across her mind, then a flattering maid to dress her in brilliant, soft-falling silks, like butterflies.

"Well?" Emily demanded, crashing through her thoughts with reality. "What is it? What has happened? Don't just sit there keeping me in suspense! I haven't heard a decent scandal in months. All I get is endless love affairs that were perfectly predictable to anyone with eyes to see! And who cares about other people's love affairs anyway? They only do it because they can't think of anything more interesting. No one really minds—I mean no one feels anything scorching! It's all a very silly game— Charlotte!" She banged her cup down with a porcelain tinkle, lucky not to chip it. "For goodness' sake, what's wrong?"

Charlotte recalled herself. Butterflies lived only a day or two anyway.

"Murder," she said bluntly.

Emily was immediately sober, sitting perfectly upright.

"Tea?" she invited, then reached for the silver bell on the table. "Who has been murdered? Anyone we know?"

The maid appeared instantly. She had obviously been on the other side of the door waiting. Emily gave her a sour look.

"Bring fresh tea, please, Gwenneth, and toast for Mrs. Pitt."

"Yes, ma'am."

"I don't need toast," Charlotte replied, thinking of getting into the butterfly silks.

"Have it anyway—off you go, Gwenneth—we don't want it at lunchtime!" Emily waited until the door was closed. "Who's been murdered?" she repeated. "And how? And why?"

"A boy called Arthur Waybourne," Charlotte answered quite bluntly. "He was drowned in the bath—and I'm not sure why—exactly."

Emily screwed up her face impatiently.

"What do you mean 'exactly'? Do you mean 'approximately,' then? You aren't making a lot of sense, Charlotte. Who would want to kill a child? He's not an unknown baby that might embarrass someone, because you just told me his name."

"He was not a baby at all. He was sixteen."

"Sixteen! Are you trying to be irritating, Charlotte? He probably drowned quite accidentally. Does Thomas think it was murder, or are you just doing this by yourself?" Emily sat back, a shadow of disappointment in her eyes.

The whole dark, miserable story was suddenly very real again.

"It's very unlikely he drowned by accident," Charlotte replied, looking across the table spread with fine bone china, fruit preserves in jars, and a scatter of crumbs. "And he certainly did not put his own body down a manhole into the sewers!"

Emily caught her breath and choked.

"Down the sewers!" she cried, coughing and banging her chest. "Did you say sewers?"

"Quite. He also had been homosexually abused, and had caught a most unpleasant disease."

"How disgusting!" Emily took a deep breath and a sip of lukewarm tea. "What sort of a person was he? I presume he came from the city somewhere, one of those areas—"

"On the contrary," Charlotte interrupted. "He was the eldest son of a gentleman of—"

At that point, the door opened and the parlormaid came in with fresh tea and a rack of toast. There was utter silence while she set them on the table, paused for a moment or two in case the conversation continued, then met Emily's frozen glance and left with a swing of skirts.

"What?" Emily demanded. "What did you say?"

"He was the eldest son of a family of distinction," Charlotte repeated clearly. "Sir Anstey and Lady Waybourne, of Exeter Street."

Emily stared, ignoring the teapot, and the fragrant steam rising gently in front of her.

"That's preposterous!" she exploded. "How in heaven's name could that happen?"

"He and his brother had a tutor," Charlotte said, beginning to tell the parts of the story that mattered. "May I have the tea? A man called Maurice Jerome, really rather an unpleasant man, very cold and very prim. He's clever and he resents being patronized by richer people with fewer brains. Thank you." She took the tea; the cup was very light and painted with flowers in blue and gold. "The younger son, the one still alive, has said that Jerome made improper advances him. And so has the son of a friend."

"Oh, dear!" Emily looked as though her tea had suddenly turned sour in her mouth. "How sordid. Do you want the toast? The apricot preserve is very good. How very nasty indeed. I really don't understand that sort of thing. In fact, I didn't even know much about it until I

195

overheard one of George's friends say something quite horrible." She pushed the butter across. "So what is the mystery? You said something rather extreme to Gwenneth about great injustice. The scandal is obvious, but unless this wretched man is going to get away with it, where is the injustice? He has been tried and he will be hanged. And so he should be."

Charlotte avoided the argument of whether anyone should be hanged or not. That would have to wait for another time. She took the butter.

"But it hasn't really been proved that he was guilty!" she said urgently. "There are all sorts of other possibilities that haven't been proved or disproved yet!"

Emily squinted at her suspiciously.

"Such as what? It all seems very plain to me!"

Charlotte reached for the apricot preserve.

"Of course it's plain!" she snapped. "That doesn't mean it's true! Arthur Waybourne may not have been as innocent as everyone is supposing. Perhaps he had a relationship with the other two boys, and they were frightened, or revolted, and they killed him."

"Is there any reason whatsoever to suppose that?" Emily was entirely unconvinced, and Charlotte had the feeling she was rapidly losing her attention.

"I haven't told you everything," she said, trying a different angle.

"You haven't told me anything!" Emily said waspishly. "Not anything worth thinking about."

"I went to the trial," Charlotte continued. "I heard all the evidence and saw the people."

"You didn't say that!" Emily exclaimed, her cheeks coloring with frustration. She sat very upright in the Chippendale chair. "I've never been to a trial!"

"Of course you haven't," Charlotte agreed with a faint flicker of spite. "Ladies of quality don't!"

Emily's eyes narrowed in a look of warning. This was

suddenly far too exciting a subject to give way to sisterly envy.

Charlotte accepted the hint. After all, she wanted Emily's cooperation; indeed, it was what she had come for. Rapidly she told her everything she could remember, describing the courtroom, the sewerman who had found the body, Anstey Waybourne, the two boys, Esmond Vanderley and the other man who gave evidence on Jerome's previous character, Albie Frobisher, and Abigail Winters. She did her best to recount accurately what they had said. She also tried as clearly as she could to explain her own mixture of feelings about Jerome himself, and about Eugenie. She ended by expounding her theories regarding Godfrey, Titus, and Arthur Waybourne.

Emily stared at her for a long time before replying. Her tea was cold; she ignored it.

"I see," she said at last. "At least I see that we don't see—not nearly enough to be sure. I didn't know there were boys who made their living like that. It's appalling—poor creatures. Although I have discovered that there are a great many more revolting things in high society than I ever used to imagine living at home in Cater Street. We were incredibly innocent then. I find some of George's friends quite repellent. In fact, I have asked him why on earth he puts up with them! He simply says he has known them all his life, and when you have grown used to a person, you tend to overlook the unpleasant things they do. They sort of creep into your knowledge one by one, and you don't ever realize just how horrible they are, because you half see the person the way you remember them and don't bother to look at them properly anymore—not as you would someone you have just met. Maybe that's what happened with Jerome. His wife never noticed how big the change was in him." She raised her eyebrows and looked at the table, reached for the bell, then changed her mind.

197

"That could just as easily be true of Arthur Waybourne," Charlotte reasoned.

"I suppose nobody was allowed to inquire." Emily screwed up her face thoughtfully. "They couldn't. I mean I can imagine the family's reaction to having the police in the house at all! Death is bad enough."

"Exactly! Thomas can't get any further. The case is closed."

"Naturally. And they will hang the tutor in three weeks."

"Unless we do something."

Emily considered, frowning. "What, for instance?"

"Well, there must be more to know about Arthur, for a start. And I would like to see those two boys without their fathers present. I should dearly like to know what they would say if they were questioned properly."

"Highly unlikely you'll ever know." Emily was a realist. "The more there is to hush up, the more their families will make sure they are not pressed too hard. They will have learned their answers by heart now and they won't dare go back on it. They'll say exactly the same thing whoever asks them."

"I don't know," Charlotte countered. "They might say it differently if they are not on their guard. We might see something, sense something."

"In fact, what you came for was to get me to find you a way into the Waybournes' house," Emily said with a little laugh. "I will—on one condition!"

Charlotte knew before she spoke. "That you come, too." She smiled wryly. "Of course. Do you know the Waybournes?"

Emily sighed. "No."

Charlotte felt her heart sink.

"But I'm sure Aunt Vespasia does, or knows someone else who does. Society is really very small, you know."

Charlotte remembered George's Great-Aunt Vespasia with a tingle of pleasure. She stood up from the table.

"Then we'd better go and see her," she said enthusiastically. She'll be bound to help us when she knows why."

Emily also stood up. "Are you going to tell her this tutor is innocent?" she asked doubtfully.

Charlotte hesitated. She needed the help desperately, and Aunt Vespasia might be disinclined to intrude herself into a grieving family, bringing two inquisitive sisters to uncover ugly secrets, unless she believed gross injustice was about to be done. On the other hand, when Charlotte recalled Aunt Vespasia, she realized that lying to her would be impossible, and worse than pointless.

"No." She shook her head. "No, I'll tell her there may be a gross injustice done, that's all. She'll mind about that."

"I wouldn't guarantee her loving truth for its own sake," Emily replied. "She'll be able to see all its disadvantages too. She's extremely practical, you know." She smiled and rang the bell at last, to permit Gwenneth to clear the table. "But then, of course, she would hardly have survived in society for seventy years if she were not. Do you want to borrow a decent dress? I suppose we'll go calling immediately, if it can be arranged. There's hardly time to lose. And, by the way, you'd better let me explain all this to Aunt Vespasia. You'll let all sorts of things slip and shock her out of her senses. People like her don't know about your disgusting rookeries and your boy prostitutes with their diseases and perversions. You were never any good at saying anything without saying everything else at the same time." She led the way to the door and out into the hall, practically falling over Gwenneth, who was balanced against the door with a tray in her hand. Emily ignored her and swept across to the stairs.

"I've got a dark red dress that would probably look better on you than it does on me anyway. The color is too hard for me—makes me look sallow."

199

Charlotte did not bother to argue, either over the dress or the insult to her tact; she could not afford to, and Emily was probably right.

The red dress was extremely flattering, rather too much so for someone proposing to call on the recently bereaved. Emily looked her up and down with her mouth pursed, but Charlotte was too pleased with her reflection in the glass to consider changing it; she had not looked so dashing since she had spent that unspeakable evening in the music hall—an incident she profoundly hoped Emily had forgotten.

"No," she said firmly before Emily spoke. "They are in mourning, but I am not. Anyway, if we let them know that we know they are, then we can hardly go at all! I can wear a black hat and gloves—that will be enough to tone it down. Now you had better get dressed, or we shall have wasted half the morning. We don't want to find Aunt Vespasia already gone out when we get there!"

"Don't be ridiculous!" Emily snapped. "She's seventy-four! She doesn't go calling on people at this hour! Have you forgotten all your breeding?"

But when they arrived at Great-Aunt Vespasia's house they were informed that Lady Cumming-Gould had been up for some considerable time, and had already received a caller that morning; the maid would have to see whether she was available to receive Lady Ashworth and her sister. They were invited to wait in a morning room fragrant with the earthy smell of a bowl of chrysanthemums, reflected in gold-edged French cheval glasses and echoed in a most unusual Chinese silk embroidery on the wall. They were both drawn to admire the embroidery in the minutes left them.

Vespasia Cumming-Gould threw open the doors and came in. She was exactly as Charlotte had remembered her: tall, straight as a lance, and as thin. Her aquiline face, which had been the among most beautiful of her generation, was now tilted in surprise, with eyebrows arched. Her hair was exquisitely piled in silver coils, and she had on a dress with delicate Chantilly lace over the shoulders and down to the waist. It must have cost as much as Charlotte would have spent on clothes in a year; yet, looking at it, she felt nothing but delight at seeing Aunt Vespasia, and a surging of spirit inside herself.

"Good morning, Emily." Aunt Vespasia walked in and allowed the footman to close the doors behind her. "My dear Charlotte, you appear extremely well. That can only mean that either you are with child again or you have another murder to meddle with."

Emily let out her breath in a gasp of frustration.

Charlotte felt all her good intentions vanish like water through a sieve.

"Yes, Aunt Vespasia," she agreed instantly. "A murder."

"That's what comes of marrying beneath you," Aunt Vespasia said without a flicker of expression, patting Emily on the arm. "I always thought it would be rather more fun—if, of course, one could find a man of any natural wit—and grace. I cannot bear a man who allows himself to be put upon. It is really very frustrating. I require people to know their places, and yet I despise them when they do! I think that is what I like about your policeman, my dear Charlotte. He never knows his place, and yet he leaves it with such panache one is not offended. How is he?"

Charlotte was taken aback. She had never heard Pitt described that way before. And yet perhaps she understood what Aunt Vespasia meant; it was nothing physical, rather a way of meeting the eyes, of not permitting himself to feel insulted, whatever the intent of others. Maybe it had something to do with the innate dignity of believing.

Aunt Vespasia was staring at her, waiting.

"In excellent health, thank you," she replied. "But very

worried about an injustice that may be about to take place—an unpardonable one!"

"Indeed?" Aunt Vespasia sat down, arranging her dress on the sofa with a single, expert movement. "And I suppose you intend to do something about this injustice, which is why you have come. Who has been murdered? Not that disgusting business with the Waybourne boy?"

"Yes!" Emily said quickly, wresting the initiative before Charlotte could provoke some social disaster. "Yes, it is not necessarily what it seems."

"My dear girl." Aunt Vespasia's eyebrows rose in amazement. "Very little ever is—or life would be insufferably boring. I sometimes think that is the whole purpose of society. The basic difference between us and the working classes is that we have the time and the wit to see that very little appears to be what it is. It is the very essence of style.

"What in particular is more than usually deceptive about this wretched business? It certainly appears plain enough!" She turned to Charlotte as she said this. "Speak, girl! I am aware that young Arthur was found in the most sordid of circumstances, and that some servant or other has been tried for the crime and, as far as I know, found to be guilty. What else is there to know?"

Emily shot Charlotte a warning glance, then abandoned hope and sat back in the Louis Quinze chair to await the worst.

Charlotte cleared her throat. "The evidence upon which the tutor was convicted was entirely the testimony of other people, nothing material at all."

"Indeed," Aunt Vespasia said with a little nod. "What could there be? Drowning someone will hardly leave tangible marks upon a bath. And presumably there was no struggle of any worth. What was this testimony, and from whom?"

"The two other boys who say Jerome tried to interfere

202

with them also—that is Godfrey, Arthur's young brother, and Titus Swynford."

"Oh." Aunt Vespasia gave a little grunt. "Knew Callantha Vanderley's mother. She was married to Benita Waybourne's uncle—Benita Vanderley, as she was then, of course. Callantha married Mortimer Swynford. Could never understand why she did that. Still, I suppose she found him agreeable enough. Never cared much for him myself—made too much of a noise about his good sense. A trifle vulgar. Good sense should never be discussed— it's like good digestion, better assumed than spoken of." She sighed. "Still, I suppose young men are bound to be pleased with themselves for some reason or other, and good sense is a better one in the long run than a straight nose, or a long pedigree."

Emily smiled. "Well, if you know Mrs. Swynford," she said hopefully, "perhaps we can call on her? We may learn something."

"That would be a distinct advantage!" Aunt Vespasia answered sharply. "I have learned precious little so far! For goodness' sake, continue, Charlotte! And come to some point or other!"

Charlotte forbore from mentioning that it was Vespasia who had interrupted her.

"Apart from the two boys," she resumed, "no one else in either family had anything ill to say about Jerome, except that they did not like him much—which nobody else does either." She took a breath and hurried on before Aunt Vespasia could break in again. "The other main evidence came from a woman"—she hesitated for an acceptable term that was not open to complete misunderstanding—"of loose behavior."

"A what?" Aunt Vespasia's eyebrows shot up again.

"A—a woman of loose behavior," Charlotte repeated rather awkwardly. She had no idea how much a lady of

Aunt Vespasia's generation might know about such things.

"Do you mean a street woman?" Aunt Vespasia inquired. "Because if you do, then for goodness' sake girl, say so! 'Loose behavior' could mean anything! I know duchesses whose conduct could well be described by such a term. What about this woman? What has she to do with it? Surely this wretched tutor did not kill the boy in jealousy over some whore?"

"Really!" Emily said under her breath, more in amazement than any moral comment.

Aunt Vespasia gave her a chilly glance.

"It is quite repellent, I agree," she said bluntly. "But then so is the idea of murder at all. It does not become nice merely because the motive is something like money!" She turned back to Charlotte. "Please explain yourself a little more clearly. What has this woman to do with it? Has she a name? I am beginning to forget whom I am speaking about."

"Abigail Winters." There was no point whatever in trying to be delicate anymore. "Arthur Waybourne was found by the police surgeon to have a disease. Since the tutor did not have it, he must have contracted it elsewhere."

"Obviously!"

"Abigail Winters said that the tutor, Jerome, had taken Arthur to her. He was a voyeur as well! Arthur contracted the disease from her—she does have it."

"How singularly unpleasant." Aunt Vespasia wrinkled her long nose very slightly. "Still, an occupational risk, I imagine. But if the boy has it, and this Jerome person was meddling with him—why did he not also have it? You say he did not?"

Emily sat upright suddenly, her face alight.

"Charlotte?" she said with a sharp lift of her voice.

"No," Charlotte said slowly. "No—and that doesn't

make sense, does it! If the affaire was still going on, he should have. Or are some people immune to it?"

"My dear girl!" Vespasia stared, fumbling for her pince-nez to observe Charlotte more closely. "How on earth should I know? I imagine so, or a great deal of society would have it who apparently do not—from what one is told. But it would bear thinking on! What else? So far, we have the words of two youths of a most unreliable age—and a woman of the streets. There must be more?"

"Yes—a—a male prostitute, aged seventeen." Her anger about Albie came stinging through her voice. "He began when he was thirteen—he was doubtless more or less sold into it. He swore Jerome had been a regular customer of his. That was the chief way we know that he is . . ." She avoided the word "homosexual" and left its meaning hanging in the air.

Aunt Vespasia was happy to allow her the liberty. Her face was somber.

"Thirteen," she repeated, frowning. "That is truly one of the most obscene offenses of our society, that we permit such things to happen. And the youth—he too has a name, presumably? He says that this wretched tutor was his customer? What about the boy, Arthur—was he also?"

"Apparently not, but then he would not be likely to admit it if he could avoid doing so," Charlotte reasoned, "since Arthur was murdered. No one admits to knowing a person who has been murdered, if they can avoid it—not if they would be suspected."

"Quite. What an extremely distasteful affair. I presume you have told me all this because you believe the tutor, what's-his-name, to be innocent?"

Now that it came to the point, it was impossible even to prevaricate.

"I don't know," Charlotte said bluntly. "But it's so convenient, it closes it up so tidily that I think we haven't bothered to prove it properly. And if we hang him, it's too late after that!"

Aunt Vespasia sighed very gently. "I imagine Thomas is not able to prove the matter any further, since the trial will be considered to have ended all questions." It was an observation rather than a request for information. "What alternative solutions do you have in mind? That this miserable child Arthur may have had other lovers—possibly even have set up in business in a mild way for himself?" Her fine mouth turned down delicately at the corners. "An undertaking fraught with all manner of dangers, one would have thought. One wonders for a start whether he procured his own custom, or whether he had a business partner, a protector, who did it for him. He can hardly have used his own home for such a concern! What order of money was involved, and what happened to it? Was money at the root of it, after all, for whatever reason? Yes, I see that there are a number of avenues to explore, none of which would be pleasing to the families.

"Emily said you were a social disaster. I fear she was being somewhat generous to you—you are a catastrophe! Where do you wish to begin?"

In fact, they began with an exceedingly formal call upon Callantha Swynford, since she was the only person connected with the affair whom Vespasia had any personal acquaintance with. And even then, it took them some mind-searching to concoct an adequate excuse, including two conversations upon that marvelous new instrument, the telephone, which Aunt Vespasia had had installed and used with the greatest enjoyment.

They drove in her carriage as soon after luncheon as was considered acceptable to visit. They presented calling cards to the parlormaid, who was duly impressed by the presence of not merely one but two titled ladies. She showed them in almost immediately.

The withdrawing room was more than pleasant; it was

both gracious and comfortable, a combination unfortunately rare. A large fire burned in the grate, giving a feeling of warmth and life. The room was cluttered with far less than the usual forest of family portraits; it was even devoid of the customary stuffed animals and dried flowers under glass.

Callantha Swynford was also a surprise, at least to Charlotte. She had expected someone portly and self-satisfied, perhaps inordinately pleased with her own good sense. Instead, Callantha was on the lean side, with white skin and freckles, which in her youth she had doubtless spent hours endeavoring to remove, or at least to mask. Now she ignored them, and they complemented her russet-colored hair in a surprisingly attractive way. She was not beautiful; her nose was too high and long for that, and her mouth too large. But she was certainly handsome, and, more than that, she possessed individuality.

"How charming of you to call, Lady Cumming-Gould," she said with a smile, extending her hand and inviting the ladies to sit down. "And Lady Ashworth—" Charlotte had not presented a card, and she was at a loss. No one helped her.

"My cousin Angelica is indisposed." Aunt Vespasia lied as easily as if she were reading the time. "She was so sorry not to renew your acquaintance in person, and told me to say how much she enjoyed meeting you. She asked me if I would call upon you instead, so you would not feel she was cool in your friendship. Since I had my niece Lady Ashworth and her sister Charlotte already in my company, I felt you would not be inconvenienced if they were to call also."

"Of course not." Callantha gave the only possible answer. "I am delighted to make their acquaintance. How very thoughtful of Angelica. I hope her indisposition is nothing serious?"

"I should imagine not." Aunt Vespasia waved it away with her hand, very delicately, as though it were something vaguely indecent to discuss. "One gets these little afflictions from time to time."

Callantha understood immediately; it was something it would be kinder not to refer to again.

"Of course," she agreed. They all knew the danger of her comparing notes with Angelica was now taken care of.

"What a delightful room." Charlotte looked about her and was able to comment quite genuinely. "I do admire your choice. I feel comfortable immediately."

"Oh, do you?" Callantha seemed quite surprised. "I am delighted you think so. Many people find it too bare. I imagine they expect rather more in the way of family portraits and such."

Charlotte seized her chance; it might not come again so felicitously.

"I always think a few pictures of quality that really catch the essence of a person are of far more value than a great number that are merely likenesses," she replied. "I cannot help observing the excellent portrait over the mantel. Is that your daughter? Great-Aunt Vespasia mentioned that you have a son and a daughter. She is quite charming, and she looks already as if she may grow to resemble you."

Callantha smiled, glancing at the painting.

"Yes, indeed, that is Fanny. It was painted about a year ago, and she is quite unbecomingly proud of it. I must curb her. Vanity is not a quality one dare encourage. And to be frank, she is not in the least a beauty. Such charm as she has will lie within her personality." She pulled a small face, a little rueful, perhaps echoing memories of her own youth.

"But that is far better!" Charlotte approved with conviction. "Beauty fades, and often disastrously quickly, whereas with a little attention, character can improve indefinitely! I am sure I should like Fanny very much."

Emily gave her a sour look, and Charlotte knew she felt

she was being too obvious. But then Callantha had no idea why they had called.

"You are very generous," she murmured politely.

"Not at all," Charlotte demurred. "I often think beauty is a very mixed blessing, especially in the young. It can lead to so many unfortunate associations. Too much praise, too much admiration, and I have seen even some of the nicest people led astray, because they were innocent, sheltered by a decent family, so did not realize the shallowness or the vice that can exist behind the mask of flattery."

A shadow passed across Callantha's face. Charlotte felt guilty for bringing up the subject so blatantly, but there was no time to waste in being subtle.

"Indeed," she continued, "I have even seen instances in my acquaintance where unusual beauty has led a young person to acquire power over others, and then quite abuse it, to their own undoing in the end—and most unfortunately, to the misfortune of those involved with them as well." She took a deep breath. "Whereas true charm of personality can do nothing but good. I think you are most fortunate." She remembered that Jerome had tutored Fanny in Latin. "And of course intelligence is one of the greatest of gifts. Foolishness can sometimes be overcome if one is safeguarded from its effects by a loving and patient family. But how much more of the world's joys are open to you if you have sensibility of your own, and how many pitfalls avoided." Did she sound as priggish as she felt? But it was difficult to approach the subject, retain a modicum of good manners, and not sound hopelessly pompous at the same time.

"Oh, Fanny has plenty of intelligence," Callantha said with a smile. "In fact, she is a better student than her brother, or either of—" She stopped.

"Yes?" Charlotte and Emily said, leaning forward in hopeful inquiry.

Callantha's face paled. "I was going to say 'either of her cousins,' but her elder cousin died some weeks ago."

"I'm so sorry." Again Emily and Charlotte spoke together, affecting total surprise. "How very hard to bear," Emily went on. "It was a sudden illness?"

Callantha hesitated, perhaps weighing the chances of getting away with a lie. In the end she decided on the truth. After all, the case had been written up in the newspapers, and although ladies of excellent upbringing would not read such things, it was impossible to avoid hearing gossip—supposing anyone were even to try!

"No—no, he was killed." She still avoided the word "murder." "I'm afraid it was all very dreadful."

"Oh, dear!" Emily was a better actress than Charlotte; she always had been. And she had not lived with the story from the beginning; she could affect ignorance. "How terribly distressing for you! I do hope we have not called at an inappropriate time?" It was really an unnecessary question. One could not cease all social life every time a relative died, unless it were in the immediate family, or else the number of one's relatives and the frequency of death would cause one to be forever in mourning.

"No, no." Callantha shook her head. "It is most pleasant to see you."

"Perhaps," Aunt Vespasia said, "it would be possible for you to come to a small soirée at my house in Gadstone Park, if you are accepting invitations. I should be delighted to see you, and your husband also, if he wishes and is free of business functions? I have not met him, but I'm sure he is charming. I will send the footman with an invitation."

Charlotte's heart sank. It was Titus and Fanny she wanted to talk to, not Mortimer Swynford!

"I am sure he would enjoy that as much as I," Callantha said. "I had intended to invite Angelica to an afternoon entertainment, a new pianist who has been much praised. I have planned it for Saturday. I hope she will

210

have recovered by then. But in any case, I should be delighted if you would all come. We shall be ladies, in the main, but if Lord Ashworth or your husband would care to come?" She turned from one to the other of them.

"Of course!" Emily glowed with anticipation. The object was achieved. The men would not come; that was understood. She darted a look across at Charlotte. "Perhaps we shall meet Fanny? I admit I am quite intrigued—I shall look forward to it."

"And I also," Charlotte agreed. "Very much."

Aunt Vespasia rose. They had been long enough for the strict duty call they professed it to be, and certainly long enough for a first visit. Most important, their purpose was achieved. With great dignity she took leave for all of them, and, after the appropriate civilities had been exchanged, swept them out to the carriage.

"Excellent," she said as they seated themselves, arranging their skirts so as to be crushed as little as possible before the next call. "Charlotte, did you say this wretched child was only thirteen when he began his disgusting trade?"

"Albie Frobisher? Yes, so he said. He looked only a little more now—he's very thin and underdeveloped—no beard at all."

"And how do you know, may I ask?" Aunt Vespasia fixed her with a cool eye.

"I was in the courtroom," Charlotte replied without thinking. "I saw him."

"Were you indeed?" Aunt Vespasia's brows shot up and her face looked very long. "Your conduct becomes more extraordinary by the moment. Tell me more. In fact, tell me everything! Or, no—not yet. We are going to visit Mr. Somerset Carlisle. I daresay you remember him?"

Charlotte remembered him vividly, and the whole unspeakable affair around Resurrection Row. He had been the keenest of all of them in fighting to get the child-poverty bill passed through Parliament. He knew as much as Pitt did of the slums—indeed he had frightened and appalled poor Dominic by taking him to the Devil's Acre, under the shadow of Westminster.

But would he be interested in the facts of one extremely unlikable tutor, who was very possibly guilty of a despicable crime anyway?

"Do you think Mr. Carlisle will be bothered over Mr. Jerome?" she asked doubtfully. "The law is not at fault. It is hardly a Parliamentary matter."

"It is a matter for reform," Aunt Vespasia replied as the carriage swayed around a corner rather fiercely and she was obliged to brace her body to prevent herself falling into Charlotte's lap. Opposite them, Emily clung on quite ungracefully. Aunt Vespasia snorted. "I shall have to speak to that young man! He has visions of becoming a charioteer. I think he sees me as a rather elderly Queen Boudicca! Next thing you know, he will have put sabers on the wheels!"

Charlotte pretended to sneeze in order to hide her expression.

"Reform?" she said after a moment, straightening up under the cold and highly perceptive eye of Vespasia. "I don't see how."

"If children of thirteen can be bought and sold for these practices," Vespasia snapped, "then there is something grossly wrong, and it needs to be reformed. Actually, I have been considering it for some time. You have merely brought it to the forefront of my mind. I think it is a cause worthy of our best endeavors. I imagine Mr. Carlisle will think so, too."

Carlisle listened to them with great attention and, as Aunt Vespasia had expected, distress for the conditions of people like Albie Frobisher in general, and for the possible injustice of the case against Jerome.

After some thought, he posed several questions and theories himself. Had Arthur threatened Jerome with blackmail, threatened to tell his father about the relationship? And when Waybourne had faced Jerome, could Jerome have told him a great deal more of the truth than Arthur had envisioned? Did he tell Waybourne of their visits to Abigail Winters—even to Albie Frobisher—and that it was Arthur himself who had introduced the two younger boys to such practices? Could it then have been Waybourne, in rage and horror, who had killed his own son, rather than face the unbearable scandal that could not be suppressed forever? The possibilities had been very far from explored!

But now, of course, the police, the law, the whole establishment had committed itself to the verdict. Their reputations, indeed their very professional office, depended upon the conviction standing. To admit they had been precipitate in duty, perhaps even negligent, would make a public exhibition of their inadequacies. And no one does that unless driven to it by forces beyond control.

Added to that, Charlotte conceded, they may well believe in all honesty that Jerome was guilty. And perhaps he was!

And would smart, clean, pink young Gillivray ever admit that he might have helped Albie Frobisher just a little in his identification, planted the seed of understanding in a mind so quick, so subtle, and so anxious to survive that Albie had grasped what he wanted and given it to him?

Could Gillivray afford such a thought, even if it occurred to him? Of course not! Apart from anything else, it would be betraying Athelstan, leaving him standing alone—and that would be cataclysmic!

Abigail Winters might not have been lying entirely. Maybe Arthur had been there; his tastes may have been more catholic than for boys only. And perhaps Abigail had tacitly accepted some immunity for herself by including Jerome in her evidence. The temptation to tie a case up conclusively that you were morally sure of anyway was very real. Gillivray may have succumbed to it—visions of success, favor, promotion dancing before his eyes. Charlotte was ashamed of the thought when she expressed it to Carlisle, but felt it should not be dismissed.

And what did they wish of him? Carlisle asked.

The answer was quite explicit. They wished to have correct and detailed facts of prostitution in general, and that of children in particular, so that they might present them to the woman of society, whose outrage at such conditions might in time make the abuse of children so abhorrent that they would refuse to receive any man of whom such a practice, or even tolerance, was suspected.

Ignorance of its horrors was largely responsible for the women's indifference to it. Some knowledge, however dependent upon imagination for the reality of its fear and despair, would mobilize all their very great social power.

Carlisle vacillated at presenting such appalling facts to ladies, but Aunt Vespasia froze him with an icy stare.

"I am perfectly capable of looking at anything whatsoever that life has to afford," she said loftily, "if there is some reason for it! I do not care for vulgarity, but if a problem is to be dealt with, then it must be understood. Kindly do not patronize me, Somerset!"

"I wouldn't dare!" he replied with a flash of humor. It was almost an apology, and she accepted it with grace.

"I hardly imagine it will be a pleasant subject," she acknowledged. "Nevertheless it must be done. Our facts must be correct—one grave error and we lose our case. I shall avail myself of all the help I can." She turned in her chair. "Emily, the best opinion to begin with is that of the people who have the most influence, and who will be the most offended by it."

"The Church?" Emily suggested.

"Nonsense! Everyone expects the Church to make noises about sin. That is their job! Therefore no one really listens—it has no novelty whatsoever. What we need is a few of the best society hostesses, the ones people listen to and imitate, the leaders of fashion. That is where you will assist, Emily."

Emily was delighted; her face shone with anticipation.

"And you, Charlotte," Vespasia continued. "You will acquire some of the information we shall need. You have a husband in the police force. Use him. Somerset, I shall speak to you again." She rose from the armchair and went to the door. "In the meanwhile, I trust you will do everything you can to look into the matter of this tutor Jerome and the possibility that there may be some other explanation. It is rather pressing."

Pitt told Charlotte nothing about his interview with Athelstan, and so she was unaware that he had tried to reopen the case. But in any event, she had not imagined it would be possible once the verdict was in. If anything, she knew better than he did that those with influence would not permit the result to be questioned, now that the law had been met.

The next thing to do was to prepare for Callantha's party, when she might have the chance to speak with Fanny Swynford. And if the occasion to speak to Titus did not offer itself gratuitously, she would then engineer some opportunity to speak with him also. At least Emily and Aunt Vespasia would be there to help her. And Aunt Vespasia was able to get away with almost any social behavior she chose, because she had the position—and, above all, the sheer style—to carry it off as if she were the rule and everyone else the exception.

She told Pitt only that she was going out with Aunt Vespasia. She knew that he liked Vespasia enough not to question it. In fact, he sent her his very best wishes in a message of what was for him unusual respect.

She accompanied Emily in her carriage, and had borrowed another dress for the day, since it was impractical for her to spend such allowance as she had for clothes on something she would wear probably only once. The minutiae of high fashion changed so frequently that last season's dress was distinctly passé this season; it was seldom more than once or twice in six months that Charlotte attended an affair like the entertainment at Callantha Swynford's.

The weather was perfectly appalling, driving sleet out of an iron-gray sky. The only way to look in the least glamorous was to wear something as gay and dazzling as possible. Emily chose light, clear red. Not wishing to look too similar, Charlotte chose an apricot velvet that made Emily slightly cross she had not chosen it herself. She was too proud, though, to demand they exchange, even though both were her gowns; her reasons would have been too obvious.

However, by the time they reached the Swynfords' hallway and were welcomed into the large withdrawing room, which had been opened into the room beyond, fires blazing, lamps bright, Emily forgot the matter and launched herself into the business of the visit.

"How delightful," she said with a brilliant smile at Callantha Swynford. "I shall look forward to meeting absolutely everyone! And so will Charlotte, I am sure. She has spoken of little else all the way here."

Callantha made the usual polite replies, and conducted them to be introduced to the other guests, all talking busily and saying very little of consequence. Just over half an hour later, when the pianist had begun to play a composition of incredible monotony, Charlotte observed a very self-possessed child of about fourteen whom she recognized from the portrait to be Fanny. She excused herself from her present company—easily done, since they were all bored with each other and had been pretending to listen to the music—and made her way between other groups until she was next to Fanny.

"Do you like it?" she whispered quite casually, as if they were long acquaintances.

Fanny looked slightly uncertain. She had an intelligent, candid little face, with the same mouth as her mother, and gray eyes, but otherwise the resemblance was less than the portrait affected. And she did not look as if lying came to her by nature.

"I think perhaps I don't understand it." She found the tactful answer with some triumph.

"Neither do I," Charlotte said agreeably. "I don't care to have to understand music unless I like the sound of it."

Fanny relaxed. "You don't like it either," she observed with relief. "Actually, I think it's awful. I can't imagine why Mama invited him. I suppose he's 'the thing' this month or something. And he looks so dreadfully serious about it I can't help thinking he doesn't like it much himself. Maybe this isn't the way he means it to sound, do you suppose?"

"Perhaps he's worried he won't be paid," Charlotte answered. "I wouldn't pay him."

Seeing her smile, Fanny burst into laughter, then realized it was completely improper, and hid her mouth with her hands. She regarded Charlotte with new interest.

"You are so pretty you don't look as if you'd say dreadful things," she observed frankly, then realized that she had added to her social mistake even further, and blushed.

"Thank you," Charlotte said sincerely. "I'm so glad you think I look nice." She lowered her voice in conspiracy. "Actually, I borrowed my dress from my sister, and I think now she wishes she'd worn it herself. But please don't tell anyone."

"Oh, I shan't!" Fanny promised instantly. "It's beautiful."

"Have you got any sisters?"

Fanny shook her head. "No, only a brother, so I can't really borrow anything much. It must be nice to have a sister."

"Yes, it is—most of the time. Although I think I might

have liked a brother, too. I have some cousins, only I hardly ever see them."

"So have I—but they're mostly boys as well. At least the ones I see are. They're second cousins really, but it's much the same." Her face became sober. "One of them just died. It was all rather horrible. He got killed. I don't really understand what happened, and nobody will tell me. I think it must be something disgusting, or they'd say—don't you think?"

Her words were quite casual, but Charlotte saw behind the puzzled, rather offhand look the need to be reassured. And reality would be better than the monsters created by silence.

Apart from her own need to press for information, Charlotte did not want to insult the child with comfortable lies.

"Yes," she said honestly. "I should think there's probably something that hurts, so people would rather not talk about it."

Fanny looked at her for several moments before speaking again, measuring her up.

"He was murdered," she said at last.

"Oh, dear, I'm so sorry," Charlotte answered with perfect composure. "That's very sad. How did it happen?"

"Our tutor, Mr. Jerome—everyone says he killed him."

"Your tutor? How appalling. Did they have a fight? Do you suppose it was an accident? Perhaps he did not mean to be so violent?"

"Oh, no!" Fanny shook her head. "It wasn't like that at all. It wasn't a fight—Arthur was drowned in the bath." She screwed up her face in bewilderment. "I simply don't understand it. Titus—that's my brother—had to give evidence in court. They wouldn't let me go, of course. They don't let me do anything really interesting! Sometimes it's awful being a girl." She sighed. "But I've thought a lot— and I can't imagine what he knows that would be any good!"

"Well, men do tend to be a bit pompous," Charlotte offered.

"Mr. Jerome was," Fanny said. "Oh, he was very stuffy, too. He had an expression as if he was eating rice pudding all the time! But he was an awfully good teacher. I hate rice pudding—it always has lumps in it and it tastes of nothing, but we have to have it every Thursday. He used to teach me Latin. I don't think he liked any of us very much, but he never lost his temper. I think he was sort of proud of that. He was terribly—I don't know." She shrugged. "He never had any fun."

"But he hated your cousin Arthur?"

"I never thought he liked him a lot." Fanny considered it carefully. "But I never thought he hated him either."

Charlotte felt a quickening of excitement.

"What was he like, your cousin Arthur?"

Fanny wrinkled up her nose and hesitated.

"You didn't like him?" Charlotte helped.

Fanny's face ironed out, the tension relieved. Charlotte guessed it was the first time the decencies of mourning had allowed her to speak the truth about Arthur.

"Not very much," she admitted.

"Why not?" Charlotte pressed, trying to hide at least some of her interest.

"He was awfully conceited. He was very good-looking, you know." Fanny shrugged again. "Some boys are very vain—just as vain as any girl. And he behaved as if he was superior, but I suppose that's just because he was older." She took a deep breath. "I say, isn't that piano dreadful? It sounds like a maid dropping a whole load of knives and forks."

Charlotte's heart sank. Just as they were really touching Arthur, the boy behind all the trappings of grief, Fanny had changed the subject.

"He was very clever," Fanny went on. "Or perhaps I mean cunning. But that isn't a reason to kill him, is it?"

"No," Charlotte said slowly. "Not by itself. Why did they say the tutor killed him?"

Fanny scowled. "Now that's what I don't understand. I did ask Titus, and he told me it was men's business, and not proper for me to know. It makes me sick! Boys really are so pompous sometimes! I'll bet it's nothing I don't know anyhow. Always pretending they know secrets that they don't." She snorted. "That's boys all the time!"

"Don't you think this time it might be true?" Charlotte suggested.

Fanny looked at her with the scorn she felt for boys.

"No—Titus doesn't know what he's talking about really. I know him very well, you know. I can see right through him. He's just being important to please Papa. I think it's all very silly."

"You mustn't monopolize our guests, Fanny." It was a man's voice, and familiar. With a light flutter of nervousness, Charlotte turned around to face Esmond Vanderley. Dear heaven—did he remember her from that awful evening? Perhaps not; the clothes, the whole atmosphere, were so utterly different. She met his eyes, and the hope died instantly.

He smiled back at her with a sharp glint of humor, so close to laughter it dazzled.

"I apologize for Fanny. I think the music bores her."

"Well, I find it a great deal less pleasing than Fanny's company," she replied a little more tartly than she intended. What was he thinking of her? He had given evidence about Jerome's character, and he had known Arthur well. If he had the charity to ignore their first meeting, she was extremely grateful, but she could not afford to retire from the battle all the same. This could be her only opportunity.

She smiled back at him, trying to take some of the sting out of her words. "Fanny was merely being an excellent hostess and relieving my solitude, since I know so few people here."

"Then I apologize to Fanny," he said pleasantly; apparently he had taken no offense.

Charlotte searched her mind for some way to keep alive the subject of Arthur without being too offensively curious.

"She was telling me about her family. You see, I had two sisters, while she has only a brother and male cousins. We were comparing differences."

"You had two sisters?" Fanny seized on it as Charlotte had hoped she would. She was ashamed to use tragedy in such a way, but there was no time to be delicate.

"Yes." She lowered her voice and did not have to strain to include the emotion. "My elder sister was killed. She was attacked in the street."

"Oh, how dreadful!" Fanny was shocked, her face full of sympathy. "That's absolutely the most awful thing I've heard for ages. That's worse than Arthur—because I didn't even love Arthur."

"Thank you." Charlotte touched her gently on the arm. "But I don't think you can say one person's loss is greater than another—we really can't tell. But yes, I did love her."

"I'm so sorry," Vanderley said quietly. "It must have been very distressing. Death is bad enough, without all the police investigation that follows. I'm afraid we've just suffered all that. But thank heaven it's over now."

Charlotte did not want to let the chance slip through her fingers. But how could she possibly pursue the less pleasant truths about Arthur in front of Fanny? And the whole subject was in appalling taste—she knew that before she even approached it.

"That must be a great relief to you all," she said politely. It was a sliding away; she was beginning to talk inanities. Where were Emily and Aunt Vespasia? Why couldn't they come to the rescue—either take Fanny away or else pursue the real nature of Arthur with Esmond

Vanderley themselves? "Of course one never gets over the loss," she added hastily.

"I suppose not," Vanderley answered civilly. "I saw Arthur quite often. One does in a family, of course. But, as I said before, I was not especially fond of him."

Suddenly, Charlotte had an idea. She turned to Fanny.

"Fanny, I'm terribly thirsty, but I don't wish to be drawn into conversation with the lady by the table. Would you be so kind as to fetch me a glass of punch?"

"Of course," Fanny said immediately. "Some of those people are awful, aren't they? There's one over there in the blue shiny gown who talks of nothing but her ailments, and it's not as if they were even interesting, like rare diseases—just vapors, like anyone else." And she left on her errand.

Charlotte faced Vanderley. Fanny would only be gone a few minutes, although with luck, since she was a child, she would be served last.

"How refreshingly honest you are," Charlotte said, trying to be as charming as she could but feeling self-conscious and rather ridiculous. "So many people pretend to have loved the dead and seen only virtue in them whatever they actually felt when they were alive."

He smiled with a slight twist. "Thank you. I admit it is a relief to confess that I saw in poor Arthur plenty that I did not care for."

"At least they have caught the man who killed him," she went on. "I suppose there is no question about it—he is definitely guilty? I mean the police are perfectly satisfied and that is an end to it? Now you will be left alone."

"No question at all." Then a thought seemed to flash into his mind. He hesitated, looked at her face, then took a deep breath. "At least I don't imagine so. There was a peculiarly persistent policeman who made the inquiries, but I cannot see what else he could want to find now."

Charlotte assumed a look of amazement. Heaven help her if he realized who she was.

"You mean he doesn't believe he has the entire truth? How dreadful! How perfectly appalling for you! If it wasn't the man they have, who can it have been?"

"God knows!" Vanderley looked pale. "Quite frankly, Arthur could be a beastly little animal! They say the tutor was his lover, you know. Sorry if I shock you." It was an afterthought; he had suddenly remembered she was a woman who might possibly not even know of such things. "They say he seduced the boy into unnatural practices. Possibly, but I wouldn't be totally surprised if Arthur was the one who did the seducing, and the poor man was drawn into it, flattered, and then ignored. Or maybe Arthur did that to someone else, and it was an old lover who killed him in a fit of jealousy. Now there's a thought! He might even have been a thoroughgoing little whore! Sorry—I am shocking you, Mrs.—I was so taken with your gown the other evening, I cannot now recall your name!"

"Oh!" Charlotte's mind raced for an answer. "I am Lady Ashworth's sister." That at least would make it seem unlikely she had any connection with the police. Again she felt her face scald with embarrassment.

"Then I apologize for such a—a violent and rather obscene discussion, Lady Ashworth's sister!" A smile of genuine amusement flickered over his face. "But you invited it, and if your own sister was murdered you are already acquainted with the less pleasant side of investigations."

"Oh, yes, of course." Charlotte said, still blushing. He was fair; she had invited it. "I'm not shocked," she said quickly. "But it is a very unpleasant thought that your nephew was such a—a warped person as you suggest."

"Arthur? Yes, isn't it. It's a pity someone has to hang for him, even a particularly unlovable Latin master with a temperament like vinegar. Poor wretch—still, I daresay if he weren't convicted, he'd have gone on and seduced other boys. Apparently, he interfered with Arthur's

younger brother, too—and Titus Swynford. Shouldn't
have done that. If Arthur dumped him, he should have
found someone else already so inclined—stuck to the
willing, not have gone scaring the sense out of some child
like Titus. He's a nice boy, Titus. A bit like Fanny, only
not so clever, thank heaven. Clever girls Fanny's age ter-
rify me. They notice everything and then remark it with
piercing clarity, at the most unfortunate times. Comes of
having too little to do."

At that point Fanny returned, proudly carrying
Charlotte's punch, and Vanderley excused himself and
wandered away, leaving Charlotte puzzled and vaguely
excited. He had sowed seeds of ideas she had hardly ever
thought of, and, she believed, neither had Pitt.

9

Pitt was quite unaware of Charlotte's enterprise. He was so preoccupied with his own doubts about the proof of Jerome's guilt that he accepted at face value her having gone calling with Great-Aunt Vespasia, something that at another time he would have regarded with sensible suspicion. Charlotte had respect and considerable affection for Aunt Vespasia, but she would not have gone calling with her for purely social reasons. It was a circle in which Charlotte had neither place nor interest.

Concern about Jerome tantalized Pitt's thoughts and made concentration on anything else almost impossible. He performed his other investigations mechanically, so much so that a junior sergeant had to point out to him his oversights, at which Pitt lost his temper, principally because he knew he was at fault, and then had to apologize to the man. To his credit, the man accepted it with grace; he recognized worry when he saw it, and appreciated a senior who could unbend enough to admit fault.

But Pitt knew it for a warning. He must do something more about Jerome or his conscience would intrude further and further until it upset all decent thought and he made some mistake that could not be undone.

Like hanging: that, too, could not be undone. A man

imprisoned wrongfully could be released, could begin to rebuild his life. But a man hanged was gone forever.

It was morning. Pitt was sitting at his desk sorting through a pile of reports. He had looked at every sheet and read the words with his eyes, but not a single fraction of their meaning penetrated his brain.

Gillivray was sitting opposite, waiting, staring.

Pitt picked the reports up again and began again at the beginning. Then he looked up. "Gillivray?"

"Yes, sir?"

"How did you find Abigail Winters?"

"Abigail Winters?" Gillivray frowned.

"That's what I said. How did you find her?"

"Process of elimination, sir," Gillivray replied a little irritably. "I investigated lots of prostitutes. I was prepared to go through them all, if necessary. She was about twenty-fifth, or something like that. Why? I can't see that it matters now."

"Did anyone suggest her to you?"

"Of course they did! How else do you think I find any prostitutes? I don't know them for myself. I got her name from some of the contacts I got the other names from. I didn't get hers from anyone special, if that's what you mean. Look, sir." He leaned forward over the desk. It was a mannerism that Pitt found particularly irritating. It smacked of familiarity, as if they were professional equals. "Look, sir," Gillivray said again. "We've done our job on the Waybourne case. Jerome has been found guilty by the courts. He was tried fairly, on the testimony of witnesses. And even if you don't have any time for Abigail Winters or her kind—or, God knows, Albie Frobisher either—you've got to admit young Titus Swynford and Godfrey Waybourne are honest and decent youths, and had no possible connection with the prostitutes. To suggest they did is just running into the absurd. The prosecution has to prove guilt beyond all reasonable doubt, not beyond all doubt at all! And with respect, Mr.

Pitt, the doubts you are entertaining now are not reasonable. They are farfetched and ridiculous! The only thing lacking was an eyewitness, and nobody commits a clever and premeditated murder in front of witnesses. Hot-blooded killings, yes—out of fear maybe, or temper, or even jealousy. But this was planned and executed with care! Now leave it alone, sir! It's finished. You'll only get yourself into trouble."

Pitt looked at his earnest face above the white collar. He wanted to hate him, and yet he was obliged to admit the advice was fair. If their roles had been reversed, it was just what he would have said. The case was over. It was bending reason to suppose that the truth was other than the obvious. In most crimes there were far more victims than just the immediate person robbed or violated; this time it was Eugenie Jerome—perhaps obscurely even Jerome himself. To expect to be able to tidy up all the injustices was to be childishly simplistic.

"Mr. Pitt?" Gillivray was looking anxious.

"Yes," Pitt said sharply. "Yes, you are quite right. To suppose that all the people, quite independently of each other, were telling the same lie to incriminate Jerome is quite ridiculous. And to imagine they had anything in common is even more so."

"Exactly," Gillivray agreed, relaxing a little. "The two prostitutes might, although it is unlikely they even knew each other—there is nothing to indicate they did. But to suppose they had anything in common with a child like Titus Swynford is twisting reason beyond any sense at all."

Pitt had no argument. He had talked to Titus and he could not imagine him even knowing of the existence of such people as Albie Frosbisher, much less having met him and conspired with him. If Titus needed an ally to defend him, he would have chosen someone of his own class, someone he already knew. And frankly, he found it hard to believe Titus had anything for which he needed defense.

"Right!" he said with more anger than he could account for. "Arson! What have we done about this damn fire?"

Gillivray immediately produced a piece of paper from his inside pocket and began to read a string of answers. They provided no solution, but several possibilities that should be investigated. Pitt assigned two of the most promising to Gillivray, and, without realizing it, chose for himself two more that took him to that area on the edge of Bluegate Fields, within half a mile of the brothel where Abigail Winters had a room.

It was a dark day. The streets dripped with a steady, fine rain; gray houses leaned together like sour old men, brooding with complaint, impotent in senility. There was the familiar smell of staleness, and he imagined he could hear the rising tide of the river in the creaking boards and the slow-moving water.

What kind of a person came here for pleasure? Perhaps a tidy little clerk who sat on a high stool all day, dipping his quill in the ink and copying figures from ledger to ledger, keeping accounts of someone else's money, and went home to a sharp-tongued wife who regarded pleasure as sin and flesh as the tool of the devil.

Pitt had seen dozens of clerks like that, pale-faced, starch-collared, models of rectitude because they dared not be anything else. Economic necessity, together with the need to live by society's rules, was a total taskmaster.

So people like Abigail Winters made a living.

The arson inquiry proved surprisingly fruitful. To be honest, he had expected Gillivray's leads to be the real ones, and it gave him a perverse satisfaction when his own turned up the answer. He took a statement, wrote it carefully, and put it in his pocket. Then, since he was only two streets away and it was still early, he walked to the house where Abigail Winters lived.

The old woman at the door looked at him with surprise.

"My, you're an early one!" she said with a sneer. "Can't yer let them girls get any sleep?"

"I want to talk to Abigail Winters," he replied with a slight smile, hoping it would soften her.

"Talk, eh? That's a new one," she said with heavy disbelief. "Well, it don't matter wot yer do—time's time just the same. Yer pays by the hour." She held out her hand, rubbing her fingers together.

"Why should I pay you?" He made no move.

"'Cause this is my 'ouse," she snapped. "And if yer wants to come in an' see one o' my girls, then yer pays me. Wot's the matter wiv yer—'aven't yer never bin 'ere before?"

"I want to talk to Abigail, nothing more, and I have no intention of paying you for that," he replied sternly. "I'll talk to her in the street, if necessary."

"Oh, will yer then, Mr. Fancy?" she said with a hard edge to her voice. "We'll see abaht that!" And she started to slam the door.

Pitt was very much larger than she was, and stronger. He put his foot next to the frame and leaned on the door.

"'Ere!" she said angrily. "You try ter force yer way in 'ere, an' I've got boys as'll do yer over till yer own muvver won't know yer! Yer no beauty now—but yer'll be a rare sight when they've finished, and that's a promise!"

"Threatening me, are you?" Pitt inquired calmly.

"Now you've got it!" she agreed. "An' I'll do it yer better believe!"

"That's a pretty serious offense—threatening a police officer." He met her sharp old eyes squarely. "I could have you up for that and put in Coldbath Fields for a spell. How would you like that? Fancy picking oakum for a while?"

She paled under the grime on her face.

"Liar!" she spat. "Yer no fuzz!"

"Oh, yes, I am. Investigating a case of arson." That was true, if not the completely so. "Now where's Abigail Winters?—before I get unpleasant, and come back with force!"

"Bastard!" she said. But the venom had gone out of her voice, and there was a certain satisfaction underlying it. Her mouth widened into a stump-toothed smile. "Well, you can't see 'er, Mr. Fuzz—'cause she ain't 'ere! Left here after that there trial. Gorn to see 'er cousin or suffink, up in the country. An' it's no use yer askin' where to, 'cause I dunno, and nor do I care! Could be any place. If'n yer wants 'er that bad, yer'd better go an' look." She gave a dry little laugh. "Course yer can come and search the place—if yer wants?" She pulled the door wider, invitingly. An odor of cabbage and drains hit his nose, but he had smelled it too often before for it to make him sick.

He believed her. And if his persistent, almost silenced suspicions were right after all, it was not unlikely Abigail had gone. All the same, it would be negligent not to make sure.

"Yes," he said. "Yes, I'll come and look." Please God her bullyboys were not inside waiting to beat him in the privacy of this warren of rooms. She might have them do it—just in revenge for the insult. Then, on the other hand, if she believed he was a police officer, such an act would be stupid, even ruinous to her business—a luxury she could most definitely not afford. The very name of Coldbath Fields was enough to sober anyone from the intoxication of revenge.

Pitt followed her inside and along the corridor. The place had a dead look about it, almost unused, like a music hall in daylight when all the tinsel and laughter has gone, and the kindness of concealing shadows.

She opened the rooms for him, one after another. He peered in at the rumpled beds, shabby in the dim light, and girl after girl turned over and stared at him out of blurred eyes, faces still smudged with paint, and swore at him for disturbing them.

"Rozzer come ter take a look atcher," the old woman said maliciously. "'E's lookin' fer Abbie. I tell'd 'im she ain't 'ere, but 'e wants 'er that bad 'e's come ter look fer 'isself. 'E don't believe me!"

He did not bother to argue. He had believed her, but he could not afford to take the one chance in a hundred that she was lying. For his own sake, he had to be sure.

"There now!" she said triumphantly at the end. "Believe me now, do yer? Owes me an apologizement, Mr. Rozzer! She ain't 'ere!"

"Then you'll have to do instead, won't you!" he said acidly, and was pleased to see the start of surprise in her face.

"I dunno nuffink! Yer don't fink no toff comes 'ere and lies wiv me, do yer? Toffs ain't no diff'rent to no one else wiv their trousers orf! They likes 'em all sorts, 'ceptin' old."

Pitt wrinkled his nose at her crudity. "Rubbish!" he said sharply. "You've never seen a real gentleman in your life—and certainly not here!"

"It's wot Abigail said, an' I 'eard 'er," the old woman argued, looking at him closely. "An' said in a court o' law she did, too. I was read it out o' the newspapers. Got a girl 'ere wot can read, I 'ave. She was in service till she lorst 'er character."

An idea materialized in Pitt's mind, suddenly and without warning.

"Did Abigail say it to you before she said it in the court, or afterwards?" he asked quietly.

"Afterwards, the thievin' little cow!" The old woman's face creased with anger and outrage. "Wasn't goin' ter tell me abaht it, she wasn't! Goin' ter keep it all fer 'erself—when I provides 'er room and lodgin' and protection! Ungrateful bitch!"

"You're getting careless." Pitt looked at her with contempt. "Letting a couple of well-heeled gentlemen in here and not collecting your share. And you must have known men dressed like that could pay—and well, too!"

"I never saw them—you fool!" she spat. "Yer fink I'd 'a let 'em walk past me if'n I 'ad, do yer?"

"What's the matter—fall asleep at your post?" Pitt's lip curled. "You're getting too old—you should give it up and let someone with a more careful eye take over. You're probably being robbed every night of the week."

"No one comes through this door wivout I knows it!" she shouted at him. "I got you quick enough, Mr. Rozzer!"

"This time," he agreed. "Any of the other girls see these gentlemen you missed?"

"If they did and didn't tell me, I'll 'ave their thievin' 'ides!"

"You mean you haven't asked them? My, but you *are* losing your hold on the game," he jeered.

"O' course I arst 'em!" she shouted. "An' vey didn't! Nobody takes me for a fool! I'll 'ave my boys beat the skin orf any girl as takes advantage—and they knows it!"

"But still Abigail did." He narrowed his eyes. "Or did you have your boys beat her for it already—maybe a little too hard—and she ended up dead in the river? Maybe we should have a better look for Abigail Winters, do you think?"

Her skin went white under the rime of dirt.

"I never touched the thievin' cow!" she shrieked. "An' neither did me boys! She gave me 'arf the money and I never touched 'er! She went into the country, I swear on me muvver's grave! You'll never prove I 'armed an 'air on 'er 'ead, 'cause I never did—none of us never did."

"How often did these particular toffs come and see Abigail?"

"Once—as I knows of—just once—that's wot she said."

"No, she didn't. She said they were regular customers."

"Then she's a liar! You think I don't know me own 'ouse?"

"Yes—I'm beginning to think so. I'd like to talk to the rest of your girls, especially this one that can read."

"You got no right! They ain't done nuffink!"

"Don't you want to know if Abigail was stealing you blind, and they were helping her?"

"I can find art me own ways—I don't need yer 'elp!"

"Don't you? Seems like you didn't even know about it at all before."

Her face narrowed with suspicion. "Wot's it to you anyway? Why should you care if Abigail cheated me?"

"Nothing at all. But I do care how often those two came here. And I'd like to know if any of your other girls recognize them." He fished in his pocket and brought out a picture of the suspected arsonist. "That him?"

"Dunno," she said, squinting at it. "So wot if it is?"

"Fetch me the girl who can read."

She obeyed, cursing all the way, and brought back a tousle-headed girl, half asleep, still looking like a housemaid in her long white nightshirt. Pitt handed her the picture.

"Is that the man who came to see Abigail, the one who brought the boy she told about in court?"

"You answer 'im, my girl," the old woman warned. "Or I'll 'ave Bert tan yer 'ide fer yer till it bleeds, you 'ear me?"

The girl took the picture and looked at it.

"Well?" Pitt asked.

The girl's face was pale, her fingers shook.

"I don't know—honest. I never saw them. Abbie just told me about it after."

"How long after?"

"I dunno. She never said. After it all came out. I s'pose she wanted to keep the money."

233

"You never saw them?" Pitt was surprised. "Who did, then?"

"No one that I know of. Just Abbie. She kept them to herself." She stared at Pitt, her eyes hollow with fear, although he did not know whether it was him she was afraid of or the old woman and the unseen Bert.

"Thank you," he said quietly, giving her a sad little half smile, all he could afford of pity. To have looked at her closely, thought about her, would have been unbearable. She was only a minuscule part of something he could not change. "Thank you—that was what I wanted to know."

"Well, I'm damned if I can tell why!" the old woman said derisively. "No use—that is!"

"You're probably damned anyway," Pitt replied coldly. "And I'll have the local rozzers keep an eye on your place—so no beating the girls, or we'll shut you down. Understand?"

"I'll beat who the 'ell I want to!" she said, and swore at him, but he knew she would be careful, at least for a while.

Outside in the street, he started back toward the main thoroughfare, and an omnibus that would take him to the station. He did not look for a hansom; he wanted time to think.

Brothels were not private places, and a procuress like the old woman did not allow men to pass in and out without her knowing; she could not afford to. The levy on their passage was her livelihood. If her girls started sneaking in customers and not paying her share of the takings, word would get around and in a month she would be out of business.

So how was it possible that Jerome and Arthur Waybourne had been there and no one had seen them? And would Abigail, with her future to think of, a roof over her head—would she have dared keep a customer secret? Many a girl had been scarred for life for retaining too much of her own earnings. And Abigail had been in the business long enough to know that; she would know of "examples" that had been made of the greedy and the overambitious. She was not stupid; neither was she clever enough to carry off such a fraud, or she would not have been working for that evil old woman.

Which left the question that had been burning at the back of his mind, inching its way forward till it came into sharp, clear focus. Had Jerome and Arthur Waybourne ever been there at all?

The only reason to suppose they had was Abigail's word. Jerome had denied it, Arthur was dead; and no one else had seen them.

But why should she lie? She had appeared out of nowhere; she had nothing to defend. If Jerome had not been there, then she had had to share with the old woman a good portion of money that she had never received.

Unless, of course, she had received it for something else. For what? And from whom?

For the lie, of course. For saying that Jerome and Arthur Waybourne had been there. But who had wanted her to say that?

The answer would be the name of Arthur's murderer. Which Pitt now clearly thought was not Maurice Jerome.

But all this conjecture was still not proof. For even a doubt reasonable enough to reopen the case, he must have the name of someone besides Jerome who might have paid Abigail. And of course he would also have to see Albie Frobisher and look a good deal more closely into his testimony.

In fact, he thought, that would be a good thing to do now.

He walked past the omnibus stop, turned the corner, and hurried down the long, drab street. He hailed a hansom and climbed in, shouting directions.

Albie's rooming house was familiar: the wet matting just past the door, then the bright red beyond, the dim stairs. He knocked on the door, aware that there might be a customer already there. But his sense of urgency would not let him wait to make a more convenient arrangement.

There was no answer.

He knocked again, harder, as if he meant to force it if he were not admitted.

Still there was no reply.

"Albie!" he said sharply. "I'll push this door in if you don't answer!"

Silence. He put his ear to the door and there was no sound of movement inside.

"Albie!" he shouted.

Nothing. Pitt turned and ran down the stairs, along the red-carpeted hallway to the back where the landlord had his quarters. This establishment was different from the brothel where Abigail worked. Here there was no procurer guarding the door. Albie paid a high rent for his room; customers came and went in privacy. But then it was a richer, different class of clientele, far more guarded with their secrets. To visit a woman prostitute was an understandable lapse, a little indiscretion that a man of the world turned a blind eye to. To pay for the services of a boy was not only a deviation too disgusting to be condoned, it was also a crime, opening one to all the nightmares of blackmail.

He knocked sharply on the door.

It opened a crack and a bilious eye looked out at him.

"'Oo are yer? Wot d'yer want?"

"Where's Albie?"

"Why d'yer want ter know? If 'e owes yer, it's nuffin ter do wiv me!"

"I want to talk to him. Now where is he?"

"Wot's it worf?"

"It's worth not being run in for keeping a brothel and aiding and abetting in homosexual acts, which are illegal."

"Yer can't do vat! I rent aht rooms. Wot vey does in 'em ain't my fault!"

"Want to prove that to a jury?"

"You can't arrest me!"

"I can and I will. You might get off, but you'll have a rough time in jail till you do. People don't like procurers, especially ones who procure little boys! Now where's Albie?"

"I dunno! Honest to God, I dunno! 'E don't tell me where 'e comes an' goes!"

"When did you see him last? What time does he usually come back—and don't tell me you don't know."

"Abaht six—'e's always back by abaht six. But I ain't seen 'im for a couple o' days. 'E weren't 'ere last night, and I dunno where 'e went. As God's me judge! An' I carn't tell yer more'n vat if yer was to send me ter Horstralia fer it!"

"We don't send people to Australia anymore—haven't done for years," Pitt said absently. He believed the man. There would be no point in his lying, and he had everything to lose if Pitt chose to harass him.

"Well, Coldbath Fields then!" the man said angrily. "It's the truth. I dunno where 'e's gorn! Nor if'n 'e'll be back. I bloody 'ope so—'e owes me this week's rent, 'e does!" Suddenly he was aggrieved.

"I expect he'll be back," Pitt said with a curious sense of misery. Probably Albie would come back. After all, why shouldn't he? As he had said himself, he had good rooms here and an established clientele. The only other possibility was if he had found some single customer who had developed into a lover, possessive, demanding—and wealthy enough to set him up somewhere for his own exclusive patronage. Such windfalls as that were pipe dreams for boys like Albie.

"So 'e'll be back!" the landlord said testily. "You plannin' to stand there in the passageway like a devil's 'ead till 'e does, then? You'll scare orf all me—visitors! It ain't good fer a place to 'ave the likes o' you standin' there! Gives a place a bad name. Makes people fink vere's suffink wrong wiv us!"

Pitt sighed. "Of course not. But I'll be back. And if you've done anything to send Albie away, or any harm has come to him, I'll have you down to Coldbath Fields quicker than your rotten little feet'll touch the ground!"

"Fancy 'im, then, do yer?" The old man's face split in a dirty grin, and he seized the chance to kick Pitt's foot out of the doorway and slam the door shut.

There was nothing else to do but go back to the police station. Pitt was already late, and he had no business being here.

Gillivray was jubilant about the arsonist, and it was a quarter of an hour before he bothered to ask Pitt what had taken him so long.

Pitt did not want to reply directly with the truth.

"What else do you know about Albie Frobisher?" he asked instead.

"What?" Gillivray frowned as though momentarily the name made no sense to him.

"Albie Frobisher," Pitt repeated. "What else do you know about him?"

"Else than what?" Gillivray said irritably. "He's a male prostitute, that's all. What else is there? Why should we care? We can't arrest all the homosexuals in the city or we'd do nothing else. Anyway, you'd have to prove it, and how could you do that without dragging in their customers?"

"And what's wrong with dragging in their customers?" Pitt asked bluntly. "They are at least as guilty, maybe more so. They're not doing it to live."

"Are you saying prostitution is all right, Mr. Pitt?" Gillivray was shocked.

Usually hypocrisy enraged Pitt. This time, because it

238

was so totally unconscious, it overwhelmed him with hopelessness.

"Of course I'm not," he said wearily. "But I can understand how it has come about, at least for many people. Are you condoning those who use prostitutes, even boys?"

"No!" Gillivray was affronted; the idea was appalling. Then the natural corollary of his own previous statement occurred to him. "Well—I mean—"

"Yes?" Pitt asked patiently.

"It's impractical," Gillivray blushed as he said it. "The men who use people like Albie Frobisher have money— they're probably gentlemen. We can't go around arresting men of that sort for something obscene like perversion! Think what would happen."

There was no need for Pitt to comment; he knew the expression on his face spoke for him.

"Lots of men have all sorts of—of perverted tastes." Gillivray's cheeks were scarlet now. "We can't go meddling into everyone's affairs. What's done privately, as long as no one is forced, is—" He took a breath and let it out heavily. "Well, it's best left alone! We should concern ourselves with crimes, with frauds, robberies, attacks, and things like that—where someone's been offended. What a gentleman chooses to do in his bedroom is his own business, and if it's against the law of God—like adultery— still best leave it to God to punish!"

Pitt smiled and looked at the window and the rain running down it, and at the gloomy street beyond.

"Unless, of course, it's Jerome!"

"Jerome wasn't prosecuted for unnatural practices," Gillivray said quickly. "He was charged with murder!"

"Are you saying that if he hadn't killed Arthur, you would have turned a blind eye to the other?" Pitt asked incredulously. Then suddenly, almost like an afterthought, he realized that Gillivray had said Jerome was charged with murder, not that he was guilty of it. Was that merely a clumsy choice of words, or an unintentional sign of some thread of doubt that ran through his mind?

"If he hadn't killed him, I don't suppose anyone would have known!" Gillivray had the perfect, reasoned answer ready.

Pitt gave no argument; that was almost certainly true. And of course if there had been no murder, Anstey Waybourne would certainly not have prosecuted. What man in his right mind exposes his son to such a scandal? He would simply have discharged Jerome without a character reference, and let that be vengeance enough. Hint, innuendo that Jerome's morals were unsatisfactory, without any specific charge, would have ruined his career, and Arthur's name would never have entered into it.

"Anyway," Gillivray continued, "it's all over now and you'll only cause a lot of unnecessary trouble if you keep on about it. I don't know anything else about Albie Frobisher, and I don't choose to. Neither will you, if you know what's good for you—with respect, sir!"

"Do you believe Jerome killed Arthur Waybourne?" Pitt said suddenly, surprising even himself with such a naïvely blunt question.

Gillivray's blue eyes were hot, curiously glazed with some discomfort inside him.

"I'm not the jury, Mr. Pitt, and it's not my job to decide a man's guilt or his innocence. I don't know. All things considered, it seems like it. And, more important, the law of the land says so, and I accept that."

"I see." There was nothing else to say. He let the subject die, and turned back to the arson.

Twice more, Pitt managed to find himself in Bluegate Fields, in the neighborhood of Albie Frobisher's rooming house, but Albie had still not returned. When he called the third time, a boy even younger than Albie, with cynical, curious eyes, opened the door and invited him in. The room had been re-let. Albie was already replaced as if he had never existed. After all, why allow perfectly good premises stand idle when they could be made to earn?

He made discreet inquiries at one or two other stations in similar areas—Seven Dials, Whitechapel, Mile End, St. Giles, the Devil's Acre—but no one had heard of Albie moving in. That in itself did not mean a lot. There were thousands of beggars, prostitutes, petty thieves drifting from one area to another. Most of them died young, but in the sea of humanity they were no more missed than one wave in an ocean, and no more distinguishable. One knew occasional names or faces, because their owners gave information, provided steady leaks from the under-world that made most police detection possible, but the vast majority stayed brief and anonymous.

But Albie, like Abigail Winters, had disappeared.

The next day, with no plan in his head, Pitt went back to Newgate Prison to see Maurice Jerome. As soon as he stepped through the gates, he was met by the familiar smell; it was as if he had been gone only a few moments since last time. Only a few moments since the vast, dripping walls had enclosed him.

Jerome was sitting on the straw mattress in exactly the same position he'd been in when Pitt had left him. He was still shaven, but his face was grayer, his bones more visible through the skin, his nose more pinched. His shirt collar was still stiff and clean. That would be Eugenie!

Suddenly, Pitt found his stomach heave at the whole slow, obscene affair. He had to swallow and breathe deeply to prevent himself from being sick.

The turnkey slammed the door behind him. Jerome turned to look. Pitt was jarred by the intelligence in the man's eyes; he had lately been thinking of him merely as an object, a victim. Jerome was as intelligent as Pitt himself, and immeasurably more so than his jailers. He knew what was going to happen; he was not some trapped animal, but a man with imagination and reason. He would probably die a hundred times before that final dawn. He would feel the rope, experience the pain in some form or other, every moment he could not concentrate enough to drive it out of his mind.

Was there hope in his face?

How incredibly stupid of Pitt to have come! How sadistic! Their eyes met and the hope vanished.

"What do you want?" Jerome said coldly.

Pitt did not know what he wanted. He had come only because time was short, and if he did not come soon, he could not come at all. Perhaps there was still a thought somewhere in his mind that Jerome would even now say something that would give him a new line to follow. To say so, to imply that there was any chance at all, would be a refinement of torture that was unforgivable.

"What do you want?" Jerome repeated. "If you are hoping for a confession to ease your sleep, you are wasting your time. I did not kill Arthur Waybourne, nor did I have, or desire"—his nostrils widened with disgust—"any physical relationship with him, or either of the other boys."

Pitt sat down on the straw.

"I don't suppose you went to Abigail Winters either, or Albie Frobisher?" he asked.

Jerome looked at him suspiciously, expecting sarcasm. It was not there.

"No."

"Do you know why they lied?"

"No." His face twisted. "You believe me? Hardly makes any difference now, does it." It was a statement, not a question. There was no lift in him, no lightness. Life had conspired against him, and he did not expect it to change now.

His self-pity provoked Pitt.

"No," he said shortly. "It makes no difference. And I don't know that I do believe you. But I went back to talk to the girl again. She's disappeared. Then I went to look for Albie, and he's disappeared too."

"Doesn't make any difference," Jerome replied, staring at the wet stones on the far side of the cell. "As long as those two boys keep up the lie that I tried to interfere with them."

"Why are they doing it?" Pitt asked frankly. "Why should they lie?"

"Spite—what else?" Jerome's voice was heavy with scorn; scorn for the boys because they had stooped to dishonesty from personal emotion, and for Pitt for his stupidity.

"Why?" Pitt persisted. "Why did they hate you enough to say something like that if it's not true? What did you do to them to cause such hatred?"

"I tried to make them learn! I tried to teach them self-discipline, standards!"

"What's hateful about that? Wouldn't their fathers do the same thing? Their entire world is governed by standards," Pitt reasoned. "Self-discipline so rigid they'd endure physical pain rather than be seen to lose face. When I was a boy, I watched men of that class hide agony rather than admit they were hurt and be seen to drop out of a hunt. I remember a man who was terrified of horses, but would mount with a smile and ride all day, then come home and be sick all night with sheer relief that he was still alive. And he did it every year, rather than admit he hated it and let down his standards of what a gentleman should be."

Jerome sat in silence. It was the sort of idiotic courage he admired, and it galled him to see it in the class that had excluded him. His only defense against rejection was hatred.

The question remained unanswered. He did not know why the boys should lie, and neither did Pitt. The trouble was Pitt did not believe they were lying, and yet when he was with Jerome he honestly did not believe Jerome was lying either. The thing was ridiculous!

Pitt sat for another ten minutes in near silence, then shouted for the turnkey and took his leave. There was nothing else to say; pleasantries were an insult. There was no future, and it would be cruel to pretend there was. Whatever the truth, Pitt owed Jerome at least that decency.

Athelstan was waiting for him at the police station the following morning. There was a constable standing by Pitt's desk with orders that he report upstairs instantly.

"Yes, sir?" Pitt inquired as soon as Athelstan's voice shouted at him to come in.

Athelstan was sitting behind his desk. He had not even lit a cigar and his face was mottled with the rage he had been obliged to suppress until Pitt arrived.

"Who the hell told you you could go on visiting Jerome?" he demanded, rising from his chair to half straighten his legs and give himself more height.

Pitt felt his back stiffen and the muscles grow tight across his scalp.

"Didn't know I needed permission," he said coldly. "Never have done before."

"Don't be impertinent with me, Pitt!" Athelstan stood straight up and leaned across the desk. "The case is closed! I told you that ten days ago, when the jury had brought in their verdict. It's none of your business, and I ordered you to leave it alone then! Now I hear you've been poking around behind my back—trying to see witnesses! What in hell do you think you're doing?"

"I haven't spoken to any witnesses," Pitt said truthfully, although it was not for the want of trying. "I can't—they've disappeared!"

"Disappeared? What do you mean 'disappeared'? People of that sort are always coming and going—jetsam, scum of society, always drifting from one place to another. Lucky we caught them when we did, or maybe we wouldn't have got their testimony. Don't talk rubbish, man. They haven't disappeared like a decent citizen might. They've just gone from one whorehouse to another. Means nothing—nothing at all. Do you hear me?"

Since he was shouting at the top of his voice, the question was redundant.

"Of course I can hear you, sir," Pitt answered, stone-faced.

Athelstan flushed crimson with anger.

"Stand still when I'm talking to you! Now I hear you've been to see Jerome—not only once, but twice! What for, that's what I should like to know—what for? We don't need a confession now. The man's been proved guilty. Jury of his peers—that's the law of the land." He swung his arms around, crossing them in front of him in a scissor-like motion. "The thing is finished. The Metropolitan Police Force pays you to catch criminals, Pitt, and, if you can, to prevent crime in the first place. It does not pay you to defend them, or to try and discredit the law courts and their verdicts! Now if you can't do that job properly, as you're told, then you'd better leave the force and find something you can do. Do you understand me?"

"No, sir, I don't!" Pitt stood stiff as a ramrod. "Are you telling me that I'm to do only exactly what I'm told, without following my own intelligence or my own suspicions—or else I'll be dismissed?"

"Don't be so damn stupid!" Athelstan slammed the desk with his hand. "Of course I'm not! You're a detective—but not on any damn case you like! I am telling you, Pitt, that if you don't leave the Jerome business alone, I'll put you back to walking the beat as a constable—and I can do it, I promise you."

"Why?" Pitt faced him, demanding an explanation, trying to back him into saying something indefensible. "I haven't seen any witnesses. I haven't been near the Waybournes or the Swynfords. But why shouldn't I talk to

Abigail Winters or Albie Frobisher, or visit Jerome? What do you think anyone is going to say that can matter now? What can they change? Who's going to say something different?"

"Nobody! Nobody at all! But you're stirring up a lot of ill-feeling. You're making people doubt, making them think there's something being hidden, something nasty and dirty, still secret. And that amounts to slander!"

"Like what, for instance—what is there still to find out?"

"I don't know! Dear God—how should I know what's in your twisted mind? You're obsessed! But I'm telling you, Pitt, I'll break you if you take one more step in this case. It's closed. We've got the man who is guilty. The courts have tried him and sentenced him. You have no right to question their decision or cast doubts on it! You are undermining the law, and I won't have it!"

"I'm not undermining the law!" Pitt said derisively. "I'm trying to make sure we've got all the evidence, to make sure we don't make mistakes—"

"We haven't made any mistakes!" Athelstan's face was purple and there was a muscle jumping in his jowl. "We found the evidence, the courts decide, and it's not part of your job to sit in judgment. Now get out and find this arsonist, and take care of whatever else there is on your desk. If I have to call you back up here over Maurice Jerome, or anything to do with that case, anything whatsoever, I'll see you back as a constable. Right now, Pitt!" He flung out his arm and pointed at the door. "Out!"

There was no point in arguing. "Yes, sir," Pitt said wearily. "I'm going."

Before the end of the week, Pitt knew why he had not been able to find Albie. The news came as a courtesy from the Deptford police station. It was just a simple message that a body that had been pulled out of the river

246

might be Albie, and if it was of any interest to Pitt, he was welcome to come and look at it.

He went. After all, Albie Frobisher was involved in one of his cases, or had been. That he had been pulled out of the water at Deptford did not mean that that was where he had gone in—far more likely Bluegate Fields, where Pitt had last seen him.

He did not tell anyone where he was going. He said simply that the Deptford station had sent a message for him, a possible identification of a corpse. That was reasonable enough, and happened all the time, men from one station assisting another.

It was one of those hard, glittering days when the east wind comes off the Channel like a whip, lashing the skin, stinging the eyes. Pitt pulled his collar higher, his muffler tighter around his throat, then jammed his hat down so the wind did not catch it under the brim and snatch it off.

The cab ran smartly along the streets, horse's hooves ringing on the ice-cold stones, the cabby bundled so high in clothes he could barely see. When they stopped at the Deptford police station, Pitt got out, already stiff with cold from sitting still. He paid the cabbie and dismissed him. He might be a long time; he wanted to know far more than the identity—if this was indeed Albie.

Inside there was a potbellied stove burning, with a kettle on it, and a uniformed constable sat near the stove with a mug of tea in his hand. He recognized Pitt and stood up.

"Morning, Mr. Pitt, sir. You come to look at that corpse we got? Like a cup o' tea first? Not a nice sight, and a wicked cold day, sir."

"No, thanks—see it first, then I'd like one. Talk about it a bit—if it's the bloke I know."

"Poor little beggar." The constable shook his head. "Still, maybe 'e's best out of it. Lived longer than some of 'em. We've still got 'im 'ere, out the back. No hurry for the morgue on a day like this." He shivered. "Reckon as we could keep 'em froze right 'ere for a week!"

Pitt was inclined to agree. He nodded at the constable and shuddered in sympathy.

"Fancy keeping a morgue, do you?"

"Well, they'd 'ave to be less trouble 'n the live ones." The constable was a philosopher. "And don't need no feedin'!" He led the way through a narrow corridor whistling with drafts, down some stone steps, and up into a bare room where a sheet covered a lumpy outline on a wooden table.

"There you are, sir. 'E the one wot you knows?"

Pitt pulled the sheet off the head and looked down. The river had made its mark. There was mud and a little slimy weed on the hair, the skin was smudged, but it was Albie Frobisher.

He looked farther down, at the neck. There was no need to ask how he had died; there were finger marks, bruised and dark, on the flesh. He had probably been dead before he hit the water. Pitt moved the sheet off the rest of him, automatically. He would be careless to overlook anything else, if there was anything.

The body was even thinner than he had expected, younger than it had seemed with clothes on. The bones were so slight and the skin still had the blemishless, translucent quality of childhood. Perhaps that had been part of his stock in trade, his success.

"Is that 'im?" the constable said from just behind him.

"Yes." Pitt put the sheet back over him. "Yes, that's Albie Frobisher. Do you know anything about it?"

"Not much to know," the constable said grimly. "We get 'em out of the river every week, sometimes every day in the winter. Some of 'em we recognize, a lot we never know. You finished 'ere?"

"Yes, thank you."

"Then come back and 'ave that cup o' tea. He led the

way back to the potbellied stove and the kettle. They both sat down with steaming mugs.

"He was strangled," Pitt said unnecessarily. "You'll be treating it as murder?"

"Oh, yes." The constable pulled a face. "Not that I suppose it'll make much difference. "'Oo knows 'oo killed the poor little beggar? Could 'ave bin anyone, couldn't it? 'Oo was 'e anyway?"

"Albert Frobisher," Pitt replied, aware of the irony of such a name. "At least that's how we knew him. He was a male prostitute."

"Oh—the one wot gave evidence in the Waybourne case—poor little swine. Didn't last long, did 'e? Killed to do with that, was 'e?"

"I don't know."

"Well—" The constable finished the last of his tea and set the mug down. "Could 'ave bin, couldn't it? Then again, in that sort o' trade you can get killed for lots o' different reasons. All comes to the same in the end, don't it? Want 'im, I suppose? Shall I send 'im up to your station?"

"Yes, please." Pitt stood up. "We'd better tidy it up. It may have nothing to do with the Waybourne case, but he comes from Bluegate Fields anyway. Thanks for the tea." He handed the mug back.

"Welcome, sir, I'm sure. I'll send 'im along as soon as my sergeant gives the word. It'll be this afternoon, though. No point in 'anging around."

"Thank you. Good day, Constable."

"'Day, sir."

Pitt walked toward the shining stretch of the river. It was slack tide, and the black slime of the embankment smelled acrid. The wind rippled the surface and caught tiny white shreds of spray up against slow-moving barges. They were going up the river to the Pool of London and the docks. Pitt wondered where they had come from, those shrouded cargoes. Could be anywhere on earth: the deserts of Africa, the wastes north of Hudson Bay where it was winter six months long, the jungles of India, or the reefs of the Caribbean. And that was without even going outside the Empire. He remembered seeing the map of the world, with British possessions all in red—seemed to be every second country. They said the sun never set on the Empire.

And this city was the heart of it all. London was where your Queen lived, whether you were in the Sudan or the Cape of Good Hope, Tasmania, Barbados, the Yukon, or Katmandu.

Did a boy like Albie ever know that he lived in the heart of such a world? Did the inhabitants of those teeming, rotten slums behind the proud streets ever conceive in their wildest drunken or opium-scented dreams of the wealth they were part of? All that immense might—and they wouldn't, or couldn't, even begin on the disease at home.

The barges were gone, the water shining silver in their wake, the flat light brilliant as the sun moved slowly westward. Some hours hence, the sky would redden, giving the pall-like clouds of the factories and docks the illusion of beauty before sunset.

Pitt straightened up and started to walk. He must find a cab and get back to the station. Athelstan would have to allow him to investigate now. This was a new murder. It might have nothing to do with Jerome or Arthur Waybourne, but it was still a murder. And murder must be solved, if it can be.

"No!" Athelstan shouted, rising to his feet. "Good God, Pitt! The boy was a prostitute! He catered to perverts! He was bound to end up either dead of some disease or murdered by a customer or a pimp or something. If we spent time on every dead prostitute, we'd need a force twice the size, and we'd still do nothing else. Do you know how many deaths there are in London every day?"

"No, sir. Do they stop mattering once they get past a certain number?"

Athelstan slammed his hand on the desk, sending papers flying.

"God dammit, Pitt, I'll have your rank for insubordination! Of course it matters! If there was any chance, or any reason, I'd investigate it right to the end. But murder of a prostitute is not uncommon. If you take up a trade like that, then you expect violence—and disease—and sooner or later you'll get it!

"I'm not sending my men out to comb the streets uselessly. We'll never find out who killed Albie Frobisher. It could have been any one of a thousand people—ten thousand! Who knows who went into that house? Anyone! Anyone at all. Nobody sees them—that's the nature of the place—and you bloody well know that as well as I do. I'm not wasting an inspector's time, yours or anyone else's, chasing after a hopeless case.

"Now get out of here and find that arsonist! You know who he is—so arrest him before we have another fire! And if I hear you mention Maurice Jerome, the Waybournes, or anything else to do with it again, I'll put you back on the beat—and that I swear—so help me, God!"

Pitt said nothing more. He turned on his heel and walked out, leaving Athelstan still standing, his face crimson, his fists clenched on the desk.

❧ 10 ❧

Charlotte was stunned when Pitt told her that Albie was dead; it was something she had not even considered, in spite of the terrifying number of deaths she had heard of among such people. Somehow it had not occurred to her that Albie, whose face and even something of his feelings she knew, would die within the space of her brief acquaintance with his life.

"How?" she demanded furiously, caught by surprise as well as pain. "What happened to him?"

Pitt looked tired; there were fine lines of strain on his face that she knew were not usually pronounced enough to see. He sat down heavily, close to the kitchen fire as though he had no warmth within.

She controlled the words that flew to her lips, and forced herself to wait. There was a wound inside him. She knew it as she did when Jemima cried, wordlessly clinging to her, trusting her to understand what was beyond explaining.

"He was murdered," he said at last. "Strangled, and then put in the river." His face twisted. "Irony in that, of a sort. All that water, dirty river water, not like Arthur Waybourne's nice clean bath. They pulled him out at Deptford."

There was no point in making it worse. She pulled herself together and concentrated on the practical. After all, she consciously reminded herself, people like Albie died all over London all the time. The only difference with Albie was that they had perceived him as an individual; they knew he understood what he was as clearly as they did—surely even more so—and shared some of their disgust.

"Are they going to let you investigate?" she asked. She was pleased with herself; her voice showed none of the struggle inside her, of her image of the wet body. "Or do the Deptford police want it? There is a station at Deptford, isn't there?"

Tired enough to sleep even crumpled where he sat, he looked up at her. But if she dropped the spoon she held, turned, and took him in her arms, she knew it would only make it worse. She would be treating it like a tragedy, and him like a child, instead of a man. She continued stirring the soup she was making.

"Yes, there is," he replied, unaware of her crowding thoughts. "And no, they don't want it—they'll send it to us. He lived in Bluegate Fields, and he was part of one of our cases. And no, we're not going to investigate it. Athelstan says that if you are a prostitute, then murder is to be expected, and hardly to be remarked on. Certainly it is not worth police time to look into. It would be wasted. Customers kill people like that, or procurers do, or they die of disease. It happens every day. And God help us, he's right."

She absorbed the news in silence. Abigail Winters had gone, and now Albie was murdered. Very soon, if they did not manage to find something new and radical enough to justify an appeal, Jerome would hang.

And Athelstan had closed the murder of Albie as isoluble—and irrelevant.

"Do you want some soup?" she asked without looking at him.

"What?"

"Do you want some soup? It's hot."

He glanced down at his hands. He had not even realized how cold he was. She noticed the gesture and turned back to the stove to ladle out a bowlful without waiting. She handed it to him and he took it in silence.

"What are you going to do?" she asked, dishing out her own soup and sitting down opposite him. She was afraid—afraid he would defy Athelstan and go ahead with an inquiry on his own, and perhaps be demoted, or even dismissed. They would have no money coming in. She had never been poor in her life, not really poor. After Cater Street and her parents' home, this was almost poverty—or so it had seemed the first year. Now she was used to it, and only thought about it as different when she visited Emily, and had to borrow clothes to go calling in. She had no idea what they would do if Pitt were to lose his job.

But she was equally afraid that he would not fight Athelstan, that he would accept Albie's death and disregard his own conscience because of her and the children, knowing their security depended on him. And Jerome would hang, and Eugenie would be alone. They would never know whether he had killed Arthur Waybourne, or if he had been telling the truth all the time and the murderer was someone else, someone still alive and still abusing young boys.

And that too would lie between them like a cold ghost, a deceit, because they had been afraid to risk the price of uncovering the truth. Would he hold back from doing what he believed right because he would not ask her to pay the price—and ever afterward feel in his heart that she had robbed him of integrity?

She kept her head down as she ate the soup so he could not read her thoughts in her eyes and base any judgment on them. She would be no part of this; he must do it alone.

The soup was too hot; she put it aside and went back to the stove. Absentmindedly she stirred the potatoes and salted them for the third time.

"Damn!" she said under her breath, and poured the water off quickly down the sink, filled up the pan again, and replaced it on the stove. Fortunately, she thought he was too preoccupied to ask her what on earth she was doing.

"I'll tell Deptford they can keep him," he said at last. "I'll say we don't need him after all. But I'll also tell them all I know about him, and hope they treat it as murder. After all, he lived in Bluegate Fields, but there's nothing to say he was killed there. He could still have been in Deptford. What on earth are you doing with the potatoes, Charlotte?"

"I'm boiling them!" she said tartly, keeping her back to him to hide the rush of warmth inside her, the pride— probably stupid. He was not going to let it go, and thank heaven, he was not going to defy Athelstan, at least not openly. "What did you think I was doing?"

"Well, what did you pour all the water off for?" he asked.

She swung around and held out the oven cloth and the pan lid.

"Do you want to do it, then?" she demanded.

He smiled slowly and slid farther down in the chair.

"No, thank you—I couldn't—I've no idea what you're making!"

She threw the cloth at him.

But she was a good deal less light about it when she faced Emily across the porcelain-spread breakfast table the following morning.

"Murdered!" she said sharply, taking the strawberry preserve from Emily's hand. "Strangled and then put in the river. He could have gone all the way out to sea and nobody would ever have found him."

255

Emily took the preserve back.

"You won't like that—it's too sweet for you. Have some marmalade. What are you going to do about it?"

"You haven't been listening!" Charlotte exploded, snatching the marmalade. "There isn't anything we can do! Athelstan says prostitutes are murdered all the time, and it just has to be accepted! He says it as if it were a cold in the head or something."

Emily looked at her closely, her face sharp with interest.

"You're really angry about it, aren't you?" she observed.

Charlotte was ready to hit her; all the frustration and pity and hopelessness boiled up inside her. But the table was too wide to reach her, and she had the marmalade in her hand. She had to be content with a blistering look.

Emily was quite unscathed. She bit into her toast and spoke with her mouth full.

"We shall have to find out as much about it as we can," she said in a businesslike manner.

"I beg your pardon?" Charlotte was icy. She wanted to sting Emily into hurting as much as she did herself. "If you would care to swallow your food before attempting to speak, I might know what it is you are saying."

Emily looked at her impatiently.

"The facts!" she enunciated clearly. "We must find out all the facts—then we can present them to the right people."

"What right people? The police don't care who killed Albie! He is only one prostitute more or less, and what does that matter? And anyway we can't get the facts. Even Thomas can't get them. Use your head, Emily. Bluegate Fields is a slum, there are hundreds of thousands of slum people, and none of them will tell the police the truth about anything unless they have to."

"Not who killed Albie, stupid!" Emily was beginning to lose patience. "But how he died. That's what matters!

How old he was, what happened to him. He was strangled, you said, and dropped into the river like rubbish, then washed up at Deptford? And the police aren't the people who matter, you told me that yourself." She leaned forward eagerly, toast in the air. "But how about Callantha Swynford? How about Lady Waybourne? Don't you see? If we can make them envision all that in their minds' eye, all the obscenity and pathos, then we may draw them into our battle. Albie dead may be no use to Thomas, but he's excellently useful to us. If you want to appeal to people's emotions, the story of one person is far more effective than a catalogue of numbers. A thousand people suffering is much too hard to think of, but one is very easy."

At last Charlotte understood. Of course Emily was right; she had been stupid, allowing herself to wallow in emotion. She should have thought of it herself. She had allowed her feelings to blot out sense, and that was the ultimate uselessness. She must not let it happen again!

"I'm sorry," she said sincerely. "You are quite right. That is definitely the right thing to do. I shall have to find out the details from Thomas. He didn't really tell me a lot yesterday. I suppose he thought it would upset me."

Emily looked at her through her eyelashes. "I can't imagine why," she said sarcastically.

Charlotte ignored the remark, and stood up. "Well, what are we going to do today? What is Aunt Vespasia planning to do?" she said, tweaking her skirt to make it fall properly.

Emily stood up, too, patted her lips with her napkin, and replaced it on the plate. She reached for the bell to summon the maid.

"We are going to visit Mr. Carlisle, whom I find I like— you didn't tell me how nice he was! From him I hope we shall learn some more facts—about rates of pay in sweatshops and things—so we know why young women cannot live on them and so take to the streets. Did you know that

257

people who make matches get a disease that rots away their bones till half their faces are destroyed?"

"Yes, I did. Thomas told me about it a long time ago. What about Aunt Vespasia?"

"She is taking luncheon with an old friend, the Duchess of somewhere or other, but someone everybody listens to—I don't think they dare ignore her! Apparently, she knows absolutely everyone, even the Queen, and hardly anybody knows the Queen these days, since Prince Albert died."

The maid came in, and Emily told her to order the carriage to be ready in half an hour; then she was to clear the table. No one would be home until late afternoon.

"We shall take luncheon at Deptford," Emily said, answering Charlotte's look of surprise. "Or else we shall go without." She surveyed Charlotte's figure with a mixture of envy and distaste. "A little self-denial will not harm us in the least. And we shall inquire of the Deptford policemen as to the state of the body of Albie Frobisher. Perhaps we may even be permitted to see it."

"Emily! You can't! Whatever reason could we give for such a bizarre thing? Ladies do not go to view the corpses of prostitutes pulled out of the river! They wouldn't allow us."

"You will tell them who you are," Emily replied, crossing the hall and beginning up the stairs so they could prepare their appearance for the day. "And I shall tell them who I am, and what my purpose is. I am collecting information on social conditions because it is desired that there should be reform."

"Is it?" Charlotte was not put off; it was merely a remark. "I thought it wasn't. That is why we must excite people's sympathy—and anger."

"It is desired by me," Emily replied with literal truth. "That is sufficient for a policeman in Deptford!"

Somerset Carlisle received them without surprise. Apparently, Emily had had the forethought to warn him of their coming, and he was at home with the fire piled high and hot chocolate prepared. The study was littered with papers, and in the best chair a long, lean black cat with topaz eyes lay stretched, blinking unconcernedly. It seemed to have no intention of moving even when Emily nearly sat on it. It simply allowed her to push it to one side, then rearranged itself across her knee. Carlisle was so accustomed to the creature he did not even notice.

Charlotte sat in the chair near the fire, determined that Emily should not dictate this conversation.

"Albie Frobisher has been murdered," she said before Emily had time to approach the subject with any delicacy. "He was strangled and put in the river. Now we shall never be able to question him again to see if he changes his testimony at all. But Emily has pointed out"—she must be fair, or she would make a fool of herself—"that his death will be an excellent tool to engage the sympathy of the people whose influence we wish for."

Carlisle's face showed his disgust at the event, and an unusually personal anger.

"Not much use to Jerome!" he said harshly. "Unfortunately, people like Albie are murdered for too many reasons, and most of them perfectly obvious, to assume it related to any particular incident."

"The girl prostitute has gone, too," Charlotte continued. "Abigail Winters. She's disappeared, so we can't ask her either. But Thomas did say that he thinks neither Jerome nor Arthur Waybourne ever went there, to her rooms, because there is an old woman at the door who watches everyone like a rat, and she makes them all pay her to pass. She never saw them, and neither did any of the other girls."

Emily's mouth curled in revulsion as her imagination conjured up the place for her. She put out her hand and stroked the black cat.

"There would be a procuress," Carlisle said, "and no

doubt a few strong men around to deal with anyone who caused trouble. It's all part of the mutual arrangement. It would be a very sly girl indeed who managed to smuggle in private customers—and a brave one. Or else a fool!"

"We need more facts." Emily would not allow herself to be excluded from the conversation any longer. "Can you tell us how a girl who begins as respectable ends up on the streets in places like these? If we are to move people, we must tell them about the ones they can feel sorry for, not just the ones born in Bluegate Field and St. Giles, whom they imagine never desire anything else."

"Of course." He turned to his desk and shuffled through piles of papers and loose sheets, coming up at last with the ones he wanted. "These are rates of pay in match factories and furniture shops, and pictures of necrosis of the jaw caused by handling phosphorus. Here are the piecework rates for stitching shirts and ragpicking. These are conditions for entry into a workhouse, and what they are like inside. And this is the poor law with regard to children. Don't forget a lot of women who are on the streets are there because they have children to support, and not necessarily illegitimate by any means. Some are widows, and the husbands of some have just left, either for another woman or simply because they couldn't stand the responsibility."

Emily took the papers and Charlotte moved beside her to read over her shoulder. The black cat stretched luxuriously, kneading its claws in the arm of the chair, pulling the threads, then curled up in a ball again and went back to sleep with a small sigh.

"May we keep these?" Emily asked. "I want to learn them by heart.

"Of course," he said. He poured the chocolate and passed it to them, his wry face showing he was not unaware of the irony of the situation: sitting by the blazing fire in this infinitely comfortable room, with its superb

Dutch scene on the wall and hot chocolate in their hands, while they talked about horrendous squalor.

As if reading Charlotte's thoughts, Carlisle turned to her.

"You must use your chance to convince as many other people as possible. The only way we'll change anything is to alter the social climate till child prostitution becomes so abhorred that it withers of itself. Of course we'll never get rid of it altogether, any more than any other vice, but we might reduce it massively."

"We will!" Emily said with a deeper anger than Charlotte had heard in her before. "I'll see that every society woman in London is so sickened by it she'll make it impossible for any man with ambition to practice it. We may not have a vote or pass any laws in Parliament, but we can certainly make the laws of society and freeze to death anyone who wants to flout them for long, I promise you!"

Carlisle smiled. "I'm sure," he said. "I never underestimated the power of public disapproval, informed or uninformed."

Emily stood up, carefully depositing the cat in the round hollow she had left. It barely stirred to rearrange itself.

"I intend to inform the public." She folded the papers and slipped them into her embroidered reticule. "Now we shall go to Deptford and look at this corpse. Are you ready, Charlotte? Thank you so much, Mr. Carlisle."

The Deptford police station was not easy to find. Quite naturally, neither Emily's footman nor her coachman was acquainted with the area, and it took several wrong turnings on seemingly identical corners before they drew up in front of the entrance.

Inside was the potbellied stove, and the same constable sat at the desk writing up a report, an enamel mug of tea steaming at his elbow. He looked startled when he saw Emily in her green morning dress and feathered hat, and although he knew Pitt, he did not know Charlotte. For a moment he was at a loss for words.

"Good morning, Constable," Emily said cheerfully.

He snapped to attention, slid off his seat, and stood up. That at least had to be correct; one did not sit on one's behind to speak with ladies of quality.

"Good morning, ma'am." His eye took in Charlotte. "Ma'am. Are you lost, ladies? Can I 'elp you?"

"No, thank you, we are not lost," Emily replied briskly, with a smile so dazzling the constable was completely disconcerted again. "I am Lady Ashworth, and this is my sister Mrs. Pitt. I believe you know Inspector Pitt? Good, of course you do. Perhaps you did not know there is a great desire for reform at the moment, especially with regard to the abuse of children in the trade of prostitution."

The constable blanched at a lady using so vulgar a term, and was embarrassed by it, although he frequently heard far coarser expressions used by others.

But she did not give him time to protest, or even to cogitate upon it.

"A great desire," she continued. "And for this, of course, a certain amount of correct information is required. I know that a young boy prostitute was pulled out of the river here yesterday. I should like to see him."

Every vestige of color drained out of his face.

"You can't, ma'am! 'E's dead!"

"I know he's dead, Constable," Emily said patiently. "He would be, having been strangled and dropped into the river. It is the corpse that I wish to see."

"The corpse?" he repeated, stupefied.

"Exactly," she said. "If you will be so kind?"

"I can't! It's 'orrible, ma'am—quite 'orrible. You can't 'ave any idea, or you wouldn't ask. It's not for any lady at all to see, let alone the likes o' you!"

Emily opened her mouth to argue, but Charlotte could see that the whole initiative was going to slip away if she did not intervene.

"Of course it is," she agreed, adding her own smile to Emily's. "And we appreciate your sensitivity to our feelings. But we have both seen death before, Constable. And if we are to fight for reform, we must make people aware that it is not pleasant—indeed as long as they are permitted to deceive themselves that it is unimportant, so long will they fail to do anything about it. Do you not agree?"

"Well—well put like that, ma'am—but I can't let you go and look at something like that! 'E's dead, ma'am—very dead indeed!"

"Nonsense!" Emily said sharply. "It's freezing cold! We have seen bodies before that were far worse than this one can possibly be. Mrs. Pitt once found one over a month old, half burned and full of maggots."

That left the constable speechless. He stared at Charlotte as if she had produced the article right there in front of him by some abominable sleight of hand.

"So will you be good enough to take us to see poor Albie?" Emily said briskly. "You did not send him back to Bluegate Fields, did you?"

"Oh, no, ma'am. We got a message as they didn't want 'im after all. Said as 'e'd bin took out o' the river 'ere, we 'ad as much right to 'im as anyone else."

"Then let us go." Emily began to walk toward the only other door, and Charlotte followed her, hoping the constable would not block them.

"I ought to ask my sergeant!" the constable said helplessly. "'E's upstairs. Let me go an' ask 'im if'n you can!" This was his chance to put the whole ridiculous thing into someone else's hands. He had been used to all manner of weird affairs coming in through the door, from drunks to terrified girls or practical jokers, but this was the worst of all. He knew they really were ladies; he may work in Deptford, but he knew quality when he saw it!

263

"I wouldn't dream of putting you to the trouble," Emily said. "Or your sergeant either. We shall only be a moment. Will you be kind enough to show us the way? We should dislike to find the wrong corpse."

"Lord! We only got the one!" He dived through the doorway after her and trotted behind them exactly where Pitt had gone the day before, into the small, cold room with its sheet-covered table.

Emily strode in and whipped off the cover. She looked down at the stiff, bleached, puffed corpse, and for a moment she went as white as it was; then, with a supreme effort, she controlled herself long enough to allow Charlotte to look also, but she was unable to speak.

Charlotte saw an almost unrecognizable head and shoulders. Death and the water had robbed Albie of all the anger that had made him individual. Staring at him now, the emptiness lying on the table, she realized how much the will to fight had been part of him. What was left was like a house without furniture, after the inhabitants have taken away the things that marked their presence.

"Put it back," she said to Emily quietly. They walked out past the constable, close to each other, arm in arm, avoiding his eyes so he would not see how much it had shocked them and taken all their confidence.

He was a tactful man, and whatever he saw or guessed he made no mention of.

"Thank you," Emily said at the street door. "You have been most courteous."

"Yes, thank you," Charlotte added, doing her best to smile at him; she did not succeed, but he took the intention for the deed.

"You're welcome, ma'am," he replied. "You're welcome, I'm sure," he added, because he did not know what else to say.

Outside in the carriage, Emily accepted the rug from

the footman and allowed him to wrap it around her feet and Charlotte's.

"Where to, milady?" he asked without expression. After the Deptford police station, nothing else she could say would surprise him.

"What time is it?" she inquired.

"A little after noon, milady."

"Then it is too early to go calling upon Callantha Swynford. We must find something to do in the meanwhile."

"Would you care for luncheon, milady?" The footman tried not to make it too obvious that he cared for it himself. Of course, he had not just viewed a drowned corpse.

Emily lifted her chin and swallowed.

"What an excellent idea. You had better find us somewhere pleasant, John, if you please. I do not know where such a place may be, but no doubt there is a hostelry of some sort that serves ladies."

"Yes, milady, I'm sure there is." He closed the door and went back to tell the coachman that he had succeeded in obtaining luncheon, and implied by his expression what he thought of it all.

"Oh, my God!" Emily sat back into the upholstery as soon as the door was closed. "How does Thomas bear it? Why do birth and death have to be so awfully—physical? They seem to reduce us to such a level of extremity there is no room to think of the spiritual!" She gulped again, hard. "Poor little creature. I have to believe in God, of some sort. It would be intolerable to think that was all there was—just to be born and live and die like that, and nothing before or after. It's too trivial and disgusting. It's like a joke in the worst possible taste."

"It's not very funny," Charlotte said somberly.

"Jokes in bad taste aren't!" Emily snapped. "I couldn't face eating, but I certainly don't intend to allow John to know that! We'll have to order something, and of course we shall eat separately. Please do not be clumsy enough to allow him to learn of it! He is my footman and I shall have to live with him in the house—not to mention whatever he might say to the rest of the servants."

"I have no intention of doing so," Charlotte replied. "And not eating will not help Albie." She had seen and heard of more violence and more pain than Emily, cushioned by Paragon Walk and the Ashworth world. "And of course there's a God, and probably heaven, too. And I most sincerely hope there is hell also. I have a great desire to see several people in it!"

"Hell for the wicked?" Emily said tartly, stung by Charlotte's apparent composure. "How very puritan of you."

"No—hell for the indifferent," Charlotte corrected. "God can do as He pleases with the wicked. It is the ones who don't damn well care that I want to see burn!"

Emily pulled the rug a little tighter.

"I'll help," she offered.

Callantha Swynford was not in the least surprised to see them; in fact, the usual etiquette of afternoon calling was not observed at all. There was no exchange of polite observations and trivia. Instead, they were conducted immediately into the withdrawing room set for tea and conversation.

Without preamble Emily launched into a frank description of conditions in workhouses and sweatshops, the details of which she and Charlotte had learned from Somerset Carlisle. They were gratified to see Callantha's distress as there opened up before her a whole world of misery that she had never conceived of before.

Presently they were joined by other ladies, and the wretched facts were repeated, this time by Callantha herself while Emily and Charlotte merely added assurance that what Callantha said was indeed true. By the time they left, late in the afternoon, they were both satisfied that there were now a number of women of wealth and influence who were sincerely concerned in the matter, and that Callantha herself would not forget, or dismiss easily from her thoughts, the abuse of children such as Albie, however much it distressed her.

While Charlotte was occupied with her crusade against child prostitution in general, trying to inform and horrify those who could change the climate of social opinion, Pitt was still concerned with the murder of Albie.

Athelstan kept him occupied with a case of embezzlement that involved thousands of pounds abstracted from a large company over a period of years. The incessant checking of double entries, receipts, and payments, and the questioning of innumerable frightened and devious clerks, was a kind of punishment to him for having caused so much embarrassment over the Jerome affair.

The body of Albie had not been moved from Deptford, so Pitt had nothing to act on. Deptford still had charge of the case—if there was to be a case. In order to learn even that much, he would have to go to Deptford on his own time, after his duties on the embezzlement were over for the day. And his inquiries would have to be sufficiently discreet that Athelstan would not learn of them.

It was a black evening after one of those flat, lightless days when fires do not draw because the air is too heavy, and every moment one expects the sky to fling a barrage from clouds so leaden they hang low across the city roofs and drown the horizon. Gas lamps flickered uneasily without dispelling the intensity of the darkness, and the drift of air from the river smelled of the incoming tide. There was a rime of ice on the stones of the street; the cab Pitt rode in moved briskly along while the cabbie kept up a steady hacking cough.

He stopped the cab at the Deptford police station, and Pitt had not the heart to ask him to wait, even though he knew he might not be long. No man or beast should be required to stand idle in that bitter street. After the heat of movement it could kill the horse; the cabbie, whose livelihood depended on the animal, would have to walk it around and around at no profit merely to keep the sweat from freezing and chilling the animal to death.

"Night, sir." The cabbie touched his hat and moved off into the gloom, disappearing before he had passed the third gas lamp.

"Good night." Pitt turned and walked into the shelter of the station and the frail warmth of the potbellied stove. It was a different constable on duty this time, but the usual steaming mug of tea was by his elbow. Perhaps it was the only way to keep warm in the enforced stillness of desk duty. Pitt introduced himself and mentioned his earlier visit to identify Albie's body.

"Well, Mr. Pitt, sir," the constable said cheerfully. "Wot can we do for yer tonight? No more corpses as'd interest you, I reckon."

"I don't want any, thank you," Pitt replied. "I didn't even get that one. Just wondered how you were doing with it. I might be able to help a little, since I knew him."

"Then you'd better talk to Sergeant Wittle, sir. 'E's 'andlin' the case, such as it is. Although, to be honest, I don't reckon we've much chance of ever knowing who done it. You know yerself, Mr. Pitt, poor little beggars like that get done in every day, fer one reason or another."

"Get a lot of them, do you?" Pitt asked conversationally. He leaned a little on the desk, as though he were in no hurry to pursue a more senior officer.

The constable warmed to the attention. Most people preferred to ask the opinion of a sergeant at least, and it was very pleasant to be consulted by an inspector.

"Oh, yes, sir, from time to time. River police brings 'em in 'ere quite a lot—'ere an' Greenwich. And o' course Wapping Stairs—sort o' natural place, that is."

"Murdered?" Pitt asked.

"Some o' them. Although it's 'ard to tell. A lot o' them

is drowned, and who knows whether they were pushed, or fell, or jumped?"

"Marks?" Pitt raised his eyebrows.

"Gawd 'elp us, most of 'em is pretty marked anyway, long before they gets as far as the water. There's some people as seems to get their pleasures out o' beating other people, instead o' what any natural man would. You should see some o' the women we get, and no more'n bits o' kids, lot o' them—younger than my wife was when I married 'er, and she was seventeen. Then, o' course, some o' them girls gets beat by their own pimps, if they've bin 'olding back on the money. All that, and wot with the tides and knockin' around the bridges, some o' them yer'd 'ardly recernize as they was 'uman bein's. I tell yer, it'd fair make yer weep sometimes. Turns me stomach, it does, and it takes a deal ter do that."

"A lot of brothels in the docks," Pitt said quietly after a moment's silence while they pursued their private memories of horror. It was more an observation than a question.

"'Course," the constable agreed. "Biggest port in the world, London." He said it with some pride. "What else d'y'expect? Sailors away from 'ome, after a long spell at sea, and the like. An I s'pose when yer gets the supply o' women, and boys, fer them that's that way inclined"—he grimaced—"then it's natural yer gets others come in from outside the harea, knowin' as they'll find whatever they wants 'ere. There's a few times yer'll see some smart gents get down from a cab outside some very funny 'ouses. But then I reckon yer knows that fer yerself, bein' near that kind o' harea, too!"

"Yes," Pitt said. "Yes." Although since his promotion to inspector he had had to do with more serious cases, and the ordinary, rather pedestrian duties of keeping a modicum of control over vice had not fallen his way.

The constable nodded. "It's when I sees children involved that I gets the sickest about it. I reckon most adult

269

people can do as they wants, although I 'ates ter see a woman lower 'erself—always makes me think o' me muvver—but kids is diff'rent. Funny, yer know, they was two ladies—and I means *ladies*, all dressed and spoke like real quality they was, and 'andsome as duchesses. They came in 'ere just yesterday, a-sayin' as they wanted ter do somethin' about child prostitution. Wanted ter make people sit up and take notice. Don't reckon as they've much chance." He smiled wanly. "It's a lot the quality as pays the money that makes it worth the procurers' while—up the better end, any'ow. No good pretending the gents wot matters don't already know about it! Still, yer can't tell ladies as their own kind does that kind o' thing, can yer? I never saw them meself, but Constable Andrews, as was on duty at the time, 'e said they wanted ter look at the corpse what was brought out o' the river—the one as yer come about. White as sheets, they went, but never lorst their nerve, nor fainted. Yer've gotta admire them. Just looked and thanked 'im, polite as yer like, and went out again. Yer've got to 'and it to 'em, they got spirit!"

"Indeed!" Pitt was startled. Half of him was furious, the other half idiotically proud. He did not even bother to ask if the ladies had left any names, or indeed what they had looked like. He would reserve his comments on the matter until he got home.

"Reckon as yer'd like ter see Sergeant Wittle?" the constable said matter-of-factly, unaware of Pitt's thoughts, or even that they had left the immediate subject. "'E's just up them stairs, first door you comes to, sir. Can't miss it."

"Thank you," Pitt said. He smiled and left the constable, who picked up the mug of tea again, before it lost the last of its warmth.

Sergeant Wittle was a sad man, with a dark face and remnants of black hair draped thinly across the top of his head.

"Ah," he sighed when Pitt explained his call. "Ah—well, I don't think we'll get much there. 'Appens all the time, poor sods! Can't tell you 'ow many I've seen, over the years. O' course, most aren't murdered, leastways not directly—just sort o' sideways, like, by life. Sit down, Mr. Pitt. Not that it'll do you any use."

"It's not official," Pitt said hastily, pushing the chair closer to the stove and settling in it. "The case is yours. Just wondered if I could help—off the books?"

"You know suffin', then?" Wittle's eyebrows rose. "We know where 'e lived, but that don't tell us anything at all. Anonymous sort o' place. Anyone could come or go— part o' the whole thing! Nobody wants ter be seen. Who would—frequenting a place like that? An' all the other residents pretty much mind their own business. Anyway, they're inside plyin' their own trade, which by its nature 'as ter be private. Like bitin' the 'and that feeds you, letting anyone know who goes in and out o' that place."

"Do you have anything at all?" Pitt asked, trying not to hope.

Wittle sighed again. "Not much. Treating it as murder, o' course at least for a while. It'll probably get filed with all the other unsolveds, but we'll give it a week or two. Seems like 'e was a plucky little bastard—spoke out more'n most. 'E was known. Kept some 'igh-class company, according to some, if they're tellin' the truth."

"Who?" Pitt leaned forward urgently, his throat tight. "Who was this high-class company?"

Wittle smiled sadly. "Nobody as you'd know, Mr. Pitt. I read the newspapers. If it 'ad bin anyone in your case, I'd 'a' sent and told you—just a matter o' politeness, like. Not that I can see as it'd do you any good. Already got yer man. Why d'ya still care?" He screwed up his eyes. "Reckon as there's more?" He shook his head. "Always is, on these things, but you'll never find it. Very close, the quality, when it comes to 'iding their family problems. Reckon young Waybourne was doin' a spot o' slummin' of 'is own, do you? Well—what does it matter now? Poor

271

little sod's dead, an' provin' there was a few lies told 'ere an' there won't 'elp no one now."

"No," Pitt said with as much grace as he could muster. "But if you find proof he kept company with anyone in our area that you want to know about, there may be something useful I could tell you that is only suspicion—and not on record."

Wittle smiled, for the first time showing genuine amusement.

"Ever tried proving a gentleman 'ad even a passin' acquaintance with somebody like Albie Frobisher, Mr. Pitt?"

There was no need for an answer. They both knew that such a piece of professional crassness would be without point; indeed, the officer who made the charges would probably suffer for his foolishness more than the gentleman he made it against. Although of course there would be embarrassment all around, not least to his superiors in the force for having employed so clumsy a man, an oaf so unaware of what may be said, and what may only be supposed, that he would voice such a thought.

"Even if it's proof you can't use," Pitt said at last, "I'd like to know."

"Just fer interest, like?" Wittle's smiled widened. "Or do you know suffin' as I don't?"

"No." Pitt shook his head. "No, I know frighteningly little. The more I learn, the less I think I really know. But thank you anyway."

It took him ten minutes' walking in the cold before he found another cab; he directed it and climbed in, then realized his mind had translated into words the thought that had barely played itself into his consciousness. He was going back to Abigail Winters's rooms to see if any of the girls knew exactly where she had gone. He was afraid for her, afraid she too was lying dead and bloated in some dark backwater of the river, or perhaps already washed out with the tide into the estuary and the sea.

*   *   *

Three days later, he received word from a police station in a little town in Devon that Abigail Winters had gone there to stay with a cousin, and was alive and in every appearance of health. The one girl at the brothel who could write had told him where she was, but he had not accepted her unsubstantiated word. He had telegraphed six police districts himself, and the second reply gave him the answer he wanted. According to the constable whose careful, unaccustomed wording he read, Abigail had retired to the country for her lungs, which suffered from the London fog. She thought the air in Devon would suit her better, being milder and free from the smoke of industry.

Pitt stared at the paper. It was ridiculous. It came from a small country town; there would be little market there for her trade, and she knew no one but a distant relative—a female at that. Doubtless she would be back in London within a year, as soon as the Waybourne case was forgotten.

Why had she gone? What was she afraid of? That she had lied, and if she stayed in London someone would press her until it was discovered? Pitt felt he knew already; the only thing he did not know was how it had come about. Had someone paid her to lie—or had it been a slow process through questioning by Gillivray? Had she realized—by implication, gesture, guess—what he wanted, and, in trade for some future leniency, given it to him? He was young, keen, more than personable. He needed a prostitute who had venereal disease. How hard had he looked, and how easy had he been to satisfy once he had found someone, anyone—who filled that need?

It was a shocking thought, but Gillivray would not have been the first man to seize a chance for evidence to convict someone he sincerely believed to be guilty of an appalling crime, a crime likely to occur again and again if the offender was not imprisoned. There was a deep, natural desire to prevent hideous crime, especially when one has only recently seen the victims. It was easy to understand. Yet it was also inexcusable.

He called Gillivray into the office and told him to sit down.

"I've found Abigail Winters," he announced, watching Gillivray's face.

Gillivray's eyes were suddenly bright and blurry. There was a heat inside him that robbed him of words. It was the guilt Pitt might not have found in an hour of interrogation, no matter how many of his suspicions he pressed or how many verbal traps he laid. Surprise and fear were so much more effective, putting the onus of reply on Gillivray before he had time to conceal the guilt in his eyes, to grasp what it was Pitt was saying.

"I see," Pitt said quietly. "I would rather not believe you openly bribed her. But you did, tacitly, lead her into perjury, didn't you? You invited her, and she accepted."

"Mr. Pitt!" Gillivray's face was scarlet.

Pitt knew what was coming, the rationalizations. He did not want to hear them because he knew them all, and he did not want Gillivray to make them. He had thought he disliked him, but now that it came to the moment, he wanted to save him from self-degradation.

"Don't," he said quietly. "I know all the reasons."

"But, Mr. Pitt—"

Pitt held up a piece of paper. "There's been a robbery, a lot of good silver taken. This is the address. Go and see them."

Silently, Gillivray took it, hesitated a moment as though he would argue again, then turned on his heel and left, closing the door hard behind him.

11

Pitt stood under the new electric lights along the Thames Embankment and stared at the dark water brilliantly dancing in the reflections, then sliding away into obscurity. The round globes along the balustrade were like so many moons just above the heads of the elegant and fashionable as they paraded in the wintry night, muffled in furs, their boots making little high, chiplike sounds on the ice-cold footpath.

If Jerome were hanged, whatever Pitt found out about the murder would be academic. And yet there would still be Albie. Whoever had killed him, it was not Jerome; he had been safely entombed in the heart of Newgate when that had happened.

Were the two murders connected? Or was it just gross and irrelevant mischance?

A woman laughed as she passed behind Pitt, so close her skirts brushed the bottom of his trousers. The man beside her, his top hat rakishly sideways on his head, leaned and whispered something. She laughed again, and instinctively Pitt knew what he had said.

He kept his back to them and stared out into the nothingness of the river. He wanted to know who had killed Albie. And he still felt that there were other lies concerning Arthur Waybourne, lies that mattered, although his brain could not tell him how, or what the answer was.

He had been back to Deptford tonight, but hadn't learned anything that really mattered, just a lot of detail that he might as easily have guessed. Albie had some wealthy customers, men who might go to a considerable length to keep their tastes from becoming known. Had Albie had been foolish enough to try enhancing his standard of living by a little selective blackmail, an insurance against the time when he could no longer command a price?

But still, as Wittle had pointed out, far more likely he had had some sort of lovers' quarrel and been strangled in the heat of jealousy or unsatisfied lust. Or perhaps it was as commonplace as a fight over money. Maybe he had simply been greedy.

Yet Pitt wanted to know; the untidy ends trailed across his mind, irritating his thoughts like a constant nagging pain.

He straightened up and began to walk along the row of lights. He walked faster than the strollers, muffled against the bitter air, carriages beside them to pick them up when they were tired of their diversion. It was not long before he hailed a hansom and made his way home.

The following day at noon, a constable anxiously knocked on Pitt's door and told him that Mr. Athelstan required him to report upstairs immediately. Pitt went unsuspectingly, his mind currently engaged on a matter of recovering stolen goods. He thought Athelstan would be inquiring into the likelihood of a conviction in the case.

"Pitt!" Athelstan roared as soon as Pitt was inside the door. He was already standing and a cigar lay squashed in the big polished stone ashtray, tobacco bursting out of its sides. "Pitt, by God I'll break you for this!" His voice rose even higher. "Stand to attention when I talk to you!"

Pitt obediently drew his feet together, startled by Athelstan's scarlet face and shaking hands. He was obviously on the edge of completely losing control of himself.

"Don't just stand there!" Athelstan came around the side of the desk to face him. "I won't have dumb insolence! Think you can get away with anything, don't you? Just because some jumped-up country squire had the ill-judgment to have you educated with his son, and you think you speak like a gentleman! Well, let me disabuse you, Pitt—you are an inspector of police, and you are subject to the same discipline as any other policeman. I can promote you if I think you are fit, and I can just as easily put you down to sergeant—or to constable, if I see a reason. In fact, I can have you dismissed altogether! I can have you thrown out onto the street! How would you like that, Pitt? No job, no money. How would you keep your lady wife then, with her highborn ideas, eh?"

Pitt almost laughed; this was ridiculous! Athelstan looked as if he might have a fit if he wasn't careful. But Pitt was also afraid. Athelstan might look ludicrous standing in the middle of the floor with crimson face, bulging eyes, neck like a turkey's over his strangle-stiff white collar, but he was just close enough to the borders of his control that he might very well dismiss him. Pitt loved his job; untangling the threads of mystery and discovering truth—sometimes an ugly truth—held a certain value. It gave him his sense of worth; when he woke every morning, he knew why he got up, where he was going, and that he had a purpose. If anyone stopped him and asked "Who are you?" he could give them an answer that summed up what he was, and why—not merely the vocational label, but the essence. To lose his job would rob him of far more than Athelstan could comprehend.

But, looking at Athelstan's purpled face, he knew that some measure of its importance to him was very well understood. Athelstan meant to frighten him, meant to cow him into obeying.

It had to be Albie again, and Arthur Waybourne. There was nothing else important enough.

Athelstan suddenly reached out his hand and slapped the flat of his palm across Pitt's cheek. It stung sharply; but Pitt felt foolish to have been surprised. He stood perfectly still, hands by his sides.

"Yes, sir?" he said steadily. "What is it that has happened?"

Athelstan seemed to realized he had lost every shred of dignity, that he had allowed himself to indulge in uncontrolled emotion in front of a subordinate. His skin was still suffused with blood, but he drew in his breath slowly and stopped shaking.

"You have been back to the Deptford police station," he said in a much lower voice. "You have been interfering in their inquiries, and asking for information about the death of the boy prostitute Frobisher."

"I went in my own time, sir," Pitt replied, "to see if I could offer them any help, since we already know a good deal about him and they do not. He lived nearer our area, if you remember?"

"Don't be insolent! Of course I remember! He was the perverted whore that that man Jerome patronized in his filthy habits! He deserved to die. He brought it on himself! The more vermin like that that kill each other off, the better for the decent people of this city. And it is the decent people we are paid to protect, Pitt! And don't you forget it!"

Pitt spoke before he thought. "The decent ones being those who sleep only with their wives, sir?" He allowed the sarcasm to creep into his voice, although he had intended it to sound naïve. "And how shall I know which ones those are, sir?"

Athelstan stared at him, the blood ebbing and flowing in his face.

"You are dismissed, Pitt," he said at last. "You are no longer in the force!"

Pitt felt the ice drench over him as if he had toppled and fallen into the river. His voice replied like a stranger's, involuntarily, full of bravado he did not feel.

"Perhaps that's just as well, sir. I could never have made the suitable judgments as to whom we should protect and whom we should allow to be killed. I was under the misapprehension that we were to prevent crime or to arrest criminals whenever possible, and that the social standing or the moral habits of the victim and the offender were quite irrelevant—that we should seek to enforce the law—something about 'without malice, fear, or favor.'"

A hot tide rose again in Athelstan's face.

"Are you accusing me of favor, Pitt? Are you saying that I am corrupt?"

"No, sir. You said it," Pitt replied. He had nothing to lose now. Everything that Athelstan could give or take had already gone. He had used all his power.

Athelstan swallowed. "You misunderstood!" he said with tight fury, but softly, suddenly startled into control again. "Sometimes I think you are deliberately stupid! I said nothing of the sort. All I meant was that people like Albie Frobisher are bound to come to a bad end, and there is nothing we can do about it, that's all."

"I'm sorry, sir. I thought you said that there was nothing we ought to do."

"Nonsense!" Athelstan waved his hands as if to obliterate the idea. "I never said anything of the kind. Of course we must try! It is just that it is hopeless. We cannot waste good police time on something that has no chance of success! That is only common sense. You will never make a good administrator, Pitt, if you do not understand how best to use the limited forces at your disposal! Let it be a lesson to you."

"I am hardly likely to make an administrator of any sort, since I have no job," Pitt pointed out. Now the coldness of reality was setting in. Through the shock he began to glimpse the wasteland of unhappiness beyond. Ridiculously, childishly, there was a constricting ache in his throat. In that moment he hated Athelstan so much he wanted to hit him, to beat him until he bled. Then he would go out of the station where everyone knew him, and walk in the gray, hiding rain until he could control the desire to weep. Except that, of course, it would all come back again when he saw Charlotte, and he would make a weak, undignified fool of himself.

"Well!" Athelstan sniffed irritably. "Well—I'm not a vindictive man—I'm prepared to overlook this breach if you'll behave yourself more circumspectly in the future. You may consider yourself still employed in the police force." He glanced at Pitt's face, then held up his hand. "No! I insist, don't argue with me! I am aware that you are overimpulsive, but I am prepared to allow you a certain latitude. You have put in some excellent work in the past, and you have earned a little leniency for the occasional mistake. Now get out of my sight before I change my mind. And do not mention Arthur Waybourne or anything whatsoever connected with that case—however tenuously!" He waved his hand again. "Do you hear me?"

Pitt blinked. He had an odd feeling that Athelstan was as relieved as he was. His face was still scarlet and his eyes peered back anxiously.

"Do you hear me?" he repeated, his voice louder.

"Yes, sir." Pitt answered, straightening up again to some semblance of attention. "Yes, sir."

"Good! Now go away and get on with whatever you are doing! Get out!"

Pitt obeyed, then stood outside on the matting on the landing feeling suddenly sick.

Meanwhile, Charlotte and Emily were pursuing their crusade with enthusiasm. The more they learned, from Carlisle and other sources, the more serious their cause became—and the deeper and more troubled their anger.

They developed a certain sense of responsibility because fate—or God—had spared them from such suffering themselves.

In the course of their work, Charlotte and Emily visited Callantha Swynford a third time, and it was then that Charlotte at last found herself alone with Titus. Emily was in the withdrawing room discussing some new area of knowledge with Callantha, while Charlotte had retired to the morning room to make copies of a list to be conveyed to other ladies who had become involved in their cause. She was sitting at the small rolltop desk, writing as neatly as she could, when she looked up and saw a rather pleasant-faced youth with golden freckles like Callantha's.

"Good afternoon," she said conversationally. "You must be Titus." For a moment she had not recognized him; he looked more composed here in his own house than he had in the witness box. His body had lost the graveness and reluctance it had expressed then.

"Yes, ma'am," he replied formally. "Are you one of Mama's friends?"

"Yes, I am. My name is Charlotte Pitt. We are working together to try to stop some very evil things that are going on. I expect you know about it." It was partly intended to compliment him, make him feel adult and not excluded from knowledge, but also she recalled how she and Emily had frequently listened at the door to her mother's tea parties and afternoon callers. Sarah had considered herself too dignified for such a pursuit. Not that they had often heard anything nearly as startling or titillating to the adolescent imagination as the fight against child prostitution.

Titus was looking at her with frankness tinged with a degree of uncertainty. He did not want to admit ignorance; after all, she was a woman, and he was quite old enough to begin feeling like a man. Childhood with its nursery humiliations was rapidly being discarded.

"Oh, yes," he said with a lift of his chin. Then curiosity

gained the upper hand. This was a chance too good to waste. "At least I know part of it. Of course, I have had my own studies to attend to as well, you know."

"Of course," she agreed, laying down her pen. Hope surged up inside her. It was still not too late—if Titus were to alter his evidence. She must not let him see her excitement.

She swallowed, and spoke quite casually. "One has only so much time, and one must spend it wisely."

Titus pulled up a small padded chair and sat down.

"What are you writing?" He had been well brought up and his manners were excellent. He made it sound like friendly interest, even very faintly patronizing, rather than anything as vulgar as curiosity.

She had had every intention of telling him anyway—his curiosity was a pale and infant thing compared with hers. She glanced down at the paper as if she had almost forgotten it.

"Oh, this? A list of wages that people get paid for picking apart old clothes so that other people can stitch them up again into new ones."

"Whatever for? Who wants clothes made up out of other people's old ones?"

"People who are too poor to buy proper new ones," she answered, offering him the list she was copying from.

He took it and looked at it.

"That's not very much money." He eyed the columns of pence. "It doesn't seem like a very good job."

"It isn't," she agreed. "People can't live on it and they often do other things as well."

"I'd do something else all the time, if I were poor." He handed it back to her. By poor, he meant someone who had to work at all, and she understood that. To him, money was there—one did not have to acquire it.

"Oh, some people do," she said quite casually. "That is what we are trying to stop."

She had to wait several moments of silence before he asked the question she had hoped for.

"Why are you trying to do that, Mrs. Pitt? It doesn't seem fair to me. Why should people have to unpick old clothes for pennies if they could earn more money doing something else?"

"I don't want them to pick rags." She used the term quite familiarly now. "At least not for that sort of money. But I don't want them to be prostitutes either, most particularly not if they are still children." She hesitated, then plunged on. "Especially boys."

The pride of man in him did not want to admit ignorance. He was in the company of a woman, and one whom he considered very handsome. It was important to him that he impress her.

She sensed his dilemma and pushed him into an emotional corner.

"I expect when it is put like that, you would agree?" she asked, meeting his very candid eyes. What fine, dark lashes he had!

"I'm not sure," he hedged, a faint blush coloring his cheeks. "Why especially boys? Perhaps you would give me your reasons?"

She admired his evasion. He had managed to ask her without sounding as if he did not know, which she now was almost sure was so. She must be careful not to lead him, to put words into his mouth. It took her longer than she had expected to frame just the right answer.

"Well, I think you would agree that all prostitution is unpleasant?" she began carefully, watching him.

"Yes." He followed her lead; the reply she expected was plain enough.

"But an adult has more experience of the world in general, and therefore has more understanding of what such a course will involve," she continued.

Again the answer suggested itself.

"Yes." He nodded very slightly.

"Children can much more easily be forced into doing things they either do not wish or else of which they cannot foresee the full consequences." She smiled very faintly so she would not sound quite so pompous.

"Of course." He was still young enough to feel echoes of the bitterness of authority, governesses who gave orders and expected early bedtimes, all vegetables eaten—and rice pudding—no matter how much one disliked them.

She wanted to be gentle with him, to let him keep his new, adult dignity, but she could not afford it. She hated having to shred it from him like precious clothes, leaving him naked.

"Perhaps you do not argue that it is worse for boys than for girls?" she inquired.

He flushed, his eyes puzzled. "What? What is worse? Ignorance? Girls are weaker, of course—"

"No—prostitution—selling their bodies to men for the most familiar acts."

He looked confused. "But girls are. . ." The color deepened painfully as he realized how acutely personal a subject they were touching.

She said nothing, but picked up the pen and paper again so he could have an excuse to avoid her eyes.

"I mean girls—" He tried again: "Nobody does that sort of thing with boys. You're making fun of me, Mrs. Pitt!" His face was scarlet now. "If you are talking about the sort of thing that men and women do, then it's just stupid to talk about men and other men—I mean boys! That's impossible!" He stood up rather abruptly. "You are laughing at me and treating me as if I'm a baby—and I think that is very unfair of you—and most impolite!"

She stood up, too, bitterly sorry to have humiliated him, but there had been no other way.

"No, I'm not, Titus—believe me," she said urgently. "I swear I am not. There are some men who are strange and different from most. They have those sorts of feelings towards boys, instead of women."

"I don't believe you!"

"I swear it's true! There is even a law against it! That is what Mr. Jerome was accused of—did you not know that?"

He stood still, eyes wide, uncertain.

"He was accused of murdering Arthur," he said, blinking. "He's going to be hanged—I know."

"Yes, I know, too. But that is why he is supposed to have murdered him, because he had that kind of relationship with him. Did you not know that?"

Slowly he shook his head.

"But I thought he attempted to do the same thing with you." She tried to look just as confused, even though the knowledge was hardening in her mind every moment. "And your cousin Godfrey."

He stared at her, thoughts racing through his mind so visibly she could almost have read them aloud: confusion, doubt, a spark of comprehension.

"You mean that was what Papa meant—when he asked me—" The color rushed back to his face again, then drained away, leaving him so white the freckles stood out like dark stains. "Mrs. Pitt—is—is that why they are going to hang Mr. Jerome?"

Suddenly he was totally a child again, appalled and overwhelmed. She disregarded his dignity entirely and put both arms around him, holding him tightly. He was smaller than he looked in his smart jacket, his body thinner.

He stood perfectly still for several moments, stiff. Then slowly his arms came up and held on to her, and he relaxed.

She could not lie to him and tell him it was not.

"Partly," she replied gently. "And partly what other people said as well."

"What Godfrey said?" His voice was very quiet.

"Didn't Godfrey understand what the questions meant either?"

"No, not really. Papa just asked us if Mr. Jerome had ever touched us." He took a deep breath. He might be clinging to her like a child, but she was still a woman, and decencies must be kept; he did not even know how to break them anyway. "On certain parts of the body." He found the words inadequate, but all he could say. "Well, he did. I didn't think there was anything wrong in it at the time. It sort of happened quickly, like an accident. Papa told me it was terribly wrong, and something else was meant by it—but I didn't really know what—and he didn't say! I didn't understand about anything like—like that! It sounds horrible—and pretty silly." He sniffed hard and pulled away.

She let him go immediately.

He sniffed again and blinked; suddenly his dignity had returned.

"If I've told lies in court, will I go to prison, Mrs. Pitt?" He stood very straight, as though he expected the constables with manacles to come through the door any moment.

"You haven't told lies," she answered soberly. "You said what you believed to be the truth, and it was misunderstood because people already had an idea in their minds and they made what you said fit into that idea, even though it was not what you meant."

"Shall I have to tell them?" His lip quivered very slightly and he bit it to control himself.

She allowed him the time.

"But Mr. Jerome has already been sentenced and they will hang him soon. Shall I go to hell?"

"Did you mean him to hang for something he did not do?"

"No, of course not!" He was horrified.

"Then you will not go to hell."

He shut his eyes. "I think I would rather tell them anyway." He refused to look at her.

"I think that is very brave of you," she said with absolute sincerity. "I think that is a very manly thing to do."

He opened his eyes and gazed at her. "Do you honestly?"

"Yes, I do."

"They'll be very angry, won't they?"

"Probably."

He lifted his chin a little higher and squared his shoulders. He could have been a French aristocrat about to step into a tumbril.

"Will you accompany me?" he asked formally, making it sound like an invitation to the dinner table.

"Of course." She left the pen and papers lying on the desk and together they walked back to the withdrawing room.

Mortimer Swynford was standing with his back to the hearth, warming his legs and blocking a good deal of the fire. Emily was nowhere to be seen.

"Oh, there you are, Charlotte," Callantha said quickly. "Titus—come in. I do hope he has not been disturbing you." She turned to Swynford by the fire. "This is Mrs. Pitt, Lady Ashworth's sister. Charlotte, my dear, I believe you have not met my husband."

"How do you, do, Mr. Swynford," Charlotte said coolly. She could not bring herself to like this man. Perhaps it was quite unfair of her, but she associated him with the trial and its misery and now it seemed, its unjustice.

"How do you do, Mrs. Pitt." He inclined his head very slightly, but did not move from the fireplace. "Your sister has been called away. She went with a Lady Cumming-Gould, but she left her carriage for you. What are you doing, Titus? Should you not be at your studies?"

"I shall return shortly, Papa." He took a very deep breath, caught Charlotte's eye, then breathed out again and faced his father. "Papa, I have something to confess to."

"Indeed? I hardly think this is the time, Titus. I am sure Mrs. Pitt does not wish to be embarrassed by our family misdeeds."

"She already knows. I have told a lie. At least I did not exactly realize it was a lie, because I did not understand about—about what it really is. But because of what I said, which was not true, maybe someone who was innocent will be hanged."

Swynford's face darkened and his body grew tight and solid.

"Nobody innocent will be hanged, Titus. I don't know what you are talking about, and I think it is best you forget it!"

"I can't, Papa. I said it in court, and Mr. Jerome will be hanged partly because of what I said. I thought that—"

Swynford swung around to face Charlotte, his eyes blazing, his thick neck red.

"Pitt! I should have known! You're no more Lady Ashworth's sister than I am! You're married to that damned policeman—aren't you? You've come insinuating your way into my house, lying to my wife, using false pretenses because you want to rake up a little scandal! You won't be content until you've found something to ruin us all! Now you've convinced my son he's done something wicked, when all the child has testified to is exactly what happened to him! God damn it, woman, isn't that enough? We've already had death and disease in the family, scandal and heartbreak! Why? What do hyenas like you want that you go picking over other people's griefs? Do you just envy your betters and want to shovel dirt over them? Or was Jerome something to you—your lover, eh?"

"Mortimer!" Callantha was white to the very roots of her hair. "Please!"

"Silence!" he shouted. "You have already been deceived once—and allowed your son to be subjected to this

288

woman's disgusting curiosity! If you were less foolish, I should blame you for it, but no doubt you were entirely taken in!"

"Mortimer!"

"I have told you to be silent! If you cannot do so, then you had better retire to your room!"

There was no decision to be made; for Titus' sake and Callantha's, as well as for her own, Charlotte had to answer him.

"Lady Ashworth is indeed my sister," she said with icy calm. "If you care to inquire of any of her acquaintance's, you will quite easily ascertain it. You might ask Lady Cumming-Gould. She is also a friend of mine. In fact, she is my sister's aunt by marriage." She stared at him with freezing anger. "And I came to your house quite openly, because Mrs. Swynford is concerned, as are the rest of us, to try to put some curb on the prostitution of children in the city of London. I am sorry it is a project which does not meet with your approval—but I could not have foreseen that you would be against it any more than Mrs. Swynford could have. No other lady involved has met with opposition from her husband. I do not care to imagine what your reasons might be—and no doubt if I did you could accuse me of slander as well."

Blood vessels stood out in Swynford's neck.

"Do you leave my house of your own will?" he shouted furiously. "Or must I call a footman to have you escorted? Mrs. Swynford is forbidden to see you again— and if you call here you will not be admitted."

"Mortimer!" Callantha whispered. She reached out to him, then dropped her hands helplessly. She was transfixed with embarrassment.

Swynford ignored her. "Do you leave, Mrs. Pitt, or shall I be obliged to ring for a servant?"

Charlotte turned to Titus, standing rigid and white-faced.

"You are in no way to blame," she said clearly. "Don't

289

worry about what you have said. I shall see for you that it reaches the right people. You have discharged your conscience. You have nothing now to be ashamed of."

"He had nothing at any time!" Swynford roared, and reached for the bell.

Charlotte turned and walked to the door, stopping a moment when she had opened it.

"Goodbye, Callantha, it has been most pleasant knowing you. Please believe I do not bear you any grudge, or hold you responsible for this." And before Swynford could reply she closed the door and collected her cloak from the footman, then went outside to Emily's carriage, stepped in, and gave the coachman directions to take her home.

She debated whether or not to tell Pitt about it. But when he came in she found that, as always, she was incapable of keeping it to herself. It all came out, every word and feeling she could remember, until her dinner was cold in front of her and Pitt had completely eaten his.

Of course there was nothing he could do. The evidence against Maurice Jerome had evaporated until there was none left that would have been sufficient to convict him. On the other hand, there was no other person to put in his place. The proof had disappeared, but it had not proved his innocence, nor had it given the least indication toward anyone else. Gillivray had connived at Abigail's lies because he was ambitious and wished to please Athelstan—and possibly he had genuinely believed Jerome to be guilty. Titus and Godfrey had not lied in any intentional sense; they were merely too naïve, as any young boys might be, to realize what their suggestions meant. They had agreed because they did not understand. They were guilty only of innocence and a desire to do what was expected of them.

And Anstey Waybourne? He had wanted to find the

least painful way out. He was outraged. One of his sons had been seduced; why should he not believe the other had been also? It was most probable he had no idea that, by his own outrage and his leap to conclusions, he had led his son into the statement that damned Jerome. He had expected a certain answer, conceiving it in his wounded imagination first, and made the boy believe there had been an offense that he was simply too young to understand.

Swynford? He had done the same—or had he? Perhaps he now guessed that it had all been a monumental catastrophe of lies; but who would dare admit such a thing? It could not be undone. Jerome was convicted. Swynford's fury was gross and offensive, but there was no reason to believe it was guilt of anything but connivance at a lie to protect his own. Accessory perhaps to the death of Jerome? But not the murder of Arthur.

So who—and why?

The murderer was still unknown. It could be anyone at all, someone they had never even heard of—some anonymous pimp or furtive customer.

It was some days before Charlotte learned the truth, which was waiting for her when she returned home from a visit to Emily. They had been working on their crusade, which had by no means been abandoned. There was a carriage pulled up in the street outside her door, and a footman and a driver were huddled in it as if they had been there long enough to grow cold. Of course, it was not Emily's, since she had just left Emily, nor was it her mother's or Aunt Vespasia's.

She hurried inside and found Callantha Swynford sitting by the fire in the parlor, a tray of tea in front of her and Gracie hovering anxiously, twisting her fingers in her apron.

Callantha, her face pale, stood up as soon as Charlotte came in.

"Charlotte, I do hope you will forgive my calling upon you, after—after that distressing scene. I—I am most deeply ashamed!"

"Thank you, Gracie," Charlotte said quickly. "Please bring me another cup, and then you may leave to attend to Miss Jemima." As soon as she had gone, Charlotte turned back to Callantha. "There is no need to be. I know very well you had no desire for such a thing. If you have called because of that, please put it out of your mind. I bear no resentment at all."

"I am grateful." Callantha was still standing. "But that is not my principal reason for coming. The day you spoke with Titus, he told me what you had said to each other, and ever since then I have been thinking. I have learned a great deal from you and Emily."

Gracie came in with the cup and left in silence.

"Please, would you not care to sit down?" Charlotte invited. "And perhaps take more tea? It is still quite hot."

"No, thank you. This is easier to say if I am standing." She remained with her back half towards Charlotte as she looked out the French windows into the garden and the bare trees in the rain. "I would be grateful if you would suffer me to complete what I have to say without interrupting me, in case I lose my courage."

"Of course, if you wish." Charlotte poured her own tea.

"I do. As I said, I have learned a great deal since you and Emily first came to my house—nearly all of it extremely unpleasant. I had no idea that human beings indulged themselves in such practices, or that so many people lived in poverty so very painful. I suppose it was all there for me to see, had I chosen to, but I belong to a family and a class that does not choose to.

"But since I have been obliged to see a little, through the things you have told me and shown me, I have begun to think for myself and to notice things. Words and expressions that I had previously ignored have now come to have meaning—even things within my own family. I have told my cousin Benita Waybourne about our efforts to make child prostitution intolerable, and I have enlisted her support. She, too, has opened her eyes to unpleasantness she had previously allowed herself to ignore.

"All this must seem very pointless to you, but please bear with me—it is not.

"I realized the day you spoke to Titus that both he and Godfrey had been beguiled into giving evidence against Mr. Jerome which was not entirely true, and certainly not true in its implication. He was deeply distressed about it, and I think a deal of his guilt has come to rest upon me also. I began to consider what I knew of the affair. Up until then, my husband had never discussed it with me— indeed, Benita was in the same circumstance—but I realized it was time I stopped hiding behind the convention that women are the weaker sex, and should not be asked even to know of such things, far less inquire into them. That is the most arrant nonsense! If we are fit to conceive children, to bear and to raise them, to nurse the sick and prepare the dead, we can certainly endure the truth about our sons and daughters, or about our husbands."

She hesitated, but Charlotte kept her word and did not interrupt. There was no sound but the fire in the grate and the soft patter of rain on the window.

"Maurice Jerome did not kill Arthur," Callantha went on. "Therefore someone else must have—and since Arthur had had a relationship of that nature, that also must have been with someone else. I spoke to Titus and to Fanny, quite closely, and I forbade them to lie. It is time for the truth, however unpleasant it may be. Lies will all be found out in the end, and the truth will be the worse for having been festering in our consciences and begetting more lies and more fears until then. I have seen what it has done to Titus already. The poor child cannot carry the weight alone any longer. He will grow to feel he is guilty of some complicity in Mr. Jerome's death. Heaven knows, Jerome is not a very pleasant man, but he does not deserve to be hanged. Titus awoke the other night, having dreamed of hanging. I heard his cry and went to him. I cannot let him suffer like that, with his sleep haunted by visions of guilt and death." Her face was very white, but she did not hesitate.

"So I began to wonder, if it was not Jerome, then with whom did Arthur have this dreadful relationship? As I told you, I asked Titus many questions. And I also asked Benita. The further we progressed in our discoveries, the more did we find that one single fear became clearer in our minds. It was Benita who spoke it at last. It will do you no good"—she turned to look at Charlotte—"because I do not think there is any way you will ever be able to prove it, but I believe it was my cousin Esmond Vanderley who was Arthur's seducer. Esmond has never married, and so of course he has no children of his own. We have always considered it most natural that he should be extremely fond of his nephews, and spend some time with them, the more with Arthur because he was the eldest. Neither Benita nor I saw anything amiss—thoughts of a physical relationship of that nature between a man and a boy did not enter our minds. But now, with knowledge, I look back and I understand a great deal that passed by me then. I can even recall Esmond having a course of medical treatment recently, medicine he was obliged to take which he did not discuss and which Mortimer would not tell me of. Both Benita and I were concerned, because Esmond appeared so worried and short in temper. He said it was a complaint of the circulation, but when I asked Mortimer, he said it was of the stomach. When Benita asked the family doctor, he said Esmond had not consulted him at all.

"Of course, you will never be able to prove that either, because even if you were to find the doctor concerned—and I have no idea who he might be—doctors do not allow anyone else to know what is in their records, which is perfectly proper.

"I'm sorry." She stopped quite suddenly.

Charlotte was stunned. It was an answer—it was probably even the truth—and it was no use at all. Even if they could prove that Vanderley had spent a lot of time with Arthur, that was perfectly natural. No one could be found who had seen Arthur the night he was killed; they had already looked, long and pointlessly. And they did not know which doctor had seen Vanderley when the symptoms of his disease had first appeared, only that it was not the family doctor, and either Swynford did not know what it was or he knew and had lied—probably the former. It was a disease that aped many others, and its symptoms, after the initial eruptions, frequently lay dormant for years, even decades. There was amelioration, but no cure.

The only thing they might possibly do would be to find proof of some other relationship he had had, and thus show that he was homosexual. But since Jerome had been found guilty and condemned by the court, Pitt could not investigate Vanderley's private life. He had no reason.

Callantha was right; there was nothing they could do. It was not even worth telling Eugenie Jerome that her husband was innocent, because she had never believed him to be anything else.

"Thank you," Charlotte said quietly, standing up. "That must have been extremely difficult for you, and for Lady Waybourne. I am grateful for your honesty. It is something to know the truth."

"Even when it is too late? Jerome will still be hanged."

"I know." There was nothing more to say. Neither of them wished to sit together and discuss it anymore, and it would have been ridiculous, even obscene, to try to talk of anything else. Callantha took her leave on the doorstep.

"You have shown me much that I did not wish to see,

and yet now that I have, I know it is impossible to go back. I could not be again the person that I was." She touched Charlotte on the arm, a quick gesture of closeness, then walked across the pavement and accepted her footman's hand into her carriage.

The following day Pitt walked into Athelstan's office and closed the door behind him.

"Maurice Jerome did not kill Arthur Waybourne," he said bluntly. When Charlotte had told him the previous evening, he had made up his mind then, and had forced it from his thoughts ever since, lest fear should make him draw back. He dared not even think of what he might lose; the price might rob him of the courage to do what his first instinct told him he must, however uselessly.

"Yesterday, Callantha Swynford came to my house and told my wife that she and her cousin Lady Waybourne knew that it was Esmond Vanderley, the boy's uncle, who had killed Arthur Waybourne but they could not prove it. Titus Swynford admitted he did not know what he was talking about in the witness box. He merely agreed to what his father had suggested to him, because he believed his father must be right—Godfrey the same." He allowed Athelstan no chance to interrupt him. "I went to the brothel where Abigail Winters worked. No one else ever saw either Jerome or Arthur Waybourne in the place, not even the old woman who keeps the door and watches it like a hawk. And Abigail has suddenly vanished to the country, for her health. And Gillivray admits he put the words into her mouth. And Albie Frobisher has been murdered. Arthur Waybourne had venereal disease and Jerome has not. There is no longer any evidence against Jerome at all—nothing! We can probably never prove Vanderley killed Arthur Waybourne—it appears to have been an almost perfect crime—except that for some reason or other he had to kill Albie! And by God I intend to do everything I can to get him for that!

"And if you don't ask Deptford for the case back, I shall tell some very interesting people I know that Jerome is innocent, and we shall execute the wrong man because we accepted the words of prostitutes and ignorant boys without looking at them hard enough—because it suited us to have Jerome guilty. It was convenient. It meant we did not have to tread on important toes, ask ugly questions, risk our own careers by embarrassing the wrong people." He stopped, his legs shaking and his chest tight.

Athelstan stared at him. His face had been red, but now the color drained and left him pasty, beads of sweat standing out on his brow. He looked at Pitt as if he were a snake that had crawled out of a desk drawer to menace him.

"We did everything we could!" He licked his lips.

"We did not!" Pitt exploded, guilt running like fire through his anger. He was even more guilty than Athelstan, because part of him had never entirely believed Jerome had killed Arthur, and he had suppressed that voice with the smooth arguments of reason. "But God help me, we shall now!"

"You'll—you'll never prove it, Pitt! You'll only make a lot of trouble, hurt a lot of people! You don't know why that woman came to you. Maybe she's a hysteric." His voice grew a little stronger as hope mounted. "Maybe she has been scorned by him at some time, and she is—"

"His sister?" Pitt's voice was thick with contempt.

Athelstan had forgotten Benita Vanderley.

"All right! Maybe she believes it—but we'll never prove it!" he repeated helplessly. "Pitt!" His voice sank to a moan.

"We might be able to prove he killed Albie—that'll do!"

"How? For God's sake, man, how?"

"There must have been a connection. Somebody may have seen them together. There may be a letter, money, something. Albie lied for him. Vanderley must have thought he was dangerous. Perhaps Albie tried a little blackmail, went back for more money. If there is anybody or anything at all, I'm going to find it—and I'm going to hang him for Albie's murder!" He glared at Athelstan, daring him to prevent him, daring him to protect Vanderley, the Waybournes, or anyone else any longer.

This was not the time; Athelstan was too shaken. In a few hours, perhaps by tomorrow, he would have had a chance to think about it, to balance one risk against another and find courage. But now he had not the resolve to fight Pitt.

"Yes," he said reluctantly. "Well, I suppose we must. Ugly—it's all very ugly, Pitt. Remember the morale of the police force, so—so be careful what you say!"

Pitt knew the danger of argument now. Even a hint of indecision, of vacillation, would allow Athelstan the chance to gather his thoughts. He gave him a cold, withering look.

"Of course," he said sharply, then turned and went to the door. "I'm going to Deptford now. I'll tell you when I learn something."

Wittle was surprised to see him. "Morning, Mr. Pitt! You're not still on about that boy as we got out o' the river, are you? Can't tell you anythin' more. Goin' to close the case, poor little sod. Can't waste the time."

"I'm taking the case back." Pitt did not bother to sit down; there was too much emotion and energy boiling inside him to permit it. "We discovered Maurice Jerome did not kill the Waybourne boy, and we know who did, but we can't prove it. But we may be able to prove he killed Albie."

Wittle pulled a sad, sour face. "Bad business," he said softly. "Don't like that. Bad for everybody, that is. 'Anging's kind o' permanent. Can't say you're sorry to a bloke as you've already 'anged. Wot can I do to 'elp?"

Pitt warmed to him. He seized a chair and swung it around to face the desk, then sat down close, leaning his elbows on the littered surface. He told Wittle all he knew and Wittle listened without interruption, his dark face growing more and more somber.

"Nasty," he said at the end. "Sorry for the wife, poor little thing. But wot I don't understand—why did Vanderley kill the Waybourne boy at all? No need, as I see it. Boy wouldn't a' blackmailed 'im—was just as guilty 'isself. Who's to say 'e didn't like it anyway?"

"I expect he did," Pitt said. "Until he discovered he had contracted syphilis." He recalled the lesions the police surgeon had found on the body, enough to frighten any youth with the faintest clue of their meaning.

Wittle nodded. "'O course. That would change it from being fun to suffin' quite different. I s'pose 'e panicked and wanted a doctor—an' that panicked Vanderley. Would do! After all, you can't 'ave yer nephew runnin' around sayin' as 'e picked up syphilis from 'avin' unnatural relations wiv yer! That'd be enough to provoke most men into doin' suffink permanent. Reckon 'e just grabbed 'is feet and, woops-a-daisy, 'is 'ead goes under an' in a few minutes 'e's dead."

"Something like that," Pitt said. The scene was easy to imagine; the bathroom with big cast-iron tub, perhaps even one of those newfangled gas burners underneath to keep it hot, towels, fragrant oil, the two men—Arthur suddenly frightened by the sores on his body, something said that brought the realization of what they were—the quick violence—and then the corpse to be disposed of.

It had probably all happened in Vanderley's own house—a servants' night off. He would be alone. He would wrap the corpse in a blanket or something similar, carry it to the street in the dark, find the nearest manhole that was out of sight of passersby, and get rid of the body, hoping it would never be found. And, but for chance, it never would have been.

It was disgusting, and so easy to see, now that he knew.

How could he ever have believed it was Jerome? This was so much more probable.

"Want any 'elp?" Wittle asked. "We still got a few of Albie's things from the rooms 'e 'ad. We didn't find any use in them, but you might, since you might know what you was looking for. Weren't any letters or anythin' like that."

"I'll look anyway," Pitt said. "And I'll go back to the rooms and search them again—might be something hidden. You found he knew quite a few high-class customers, you said. Can you give me their names?"

Wittle pulled a face. "Like to make yerself unpopular, do yer? There'll be a rare lot o' squealin' and complainin' goin' on if you go and talk to these gentlemen."

"I daresay," Pitt agreed wryly. "But I'm not going to give up on this as long as there's anything at all that I can still do. I don't care who screams!"

Wittle fished among the papers on the desk and came up with half a dozen.

"There's the people as Albie knew that we know of." He grimaced. "O' course there's dozens more we'll never know. That's just about all we done to date. An' 'is things that we got are in the other room. Not much, poor little swine. Still, I suppose 'e ate reg'lar, and that's suffink. An' 'is rooms was comfortable enough, and warm. That'd be part of 'is rent—can't 'ave gentlemen comin' in ter bare their delicate bodies to the naked an' the room all freezin' chill, now, can we?"

Pitt did not bother to reply. He knew they had an understanding about it. He thanked Wittle, went to the room where Albie's few possessions were, looked through them carefully, then left and caught an omnibus back to Bluegate Fields.

The weather was bitter; shrill winds howled around the angles of walls and moaned in streets slippery with rain and sleet. Pitt found more and more pieces of Albie's life.

300

Sometimes they meant something: an assignation that took him closer to Esmond Vanderley, a small note with initials on it found stuffed in a pillow, an acquaintance in the trade who recalled something or had seen something. But it was never quite enough. Pitt could have drawn a vivid picture of Albie's life, even of his feelings: the squalid, jealous, greedy world of buying and selling punctuated by possessive relationships that ended in fights and rejections, the underlying loneliness, the ever-present knowledge that as soon as his youth was worn out his income would vanish.

He told Charlotte a lot of it. The sadness, pointlessness lay heavy on his mind, and she wanted to know, for her own crusade. He had underestimated her strength. He found he was talking to her as he might have someone who was purely a friend; it was a good feeling, an extra dimension of warmth.

Time was growing desperately short when he found a young fop who swore, under some pressure, that he had attended a party where both Albie and Esmond Vanderley had been present. He thought they had spent some time together.

Then a call came to the police station, and shortly afterward Athelstan strode into Pitt's office where he was sitting with a pile of statements trying to think whom else he could interview. Athelstan's face was pale, and he closed the door with a quiet snap.

"You can stop all that," he said with a shaking voice. "It doesn't matter now."

Pitt looked up, anger rising inside him, ready to fight—until he saw Athelstan's face.

"Why?"

"Vanderley's been shot. Accident. Happened at Swynford's house. Swynford keeps sporting guns or something. Vanderley was playing about with one, and the thing went off. You'd better go around there and see them."

"Sporting guns?" Pitt said incredulously, rising to his feet. "In the middle of London! What does he shoot—sparrows?"

"God dammit, man, how do I know?" Athelstan was exasperated and confused. "Antiques, or something! Antique guns—they're collectors' things. What does it matter? Get out there and see what's happened! Tidy it up!"

Pitt walked to the hatstand, picked off his muffler, and wound it around his neck, then put on his coat and jammed his hat on hard.

"Yes, sir. I'll go and see."

"Pitt!" Athelstan shouted after him. But Pitt ignored him and went down the steps to the street, calling for a hansom, then running along the pavement.

When he arrived at the Swynford house, he was let in immediately. A footman had been waiting behind the door to conduct him to the withdrawing room, where Mortimer Swynford was sitting with his head in his hands. Callantha, Fanny, and Titus stood close together by the fire. Fanny clung to her mother without any pretense at being adult. Titus stood very stiff, but under the disguise of supporting his mother, he was holding her just as tightly.

Swynford looked up as he heard Pitt come in. His face was ashen.

"Good afternoon, Inspector," he said unsteadily. He climbed to his feet. "I am afraid there has been an—an appalling accident. My wife's cousin Esmond Vanderley was alone in my study, where I keep some antique guns. He must have found the case of dueling pistols, and God knows what made him do it, but he took one out and loaded it—" He stopped, apparently unable to keep his composure.

"Is he dead?" Pitt inquired, although he knew already that he was. A strange sense of unreality was creeping over him, over the whole room, as if it were all merely a

302

rehearsal for something else and in some bizarre way they all knew what each person would say.

"Yes." Swynford blinked. "Yes, he's dead. That is why I sent for you. We have one of these new telephones. God knows I never thought I would use it for this!"

"Perhaps I had better go and look at him." Pitt went to the door.

"Of course." Swynford followed him. "I'll show you. Callantha, you will remain here. I shall see that it is all taken care of. If you would prefer to go upstairs, I am sure the Inspector will not mind." It was not a question; he was assuming Pitt would feel unable to argue.

Pitt turned in the doorway; he wanted Callantha there. He was not sure why, but the feeling was strong.

"No, thank you." She spoke before Pitt had time to speak. "I prefer to stay. Esmond was my cousin. I wish to know the truth."

Swynford opened his mouth to argue, but something in her had changed and he saw it. Perhaps he would reassert his authority as soon as Pitt had gone, but not now—not here in front of him. This was not the time for a battle of wills he might not win immediately.

"Very well," he said quickly. "If that is what you prefer." He led Pitt out and across the hallway toward the rear of the house. There was another footman outside the study door. He stood aside and they went in.

Esmond Vanderley was lying on his back on the red carpet in front of the fire. He had been shot in the head and the gun was still in his hand. There were powder burns on his skin, and blood. The gun lay on the floor beside him, his fingers crooked loosely around the butt.

Pitt bent down and looked, without touching anything. His mind raced. An accident—to Vanderley—now, of all times, when he was at last finding the first shreds of evidence to connect him with Albie?

But he was not close enough yet—not nearly close

enough for Vanderley to panic! In fact, the more he knew of the garish half-world that Albie had lived in, the more he doubted he would ever have proof he could bring to court that Vanderley had killed Albie. Surely Vanderley knew that too? He had stayed calm through all the investigation. Now, with Jerome about to be hanged, suicide was senseless.

In the original case, it was Arthur who had panicked, at his understanding of those lesions—not Vanderley. Vanderley had acted quickly, even adroitly, in an obscene way. He played any game to the last card. Why suicide now? He was far from being cornered.

But he would have known that Pitt was after him. Word would have spread—that was inevitable. There had never been any chance of stalking him, surprising him.

But it had been too soon for panic—and infinitely too soon for suicide. And an accident was idiotic!

He stood up and turned to face Swynford. An idea was gathering in his mind, still shapeless as yet, but becoming stronger.

"Shall we go back to the other room, sir?" he suggested. "It is not necessary to discuss it in here."

"Well—" Swynford hesitated.

Pitt affected a look of piety. "Let us leave the dead in peace." It was imperative that he say what he intended in front of Callantha, and even in front of Titus and Fanny, cruel though it was. Without them it was all academic—if he was right.

Swynford could not argue. He led the way back to the withdrawing room.

"You surely do not require my wife and children to remain, Inspector?" he said, leaving the door open for them to leave, although they showed no sign of wishing to.

"I am afraid I shall have to ask them some questions." Pitt closed the door firmly and stood in front of it, blocking the way. "They were in the house when it happened. It is a very serious matter, sir."

"Dammit, it was an accident!" Swynford said loudly. "The poor man is dead!"

"An accident," Pitt repeated. "You were not with him when the gun went off?"

"No, I wasn't! What are you accusing me of?" He took a deep breath. "I'm sorry. I am extremely distressed. I was fond of the man. He was part of my family."

"Of course, sir," Pitt said with less sympathy than he had intended. "It is a most distressing business. Where were you, sir?"

"Where was I?" Swynford looked momentarily confused.

"A shot like that must have been heard all over the house. Where were you when it went off?" Pitt repeated.

"I—ah." Swynford thought for a moment. "I was on the stairs, I think."

"Going up or coming down, sir?"

"What in God's name does it matter!" Swynford exploded. "The man is dead! Are you totally insensitive to tragedy? A moron who comes in here in the midst of grief and starts asking questions—idiotic questions as to whether I was going upstairs or downstairs at the instant?"

Pitt's idea was growing stronger, clearer.

"You had been with him in the study, and had left to go upstairs for some purpose—perhaps to the bathroom?" Pitt ignored the insult.

"Probably. Why?"

"So Mr. Vanderley was alone with a loaded gun, in the study?"

"He was alone with several guns. I keep my collection in there. None of them was loaded! Do you think I keep loaded guns around the house? I am not a fool!"

"Then he must have loaded the gun the moment you left the room?"

"I suppose he must! What of it?" Swynford's face was flushed now. "Can you not let my family leave? The discussion is painful—and, as far as I can see, totally pointless."

Pitt turned to Callantha, still standing close to her children.

"Did you hear the shot, ma'am?"

"Yes, Inspector," she said levelly. She was ashen white, but there was a curious composure about her, as if a crisis had come and she had met it and found herself equal to it.

"I'm sorry." He was apologizing not for the question about the shot but for what he was about to do. Word had come back that Pitt was coming closer in his pursuit; that he knew. But it was not Esmond Vanderley who had panicked—it was Mortimer Swynford. It was Swynford who had been the architect of Jerome's conviction—and he and Waybourne were all too willing to believe in it, until the appalling truth was uncovered. If the conviction was overturned, even questioned by society, and the truth came out about Vanderley and his nature, not only Vanderley would be ruined but all his family as well. The business would disappear; there would be no more parties, no more easy friendships, dining in fashionable clubs—everything Swynford valued would fray away like rotten fabric and leave nothing behind. In the quiet study, Swynford had taken the only way out. He had shot his cousin.

And again Pitt could certainly never prove it.

He turned to Swynford and spoke very slowly, very clearly, so that not only he would understand, but Callantha and his children also.

"I know what happened, Mr. Swynford. I know exactly what happened, although I cannot prove it now, and perhaps I never could. The boy prostitute Albie Frobisher,

306

who gave evidence at Jerome's trial, has also been murdered—you knew that, of course. You threw my wife out of your house for discussing it! I have been investigating that crime also, and have discovered a great deal. Your cousin Esmond Vanderley was homosexual, and he had syphilis. I could not prove to a court that it was he and not Jerome who seduced and murdered Arthur Waybourne." He watched Swynford's face with a satisfaction as hard and bitter as gall; it was bloodlessly white.

"You killed him for nothing," Pitt went on. "I was close behind Vanderley, but there was no witness I could bring to court, no evidence I would have dared to call, and Vanderley knew that! He was safe from the law."

Suddenly the color came back into Swynford's skin, deep red. He sat up a little straighter, avoiding his wife's eyes.

"Then there is nothing you can do!" he said with a flood of relief, almost confidence. "It was an accident! A tragic accident. Esmond is dead, and that is the end of it."

Pitt stared back at him. "Oh, no," he said, his voice grating with sarcasm. "No, Mr. Swynford. This was not an accidental death. That gun went off almost the moment you had left the room. He must have loaded it as soon as your back was turned—"

"But it was turned!" Swynford stood up, smiling now. "You cannot prove it was murder!"

"No, I cannot," Pitt said. He smiled back, an icy, ruthless grimace. "Suicide. Esmond Vanderley committed suicide. That is how I shall report it—and let people make of it what they please!"

Swynford scrabbled after Pitt's sleeve, his face sweating.

"But good God, man! They'll say he killed Arthur, that it was remorse. They'll realize—they'll say that—"

"Yes—won't they!" Pitt still smiled. He put Swynford's hand off his arm as if it were a dirty thing, soiling him. He turned to Callantha. "I'm sorry, ma'am," he said sincerely.

She ignored her husband as if he had not been there, but kept her hands tightly on her children.

"We cannot make amends," she said quietly. "But we shall cease to protect ourselves with lies. If society chooses no longer to know us and all doors are closed, who can blame them? I shall not, nor shall I seek to excuse us. I hope you can accept that."

Pitt bowed very slightly. "Yes, ma'am, of course I can accept it. When it is too late for reparation, some part of the truth is all that is left us. I shall send for a police doctor and a mortuary wagon. Is there anything I can do to be of service to you?" He admired her profoundly, and he wished her to know it.

"No, thank you, Inspector," she said quietly. "I shall manage everything that needs to be done."

He believed her. He did not speak again to Swynford, but walked past him out into the hall to instruct the butler to make the necessary arrangements. It was all over. Swynford would not be tried by law, but by society—and that would be infinitely worse.

And Jerome would at last be acquitted by that same society. He would walk out of Newgate Prison to Eugenie, her loyalty—perhaps even her love. Through the long searching for a new position, perhaps he would learn to value his life.

And Pitt would go home to Charlotte and the warm, safe kitchen. He would tell her—and see her smile, hold her tight and hard.

fireandwater

The book lover's website

www.fireandwater.com

The latest news from the book world

Interviews with leading authors

Win great prizes every week

Join in lively discussions

Read exclusive sample chapters

Catalogue & ordering service

www.fireandwater.com
Brought to you by HarperCollins*Publishers*

Collins Crime

For all criminal investigations

www.collins-crime.com

The latest news from the crime world

Exclusive author interviews

Read extracts from the latest books

All the latest signing dates

Solve clues to win prizes

Full catalogue & ordering

www.collins-crime.com